OUTLAW

OUTLAW

Angus Donald

SPHERE

First published in Great Britain as a paperback original in 2009 by Sphere

A CIP catalogue record for this book
is available from the British Library.

ISBN 978-0-7515-4208-0

Papers used by Sphere are natural renewable and recyclable
products sourced from well-managed forests and certified
in accordance with the rules of the Forest Stewardship Council.

Mixed Sources
Product group from well-managed
forests and other controlled sources
www.fsc.org Cert no. SGS-COC-004081
© 1996 Forest Stewardship Council
FSC

Typeset in Goudy by Palimpsest Book Production Limited,
Grangemouth, Stirlingshire
Printed and bound in Great Britain by Clays Ltd, St Ives plc

Sphere
An imprint of
Little, Brown Book Group
100 Victoria Embankment
London EC4Y 0DY

An Hachette UK Company
www.hachette.co.uk

www.littlebrown.co.uk

For my lovely wife Mary,
who makes everything possible

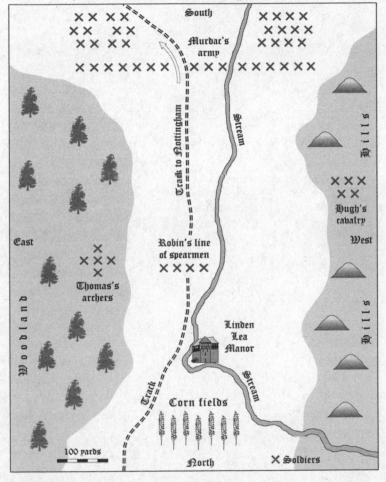

Battle of Linden Lea, mid-morning, 20 July 1189

South

Murdac's army

Stream

Track to Nottingham

Hills

Hugh's cavalry

West

East

Robin's line of spearmen

Thomas's archers

Woodland

Linden Lea Manor

Stream

Hills

Track

Corn fields

100 yards

North

✕ Soldiers

Chapter One

A thin, sour rain is falling on the orchard outside my window, but I thank God for it. In these lean times, it is enough to warrant a fire in my chamber, a small blaze to warm my bones as I scratch out these lines in the grey light of a chill November day. My daughter-in-law Marie, who governs this household, is mean with firewood. The manor is mine, and there would be a decent, if not lavish living to be had for us on these lands if there were a young man or two to work them. But since my son Rob died last year of the bloody flux, a kind of weariness has settled upon me, robbing me of purpose. Though I am still hale and strong, thank the Lord, each morning it is a struggle to rise from my bed and begin the daily tasks. And since Rob's death, Marie has become bitter, silent and thrifty. So, she has decreed, no chamber fires in daylight, unless it rains; meat but once a week; and daily prayers for his soul, morning and night. In my melancholy state, I cannot find the will to oppose her.

On Sundays, Marie doesn't speak at all, just sits praying

and contemplating the sufferings of Our Lord in the big, cold hall all day and then I rouse myself and take my grandson, my namesake Alan, out to the woods on the far edge of my land where he plays at being an outlaw and I sit and sing to him and tell him the stories of my youth: of my own carefree days outside the law, when I feared no King's man, no sheriff nor forester, when I did as I pleased, took what I wanted, and followed the rule of none but my outlaw master: Robert Odo, the Lord of Sherwood.

I feel the cold now, at nearly three score years, more than I ever did as that young man, and the damp; and now my old wounds ache for most of the winter. As I watch the grey rain drifting down on to my fruit trees, I clutch my fur-lined robe tighter against the chill air and my left hand drifts up the sleeve, over the corded swordsman's muscles and finds its way to a long, deep scar high on my right forearm. And stroking the tough, smooth furrow, I remember the terrible battle where I earned that mark.

I was on my back in a morass of blood and churned earth, half-blinded by sweat and my helmet, which had been knocked forward, my sword held pointing up at the sky in a hopeless gesture of defence as I gasped breathless on the ground. Above me, the huge, grey-mailed swordsman was slashing at my right arm. Time slowed to a crawl, I could see the slow sweep of his blade, I could see the bitter rage on his face, I could feel the bite of the metal through the padding of my sleeve into the flesh of my right arm, and then, out of nowhere, came Robin's blocking sword-stroke, almost too late, but stopping the blade from slicing too deeply.

And, later, I recall Robin bandaging the wound himself, sweat-grimed, his own wounded face bleeding, and grinning at me as I winced in pain. He said, and I will remember his words until my death: 'It seems that God really wants this hand, Alan. But I have denied it to him three times – and He shall never take it while I have strength.'

It was my right hand, my quill hand that he saved, and with this hand I plan to repay my debt to him. With this instrument, the Lord willing, I will write his story, and my story, and set before the world the truth about the vicious outlaw and master thief, the murderer, the mutilator and tender lover, the victorious Earl and commander of an army, and, ultimately, the great magnate who brought a King of England to a table at Runnymede and made him submit to the will of the people of the land; the story of a man I knew simply as Robin Hood.

Everyone in our village knew Robin was coming. Since the lord of the manor's death last winter, the village had an almost perpetual holiday atmosphere: there was no authority to force them to work on the lord's demesne and, after tending their own strips of land, the villagers had time on their hands. The alewife's house was full all day and buzzing with talk of Robin's exploits, adventures and atrocities. But very little truth was spoken and news was scant: merely that he would be arriving at dusk and he would see anyone who had business with him at the church that night, where he would hold his court.

I was above all this noise and nuisance, quite literally, as I was hiding in the hayloft above the stable at the back of my mother's crumbling cottage in a den I'd built in the hay. I was thirteen summers old, I had a throbbing knot the size of a walnut on my forehead, a bloody nose, a bad cut on my cheek, and I was treating the terror that I felt with a large dose of absolute boredom. I'd been there since mid-afternoon when I had stumbled into our home, breathless, cut and bruised, having escaped the rough hands of the law and run the dozen miles from Nottingham across the fields all the way home.

We were poor, almost destitute and, after seeing my mother weeping with exhaustion one too many times after a day scratching a meagre living gathering and selling firewood to her neighbours, I had decided to become a thief, more precisely a cut-purse: I cut the leather straps that secured men's purses to their belts with a small knife that I kept as keen as a razor. Nine times out of ten, they never noticed until I was twenty yards away and lost in the thick crowds of Nottingham's market place. When I returned home with a handful of silver pennies and placed them before my mother, she never asked where they had come from, but smiled and kissed me and hurried out to buy food. Though it had been necessity that drove me to take my daily bread from others, I found, God forgive me, that I was good at it, and liked it. In fact, I loved the thrill of the hunt; following a fat merchant as he waded through the market-day crowds, silent as his shadow, then the rough jostle, as if by accident, a quick slice and away before the man knew his purse was gone.

That day, however, I'd been stupid and I'd tried to steal a pie – a rich, golden-crusted beef pie, as big as my two fists – from a stall. I was hungry, as always, but overconfident too.

It was a ruse I had used before: I stood behind a blowsy alewife who was poking the wares on the stall and grumbling about their price; surreptitiously lobbed a small stone at the next stallholder along – a cheesemonger, if I remember rightly – hitting him full on the ear; and in the ensuing recriminations between stallholders, I swept

4

the pie off the board and into my open satchel and sauntered away.

But the pieman's apprentice, who'd been taking a piss behind their cart, came out just as I was scooping up my dinner and shouted: 'Hi!' And everybody turned. So then it was 'Stop thief!' and 'Catch him, somebody!' as I squirmed like a maddened eel through the press of towns-folk until – crack! – I was knocked down by a cudgel to the forehead from some yokel and then grabbed round the neck by a passing man-at-arms. He punched me twice full in the face with his great mailed fist and my legs went limp.

When I came round, moments later, I was lying on the ground at the centre of a jabbering crowd. Standing over me was the soldier, who wore the black surcoat with red chevrons of Sir Ralph Murdac, by the wrath of God, High Sheriff of Nottinghamshire, Derbyshire and the Royal Forests. And suddenly I was seized rigid with terror.

The soldier hauled me to my feet by my hair and I stood dazed and trembling while the scarlet-faced apprentice yammered out the tale of the stolen pie. My satchel was torn open and the circle of onlookers craned to see the incriminating object steaming gently, deliciously, at my waist. I still get jets of saliva in my mouth when I remember its glorious aroma.

Then, a wave of jostling and shouting, and the crowd parted, swept aside by the spears of a dozen men-at-arms, and into the space stepped a nobleman, dressed entirely in black, who seemed to move in his own personal circle of awe.

Though I had never seen him before, I knew immedi-ately that this was Sir Ralph Murdac himself: the magnate who held Nottingham castle for the King and who also held the power of life and death over all the people in a huge swathe of central England. The crowd fell silent and I gawped at him, terrified, as he gazed calmly up and down my thin body, taking in my dirty blond hair, muddy face and ragged clothes. He was a slight man, not tall but handsome, with an athletic body clad in black silk tunic and hose, and a pitch-dark cloak, fixed with a golden clasp at his throat. In his right hand he held a riding whip; a yard-long black leather-covered rod tapering from an inch thick at the butt to the width of a bootlace. At his left side hung a silver-handled sword in a black leather scabbard. His face was clean-shaven, finely carved and framed with pure black hair, cut and curled neatly into a bowl shape. I caught a whiff of his perfume: lavender, and something musky. The palest blue eyes I had ever seen, cold and inhuman, seemed to glitter like frost beneath dark eyebrows. He pursed his red lips as he considered me. And suddenly all my fear receded, like a wave pulling back from the shingle of the beach . . . and I discovered that I hated him. I was filled with a cold stony loathing: I hated what he and his kind had done to me and my family. I hated his wealth, I hated his expensive clothes, his good looks, his perfumed perfection, and the arrogance that he was born to. I hated his power over me, his assumption of superiority, the truth of his superiority. I focused my hate in my stare. And I think he must have recognised my animosity. For an instant our eyes locked and then, with a jerk of his perfectly square chin, he looked away. At that moment, I sneezed, a colossal nasal bark so loud and sudden that it shocked everyone. Sir Ralph started, and glared at me in astonishment. I could feel snot and blood mingling in my battered nose. It began to run down the side of my mouth and on to my chin. I resisted the urge to lick at it. Murdac was silent, staring at me with utter contempt. Then he spoke very quietly: 'Take this . . . filth . . . to the castle,' he said in English, but in a lisping French-accented whisper. And then, almost as an after-thought, he said directly to me: 'Tomorrow, you disgusting fellow, we shall slice off that thieving hand.'

I sneezed again and a plump gobbet of bloody phlegm shot out and splattered on to his immaculate black cloak. He looked down in horror at the red-yellow mess, then, quick as a striking adder, he lashed me full in the face with his riding whip. The blow knocked me to my knees, and blood started to pour from a two-inch cut on my cheek. Through eyes misty with rage and pain, I looked up at Sir Ralph Murdac. He stared back at me for a second, his blue eyes strangely blank, then he dropped the riding whip in the mud, as if it had been contaminated with plague, turned smoothly away, hitched his cloak to a more comfortable position and swept through the surrounding rabble of townsfolk, who parted before him like the Red Sea before Moses.

As the man-at-arms started to drag me away by my wrist, I heard a woman cry: 'That's Alan, the widow Dale's son. Have pity on him, he's only a fatherless boy!' And the man paused, turning to speak to her, with my arm gripped in only one of his fists. And, as he turned, I focused my hatred, my anger, and I twisted my wrist against his grip, ripped it free, squirmed through a pair of legs and took to my heels. A fury of bellowing erupted behind me: men-at-arms shoving and cursing the people obstructing their path. I jinked right and left, sliding through the crowd, shoving past stout yeomen, dodging around the goodwives and their baskets. I created a tornado of confu-sion as the people reacted angrily to my passing. Men and women turned fast, furious at being shoved so roughly. Carts were knocked flying; pottery crashed to the ground; the hurdles containing a herd of sheep were smashed and the animals let loose to add their bleating to the tumult; and I was away and racing down a side alley, bursting through a blacksmith's forge and out the other side, up a narrow street, squeezing between two big townhouses, and turning left down another street until the noise subsided behind me. I stopped in the doorway of a church by the town wall and recovered my wind. There appeared to be no pursuit. Then, fighting to calm my hammering heart, I walked as coolly as I could, my hood pulled forward, a hand held casually over my cut and bruised face, out of the town gate, past the dozing watchman, and on to the winding road that led into the thick woodland. Once out of sight, I ran. I ran like the wind, despite my pounding head, and a sick feeling churning my guts. I gave it my all till our village came into sight around a bend in the road. As I paused to catch my breath, I found I was clutching my right wrist tightly. I still had my arm, praise God, I still had my light fingers. I still had the pie, too.

As I lay in the hayloft, nursing my cut and bruised face, I ran images of the day again in my head. There had been no pursuit on the road out of Nottingham, as far as I could tell, but the woman in the market had known me and so it wouldn't be long, I realised – probably the next morning – before the sheriff's men came for me at my mother's cottage.

So that night, my mother took me to see Robin.

The village was dark, except for a ring of torches around the old church at the northern end of the village. Our church was not grand – it was not much bigger than a village house, but built of thick stone with a thatched roof. We had no priest as the village was too poor to support his living – it was scarcely more than a hamlet, truth be told. But on holy festivals, Easter, Michaelmas, Christmas and the like, a junior cleric would come from Nottingham and hold a Mass. And, sure as man is born to die, after the harvest, the Bishop's man would come to collect our tithes.

As it was the largest, most solid building in the village, we also used it for meetings and, in the recent Anarchy between King Stephen and the Empress Maud, it had sheltered the villagers from roving bands of warriors intent on slaughter and pillage. In those dark days, a wise man, the saying went, kept his coin buried, his dress plain and his daughters inside.

Since King Henry came to the throne, thirty-four years ago, England had known a kind of peace. We no longer had to contend with marauding bands of rebel soldiers, but we did have to bow our heads to Sir Ralph Murdac's men-at-arms. And they could be just as rapacious, especially now that the King was abroad, fighting against his son Duke Richard of Aquitaine and Philip Augustus, the King of France. Our Henry had appointed Ranulf de Glanville to rule as Justiciar and England, many a villager muttered, was no longer well governed. Ranulf, it was said, loved silver and gold and would appoint anyone – even the Devil himself – to the post of sheriff if he could pay, and continue paying handsomely for the office. He had been a sheriff himself and he knew exactly how much tax silver could be squeezed from a county. And so we were squeezed until the pips squeaked. Certainly Ralph Murdac, who had been appointed by Glanville, was said to be making a goodly fortune for the Justiciar, and for himself.

9

On that spring night, a throng of villagers had gathered outside the church and a few at a time were going inside as others came out. My mother pushed through the crowd, dragging me in her wake. And as we approached the great door of the church, I saw that it was guarded by a giant. He didn't speak but held out one vast hand, palm facing us. And we stopped as if we had run into an invisible wall.

The doorkeeper was a truly enormous man, yellow-haired, with a quarterstaff in one great paw and a long dagger, almost a sword, at his belt. He looked down on us, nodded and, with a half-smile, said: 'Mistress, what brings you here – what business have you with him?'

My mother answered: 'It's my son, Alan.' She gestured at me. 'They are coming for him, John.'

The giant nodded again: 'Wait over there,' he rumbled, and indicated a group of twenty or so, men and women, some children too, waiting by the side of the church.

We stood with the others and my mother spat on to a scrap of cloth and began to dab at my face trying to clean off some of the dirt and caked blood. I lived pretty wild then – rarely returning home unless I had a little silver or food to bring my mother, sleeping rough in ill-lit corners of Nottingham town or in country hayricks and barns. Since my father Harry died, four years ago, hanged by Murdac's soldiers, I had rarely bothered with ablutions and, to be honest, I was filthy. My father had been an odd man, learned and musical, wise and courteous, and strangely fastidious about having clean nails and hair. But when I was nine years old, they had hanged him as a common thief.

The soldiers had burst through the door of our cottage just before dawn and grabbed my father, ripping him from the big straw mattress on which the whole family slept, and bundling him out on to the street. Without the slightest formality, they tied his hands behind his back and strung him up by the neck on the big spreading oak tree in the centre of the village, next to the ale house, as an example to the rest of us. He took many minutes to die and he soiled himself – piss dripping from his kicking bare heels – as he swung twitching from the rope in the half-light. My father tried to keep eye contact with me as he died, but, God forgive me, I turned away from his hideous swollen face and bulging eyes and hid my face in my hands. May the Lord have mercy on his soul. And mine.

When the soldiers had gone, we cut him down and buried him and I don't believe I ever saw my mother happy again after that day. She told me many stories about him, an effort, I think, to keep his memory alive in his children. He had travelled the world, my mother said, and been well educated; at one time he had been a cleric in France, a singer in the great new cathedral of Notre Dame that they are building in Paris. Before he died, my father had made efforts to teach me to read and write in English, French and Latin. He had beaten me on many occasions, though never hard, to get the words to take root in my head but, at the end of many, many hours I was still more interested in running free in the countryside than slaving over a slate. I will always remember his music, though, even as his face grows hazy after so many years, and how his singing filled the house with joy. I remember how we would sing, the whole family, by the fire of an evening; my mother and father so happy together.

As she pawed at my dirty face with her spit-dampened cloth, I saw that the tears were once again running down my mother's face. I was the last of her family: my father dead; my younger sisters Aelfgifu and Coelwyn both died within weeks of each other two summers ago after a short, agonising illness in which they had vomited blood and voided a black stinking liquid. And now I, her only surviving child, might be taken by the law tomorrow and have my hand hacked off. Or worse: hanged like my father as a thief.

I must confess that, at that moment, outside the church with my weeping mother, I felt not fear of the sheriff's men, nor sorrow at the deaths of my father and sisters – the uppermost emotion in my heart was excitement. Robert, Lord of Sherwood, was here; Robin Hood: that great and terrible man, feared by Norman lords and English villagers alike. He was a man who preyed on the rich, stealing their silver and killing their servants as they passed through his realm; a man who, scorning Sir Ralph Murdac, did as he pleased in the great Royal Forest of Nottingham, who was, in fact, its true ruler. And in a short while, I would be before him.

As I looked up at the church door, I noticed something amiss. A dark lump had been affixed above the lintel. In the flickering light of the torches, I could just make out what it was. It was the severed head of a young wolf, eyes still open and glittering madly in the torchlight. A huge nail had been hammered through its forehead, transfixing it to the wood. Either side of the head and on the doorposts, black blood had been smeared. I felt a sense of almost unbearable excitement, a euphoria soaring up through my lungs and into my head. He had dared to desecrate the church with the body of an animal, to make it, for one night, his own. He dared to risk his immortal soul with a pagan symbol in the sacred precincts of our Mother Church. This was a fearless man indeed.

At last, after what seemed several hours, the giant beckoned us and pushed open the doors of the church. My excitement had reached a fever pitch and, although my bruised head was throbbing, I held it high as we walked inside.

Scores of thick tallow candles had been lit and, after the darkness outside, it was surprisingly bright in the church, which was half-filled with villagers and a sprinkling of grim-looking strangers, with hoods pulled forward over their faces, some standing, some seated on wooden benches around the walls. A clerk, a middle-aged man of thirty or so, sat at a small table to one side of the church, scribbling on a roll of parchment. And a great wooden chair had been set immediately below the altar.

In the chair sat an ordinary-looking young man, slim, in his early twenties, with nondescript brown hair, and dressed in a badly dyed, patched dark green tunic and hose and partially wrapped in a grey cloak. His clothes were no different to any man in our village – they were, perhaps, even more drab. It was a shock. Where was the great man? Where was the Lord of the Wood? He wore no sword, no gold, no rings, no signs at all of his status and power, except that behind him stood two tall, hooded men each with a long-sword and six-foot bow. I was deeply unimpressed; this was no outlaw lord; he looked like a villein, like me. An image of Sir Ralph Murdac leapt into my mind: his costly black silks, his lavender scent, his air of superiority. And then I looked again at the ordinary man in front of me.

He was leaning forward, eyes closed, elbow on the arm of the chair, his chin cupped in his hand, fingers wrapped

13

around his cheek, listening to a short, very broad man with reddish brown hair, in the coarse robes of a monk, who was speaking quietly and earnestly into his ear. The monk finished speaking and came over to us. Robin sat back, sighed, and opened his eyes. He looked directly at me and I saw that his eyes were as grey as his cloak, almost silver in the candlelight. Then he closed his eyes again and fell back into contemplation.

'My name is Tuck,' said the monk in a strange, sing-song accent, which I took to be Welsh. 'How can I be of service to you?'

My mother held out her hand to the monk: in it was a single hen's egg. 'It's my son,' she said, all in a rush. 'The sheriff's men are coming for him; and they'll cut his hand off or hang him for sure. Take him with you, Brother. Keep him safe under the protection of the Lord of the Wood. Sanctuary, Brother. For the love of God, give him sanctuary in the forest.'

I looked into the Welsh monk's eyes: they were mellow, light brown, the colour of hazelnuts, sad and kind. He took the egg and slipped it into an open pouch on his belt, not bothering to buckle it shut.

'Why are they coming for you?' he asked me.

My mother began gabbling: 'It's all a misunderstanding; a mistake; he's a good boy, naughty sometimes, yes . . .'

Brother Tuck ignored her. He asked again: 'Why are they coming for you, boy?'

I looked him straight in the eye: 'I stole a pie, sir,' I said as calmly as I could, my heart beating like a Moorish drum.

'Do you know that stealing is a sin?' he asked.

'Yes, sir.'

'And yet you stole anyway – why?'

'I was hungry and, and . . . it's what I do – thieving. It's what I do best. Better than almost anyone.'

Tuck snorted, amused. 'Better than almost anyone, eh? I very much doubt that. You were caught, weren't you? Well, there must be penance. All sins must be paid for.'

'Yes, sir.'

Tuck took me by the arm, not unkindly, and led me forward to Robin's chair. The Lord of the Wood opened his eyes and looked at me again. And I completely forgot his drab exterior, his homespun villein's garb. His eyes were extraordinarily bright: it was like staring at the full moon, two silver full moons. The rest of the world dissolved, time stood still, and it was just me and Robin in a dark universe lit only by his eyes; he seemed to be drinking me in through his stare, discovering me, understanding my sins and my strengths.

When he spoke it was in a musical voice, light but strong: 'They tell me you chanced your arm for a pie?'

I nodded. He said: 'And you wish to serve me? You wish me to take you under my protection?' I was mute; I made the barest tilt of my head.

'Why?'

I was taken aback by his question: he must know that I needed to escape the law, that I needed sanctuary, and yet I sensed that he wanted a less obvious answer. I looked into his silver eyes and decided to tell the truth, as I had to Tuck. 'I am a thief, sir,' I said, 'and I would serve under the greatest thief of all, the better to learn my trade.'

There was a sharp intake of breath, all around the church. It occurred to me belatedly that perhaps Robin did not care to regard himself as a common felon. One of the hooded men behind Robin half-drew his sword but stopped when Robin raised a pacifying hand.

'You flatter me,' said the Lord of the Wood. His voice had grown cold, his extraordinary eyes now blazed like naked steel. 'But that was not what I meant by my question. I did not mean why would *you* wish to serve *me*. I meant why should *I* take *you* on; why should I burden myself with another hungry mouth?'

I could think of no reason. So I hung my head and said nothing. He continued, his voice as chill as a grave: 'Can you fight like a knight, clad in hard steel, dealing death to my enemies from the back of a great horse?'

I remained silent.

'Can you draw a war bow to full stretch, and kill a man with one arrow at two hundred paces?'

He knew that I could not; few grown men could achieve such a feat, and I was then a slight boy.

'So what can you offer me, little thief?' The mockery dripped from his voice.

I lifted my chin and stared back at him, little spots of anger on my cheeks. 'I will give you my skill as a cut-purse, my willingness to fight for you as best I may, and my absolute loyalty until death,' I said, far too loudly for the confines of the small church.

'Loyalty until death?' said Robin. 'That truly is a rare and valuable thing.' His voice seemed to have lost its scorn. He considered me for a few heartbeats. 'That was a good answer, thief. What is your name?'

'I am Alan Dale, sir,' I said.

He looked surprised. 'Is your father's name Henry?' he said. 'The singer?' I nodded. I couldn't bring myself to tell Robin that my father was dead. He was silent for a while, regarding me with those great silver eyes. Then he said: 'He's a good man. You have his resemblance.' Suddenly, he smiled – as shocking as a blast of a trumpet – white

16

teeth gleaming in the dim church. His coldness slid away like the shedding of a cloak, and he was transformed. I knew by his sudden warmth that he would take me and I felt my heart bound with joy.

'And by the way, young Alan, I am not a thief,' said Robin, still smiling. 'I merely take what is my rightful due.' There was a murmur of gentle laughter around the church.

Tuck lightly touched my elbow, guiding me away from the great chair: 'Say God-be-with-you to your mother, boy, you're with us now.'

As we walked back to my mother by the church door, I found my legs had become weak and shaky beneath me and I stumbled against Tuck's side before he caught me and held me upright. Then I kissed my mother, hugged her, muttered goodbye, and watched as she walked outside into the dark and out of my life for ever.

As the church door closed behind her, Tuck said: 'Not bad, little thief. But I'll have that egg back now, boy, if you please.' And, as he held out his open palm, he was smiling.

I waited at the side of the church on a bench next to the clerk and his table of parchments. On the far side of the table was a heap of produce from local farms, tribute offered to Robin: several cheeses; loaves of bread; a basket of eggs; two barrels of ale; a honeycomb in a wooden bowl; two chickens, tied together at the legs; numerous sacks of fruit and even a purse of silver pennies; a kid was tied to the table leg and it kept trying to nibble the parchment – at which the clerk would slap at its muzzle without raising his head. He was a thin man, balding, and his long fingers were covered in ink spots. Then he looked up from his

17

scribbling: 'I'm Hugh Odo,' he said, smiling kindly at me. 'Robert's brother. Wait quietly here until our business is concluded.'

I looked to my right and noticed a human form on the floor in the corner of the church and a tall hooded man next to him, armed with long sword and a great bow, standing guard. The man on the floor was bound tightly, hands and legs. I noticed that he was actually shaking with fear. He was moaning inaudibly through a cloth gag. His wild staring gaze caught mine for a few moments and I looked away, embarrassed and a little frightened by his naked terror.

The rest of the night, I waited, sitting there in silence at the side of the church, watching Robin hold his court. A steady stream of villagers came in, spoke respectfully to Robin, received his judgement and paid their fines to Hugh. It was a shadowy night-time version of the manorial court in which, before his death, our local lord had dispensed justice. One woman's herd of pigs had damaged a neighbour's crops; she was ordered to pay a fine to the neighbour, four piglets, and to pay Robin a piglet for his justice. She agreed to pay without question. The man who had seduced his best friend's wife had to pay him a milk cow in compensation, and a fresh cheese to Robin. Again there was no argument.

As Robin dispensed petty justice all that long night, the mound of produce became larger: some, as poor as my mother, paid only an egg or two; one man, who had accidentally killed another in an ale house fight, led a bull calf over to the table and tied it next to the goat. I eyed the purse of silver; it was lying on the table near to where I was sitting. Hugh the clerk was busy in his parchment roll and I could have had it easily. But some instinct stayed

18

my arm. Finally there were no more supplicants and Robin rose from his chair and came over to the table to look down on the bound man.

'Take him outside; do it there in front of everyone,' he said to the hooded man-at-arms, his voice flat. And then he turned aside to talk to Hugh, who began showing him the parchment roll. The bound man was lifted on to his feet by two men; at first he was docile and then he began struggling wildly, writhing, twisting his body like a man possessed, as he realised he was about to meet his fate. One of the hooded men punched him in the stomach, a blow that knocked him breathless to the floor, and then he was dragged outside.

Tuck came over and took me by the arm; he led me out of the door and round the corner of the church. There, as I looked on, Robin's men forced the bound wretch to his knees. He was sobbing and choking on the cloth that had been shoved into his mouth and tied there with a long strip of leather.

'You must watch this,' said Brother Tuck. 'This is your penance.' A small crowd had formed to observe. The man's eyes, huge with terror, rolled in his head. John the giant came over to the man. He pulled the sodden gag out of his mouth and wedged a thin iron bar, crossways, at the back of his mouth, over his tongue, hard up against the hinge of his teeth. One of the men-at-arms strapped the bar in place, with the leather strip that had been used to gag him. The victim was moaning loudly, half-choking and writhing his body, eyes closed, mouth grotesquely forced open by the iron bar. He might have been laughing. The two men behind the wretch steadied his head, and held it still with the iron bar. John produced a pair of iron tongs from his pouch and seized the man's tongue

19

by the tip. In his other hand he held a short knife, razor sharp.

I knew what was coming and a wave of nausea burned my stomach. In my mind, my own right arm was on a block in Nottingham castle, an axeman standing over me, the axe swinging high and . . . I turned my head away from the victim before me, choking back bile . . . Then I felt two strong hands grasp my own jaws and force my head back towards the scene in front of me. The victim's eyes opened and he stared at me for an instant. He was grotesque, like a stone demon on the side of a church: huge gaping mouth and his tongue pulled out by the tongs. 'This is your penance,' repeated Tuck quietly, keeping his powerful hands round my face, forcing me to look. 'See how Robin serves those who inform on him to the sheriff. Watch and take heed!' And John the giant sliced through the thick root of the tongue, with one sweep, and then dodged quickly as a fountain of blood roared from the man's mouth. The man was screaming, a bubbling liquid howl of livid pain and, released by his captors, he fell to the ground, still tightly trussed, bellowing and jetting gore from the bloody cave of his gaping mouth.

I wrenched my head away from Tuck's hands and staggered to the wall of the church where, my head reeling with disgust and horror, I retched and puked, and brought up the remains of the beef pie that had brought me to this present situation. After a while, when there was nothing more in my stomach, I leaned my forehead on the cool stone of the church wall and gulped down the cold night air.

As my head cleared, I realised fully for the first time what I had promised when I swore loyalty until death to

Robin. I was now bound for life to a monster, a devil who mutilated others for merely speaking to the sheriff's men. I knew then that I had left the world of ordinary men.

I had become an outlaw.

Chapter Two

Now, as I look back after nearly sixty winters, I can hardly believe how soft I was then. I was to see worse in my time with Robin, much worse. And although I never enjoyed watching another's pain, as some in our band did, I did learn to hide that weakness in time, as becomes an outlaw, or any man. On that spring night, however, I was young, only thirteen summers old. I knew little of the world and its cruelties, I knew very little about anything. But I was about to learn a great deal.

As I leaned my head on the church wall, staring down at the remains of the beef pie, I could sense a stir of activity behind me: a sudden busy-ness. There were men gathering the tribute and loading it into ox-carts, horses being brought, outlaw-soldiers shooing away the curious villagers, and Robin was there, mounted and giving orders. A man pulled the bloody wolf's head off the church lintel and threw it away into some bushes. The candles were extinguished, the church door locked and it seemed that within minutes we were packed up and on our way. There was no horse for me, I was a poor rider anyway, but Tuck stumped along beside me, leaning on a staff, as we joined the slow-moving cavalcade of carts and mounted men and beasts that snaked away into the woodland.

Dawn was just breaking as we moved off north-west, out of the village and along the farm tracks until we joined the road that wound north through Sherwood Forest. This great wood of the shire of Nottingham was a royal hunting preserve that stretched for a hundred miles north of our village. It was a huge expanse of territory, at some points being fifty miles wide, containing many villages and hamlets, fields and commons; but most of the land was woodland, home to badgers, rabbits, wolves and wild boar, and, of course, the King's deer. To hunt King Henry's deer was a capital offence, punishable by hanging if a man was caught 'red handed', stained with the deer's blood; even to be caught with a hunting dog in the forest could bring you branding or mutilation. And two toes from each of the dog's front paws would be hacked off to stop it running swiftly again. Not that this constrained Robin's followers, I soon learnt. If they were captured they were dead men, anyway. But they seemed to take a special pleasure in flouting the forest laws, murdering the King's foresters and eating as much venison as they wished. It was almost part of the band's identity. 'We were Robin's men; we ate the red deer, and we laughed at the law,' one grizzled outlaw told me simply, but with immense pride, years later.

As I walked along on that morning, through the sharp spring sunshine, through the tall alders and kindly beech, and the thick trunks of ancient oak trees, with the feathery fingers of lush green fens caressing my legs, the horrors of the night receded and Tuck, who walked beside me leaning on his staff, began to talk. About nothing at first – just talking as we walked through the peaceful woodland.

'I have met hot men,' he said. 'Men who could become angry in an instant; some say they have too much yellow bile in their bodies; too much of the element of fire. These are violent, angry men, who in their passion would strike you dead. Our own King Harry is one; an intemperate fellow. In his rages, he will roll upon the ground, you know; quite literally biting the rushes on the floor. Chewing them. Rush-muncher, his servants call him, when his back is turned, when they think it's safe to joke about their lord.'

I stared at him: the King? Who would dare to mock the King? And Tuck went on: 'And I have met cold men, so-called phlegmatic types, with too much water in their veins. A man who would take a blow to the face from a man who had seduced his wife. And he would say naught, but then have his wife quartered and send the seducer a severed leg tied with her garter ribbons. Oh yes, and smile at dinner with him, drink a toast to the man's health.

'Both are dangerous, of course, but the worst men are the ones who appear cold, but inside they are hot. They have the raging power of anger but the icy control of a calm man. This cold-hot man, this phlegmatic-choleric man, is the one to fear.'

'And my master,' I asked. 'Is he a cold-hot man?'

Tuck shot me a sideways look. 'Well done, boy. You're quick, I see. Yes, Robin is such a man. He's cold-hot. And when he is very angry, that's when he is at his coldest. And then God help his enemies, whoever they are, for Robin will have no mercy on them.'

'Is he a good man?' I asked. Forty-odd years later the question still makes me blush. The monk just laughed. 'Is he a good man?' he repeated. 'Yes, I suppose, he's a good man.

24

He's a sinner, of course. We all are. But a good man, too. If you asked me is he a godly man, I'd have to say no. He has his own peculiar notions about God but he has no love, no love at all for Mother Church. Oh, quite the opposite. He mocks it. And takes pleasure in robbing and tormenting its servants.' Tuck crossed himself. 'I pray the Lord Jesus will open his eyes to the truth one day.' Piously, I crossed myself too, but what I was feeling was an intoxicating shock of excitement. Such boldness, to mock God's representatives on Earth; what contempt for his immortal soul, of Hell itself. Like the wolf's head nailed to the church door, it was dizzying.

'I'll tell you a story,' Tuck continued, 'A few months ago, Robin, Hugh and a handful of his men ambushed the Bishop of Hereford as he was travelling with a considerable armed retinue through Sherwood. After a brief and bloody fight, the Bishop and his followers were subdued. Robin took three hundred pounds in silver pennies off them; then he ordered the Bishop to sing Holy Mass for his men. I was away at my duties in the north and the men had been without the comfort of a religious service for some time.

'Well, the Bishop, a stupid, arrogant man, refused to celebrate Mass in the wilderness at the command of outlaws. So Robin ordered the slaughter, one by one, of all the priests and monks who had the bad luck to be accompanying the Bishop on that day. He didn't touch the captured men-at-arms or the female servants, but the clerics, he killed them all, one after the other, as the Bishop looked on and prayed for their souls. When they were all dead, the corpses lying in a stinking blood-spattered pile, they stripped the Bishop to his drawers and put a sword to his throat, and only then did he consent to sing Mass for the outlaws, shivering in his skimpy braies, in the gloom of the wild wood. Then Robin sent the Bishop on his way, almost naked and alone, stumbling all the way on foot twenty miles to Nottingham. Of course, Robin's men loved it, if only for the entertainment. And, some felt their souls were more secure after the Mass.'

'And yet you serve him?' I asked. 'You, a monk, serve a man who mocks Mother Church, who kills priests . . .'

'Aye, well, actually, I do *not* serve him. I serve only God. But I'm his friend and so I sometimes help him. I help him and his men, God forgive me, because all men need Jesus's love, even godless outlaws. And I regard the wild places in Sherwood as my parish. These men, if you like, are my parishioners, my flock. Remember, boy, we are all sinners to one degree or another. And Robin is not a bad man; he has done many bad things, no doubt. But I have faith that he will come to see the light of Our Lord Jesus Christ in time. I'm sure of that as I am of Salvation.'

He fell silent. As we walked along, I thought about hot men and cold men and cold-hot murderers. And good men. And bad men. And sinners. And Hell.

The morning passed and it grew hot under the sunshine. I wanted to ask Tuck so many things. But he had begun to sing a psalm to himself under his breath as we walked and I did not dare to disturb his thoughts. So for an hour or two we strolled along in companionable silence, keeping our place in the great slow-moving column and saving our breath.

A horseman, well-mounted but in shabby homespun clothes, came riding up the column to Hugh, who was on a grey mare a few paces ahead of us. The rider's hood was pulled far forward so as to conceal his face unless you were looking directly at him. In the full sunlight of a spring

26

morning he still managed to look shadowy and sinister, as if he had somehow wrapped the night around himself. He drew his horse alongside Hugh's and, leaning forward, whispered something into the clerk's ear. Robin's brother nodded, asked a question and learnt its answer. He handed the shadow man a small leather purse, said something inaudible to him and then Hugh spurred forward and galloped to the head of the column where Robin was riding. The hooded man turned his horse and trotted back the way we had come towards Nottingham. Tuck paid him no mind. He continued to plod along in that steady mile-eating pace, barely using his staff at all. Then, suddenly, a trumpet, shockingly loud, sounded from the head of the column. I started, looked around for an alarm but everything seemed normal. The cavalcade came to a halt. The people were chatting to each other unconcerned. The armed men leaning on their bow staves. The cheerful sun looked down from above: it was noon.

'Time for dinner,' said Tuck, with a great deal of relish. He rummaged in the nearest cart and pulled out a dirty white sack and huge stone bottle. 'Let's sit over here,' he said, and we sat down in the shade of a wide chestnut tree. All around us men and women from the column were unpacking bags and satchels and spreading blankets on the grass. Out of our sack, like a travelling magician I had once seen at a Nottingham fair, Tuck started to pull wonderful things, luxuries of the kind that I rarely saw then and very seldom ate: a loaf of fine-milled white bread; a whole boiled chicken; smoked gurnard; cold roast venison; a round yellow cheese; hard-boiled eggs; salted cod; apples, stored in straw since the previous autumn . . . He gestured at the stone bottle, inviting me to drink, and I pulled out the wooden stopper and took a long swallow

27

of cider. This was a feast fit for a royal household: my normal noon-day meal, if there was anything to eat in our house, which was seldom, consisted of coarse rye bread, ale, pottage and, if we were lucky, some cheese. Meat we rarely ate, perhaps a rabbit poached from the lord of the manor's warren once in a while. The monk tore a leg off the plump chicken and tossed it to me. I grabbed a handful of the soft white bread, ripped off a hunk and quickly began to fill my belly.

Tuck cut himself a large slice of cheese, wrapped it in bread, took a deep swallow of cider, and sighed happily. His mouth full, he gestured at me to eat and drink. And he further encouraged my gluttony by cutting me a large chunk of smoked fish. The food and drink seemed to loosen his tongue once again, and between mouthfuls he said: 'You asked how I, a man of God, come to help Robin, a godless murderer. Well, I shall tell you . . .' And he began.

'I have known Robin these nine years past; since he was but a boy, not much older than you. He had been sent to stay with the Earl of Locksley, to learn the skills of a knight, but he was a wild one even then, forever running off into Barnsdale forest when he should have been attending to his lessons. But he was not an outlaw, not the Lord of the Wood you see today, whom everyone must obey on pain of death.' He lifted his chin towards a distant group of figures – Robin, his brother Hugh and John – sitting on the ground, laughing and eating, joking with each other in a carefree way, but surrounded by a ring of grim armed men. 'But he despised the Church, even at that age,' he continued, 'and when we first met, to him I was no more than a symbol of a tyrannical and corrupt institution.' He paused and took another huge swig of cider.

'I was a wayward monk, a sinner, who had been sent away from Kirklees Priory – yes, I know it is more famous as a nunnery, but a certain number of monks lived in an adjoining brother house – what was I saying? Yes, I was sent away to live alone in a cell in the woods. What was my sin, you ask? Not what you suspect, you horny young rascal, with the nuns and monks living next to each other; it was plain greed. I could not control my appetite on fast days. And, in those days, under old Prior William, almost every day at Kirklees was designated a fast day: Wednesdays, Fridays, Saturdays, and all those interminable, joyless holy days.'

Tuck gave me a grin, to let me know that he was joking, and stuffed a whole leg of chicken into his mouth, stripping the flesh from the bone with his strong white teeth. 'I have always been afflicted with a large appetite,' he said, with his mouth full. 'So, for my sin, I was sent off to a hermit's cell in the forest where there was a ferry owned by the Priory. I was alone, and my duty was to act as the ferryman, conveying travellers safely across the river. I was to take my meagre living from their small gifts of food. Prior William thought it would teach me a lesson. Perhaps cure my gluttony.

'One sunny day I was lying under a tree, eyes closed, in deepest contemplation, when a young man rode up on a horse. It was Robin. His shouts of greeting roused me from my meditation. He was well dressed and armed with a fine sword in a gold-chased scabbard. I could tell he came from money. "Good morning, Brother," he sings out. And then I realised he was also very drunk and I noticed that his face was badly bruised. "Will you carry me across this river safely to the far bank?" Robin said cheerily, nearly falling off his horse.

'I scrambled to my feet and said that I would, if he would grant me alms, food or drink as payment. He said: "I shall give you what you deserve for this service." Then he walked his horse on to the ferry. I was wary of him: drunken, heavily armed young men usually mean trouble for someone. I know because I was not always a monk. Before I took my vows, I was a soldier in Wales, a bowman and a damned good one, though I say so myself, fighting for Prince Iorweth, and in those days I did my full share of swaggering about in drink.

'The ferry was a simple floating platform linked to a rope that stretched across the river. The rider or pedestrian just walked on to the platform and I punted them a dozen yards across to the other side with a sturdy pole. Robin said nothing as I heaved the ferry across the calm brown water, but he took a long pull from a flask of wine at his belt. When we were still a few yards from the other bank, I stopped the ferry. It floated downstream a yard or two until it came to rest, held against the gentle current by the rope.

'"I'll take that payment now, if it pleases you, sir," I said. Robin stared at me, then his handsome young face contorted in anger and he snarled: "I will pay you what you deserve, monk: and that is nothing, you brown parasite. You and your filthy brethren have been sucking the blood of good men for too long, threatening them with damnation unless they offer up their wealth, their food, their toil and even their bodies. I say you are all bloodsuckers and I will not allow you another drop of mine. Take me to the bank and then get you to Hell."

'I said nothing but merely shoved my pole into the mud of the river and began to move the ferry back to the original riverbank. "What are you doing, you God-cursed tub of shit, you prick-sucking pig," Robin was spitting at me in his rage. I stayed silent. But with two or three good shoves on the pole we were back where we had started, the ferry nudging up against the bank. "If you will not pay," I said. "You shall not cross."

'At this Robin drew his sword. It was a beautiful blade, I remember thinking, far too good for the drunken lout who held it. "You will carry me across this river or I will have your life, you soul-selling leech," Robin said, holding the sword to my throat. I looked into his grey eyes and I saw that, drunk or not, he meant what he said. My life hung by a thread. And so I shoved the pole into the riverbed and we began to cross once again. Robin relaxed; he still held the sword, but it was no longer tickling my throat.' Tuck paused at this point and took a bite from a wrinkled apple.

'Now, Alan, have a care about repeating what I tell you next. It is a sensitive issue with Robin. He's a proud man and he can be very dangerous in defence of his reputation.' I nodded and he continued. 'About halfway across the river, he holding out the sword and with his back to the other bank, I suddenly shouted, "My good sweet Christ," and pointed over his shoulder at the edge of the wood behind. Robin spun drunkenly around in alarm to see what I was pointing at . . . and, holding the punting pole like a spear, I smashed the blunt end of it into the side of his head, exactly on the temple. He dropped like a sack of onions and slid off the ferry into the slow brown river.'

I stared at Tuck, my mouth agape. Then I started laughing. 'Are you serious?' I asked, between gasps of breath. 'Robin Hood fell for that old trick? "I say, what's that behind you?" A ruse that was well into its dotage when Cain killed Abel?'

Brother Tuck nodded. 'He swallowed it. But try not to mention it to anyone. The poor boy is still very sensitive about it. He was very young, you must remember, and thoroughly drunk.'

I controlled my snorts of laughter with a mouthful of cider: 'What happened next?'

'Well, I fished him out, of course,' said Tuck. 'He was quite unconscious, and so I wrapped him up in a blanket and let him sleep in my cell for the rest of that day and the whole night.

'In the morning he was awake, with an aching head and a mouthful of apologies, and I fed him broth and we talked, and made peace between ourselves. We have been friends ever since. And, a few years later, after he was declared outlaw – which is a story for another day – he would visit me quite often, and sometimes leave wounded comrades at the cell for me to tend. Until he found someone who could heal them better than I. But that too is another story. Anyway, I have never seen Robin the worse for drink since that day. And I have never seen him openly display his anger. But he is angry inside – why, I do not know, but inside he is boiling and outside, these days at least, he is ice. He is the quintessential cold-hot man.'

The noon meal was over. All along the column Robin's people were packing away food sacks into the carts, sweeping crumbs off clothes, throwing away scraps. I was feeling full and not a little sleepy after such a huge meal. I had not slept the night before, though the hideous scenes with the man whose tongue was carved out seemed like no more than a nightmare in the glorious afternoon sunshine. Tuck noticed my tiredness and suggested I ride in one of the carts for a while. So I made myself a nest among the sacks of grain and bales of hay in the largest cart and lay back as the cavalcade moved off down the road. I thought about Tuck's story; trying to imagine Robin, the calm, controlled man that I had met last night, as that raging drunken youth, but it seemed incredible, so I dismissed it from my mind and very soon the swaying of the cart and the soft familiar noises of the cavalcade lulled me to sleep.

When I awoke it was dark, a crescent moon was high in the sky and the cart was in the courtyard of what looked like a large farmstead: a long hall with stables and various outbuildings. I must have slept all afternoon and for the early part of the night. There was nobody around, but the horses were housed, next to a dovecote, in an open shed, one of many off to the side of the hall itself. One of the horses was more striking than the others: pure white and more richly caparisoned than any I had seen on our journey here or, in fact, ever: it was the mount of a lady, not some well-to-do farmer's wife, but a noblewoman. I stared at the horse for a while thinking that the bridle alone would be worth five marks, and, very briefly, I considered lifting it. I was hungry again and there were sounds of revelry – great gusts of raucous laughter and music – and a strong smell of roasting meat and spilled ale coming from a partially open door at the side of the house. I'd never get away with the bridle, I thought. I didn't even know where I was exactly, and I had nowhere to run to, and nowhere to sell the loot. So, scrambling out of the cart, I brushed the hay and seeds off myself and went to the half-open door in search of food.

Inside the hall was a scene to make the Devil blush: a big, hot, noisy communal room with a huge fireplace at one end; a haunch of venison on the spit at the fire being turned by a sweaty, grubby, half-naked boy; Robin's men and women sprawled around the room or slumped drunkenly at a table, which was littered with the remains of their feast – broken bread, a small lake of spilled ale, piled greasy wooden platters, scraps and animal bones. In one corner of the hall a couple were mating like beasts, the girl, a redhead not much older than me, leaning with her palms against the wall, her skirts rucked up around her waist, with her paramour thrusting and grunting from behind. The noise was deafening, crimson-faced men shouting jests at each other across the table; three women were screaming at each other, waving their fists; a drunken oaf was blowing a wailing stream of pain from a set of bagpipes. The redhead being serviced in the corner suddenly turned her head and looked directly at me as I hovered in the doorway. She had huge, gorgeous eyes the colour of spring grass and she held my gaze for a few heartbeats before smiling and raising a suggestive eyebrow. Her look was like a physical blow, those mesmerising, bright green eyes and her air of cynical detachment from the heaving beast behind her, inside her. I looked away quickly, but not before I felt a disturbing and distinctly pleasurable stirring in my virgin loins.

I took a step back and averted my gaze and my eyes alighted on two men seated at a small table near the door talking quietly – an oasis of sober calm in the maelstrom of drunken tumult. It was the giant John with his back to me and Hugh, the clerk, deep in some private conversation. A man stumbled over to their table, body swaying like a young silver birch in a gale, with a full pot of ale in his fist. He leaned towards the centre of the table, pushing his face between John and Hugh and shouting

34

something that I didn't catch. The clerk just leaned back and John, without even rising from his seat, smashed his huge left fist across his body full into the face of the drunken man, hurling him across the room away from their table. The drunk sat down hard on the floor, and slid into oblivion. John didn't even turn his head to see the results of his handiwork.

I heard the giant say: 'So what does your brother want with all this? Deep in his heart, I mean,' and he flapped an enormous arm to indicate the howling mass of boozing outlaws. Hugh shrugged. 'It's quite simple. He wants what all men want: to be greater than his father.' Then he saw me hovering nervously and rose from his chair: 'Greetings, Alan,' he said. 'Join us.' He found me a stool and ushered me to the table with John. I could barely look at the giant, for fear he would smash my skull, like the drunken intruder, for my effrontery, so when a serving girl brought me a pot of ale and a cut of roast venison – meat twice in one day! – I buried my face in my food and held my tongue.

Hugh and John watched me eat for a while in silence and then, when I had nearly finished the plate, the clerk said: 'So how do you like our little company?' I looked at him, my mouth full of rich venison, bloody gravy running down my chin, and nodded, trying to indicate that I found the company agreeable.

'He likes the food, at any rate,' said John and laughed – a deep booming big-man's laugh that seemed to shake the room. I nodded again, more vigorously, and took a great slurp of ale to wash down the meat.

'Well, your table manners need a little polishing,' said Hugh, 'but you seem to know how to keep your mouth shut. It's the most important lesson any man can learn – keep

35

your mouth shut, and never tell on your friends. Has anyone told you your duties?'

I just stared at him, wiping my chin, and stayed mute. He continued: 'So, you are sworn to Robert, your master – and so he will arrange for your training and education. He will also clothe, arm and feed you. Till we sort out what to do with you, you'll be his body servant; it's your duty to protect him, serve him meals, run errands for him – and try not to annoy him too much. Keeping your mouth shut at all times is a pretty good rule,' he added, but not unkindly.

'You can start by taking him some supper,' he went on. 'There's a tray on the sideboard there already prepared and he's in the chamber yonder. Off you go.' He jerked his thumb at the dark opening of a passageway.

As I rose to leave, he added: 'Oh, and knock before you enter his chamber. He may be . . . occupied.'

At this, John slapped the table and started roaring with laughter. Hugh frowned: 'And don't forget what I said about keeping your mouth shut.'

I was nettled by his last remarks – did he think I was an oaf who would barge in on his master without a by-your-leave? Who couldn't understand a simple instruction to be silent? And what was so funny, anyway?

I collected the heavily laden tray – venison, cheese, bread, fruit and a jug of wine – from a board at the side of the hall which was sagging with good things to eat, whipping a couple of apples into my pouch, purely from habit, as I did so, and hefted it along the corridor that Hugh had indicated. It was a long corridor and, as the drunken hubbub from the hall diminished, I could clearly hear the sound of a woman singing. It grew louder as I approached and it was beautiful: the notes

36

high and so pure, the tune flowing like an icy, crystal stream in winter, frothily cascading over rocks, the words of the song like drops of water sparkling in the sunlight, slowing to a clear stream, idling in a moss-fringed pool and then quickening, sliding elegantly along again as the pace of the music grew . . .

I stopped, put down the tray, and stood by the door to listen. It was a song I knew well, 'The Maiden's Song', which my mother used to sing as she spun by the fire in our cottage in the happy days before my father was taken. My father had taught us all to sing in the style of the monks of Notre Dame in Paris, not all singing the same note but each making slightly different notes that blended together in a pleasing way. Nobody else in the village could do this and we were proud of the way our family could make this distinctive new kind of music together.

I felt a lump in my throat as 'The Maiden's Song' came to an end. I felt so far from home. 'Sing another, sing again,' I wanted to shout but I held my tongue. Emotion was roaring around my chest. I felt very close to tears. Beyond the door there were a few murmured words of conversation and then another voice, a man's, began: it was the old ballad 'My Love is Beautiful as a Rose in Bloom'.

The old version of the song is not much sung these days: from time to time some fresh-faced bard comes up with a newfangled version but the original is rarely heard. The verses are sung alternately by a man and woman and the story is of a man trying to woo his lover by comparing her beauty to various objects of wonder in the natural world. I'm sure you've heard it. We had sung it in my family: my father taking the male part, my mother the female, but he had taught the children to sing along in a harmonious way to both parts. Listening to the man sing his verse praising the woman's beauty made me realise, for the first time, that I would probably never see my mother again, and I was only a whisker away from sobbing out loud when the woman came in to sing her verse.

Before I knew what I was doing, I had joined in, singing the harmonies that accompany the female line as well as I could and, even with the door between us, our two voices twisted and melded together as solemn and bright and beautiful as a cathedral choir. There was a slight pause at the end of the woman's verse, just a couple of beats longer than was usual, but then the man began to sing and I accompanied him as well. We worked through the full eight verses, carolling away in harmony, all the way to the bitter-sweet end of the ballad with half an inch of English oak between me and the couple. As the angelic notes of the final verse died away, we fell into peaceful silence for a few moments – and then the door was jerked open and there was Robin, his silver eyes shining in the candlelight. He said nothing but he was staring at me as if I were a spirit or ghost.

'I've brought your supper, sir,' I said, and I bent down to pick up the tray. And then I burst into tears.

Chapter Three

It seems incredible, now as I look back, that I had the nerve as a beardless boy to join in the private carolling of my master, the murderous outlaw Robin of Sherwood, and his lady. But I believe that my actions were inspired by God, for I know that He loves music. And, as events proved, it was one of the most important performances of my life. In fact, if I had not forced my harmonies on my master, my life would have taken an entirely different path.

I stood there, weeping like an infant on the threshold and holding out the tray of food, until Robin opened the door fully and ushered me into the room. So then I set the tray down and, drying my eyes, I looked around the candle lit chamber. Sitting on a ledge by the window was the most radiant, transcendently beautiful woman I have ever seen – and I have bedded many a lovely wench in my time. But, that night she . . . she was perfection, a living angel. She looked like paintings I have seen of Mary, the mother of God, but a little younger. She was dressed simply in a long bright blue dress, embroidered with gold thread, and a white headdress, which flowed from a silver band around her forehead, above a perfect heart-shaped face. She smiled at me and my own heart gave a lurch. Her hair, a coil of which peeped out from under her headdress, was a glossy brown, the colour of chestnuts fresh from their casings. Her eyes were innocent, happy and blue, like a cloudless summer sky.

It was a plain room, as you would expect in a farmer's house deep in the countryside, but far grander than any I had been invited into before: a comfortable-looking four-poster bed, with the curtains tied back, and a chamber pot on the floor underneath, just showing; a table strewn with sheets of music with a bowl of fruit pushed to the back; two wooden chairs and a chest for clothes. That was it. It smelled of beeswax and warm wine, honest sweat and old wood: the smell of an old much-loved spade's handle; and the merest whiff, a spike of scent, from the chamber pot, filled by a woman, by this gorgeous woman. I was, in that instant, drowned in love.

Compared with the homely austerity of the room, Robin seemed to be magnificently dressed. Gone was the shabby grey travelling apparel of the day; in its place – a peacock. He was resplendent in a brilliant emerald green satin tunic, buttoned at the neck and wrists, with a wolf's head embroidered in gold and black on the chest. His long legs were clad in tight black hose and ended in pointed dark green shoes of kidskin. His hair was combed and his face and hands were clean. It was a remarkable transformation from the shaggy outlaw dispensing justice in the church.

As I cuffed away my tears, Robin poured me a goblet of wine and bade me sit in the chair at the table.

'May I present my lady Marie-Anne, Countess of Locksley,' he said to me. 'And, my darling, this is Alan

Dale, the son of an old friend, who has newly joined our strength.'

'You have the voice of an angel,' said Marie-Anne and smiled at me with those huge happy blue eyes. She was truly lovely, about eighteen, I'd have guessed, and in the full bloom of her looks. Robin drew his chair up beside her and, entwining his hand in hers, looked at me.

'You sing just like your father,' said Robin. 'I thought you were he when I opened the door.'

'You knew him well, sir?'

'Yes, he was a good friend to me many years ago. We had many a happy evening making music together at Edwinstowe. But I could not match his skill, the way he had – that you clearly have – of pitching the notes so pleasingly to make harmony.' He smiled at me, and then frowned. 'But you said "knew". Does he no longer live?'

I dropped my gaze. 'He was hanged, sir. The sheriff's men came . . .' Suddenly the tears were pressing at my eyes again and I could not go on. I was determined not to cry again in front of my master, so I looked at the floor and fell silent. The silence lengthened and grew uncomfortable. I sniffed and rubbed my nose.

'I am sorry to hear it,' Robin said gruffly. 'He was a fine man.' There was another embarrassed pause. 'Hanged on the sheriff's orders, you say?' I said nothing, fighting back tears. 'And have you looked to avenge his death?' he said, after several moments. I remained silent. He repeated his question: 'Have you not sought vengeance?' He sounded puzzled, irritated.

'Robin . . .' said Marie-Anne. 'Can't you see he's upset . . .'

'You know who ordered your father's death, do you not? But you have done nothing against him?' Robin's voice

41

now was cold. 'Look at me, boy. Look at me.' His voice was hard, compelling. I lifted my head. 'A man does not snivel when a member of his family has been murdered.' His cold silver eyes were blazing again, boring into mine. 'A man does not cry like a babe, seeking pity from those around him for a wrong he has suffered. He takes his revenge. He makes the guilty men, the men who took that kinsman's life, weep in pain; he makes their widows sob themselves to sleep at night. Else he is no man. You should have come to me. If you had come to me, we would have had the vengeance that his spirit cries out for.'

'I will avenge him, sir,' I interrupted hotly. 'I need no man's help in this. I swear it on the Holy Cross of Our Lord Jesus Christ.'

Robin snorted. 'Jesus would have you turn the other cheek. The Christ would have you forgive him,' he almost spat out the word 'forgive', then continued. 'I have little time for such a womanish religion. But I believe you shall have your vengeance, if you truly seek it, and you shall have my help in this matter of honour whether you wish it or not. You are my sworn man now, loyal until death, remember? And so my enemies are yours, just as yours are mine.'

'He's just a boy,' said Marie-Anne. 'Too young for all your blood-thirsty talk. All these bold words of vengeance and calls for death.'

'I need men-at-arms, not milksops,' said Robin shortly, glancing at his lady. And I blushed with anger.

'I am no milksop, sir,' I said angrily. 'And I will have the hides of those who killed my father. I am no warrior, it is true, but I shall become one and one day I shall dance in the blood of Sir Ralph Murdac – I shall crush him like, like . . .' I could not think of how I would crush him, and so I stopped.

'Well said,' said Robin. 'Spoken like a man. And we shall make a warrior of you before too long. I am sending you to a seasoned fighter who, though no longer as spry as he once was, will teach you his trade . . .' His voice trailed away, he was clearly lost in thought. 'But we can make more of you than just a soldier, I think . . .'

Silence fell again on the three of us. Then Robin slapped the table. 'Enough of this grim talk.' He smiled apologetically at Marie-Anne, who took hold of his hand.' Let us have some more wine . . . and some more music.'

Though I had lost much of my appetite for song, we worked easily through 'The Thrush and the Honey-Bee', our voices mingling well together, and then Marie-Anne sang us a French lament called 'Le Rêve d'Amour'. And we all sang 'My Love is Beautiful' a second time. As the last sweet notes faded into the corners of the room, Robin took my arm and looked into my face. 'A voice such as yours should not be wasted,' he said, kindness once again shining from his silver eyes. 'You truly have a gift.

'Now, it is late,' he went on, 'and you need to rest. Be so good as to ask Hugh to direct you to your sleeping place and ask him to attend me for a few moments.'

'Yes, sir,' I replied. Marie-Anne wished me a good night and I found myself closing the door and walking down the dark corridor in a state of confused euphoria, feeling that I was truly honoured to serve such a man, and yet fearful that I would disappoint him. He had that effect on people, did Robin, as I was to witness many times in the future, something about the way he looked at you made you forget his rough mockery, his hardness, his cruelty, and feel, at that moment, as if you were the most important person in the world to him. It was like a spell, a kind of magic and, as everybody knows, magic is dangerous.

I told Hugh that Robin wished to see him and made my way through the parlour, the floor of which was now littered with sleeping, snoring men and women, and out to the stable, to make my bed in the straw. As I drifted off to sleep in a warm mound of fodder, I looked again at the lovely white lady's horse. I dreamed of Marie-Anne.

We were on the road again at dawn the next day, the motley cavalcade clattering out of the gates of the farm compound, oxen roaring, carts creaking, hung-over men cursing the hour, as the cocks were bawling a noisy message about their masculinity to the heavens. Marie-Anne had departed long before the column began lumbering its way north up the forest road. And, catching my eye, she had smiled at me and waved before cantering off on her white mare, flanked by the half a dozen mounted men-at-arms.

Her departure left me feeling strangely flat. Robin, back in his shabby travelling outfit, rode at the head of our column, in earnest conversation with Hugh and Tuck. At something of a loss, I trudged along alone behind a swaying cart full of household goods, chairs, tables and chests with a wicker chicken coop filled with squawking chickens on the top. A piglet, tied by a rope round its neck to the cart, trotted happily beside me. I felt neglected and low after the excitement of the night before: had I really interrupted my lord at his music-making and joined him and his lady as an equal? It seemed unreal. The reality was not the peacock, glorious in satin and silk, warbling with his lady; the reality was the ragged outlaw at the head of this drab column, trotting along with his rascally followers.

My mood soon lightened. It was a perfect spring day and the forest was bursting with new life and fresh hope:

jewelled butterflies danced in the bright sunlight slanting through the green lattice of branches above us; on either side of the road the forest floor was a gorgeous carpet of bluebells; young coneys raced away from the column's approach; wood pigeons called to each other: *ca-cow-ca, ca-cow-ca, ca-cow-ca* . . . and I began to take notice properly of the company in which I journeyed.

We were about fifty souls in all: Robin, Hugh and Tuck were all mounted and rode at the head of the column under Robin's simple banner, a black and grey wolf's head on a white background. The banner was apt: outlaws were known as 'wolf's heads', because they could be killed by anybody, as peasants killed wolves and took their heads. Up and down the column's length, evenly spaced, were a dozen mounted men-at-arms armed with sword, shield and long spear; and a similar number of squat, hard-looking men on foot carrying big war bows made of yew, with full arrow bags strapped at their waists. Some of the fighting men looked a little grey after too much ale the night before but all were alert; keeping their heads up and scanning the woodland either side of the broad road on which we marched. A dozen paces ahead of me strode John the giant. He was talking to another big man, a blacksmith, I guessed from his thick leather apron and brawny forearms, and periodically John's great booming laugh would echo over the cavalcade. There was a farrier driving a heavy wagon, a pedlar walking under a great pack of goods, an alewife carting an enormous barrel of beer. There were mothers with babies and young children, older children playing games of tig around the slow-moving wagons, shy-saucy lasses walking proudly beside the bowmen or men-at-arms, cows bellowing and lumbering along tied to carts, sheep being prodded along by herdsmen. There was even a cat, curled up on a sack in the cart in front of me, seemingly asleep but with one speculative eye on the chicken coop. It was almost like a travelling village – I say almost because there were too many armed men for any village to tolerate in peace. But, for a column of desperate outlaws, it was far more domestic than dangerous-looking.

As I looked around me, I suddenly became aware of the mud-spattered rider I'd seen yesterday, spurring madly along the edge of the road, galloping as if the Devil himself were after him. He headed straight for Hugh at the head of the column, reined in savagely and began to make a hurried report. After a brief conversation with Hugh, just as he had done yesterday, he pulled his horse round and galloped back down the road to Nottingham the way he had come. Robin and Hugh conferred, our leader lifted his hand, the trumpet blew, and everyone came to an abrupt halt. Riders trotted up and down the column issuing orders; there was stir and bustle all along its length; and word spread: soldiers were coming; mounted men-at-arms, the sheriff's men from Nottingham. And they were approaching fast.

I felt a clutch of terror in my stomach: they were coming for me, certain-sure. They were coming to cut off my hand, to hack it off at the wrist and leave me with a spurting stump. I felt close to panic, sick to my stomach, fighting the urge to run, just to sprint into the welcoming gloom of the forest, off the main road, away from Robin and this slow column of condemned men and women.

Somehow, I managed to control my shaking legs and push my terrors to a dark cellar in my mind and lock them in. I was sworn to Robin, it was my duty to stay with him. But I was also calmed by the matter-of-fact reaction of my fellow travellers: there was no panic, little fuss at the news that the forces of the law were approaching bent on bloody retribution. People seemed businesslike, cheerful, as if this were a welcome break in a tedious day's march. In a great clearing by the side of the road, probably cleared by the King's foresters to deter villainous outlaws such as we from surprising honest travelling folk in an ambush, Robin rammed the sharpened end of his wolf banner pole in the centre of a smooth patch of turf about a hundred yards from the highway, close to the treeline where the dark wood began. The wagons rumbled off the road, oxen goaded to more speed with sharp sticks, made their way past him and formed a great circle with the banner at the centre. Everyone seemed to know what was expected. The oxen were pulled roughly into position and tied to the wagon in front to form a continuous hoop of beasts and wide, wooden vehicles. Women and children, animals and baggage went into the centre of this defensive ring. The unarmed men began unpacking axes, mattocks, hoes; some were at the forest's edge cutting long, fat quarterstaves from young trees, a few were even picking up round fist-sized stones.

There was an air of expectancy, controlled excitement. 'Little' John, as I'd heard him referred to – a feeble joke about his size – had acquired a huge double-bladed axe and he was swinging it in great hissing sweeps to loosen his muscles for the fight. His friend the blacksmith was holding two great hammers in his hairy fists, two-foot oak shafts with a couple of pounds of iron at the end, secured by stout leather straps to his wrists. I checked that my small purse-cutting knife was still in its sheath at my waist and, swallowing my fear, hurried forwards towards Robin: as his sworn man my place in battle was beside him. I hoped somehow to impress him in the coming fight.

Robin was too busy to notice me. He was unhorsed and

issuing orders to Hugh and the mounted men-at-arms, all of whom were now equipped with swords, helmets and kite-shaped wood-and-leather shields painted white with lime wash and marked with Robin's wolf device. Some carried war axes, some wore *cuir-bouilli* breastplates – front-and-back chest armour of tough boiled leather; others had chain-mail leggings or gauntlets to protect feet and hands. Each man was holding a twelve-foot spear of pale ash tipped with bright, freshly sharpened steel. And over their armour, they all wore a surcoat of the same dark green hue: a badge of their allegiance to Robin, as if he were a great noble rather than a condemned ruffian. These men might have been outlaws, thieves, murderers, men of the worst character . . . but they were also warriors – a dozen tough, proud, bearded cavalrymen, as at home on horseback in a mêlée as I was on two feet in a peaceful, grassy field. They were fearsome.

Hugh leaned down from his horse towards Robin and they clasped hands and then Hugh led the men-at-arms away from the clearing, cantering into the greenwood and disappearing into the trees. I was appalled: where were they going? Robin must have seen my gaping incredulity because he laughed and said: 'Don't worry, Alan. They'll be back . . . *à la traverse!*' he chuckled; a light, golden re-assuring sound. I had no idea what he meant, but his laughter comforted me and before I could ask him anything he turned away and bellowed: 'Archers! To me! Archers!'

From all parts of the glade, bowmen came hurrying, and with them came Tuck, a long brown stave clutched in his hand that was taller than him. Each end was tipped with cow's horn with a notch cut in its side that would hold the bowstring. As I watched, Tuck strung the bow, and I remembered that he had been a soldier in Wales before

48

he was a monk. This was no light hunting-bow for skewering rabbits; this was a war bow: six foot of strong wood from a young yew tree. The part of the bow facing the enemy, known as the 'back', was made from the lighter sapwood near the bark of the yew. This outside part of the yew tree resists being stretched when the bow is bent. The inside of the bow, its 'belly', as Robin's archers called it, was made of the dark-coloured heartwood from the centre of the tree. This inner, harder wood resists being compressed as the bowstring is pulled back. The resistance from both types of wood gave the bow its tremendous power. It took enormous strength to bend the yew wood even slightly but Tuck, though short, was immensely strong. And, after a moment's effort, he slipped the loop of bowstring into the notch in the horn – and held a man-killing machine in his hands.

Little John wandered over from the circle of wagons, his enormous axe held casually, the double-blade behind his neck, the long shaft resting on a brawny shoulder. Robin drew his sword and thrust it into the turf about five paces from the wagon circle. 'Archers here, I think,' he said. About ten burly bowmen began to form a ragged line on the sword, facing towards the road. Their leader, a squat man called Owain, spoke to them in a language I could not understand, but which I assumed was Welsh. These men had been lured from their mountains in the West by Robin, with Tuck's help, to form the core of his fighting force, and to teach his English outlaws the art of the great bow. As I watched, some of these Welshmen were still stringing their bows, others were removing arrows from the box-like linen bags at their waists and planting them point first in the turf in front of their position. Robin looked at John and asked: 'All well?' The giant just grunted.

And Robin said: 'Remember, John, keep them on a leash – don't let them out until after our charge.'

'God's holy toenails,' bellowed John in exasperation. 'Do you think I haven't done this a score of times before?'

Robin soothed him: 'Yes, John, I know, but you will agree that they do tend to get a bit overexcited . . . Be a good fellow and keep them on a leash until after the charge.'

The giant stomped away back into the circle of wagons, which was aswarm with women, children, men and beasts in a cacophonous muddle.

Tuck plucked at my sleeve. 'You shouldn't really be here,' he said. 'Your place is inside the wagons.'

I shook my head. 'My place is beside my lord,' I said gesturing with my chin at Robin who was stringing his own bow.

'Well,' said Tuck, 'I thought you might say that, so if you are determined to play the warrior, you might as well look the part,' and he handed me a heavy brown sack. It clanked.

For a young man there will always be something special, something magical, about his first sword, whether it is a small, notched rusty thing, little better than a long butcher's knife, or the finest Spanish steel blade, engraved with gold and fit for a king. It is a symbol of power, of manliness – indeed, troubadours and *trouvères*, when they weave their songs about knightly love, often use the word 'sword' as an alternative word for the male member. And when they sing about sliding a sword into its sheath . . . Well, I'm sure you understand, you've no doubt heard the salacious *cansos* and bawdy *fabliaux* . . . A sword is an icon of manhood; to be given a sword is to have manhood granted to you.

My first sword, which I found inside the sack along with

a dark green cloak and battered helmet, was a standard yard of tapered steel, a little scratched but sharp, with a fuller, a groove, running from the handle three-quarters of the way down the blade on both sides. It had a straight five-inch steel cross-piece, a wooden handle, and a rounded iron pommel. It was an ordinary weapon, like the ones carried by thousands of men-at-arms across England, but to me it was Excalibur. It was a magical blade forged by the saints and blessed by God. And it was mine. The sword came with a scuffed leather sheath attached to a worn leather sword belt. As I buckled the belt around my waist and then pulled out the blade, I felt as tall as Little John, a hero, the noble warrior who would defend his lord until death. I slashed the sword through the air in front of me, experimentally slaying invisible dragons.

Tuck who had been watching my hay-making with a kindly eye said: 'Just try not to kill any of our folk.'

His words sobered me and, as he helped put on the cloak and helmet, I realised that I really might be expected to kill, to shove this blade into a living human body, to spill a real person's guts on the green grass of this peaceful glade. And that he would be trying to spill mine.

I put the sword back in its sheath, and, as I turned to thank Tuck for his gifts, the mud-spattered spy came galloping around the bend on the road and this time headed straight for our little circle of wagons. He pulled up his sweating horse next to Robin and his thin line of archers, jumped off the beast and said breathlessly to Robin: 'They're coming, sir, hard on my heels; Ralph Murdac's men. About thirty of the bastards . . .'

Robin nodded and said: 'Fine, good; get yourself and the animal inside the cart-ring.' The man bobbed his head and led the horse away. Robin, turning to the archers who stood in a ragged line looking at him expectantly, said: 'Right lads, let's not play with them. When you see the bastards, start killing them. And when they get to that bush,' and he pointed to a scrubby alder fifty paces away, 'get inside the ring as fast as you can. Get in the cart-ring if you want to live – but not before they get to that bush. Does everybody understand?' He glanced at me and I nodded, not wanting to speak in case my voice revealed my fear.

Then we waited. Robin was sticking arrows needle-point down into the turf in front of his place, idly arranging the pattern so that it was symmetrical; the Welsh archers leaned lightly on their bow staves, chatting to each other quietly, perfectly calm. They were a very muscular lot, though few were very tall, I noticed. Many of them had a similar body shape, as if related by blood: short and squat, with thickly muscled arms and deep chests. Tuck walked down the line blessing their bows. I stood there clutching the hilt of my sword, awaiting blessing and sweating with fear and excitement in the spring sunshine. I desperately wanted to piss. Time seemed to stand still. The hubbub from the circle of wagons seemed to quieten, though an ox would occasionally moan or a chicken squawk. I wondered if the spy had been mistaken. Where were they? Robin was cleaning his fingernails with a small knife and humming under his breath – it was 'My Love is Beautiful as a Rose in Bloom', but last night and our cosy harmonies seemed a thousand miles and many lifetimes away. Tuck was on his knees praying. I closed my eyes but, from nowhere, the image of the green-eyed girl coupling with her drunken beau in the farmhouse came into my mind. I opened my eyes quickly, and crossed myself. If I were to die I did not want my last thoughts to be of those sinners.

And then, at last, at long last, I heard the drumming of hooves on a dry road and the enemy came into sight around the bend. A clattering mass of heavy horsemen, wrapped in steel and malice, and seeking our deaths.

They were a terrifying sight. Thirty stone-hard men-at-arms, mounted on big, well-trained warhorses, each man wrapped in chain mail from toe to fingertip and crowned with a flat-topped riveted steel helmet with a metal grill that completely covered his face. Soldiers such as these had hanged my father. On top of their mail they wore black surcoats, slashed with red chevrons, and they carried twelve-foot-long steel-tipped lances, man-killers, and kite-shaped wooden shields, faced with leather and painted with the red and black arms of Sir Ralph Murdac. Long swords and shorter daggers were strapped to their waists; spiked maces and razor-sharp battleaxes hung from their saddles. They were skilled killers, the lords of the battle-field, and they knew it.

They paused about two hundred yards away, their chargers snorting and pawing the grass, and they stared at our pathetic huddle of wagons, beasts, anxious peasant mothers and children, and our thin line of stunted bowmen. They looked like the steel monsters of some terrible legend, not flesh-and-blood men. Horsemen such as these had spread terror among the English folk for more than two hundred years, since William the Bastard came to take our land. Riders such as these had smashed the housecarls' shield wall at Hastings, and, since then, their descendants had been hunting down the wretches who could not pay their taxes, slaughtering honest yeomen who stood in their way, raping any girl they took a fancy to, crushing English spirits beneath their steel-shod hooves.

Two knights rode out in front of the horsemen, the

53

leaders of the conroi, as these cavalry units are called, each with a dyed-black-and-red goose-feather plume atop his helmet. They began to order the troop into two ranks of about fifteen men each. As I watched the superbly trained horses shuffle and jostle into position, I heard Robin murmur: 'Stand fast, lads . . .' His archers drew their bowstrings back to their ears. ' . . . and loose.' There was a rushing sound like a flight of swallows and a handful of arrows sped away, thin grey streaks against the blue sky. I heard Robin say again, perfectly calmly, 'Fast . . . and loose,' and then I watched in amazement as the first barrage smashed into the ranks of the conroi. Which erupted into screaming bloody chaos. Horses cried in agony, kicking out savagely at random as a dozen yards of fire-hardened ash wood, tipped with razor-sharp bodkin arrowheads, slammed deep into their chests and flanks. Two men-at-arms fell dead from their horses, killed by the arrows that punched through their hauberks into heart and lungs. What had, moments before, been menacing, orderly ranks of mounted men preparing for the charge, lances held vertically, perfectly in line, like the palings of a village fence, was now a circus of rearing terrified horses and cursing gore-splashed men. Yet more arrows sliced into them. I saw one man, unhorsed, on hands and knees, skewered by a shaft through his throat, collapse on the green turf, clutching his neck and coughing blood. Another was cursing, a vile string of obscenity, damning God himself as he tried to pull a shaft from the muscle of his thigh. A riderless horse, lashing out with his hind hooves, caught his unseated owner plumb in the chest with an audible crack of bone and the man was hurled backwards and did not rise again.

But these were no ordinary soldiers. These men were

proud horse warriors, Sir Ralph Murdac's hand-picked men-at-arms, feared in two counties, disciplined by hours of practice with horse and lance and sword and shield. The arrows were still scything into them but the men-at-arms had their shields up and were steadying their horses with their knees, pushing them back into some semblance of formation. The two knights, gaudy plumes nodding madly, were rallying the conroi with shouts and threats. And then I watched, heart in my gorge, as they ordered their ranks, turned their huge horses towards us and charged. The horsemen levelled their lances and began to gallop across the glade, bunching as they thundered across the grass, their massive hooves making the world vibrate, heading straight for our feeble defensive ring.

'Fast . . . and loose,' said Robin. And the steel-headed arrows, once again, slashed across the field to slam a foot deep into the charging horses. Two men were hurled backwards out of their saddles, as if their bodies had been attached to a rope tied to a tree. 'One more volley, boys, then we run. Stand fast . . . and loose.' Robin pulled a hunting horn from his belt and blew two short blasts, high and clear, and then a long one. The final handful of arrows drove into the charging conroi as it reached the alder bush and then we were all scrambling, breathless, tripping, terrified, back, back into the defensive circle of wagons. I ran, too, clutching my sword, as if the Devil were on my tail – I ran fit to burst my heart. It was only a short distance, perhaps thirty yards, but the horsemen were nearly upon us. I imagined I could feel the hot breath of an enormous beast and his steel-faced rider, the hooves crushing me; I could almost feel the pricking of the steel lance head between my shoulder blades . . . and then I was at the circle and sliding, sliding on the grass under the wheels of the nearest wagon – and into the legs of the blacksmith, still clutching his huge hammers, who peered down at me and said: 'All right there, son, you seem a bit out of breath.' And he winked at me.

The conroi was checked by the wagon circle. It was too big an obstacle for the horses to jump and, in frustration at missing the archers, the riders milled around the outside, leaning out of their saddles and stabbing with their long lances at our folk inside the ring, who dodged and parried and retreated out of reach. Robin's horn sounded again; two short notes and a long one, and out of the green wall of the forest our own blessed horsemen erupted.

They were a beautiful sight: a dozen mailed cavalrymen perfectly aligned in a single row, galloping towards our defensive ring. Hugh was in the centre with the white wolf banner fluttering above his head as his men swept across the glade. Their lances were couched, tucked under the arm and held parallel to the ground, aimed at the foe, spear points lusting for blood. One of Murdac's men had just time to shout a warning and then Hugh's men crashed into the scattered ranks of the enemy, spearing men and horses as they smashed through the milling throng, scattering the sheriff's troop like wolves running through a herd of sheep.

Robin's horn sounded again, three rising notes that set the hairs on my neck standing erect: *ta-ta-taaa, ta-ta-taaa*. 'Come on, then, lad,' said my blacksmith friend. 'That's the attack, that is.' And he leapt up on to the wagon and over the other side, swinging his two great hammers, surprisingly nimble for such a big man. Once out of our cart-ring he gave a passing enemy horse a great smash on the forehead and the poor animal tottered and sank to its knees. Quick as a weasel the smith was on his rider, even as the animal was sinking, pounding with both the great lumps of metal in turn at his square helmeted head. He must have smashed through the helmet and into the brain because, suddenly, there was a great gout of blood and greyish pink matter that splashed the front of his chest. He saw me watching, appalled at this savage display, and he smiled an enormous, battle-mad grin and shouted: 'Don't gawp, boy, get stuck in, get stuck in . . .'

Robin was to my right, standing on a wagon with another archer; both of them calmly shooting arrow after arrow into the enemy horsemen. I turned to my left and there was Little John, outside the circle, swinging his enormous axe with murderous skill. I saw him hack into the back of a rider and cut straight through his mail, severing the spine. As he tugged the double-blade loose, the man fell forward, limp as a doll, his head almost touching his foot in the stirrup as a scarlet fountain from his partially severed waist shot straight into the air.

Everywhere I looked there were Robin's followers, men, and some women too, on foot, some armed only with quarter-staves or stones, some with hoes or scythes, surrounding isolated riders and smashing them and their mounts with a near-berserk fury. A body of horsemen, disciplined and armed with the long lance, can destroy a crowd of infantry in moments; but when the horseman is alone and surrounded by a pack of blood-crazed peasants with a chance to wreak vengeance for the crimes committed against them, and their forebears, by that mounted symbol of Norman power, it's like watching a crippled spider being overrun by a pack of maddened ants. The horses were hamstrung, quick-smart, with long, sharp knives; the unfortunate man-at-arms's legs seized by many hands. He was yanked, tugged alive, from the saddle to be pulverised to bloody ruin on the steaming earth. Pounding metal, blunt tools punched into living flesh; screaming man and horse, and hot, squirting blood.

But it was not all going our way: one of the plumed knights was wreaking havoc on our people. His reins dropped over his saddle horn and controlling the horse only with his knees, he laid about him with sword and spiked mace, smashing skulls and severing arms. As I watched an arrow slammed into his thigh, and he wheeled away with a curse.

The blacksmith just in front of me had stopped hammering at his foe's mashed skull and was watching Little John, who sank his huge axe-blade with a graceful backhand into the throat of a passing horse. The unfortunate animal, spraying gore, reared with the last of its strength and dislodged the rider, who lay winded on his back on the life-drenched ground. Within a heart-beat, he was surrounded by a swarm of hacking, gouging peasantry. 'That's the way, lad,' the blacksmith grinned at me, 'no lollygagging, get stuck in.' And then his mad, happy face suddenly changed shape, paled and he sank to his knees. From the centre of his chest the bloody tip of a steel lance was protruding. He looked down in disbelief and his huge body juddered and jiggled as the man-at-arms on the other end of the spear tugged at the weapon to release it from his sucking flesh.

An image of my father's distorted hanged face leapt into my mind and I found myself screaming 'Noooo . . .!' My naked sword was in my fist and I was up and had leapt over the wagon before I could think. I charged at the rider, whose lance was still trapped in the smith's body, and swung my weapon at his leg, crazed with red fury. The blade slammed into his mailed calf and the man shouted in pain but the blow did not break through the chain armour. The man dropped the lance and swung at me, left handed, across his body, with a huge war axe. I dodged, and then another horse barged into the back of his and he staggered in the saddle, both arms flailing, the axe hanging from its strap on his left wrist. I grabbed the mailed sleeve of his right arm, my mind boiling, heaved and, with a rattle and a crash he thumped down on to the turf, his helmet knocked off, wheeling away.

I didn't think for a second about what I was to do; it was as if there was another boy controlling my body. As the enemy horseman sprawled on the ground, bareheaded, I swung the sword as hard as I could at his exposed neck and I felt the jar of the blade as it chopped into his spine at the base of his head. He screamed and his body gave a huge convulsive jerk. But my heart, my tender heart was singing. Here was vengeance, this was a blow struck for my father's memory. The man convulsed again; there was a massive spurt of bright gore and then he lay still, face up, blood pooling underneath him, with my old sword half-severing his head from his body.

I saw his face clearly for the first time. He was no steel monster from a nightmare. His blue eyes stared at Heaven, his skin was milk-white and unblemished except for a wispy blond moustache on his upper lip, his jaw slack, red mouth open revealing perfect white teeth. He was, perhaps, only two or three years older than me. Then he breathed a last sigh, like a man taking his ease after a long day of labour, a long rattling huff of air as his soul left his body.

I looked down at the first man I had ever killed. I stared at him. My eyes were pricking with tears. And I reached forward to . . . to touch him, to apologise, to beg his forgiveness for ending his young life – I don't know what.

I pulled my hand back, and looked up and away from him. I saw Robin above me, standing on the wagon, an arrow nocked at his bow, searching for a fresh victim. His eyes met mine. He nodded at me, and shouted; and above the screams of battle, I could hear his strong confident voice as clear as if he were next to me: 'A fine kill, Alan. Neatly done. We'll make a warrior of you yet.' He smiled at me, a relaxed careless grin. I stared at him, my mind whirling. And then by some strange alchemy my mood changed, I became infected with his courage. Where I had felt sick and weak at having cut short a young life, I now felt a glorious surge of blood to my limbs. I looked down again at the dead boy at my feet and I found my hand reaching for my sword. I grasped its plain wooden handle and, with a great heave, I tugged it loose from the vice of his backbone. Then I stood straight, lifted my chin, steadied my shaking legs, and looked about for more enemies to kill.

Chapter Four

The battle was done. The surviving enemy men-at-arms, and there was not above a handful, had run, some on foot, some two or even three to a horse, back down the road in the direction they had come.

I looked around the field and my stomach turned to ice: it was scattered with dying horses, crawling, staggering blood-soaked men, the air filled with bubbling screams and groans, the ground covered with so much gore that the lush clearing was green no more: a stinking midden of blood and mud, horse shit and shattered bodies. The battle smell was sharp as salt: a metallic odour, coppery and blunt at the back of the nose; with notes of dung and piss, fresh sweat and crushed grass. But above all that, above the pain and death and horror and filth, I felt a great swooping, skylarking joy at merely being alive, joy that the enemy was beaten, and that we were victorious.

Robin's ragged men and women were hurrying from body to body, cutting the throats of the enemy wounded, stifling screams and digging through their pouches and saddlebags. Only one enemy remained standing on the field. It was the knight, his helmet off, a bloody gash in his side, his chain mail clogged with blood, his left thigh pierced by an arrow, but still on his feet, sword and mace in hand, surrounded by a ring of Robin's men, some freshly wounded, who were taunting him and pelting him with stones. The mocking outlaws stayed prudently out of reach of the knight's sword and mace: I could see three bodies at his feet.

'Come on, you cowards,' the knight shouted. His English was unaccented, which was rare for a knight. 'Step forward and die like men.' A stone bounced off his chest. 'You pack of lily-livered villeins, come forward and fight!' And, in answer to his taunt, one rash outlaw, a big fellow armed with an axe, rushed at him from behind. The knight seemed to have eyes in the back of his head. He half turned to the right and blocked the man's wild axe swing with his sword. Then he changed direction, his feet as neat as a dancer's, and swinging his torso to the left, he neatly crushed the man's skull with one blow of his spiked mace. The man crumpled, jerked once, lay still. The knight had done it so casually, a killing flick of such skill and grace, that his jeering enemies were silenced.

'Come on then, who's next?' said the knight. 'Let's start a pile.'

An archer pushed his way through the ring until he was just five yards from the knight; he nocked an arrow to his bow, pulled back the hemp cord and was about to sink a yard of ash into the knight's chest when Robin, arriving at a run, shouted in his iron battle voice: 'Hold!' And, pushing through the crowd around the knight, he said: 'Sir, you have fought with courage. And now you are wounded. I am Robert Odo of Sherwood. Yield!'

The knight cocked his head on one side; he was a handsome man, about twenty-five, with a big black bushy beard and bright eyes. He replied: 'You wish to yield? Very well, I accept.' He was smiling, even in the face of death. Robin stared at him. The archer hauled back his bow cord the final inch. The knight lifted his chin, a heartbeat from his Maker. But Robin stuck out a commanding arm, palm toward the archer. And then my master began to laugh, amid the blood and death, the pain and fury, he laughed and laughed. And the knight, laughing also, dropped his mace, spun the sword in a glittering sweep in the air, caught it by the bloody tip in his mailed hand and offered the hilt to Robin. 'I am Sir Richard at Lea,' he said smiling, 'and I am your prisoner.' And, still smiling, he collapsed on the mud at Robin's feet, unconscious.

We packed up the wagons with astonishing speed. In fact, Robin's band did everything quickly, without fuss. The wounded were loaded with the baggage. The very badly wounded, only three men that I saw, after they had been given the last rites by Tuck, were dispatched with a swift dagger to the heart, administered by John. He did it with a strange gentleness, cradling their heads in his enormous hand and thrusting once, quickly, through the ribs to release a bright gout of heart's blood. It seemed that this was the custom of Robin's band. And nobody commented on the way these men were hurried on to Heaven, or the other place. Graves were dug, again with great speed, for our dead. Their dead – there were twenty-two corpses, and no wounded: all who had not run, except Sir Richard, had been executed by Robin's men and women – were stripped of anything valuable: weapons, mail, boots, clothes, money, and lined up by the side of the road; their grubby chemises, these undershirts being the only item of clothing too dirty even for Robin's men to steal, fluttered in the wind, grey, ragged flags to mark their passing to the next world. Tuck said a few brief words over the row of dead men, and I felt a pang as I caught sight of my victim's blond, blood-smirched hair. They were the enemy, but they were also warriors and men. Tuck made the sign of the cross over the bodies and turned away; Hugh, mounted and at the head of the column, gave the cry: 'Forward!' and the whole lumbering train set off again down the forest road. I looked at the sun – only an hour had passed since we had been warned by the spy. I hitched my sword belt, turned my back on the bloody clearing and walked after the column, following my victorious outlaw lord.

We turned off the Great North Road soon afterwards, and on to a series of lesser tracks, each one narrower than the last. The great green wood closed in around us until the sides of the ox-carts were whipped with branches and the sunlight was rarely seen. The rutted pathway twisted and turned so regularly that, in the gloom of the forest, I soon lost track of north and south, east and west. As darkness fell, I realised that I was hopelessly lost. But Robin clearly knew where we were heading and we plunged ever onward, travelling by the light of a few pitch-wood torches, until we arrived at an ancient hall, deep in the forest.

Robin left us there: Hugh, the wounded men-at arms, the women, the children, the livestock, the cumbersome ox-carts and their loads of tribute, Sir Richard and me. The steward of the hall, Thangbrand, a grizzled old warrior, had killed a pig and prepared a feast for Robin and his band, but I was filled with strange melancholy humours after the battle and could barely eat; I kept thinking of the blond boy I had killed – his face hung before me when I closed my eyes, red mouth smiling, showing his white teeth, as blood seeped around his neck from the hideous wound in his spine. He was too young to have been one of the men who had killed my father, yet I had no doubt he would have obeyed such an order. So I believed I had taken at least some measure of vengeance for my father in taking this man's life, even if he was only a symbol, an embodiment, of the forces that had deprived me of my parent. And I was very glad that Robin had seen me kill this enemy; but why then did I feel so miserable? It was too much to understand, so I retired to a corner of the hall, wrapped myself in my cloak and tried to block out the sound of carousing around the ale barrels and find the oblivion of sleep.

Robin and his unburdened cavalcade left the next morning. Every man was freshly mounted on horses from Thangbrand's stables. Tuck embraced me and urged me to mind my manners and consider my immortal soul every once in a while. Little John gave me a powerful slap on the back. When Robin himself came to bid me a brief farewell, I knelt and asked if I might not accompany him, but he raised me up and told me to obey Hugh in all things and attend to my lessons with him. 'You will serve me better with a little education under your belt, Alan. I need clever men around me. Learn from Thangbrand, too,' he said. 'He was once a great fighter and he has much to teach you. One kill doesn't make you a warrior, though it was a fine start, a very fine start.' He smiled and clasped my shoulder. 'I'll be back soon, never fear,' he said. 'Doubtless, I'll have need of your new skills before long.' Then he turned his horse and cantered away. As I watched him ride away through the trees, I felt suddenly uncertain, bereft, even a little afraid. I was alone among strangers in the middle of the wilderness.

Thangbrand's hall, like his name, was a throwback to Saxon times. Built of sturdy oak posts and wattle-and-daub walls, in a wide clearing hidden deep in Sherwood, it appeared to exist in a simpler time, a time before the proud Frenchmen came to these shores. A large oblong building, with a high thatched roof, the hall was the centre of a settlement of about thirty folk. A rickety wooden palisade surrounded the hall and its outbuildings: stables, granaries, workshops, a smithy, a cookhouse and several ramshackle huts where the lowlier human inhabitants slept, along with the animals. It was in one of these that Sir Richard was lain. He had sworn to Robin the night before, on his honour as a knight, that he would not try to escape until his ransom was agreed and paid by Sir Ralph Murdac. In truth, he was too much knocked about to run far. He had lost vast quantities of blood and he was only intermittently conscious. An axe blow had smashed several ribs and punctured his right side, Tuck told me, after he had tended to him to the best of his abilities. His left thigh had been pierced by an arrow, which had been removed while Sir Richard was unconscious. Fortunately, the thigh bone had not been broken. Now bandaged and pale, stripped of his armour, but with a flask of water mixed with wine at his side, he sat on the floor of a pigsty, propped against the back wall on a pile of clean straw, and observed the bustle of his rustic prison through the wide opening.

Thangbrand's household, of which Hugh had assumed temporary mastery as Robin's lieutenant, consisted of Thangbrand, his extremely fat wife Freya, their two dark, well-made sons, Wilfred and Guy, who were only a few years older than me, and a skinny daughter called Godifa, of about nine or ten summers. Another boy, William, a sturdy red-head about my age much given to oafish grinning, lived there as well, a cousin of some sort. There were also a dozen men-at-arms, some wounded from our skirmish, some I'd never seen before, and half a score of male and female servants.

Shortly after Robin left, Hugh summoned me and outlined the shape of my life there at Thangbrand's. I should learn, he told me, as much as I could from those around me. And I would be punished if I disrupted the household, if I stole anything or did not attend to my duty. If I behaved myself, and paid close attention in my lessons, and worked hard, I would receive something of inestimable value, a treasure of the mind, a *thesauros* . . . He was talking about my education.

My day, he said, would be structured thus: at dawn, before breakfast, I would do chores around the hall, feed the chickens and pigs and the doves in the dovecote, under the supervision of Wilfred, Thangbrand's elder son, for an hour or so. Then we – Wilfred, Guy, William and me – would break our fast and then be instructed in the arts of war with some of the men-at-arms by Thangbrand until noon, when we would eat the main meal of the day. Then, in the afternoon, we would be instructed in French and Latin, in grammar, logic and rhetoric, and in *courtoisie*, the correct behaviour of noble young men. I was privileged, Hugh made me understand in a stern but kindly way, to be learning the skills of a gentleman's son, despite my low birth. After supper there would be more chores, he informed me, and then an early bed.

At the feasts on high days and holidays, I was to serve at table in my best clothes, with my face washed. I was

67

not to pick my nose or my ears in sight of the guests. Nor was I to get drunk. I was to sleep every night in the hall on a straw-filled palliasse on the floor by the fire with the other men and boys. Hugh had his own hut, not far from the hall, where he slept and met his dark couriers, the shadowy men who brought him news from the four corners of the country, and Thangbrand and Freya slept in a solar at the end of the hall that was their own private chamber.

Hugh then issued me with new clothes, as mine were nearly falling off me: several pairs of linen drawers, known as braies, two pairs of green woollen hose, two chemises, an ordinary brown knee-length tunic for daily wear, a much finer green surcoat trimmed with a little squirrel fur at neck and hem for special occasions, and a hood of dark green wool, the same colour as the cloak that Tuck had given me. I was to look after them, Hugh told me, and keep them clean. I also received a pair of new leather boots, worth more than anything I had ever owned, and an aketon, or gambeson, a heavily padded coat, worn both for warmth on cold days and protection in battle. It was too large for me. But when, in private, I strapped my sword belt over the aketon, and put on my helmet, I felt more like a man-at-arms and less like a servant.

Discipline was harsh at Thangbrand's, which I soon discovered was more military training camp than peaceful backwoods farmstead. There were no light beatings of the kind my father had given me to make me mend my wild ways. Instead, the penalties for any transgressions were savage. Several days after I arrived, one of the men-at-arms, a fellow called Ralph, got drunk and raped one of the servant girls. Thangbrand dragged the rapist before Hugh, who said he was going to make an example of him. He had him beaten bloody with quarterstaves by the other outlaws until he was barely conscious, then the poor man was castrated in an awful ceremony performed in front of the entire population – I vomited at the sight once again, to my shame. Naked, bleeding from the gory hole between his legs, and barely able to walk, he was driven out of Thangbrand's settlement into the forest to starve or, more likely, be eaten alive by the wolves.

I was frightened, I admit – the man's agonised screams visited my dreams for weeks afterwards – and I vowed to behave myself and not invite punishment. So I obeyed my betters and began to learn the skills of a gentleman's son.

Wilfred, Thangbrand's eldest son, was perhaps sixteen years old, a quiet, mild youth much given to daydreaming and reading romances. He was not unkind to me but it was clear that he found me irritating. I needed to be supervised, he felt, and this took him away from his stories about King Arthur and other tales of heroic feats in battle. Despite his lurid tastes in literature, he was not at all warlike himself, and I could see that he might have made a good priest, if circumstances had been different and his father had been a Norman knight rather than a Saxon nobody living in the wilderness. As it was, he was responsible for overseeing me at my chores: simple, dull everyday jobs, such as chopping wood for the hall's great fire and bringing water to fill the household butts from a stream that ran half a mile away. I also fed the chickens, doves and pigs twice a day and swept the area of beaten earth in front of the hall on which we practised for war.

Guy, though two years younger than Wilfred, was far more bellicose: indeed, I have never come across two brothers who were less similar. Wilfred was quiet, dreamy, monk-ish; Guy was loud, self-regarding, warlike and, from

69

the moment I arrived there, he treated me with absolute contempt. Guy wished more than anything to be a knight: his name was actually Wolfram, not Guy, but he had given himself the Norman name, to his father's fury, because he believed it sounded more knightly. Everything he did reflected his desire to be a member of the Norman military class. His loathing of me, I believed, came from my peasant birth; his family, Thangbrand's ancestors, he often told me, had been lords since the dark ages. Before the Romans, even. He was my superior, he constantly pointed out, in every way.

Guy thrashed me with his fists on my third day at Thangbrand's. He attacked me from behind as I was filling a sack with wheat to take to the mill and knocked me senseless; then, slapping me back into this world, he told me, ludicrously, to stay out of his way. I did try to stay out of his way, as much as possible, but Guy and I were forced into proximity in Thangbrand's yard every morning for battle practice and every afternoon for our lessons with Hugh.

In his youth, Thangbrand may have been a great warrior. Indeed, he was apparently known as Thangbrand the Widowmaker and he claimed that his grandfather had been one of Harold Godwinson's housecarls. But little of his prowess remained now that he had seen nearly sixty summers. He taught us to use sword and shield in stiff, very simplistic, set manoeuvres. Punch forward with the shield, then hack down with the sword. Or, lunge with the sword, defend high against the counterstroke with the shield. He had us practise these dull, obvious moves for hours, me, Wilfred, Guy and William and a couple of the outlaw men-at-arms who had had little or no military training. All of us standing in line and stepping our way forward in unison

70

across the yard, while Thangbrand clapped his hands and shouted one-and-two, one-and-two, in time with our strokes. At the end of our session he would pair us up – most often Will and Wilfred and Guy and me – and we would mimic single combat. In my case, this meant cowering behind my shield enduring a storm of fury as Guy battered mercilessly at my defences. I realised that Robin had been right. One kill did not make me a warrior.

In one way this training was useful: I didn't learn much about fighting but I did discover how deeply angry Guy was. What Tuck would call a 'hot man'. And the exercise strengthened my arms – and quite possibly my mind.

The afternoon lessons were a pleasant surprise: I discovered that much of the language my father had attempted to beat into me had in fact taken root. When Hugh read out passages in Latin, I found myself half-understanding the text. When he spoke to us in French, too, I found it relatively easy to understand. And the words and phrases that I didn't know, once Hugh had explained them in English, stuck with me. Hugh was pleased; the other boys were not. When Hugh's back was turned, Guy would punch me hard on the arm, or knee me painfully in the thigh, and call me 'teacher's blondie bum-boy' or 'little yellow lick-spittle'.

William, the red-headed cousin, was a thief. He proudly told me that his nickname in his home in Yorkshire was 'Scoff-lock' or 'Scarlock' because of his skill breaking into houses and opening money chests. We all called him Will Scarlet, because of his flaming hair. His most irritating habit was to steal my food at dinner, quite blatantly: his darting hand snatching a piece of bread or meat as my head was turned and stuffing it into his mouth. I found this particularly annoying because of its absurdity – there was plenty of food to go around, and good food, too.

Indeed, we ate meat almost every day; as Thangbrand lived not by farming – although a few vegetables were grown in a plot behind the hall – but by poaching the forest. He traded meat – venison and wild boar, mainly – for grain with the nearest farmers, and occasionally he and his men would ambush travellers on the Great North Road and relieve them of their valuables and sometimes their lives. One third of the cash from these robberies was handed over to Hugh, as Robin's representative. This tribute, sometimes called Robin's Share, was stored in a great iron-bound coffer in the hall which was half full of silver pennies. Even to touch the chest was a death sentence. And, after witnessing the punishment meted out to Ralph the rapist, much as I loved to steal, I lost any inclination to help myself from it.

But Robin's Share was not the only treasure in Thangbrand's hall. Freya, Thangbrand's enormous wife had one, too; their own private hoard of valuables hidden in their chamber.

As part of my daily duties, I would bring cups of warmed wine to Freya and Thangbrand before they went to sleep an hour or two after dusk. One night when I was bringing their nightcaps, I found the door was ajar and entered their solar silently without knocking. I did not mean to surprise them but the cups were full and I was concentrating on not spilling the hot wine and so I moved carefully and, as a result, quietly. As I entered the chamber I saw Freya on her knees in the corner of the room. There was a dark hole in the floor, which I had never seen before, from which the lid of a small metal box protruded. Freya had a rush-light in one hand and, in the other . . . God forgive me, but even forty years on I still feel a rush of unholy greed when I think of it . . . in the other hand was a huge

72

oval-shaped jewel, a dark translucent red colour. It was an enormous ruby, a great gorgeous stone worth many hundreds of pounds, a baron's ransom, maybe more – although I didn't know it at the time. All I knew, with my thievish heart, was that I wanted it. Then things began to happen very fast. Freya saw me, gave a high pitched squeal and thrust the great jewel back into the box in the hole in the floor; and out of the darkness, like an avenging demon, sprang Thangbrand the Widowmaker, grasping a great dagger. His weight smashed me against the wall, cups and wine hurled into the air, and he held me there with the knife against my throat, his ageing, bloated face inches from mine. I could smell his foul breath and his eyes bored into me. I was moments from death, I could feel the cold steel pressing into the flesh of my neck; one swift lateral movement of his hand and I would be washing the beaten earth floor with my life's blood.

'What did you see?' hissed Thangbrand. The stench of his rotting teeth filled my nostrils. His yellowed eyes searched my face. 'Nothing,' I squeaked. 'Nothing, sir.'

'You lie,' he said, his blotched face working with rage. 'You lie . . .' There was a momentary increase in the pressure on my neck. Then, praise God, he pulled back his face a few inches, considering me, and then more calmly he said again: 'You lie, but, as you are under Lord Robert's protection, you shall live, for now . . .' He released me and stepped back. We stared at each other for a few heartbeats. Freya was frozen on her knees in the corner. 'Listen to me, boy,' said Thangbrand, 'listen to me if you want to live. You did see nothing, nothing at all. But if, by any chance, you were to talk to anybody about the nothing that you saw here tonight, Will, Wolfram, anybody at all, then I will slit your weasand from ear to ear while you

73

sleep, drag you out into the forest for the wolves, and no one will say a word. Do you hear me?'

'I will be silent, sir, I vow it,' I said, trying to still my shaking limbs.

'Yes,' he growled, 'be silent, and be gone.'

I felt more respect for Thangbrand after that night. He might be a dull sword instructor but he was still a fearsome man despite his age. So I tried to put what I had seen from my mind. The next day it was as if nothing had ever happened and Thangbrand treated me with the same rough affection as he had previously.

Life rolled on, spring turned into summer, and in these months my routine changed little: a round of work, meals, lessons, sleep, work . . . It would have been quite pleasant were it not for the taunts and blows from Guy, and the behaviour of his irritating shadow Will. As I've said, there was absolutely no need for William to steal from my plate, but he continued to do it anyway; I suppose he thought it was a challenge of some kind. But watching Will's chewing, bulging mouth, stuffed with my food, leering at me across the table, while he sat next to his protector Guy and dared me to say something, well, it didn't make me feel challenged – just slightly ill.

I had to do something about it, though, if only for my honour's sake. One day, palming a crust of bread, I inserted a sharp but rusty iron nail that I had found in the yard that morning, making sure it was completely hidden from view. Casually leaving the piece of bread on the edge of my plate nearest to Will, I turned away from the table to ask Thangbrand about something and when I turned back the little red-haired bastard was cursing and spitting blood. He'd bitten down hard on the nail and broken one of his teeth. Of course, he could say nothing about my part in the incident, and it stopped him filching from my plate, but it didn't exactly make us friends.

I did make one friend at Thangbrand's: the skinny little yellow-haired girl Godifa. I was trying to stay out of Guy's way after a particularly dreary Latin lesson – Guy had no ear for the language at all and to make matters worse he was badly hung-over after drinking heavily the night before with the men-at-arms. As he stumbled and stuttered his way through a passage of the Bible, I could feel Hugh's impatience growing. He loved the Word of God with all his heart and it offended him to hear it mangled so. Finally, he asked me to translate the passage correctly and I did so, fluently but with a growing realisation that this display of prowess would cost me dearly. Sure enough, once Hugh's back was turned, Guy kneed me hard in the thigh, causing my leg to go numb. After the lesson, I'm ashamed to say, I fled to avoid the inevitable beating from Guy. He stood a good head taller than me and, as I had discovered many times before, I stood no chance against him in any kind of combat.

So I had left the farmstead – it was a beautiful, warm day – and gone into the woodland to lose myself in the calm of the great trees for a while, when I came across Godifa standing by a huge old oak tree and crying her little heart out. She had adopted a kitten, which had grown into a young and daring little beast, and it was stuck up the tree. As she sobbed, it peered down at us from a low branch, miaowing piteously. It took me a dozen heartbeats to scramble up the tree and stuff the cat into my tunic before swinging down and presenting it to Godifa with a little bow and a flourish. There was an instant transformation on her face – from rain to sunshine. Beaming and cuffing away her tears she grabbed my hand and kissed it before running away, skipping with happiness. I thought little of it but, for weeks afterwards, I began to notice her following me around as I did my chores. She was very shy and would not speak to me and, if I caught her eye and smiled at her, she would immediately blush and run away.

About six months after my arrival at Thangbrand's, there was an evening feast: a saint's day, I think, though I cannot remember which one. At great feasts, my duty was to go around the table with a huge ewer of water, pour it over the outstretched hands of the guests into a salver held by Will. Then Guy would offer a clean towel. When all the guests had washed, I would help the servants bringing food from the cookhouse: we had roast boar; great haunches of venison, of course; boiled capons; pigeon pie; pease pudding; cheese and fruit. Each guest had a trencher: a wide, flat platter of baked bread on which they would eat their meat; the bread soaking up the juices. Will and I circled the great table pouring wine, removing dishes when empty, bringing in more courses from the cookhouse. We took turns to snatch a few mouthfuls in a dark corner of the hall, whenever we could.

On this occasion, when everyone had fed to their hearts' content, and we had removed all but the fruit and jugs of wine, a man I had not seen before walked to the end of the hall. He was holding a vielle, a beautifully polished wooden musical instrument with five strings, a big round belly and a tall, thin neck. Holding the vielle to his shoulder with his left hand, with a sweep of the horsehair bow in his right, he struck a single long, golden chord and gradually silence descended on the boisterous gathering.

'My friends,' he said, as bitter-sweet sound still hummed

around our head, its delicious reverberations quickening my soul, 'this is a song about love . . .'

And he began:

'I love to sing, as singing is fed by joy . . .'

As I write this line of poetry in my own language, English – he was, of course, singing in French – it seems a paltry thing, a commonplace utterance. But, then, in that ramshackle hall, deep in the ancient greenwood, it cast a shiver down my spine. It was sung with such beauty, and accompanied by the angelic notes of the vielle, that it lifted the hearts of everyone in the hall. I saw Guy's mouth drop open, exposing a mash of half-chewed meat. Hugh, who had been about to drink from his goblet, stopped with the vessel held halfway up to his face. Then the musician swept the bow smoothly across the strings, releasing another chord, and sang:

'But no one should force themselves to make a song,
When the pleasure has left a true heart.
The work is too hard, the labour is joyless.'

He was a youngish man; medium height and slender, with dark blond hair that adorned his head like a smooth, glossy helmet and a handsome open face. He was clean-shaven, a rarity in our community, and his face seemed flushed with goodness in the flickering firelight. Everything about him was strangely clean and neat, exact, from his spotless tunic of dark blue satin, with jewelled belt and knife, to his smooth green and white striped hose and kidskin boots. He stood out in the hall filled with muddy ruffians dressed in lumpy homespun like a proud, iridescent cockerel among dowdy brown chickens. The chickens were silent now, entranced.

'He whom love and desire compel to sing,
Can easily compose a good song
But no man can do it without being in love.'

I had never heard glorious music of this kind before: simple yet heartbreakingly beautiful, a waft of notes and the voice – oh, and such a pure voice – echoing the tune, repeating the vielle's refrain as the instrument moved on to a new elegant phrase. And, best of all, he sang of love: the love of a young knight for his lord's lady; not the squalid rutting of outlaws and whores, but a pure, wonderful, painful love; an impossible love that can never find expression outside song. This was the love that inspired men to do great deeds, to sacrifice their blood for an ideal, an emotion. And I knew what I wanted to do with my life: I wanted to love . . .

'Love is pure for it teaches me,
to create the purest words and music.'

. . . and I wanted to sing.

Chapter Five

Thangbrand's hall was bright with firelight and music. At one end stood the elegant musician, his vielle cradled in his silk-wrapped arms, chin high, eyes closed, his pink mouth and white teeth wide as he poured out a golden stream of sound into the room. On benches by the walls, on the chests of personal possessions, on stools and chairs at the long table, and even squatting on the rush-strewn floor, all the earth-bound inhabitants of Thangbrand's listened in absolute silence to this heavenly music. These were the exquisite notes of another life, a life of effortless beauty, of wealth and taste and power, the power to summon delight with a clap of well-fed hands. They were hearing the gorgeous sound of a great court, the music of kings and princes. And I wanted to be part of it; I wanted to own that music, to wallow in it, to drown in its heady, sumptuous liquor.

And then it happened. In the pause at the end of a perfect refrain about the beauty and pain of love, Guy sniggered. It was only a small sound, a snort of derision. But the musician stopped dead in the middle of a line: his eyes snapped open and he looked at Guy. He stared at him for an instant, his face losing all colour. Then with the merest ghost of a bow at the high chairs at the end of the hall where Hugh and Thangbrand were sitting, he strode out of the great door into the night.

There was a great collective sigh. The spell had been broken: and yet we all longed to hear more of his witch-craft. Starting with a few murmurs, talk began to flow again about the hall. Hugh, who had been chewing a chicken leg while he listened to the music, shouted 'Idiot!' and hurled the bone at Guy, hitting him squarely on the forehead. Guy raised his eyebrows and palms in a pantomime of innocence.

And, at that moment, I hated him. Before then, he had been an annoyance, and someone to avoid, but at that moment all my emotion distilled into poisonous concentrated hatred: I hated Guy with true ferocity. I wanted, not so much his death, as his total annihilation; a wiping of his being off the face of the Earth.

The French musician's name was Bernard, as I discovered the next day in an interview with Hugh after the noon meal. To my joy, Hugh told me that Robin had arranged that I should become Bernard's pupil. The Frenchman would also take over as my language teacher from Hugh, as I was far more advanced than the other students, and Bernard had also been charged with giving me lessons in arithmetic, geometry, astronomy . . . and music. I was ecstatic, bubbling with happiness: I would spend all afternoon listening to wonderful music, and learning how to make it myself, and, best of all, I would be away from Guy and Will for hours at a time.

I found Bernard in the small cottage he had been given

about half a mile from Thangbrand's farmstead in a small clearing in the greenwood. I walked there on air, dizzy with joy at my prospects, mingled with some trepidation: would I prove worthy of this great man? Hugh had let slip that separate living quarters had been a condition of Bernard's acceptance of the job as my tutor. He was a fastidious man, Hugh said, and he would not sleep in the hall with all the other flea-bitten outlaws.

He did not look particularly fastidious when I encountered him that fine early autumn afternoon, to present myself as his pupil. He was slumped on an up-ended sawn-off log outside the semi-derelict cottage; his tunic, the fine silk one from yesterday's performance, was only half buttoned, and had what looked like dried vomit down the front. He had lost one of his shoes and, as he strummed his vielle with his fingers, he giggled softly to himself, swaying on his seat. The day before I had seen him a God-like figure, courtly lover, master of music, creator of beauty: today he was ridiculous.

'Master Bernard,' I said in French, standing in front of him as he sat there head drooped over his vielle, fingering the strings. 'I am Alan Dale, and I have come to present myself to you as a pupil at the orders of my master, Robert Odo . . .'

'Shhhhhh . . .' he slurred at me, wagging a finger rapidly in my general direction. 'I am creating a masterpiece.'

He amused himself on the vielle, playing little ripples of music and occasionally appearing to nod off for a few moments, before jerking awake. I stood there for perhaps a quarter of an hour and then he looked up and said clearly: 'Who are you?'

I repeated: 'I am Alan, your pupil, and I have come to serve you at the orders—'

He interrupted me: 'Serve me, eh, serve me? Well, you can bring me some more wine, then.'

I hesitated, but he waved me away shouting: 'Wine, wine, decent wine, go on, boy, go on, go on, go on . . .' So I went back to Thangbrand's, stole a small cask of wine from the buttery when nobody was looking, brought it back on a barrow. Then I helped him to drink it.

As my tutor in arithmetic, geometry and astronomy, Bernard was a disaster. In fact, as I remember, he never even mentioned the subjects. But he did improve my French, as it was all we spoke together, and he did teach me music, God be praised: he taught me how to construct *cansos* and *sirventes*, love songs and satirical poems, how to tune and play the vielle, how to extend my voice, to control my breathing and many more technical tricks of his trade. He was a troubadour, or more properly, since he came from northern France, a *trouvère*, and his joy, he told me, was to play and sing for the great princes of Europe; to sing of love; the love of a humble knight for a high-born lady, to sing of *l'amour courtois*, courtly love, the love of a *servus* for his *domina* . . .

That afternoon, as we drank the wine, and I scrubbed the dried vomit off his tunic with a brush, he told me his life's story. He was born in the county of Champagne, the second son of a minor baron, who served Henry, the count. He had loved music from an early age, but his father, who did not care much for music or for Bernard, had disapproved. However, bullied by Bernard's mother, he had arranged for his training with one of the greatest *trouvères* in France, and had found him a place at the court of King Louis. From the first, Bernard confided in me, he was an enormous success – great ladies wept openly at his love songs, everyone guffawed at his witty *sirvantes*, which mocked court life but never went too far. Louis had showered him with gold and jewels. Everybody loved him; life was good; and for a *gentil* young man of fine looks but no fortune there was the hope of a good marriage to one of the plainer ladies of the court. It was a glittering life: hunting parties, royal feasts, poetry games and singing competitions. But, like many a young buck before him, Bernard over-reached himself. For, as well as a deep adoration of music, he also loved, and almost to the same extent, wine and women – and it was this last pleasure that had led to his downfall.

Bernard – young, handsome, funny and talented – was very popular with the ladies of the court. Several ladies, married and unmarried, had admitted him to their bedchambers, but he had kept his lovemaking light and retained his freedom from commitment to any one lover. But then he fell in love. He was utterly bewitched by the young and lovely Héloïse de Chaumont, wife of the ageing Enguerrand, Sire de Chaumont, a noted warrior much esteemed for his *preux* or prowess on the battlefield by King Louis.

'Ah, Alan, my boy, she was perfect, she was beauty made flesh,' Bernard told me, and his face gave a little twist of pain. 'Hair like corn, huge violet eyes, a slender waist swelling to generous curves . . .' Here Bernard made the usual gesture with his hands. 'How I loved her. I would have died for her – well not died, but certainly I would happily have suffered a great deal of pain for her. Well, not a *great* deal of pain, some pain. Let's just say a small amount of discomfort . . . Ah, Héloïse; she was the very air in my lungs, the breath of my life.' He took a huge gulp of wine and wiped away an oily tear. 'And she loved me, Alan, she truly loved me, too.'

For several weeks the lovers enjoyed a passionate affair and then, inevitably, Enguerrand discovered them.

The Sire de Chaumont had been out hunting with a royal party in the woods around Paris. His horse had become lame early in the morning and so he had returned, unexpectedly, to his apartments in the palace, thinking that he might return to bed and enjoy a little sport with his young wife instead. He entered his wife's bedchamber to discover Bernard naked and with an enormous erection striding up and down in front of Héloïse's bed, playing his vielle and reciting a scurrilous ditty about the King. The lady, also naked, was in fits of hysterical laughter when Enguerrand burst through the door. Unfortunately, the Sire de Chaumont had also removed his clothing and he too was in a state of obvious arousal. Then Héloïse did the wrong thing, she carried on laughing. She looked at the two naked men, one young, one old, both now with fast-shrinking erections, and she howled with laughter.

'Of course, there was no comparison,' Bernard informed me with pride. 'He might have been a lion on the battle-field but, for the bedchamber, he was equipped like a baby shrew.' Both men left the chamber at speed. Bernard grabbed his clothes and was out of the window in a couple of heartbeats. Enguerrand retreated to the antechamber to collect his dignity and summon his men-at-arms.

'It was not funny, Alan,' said Bernard sternly, as the tears rolled down my cheeks. 'It all ended very sadly. The Sire de Chaumont had Héloïse beheaded – really, in this day and age, beheaded for adultery – and he challenged me to single combat; and when I refused – I only like to wield my sword in bed – he sent his assassins to murder me. My father said he could not help me; I only escaped with my life by fleeing France and coming to this miserable rain-drenched island. And – can you believe it? – he pursued me even here! He has set a bounty on my head of fifty marks and had his noble friends in England declare me outlaw, me Bernard de Sézanne, the greatest musician in France, *un hors-la-loi*.' He fell silent, pitying himself, and so I poured him another cup of wine.

Every afternoon, after the midday meal, I would walk out to Bernard's cottage and we would explore music. It was a wonderful time and I learnt more about life and love and music and passion in those few months than I had learnt in my whole life. It was an escape from the grind of Thangbrand's, but only a temporary one. I had to return each evening to the hall and the petty bullying of Guy and Will. Wilfred had gone: packed off to an abbey in Yorkshire. Robin had arranged it. But Wilfred's departure meant little to me; he had never been a real part of my world, more like a ghost drifting through the human world awaiting his call to a more spiritual life. Apart from my few hours each day with Bernard, life at Thangbrand's seemed flat, unchanging: chores, dull meals, battle practice, more chores . . . and long hours trying to sleep in the hall while the men-at-arms snored about me.

But, despite appearances, things were changing. For one, my body was changing: I was growing taller, and the battle practice was filling my thin frame with muscle; hairs appeared in private places on my body and my voice cracked and wavered, sometimes in a girlish pipe, sometimes a masculine growl. Bernard thought this was very funny, and would imitate my squeaking and booming. But in our singing lessons he began to teach me the male parts of songs. I was becoming a man, physically, at least. And when we practised swordplay on the exercise yard I remembered

85

the blond man I had killed, and squared my shoulders, and scowled at Guy across the rim of my shield. I still ended up in the dust, of course.

There were other small changes too. Our settlement was growing. Young men, sent by Robin, had drifted into Thangbrand's in ones and twos over the summer. For the most part, they were unprepossessing: often malnourished, exhausted and with an air of desperation. But Thangbrand welcomed them, fed them and, when they had rested, they joined us on the well-swept yard for battle practice every day. Soon there were ten of us, fifteen, twenty in a line; swinging swords or using spear and shield in combination, learning battle manoeuvres, drilling endlessly, while an exasperated Thangbrand roared at some unfortunate newly arrived vagabond: 'No, you fool, it's a war spear, not a ox goad. Don't poke with it, you are supposed to be stabbing a man, not tickling him. God save us all from plough-bred peasants!'

Not all the newcomers joined us in this farcical display. The men with greater than average physical strength were trained to the bow: lifting great weights all day, rocks and sacks of grain to condition their muscles, and shooting yard-long ash arrows at round straw-filled targets a hundred paces away, not always with the greatest of success. Those men who could ride, and had brought their own or stolen horses, were trained separately, too. I was taught to ride properly by Hugh, who soon had me galloping around a paddock, jumping over small hurdles with my arms folded across my chest, gripping the horse only with my knees. He trained the cavalry contingent, too. They would gallop, with a blunt lance couched under one arm, at a quintain: a horizontal pole with a target shield at one end and a counterweight (usually a bag of grain) at the other. The pole was mounted on a vertical post and when the shield was struck from horseback by the lance the contraption would rotate at high speed and the bag of grain could sweep an unwary horseman off his seat as he rode past. Guy was fascinated by the quintain. He would watch the men practising for hours and, strangely, when they were knocked out of the saddle, though the other onlookers guffawed and wiped away tears of hilarity, Guy never did. At the end of one training session, he begged a horse for an hour and tried it himself. Of course, like all the other novices, he was tumbled into the dirt by the heavy swinging bag of grain every time he charged the machine. But he didn't give up. He worked out that speed was the essence; he had to be moving fast enough to avoid the sweep of the counterweight, but at high speed it was difficult to hit the target shield with your lance and you risked horse and rider crashing into the stout wooden block if your lance didn't jab it out of your path.

I thoroughly enjoyed watching Guy being hurled from the saddle again and again to thump into the turf of the cavalry training field. But I also felt a grudging respect. He never gave up. After each tumble, he got up, brushed the dirt from his tunic and hose, recaptured the horse and climbed stiffly back into the saddle. By the end of that first session he had managed, once, successfully to hit the target and, admittedly with a dangerous sway of his body, had ridden clear, raising his lance in triumph and shouting his victory to the greenwood. Within the week he was able to gallop past, striking the shield cleanly and with considerable force, without the swinging counterweight coming anywhere near him.

He was improving with the sword, too. Almost in spite of Thangbrand's plodding teaching methods, Guy was becoming skilled on the exercise yard. When we paired off to practise sword combat, instead of the furious storm of blows that used to batter at my defences, Guy was showing craft, cunning even. He feinted, made mock-lunges, kept me off balance and then struck; knocking me sprawling with the flat of the blade and then holding the sharp tip at my throat and demanding surrender. He no longer cursed me or tried to hurt me in petty ways on the exercise field: he was taking it seriously; not me, but the practice of war. And he was good at it.

Thangbrand noticed it and began getting Guy to demonstrate particular sword and shield manoeuvres, with me as his partner. A pattern emerged: a cut or two, a clash of shields and I'd be sprawling on the ground. One day, knocked on the flat of my back for the twentieth time, I felt a great weariness in my bones and I couldn't bring myself to get to my feet as the session ended. I just lay there listening to the sounds of the other men and boys leaving the yard: the ribald laughter, the clatter of arms, a curse or two and then blessed silence. I continued to lie there, staring up at the blue summer sky above, when a voice spoke.

'You are not all that bad, you know,' it said. 'You are not strong yet, it's true. But you are quick – very quick, I believe. The problem is that you don't move your feet. You stand like a woodsman trying to chop down a tree. Your enemy isn't a tree. He's a living, breathing, fast-moving, fighting man. And, if he knows how to move his feet, he'll kill you.'

It was a good voice, mellow and mild but with comforting depth. I turned my head and looked up at Sir Richard at Lea standing there blocking out the sunlight. He held out his hand and I scrambled to my feet.

Sir Richard had recovered well from his injuries. I had noticed him exercising with some of the other men-at-arms; I'd even seen him take a tilt at the quintain, and, of course, he struck the target beautifully dead in the centre and cantered on unscathed. He was just marking time, really, waiting for Sir Ralph Murdac to raise the money for his ransom. But there seemed to be some delay, I didn't know what. He could have escaped any time he wished; he wore a sword, had been allocated a horse, and he was almost entirely healed. But he was a gentleman, a knight, and he had given his parole to Robin.

'Watch my feet,' he said. And, drawing his sword, he executed a few elegant passes, moving lightly on the balls of his feet, back and forward on the exercise yard. It looked simple; half steps back and forward, side to side, a large quick pace before the lunge. Then he drew a circle in the dirt about a yard wide and gave me his sword. 'I'll stay in this circle,' he said. 'Try and hit me.'

'But I might hurt you,' I said. He just laughed.

So he stood unarmed in the dirt circle and I lunged half-heartedly at him with his sword. He moved easily, casually, out of the way of the blade. 'Come on, try harder,' he said. I lunged again, faster this time. He moved nimbly once more, dancing out of the way. I struck as fast as I could: a snake-quick stab at his heart. He merely twisted his body to avoid the blade. I could see how he thought this would play out, and it irritated me: I'd poke at him, the clumsy boy, he'd give a manly guffaw, and skip lightly out of my path. I was well fed with such humiliation, so I hacked hard and suddenly at his head; he ducked only just in time. Then I held the sword with two hands and, with a swirl of real anger in my gut, I swung it as hard and fast as I could at his middle. If the blow had struck his waist, it would have sliced into his body and half severed him. He stepped forward, lightning fast, to the edge of the circle, caught my double handed grip on the hilt with his left hand, half-blocking my swing, his right foot was outside my right foot, his right hand was under my left shoulder, shoving hard – and I was tumbled into the dirt once again. 'You are quick,' said Sir Richard, 'angry, too. That's good. A man needs his anger in a fight.' He helped me up again. 'Now it's your turn,' and he nodded towards the circle in the dirt.

And so Sir Richard at Lea, the renowned and noble knight, taught me to move my feet. For the rest of the morning, and then every morning after Thangbrand's battle practice for the next few weeks, I stood in the dirt circle as Richard lunged, swiped and hacked at my dodging body. He attacked slowly at first, building the basic foot movements into my mind, so that they became second nature. Then he would speed up, even try to take me by surprise. After a month, he let me use my sword to defend myself and he started by teaching me the basic blocks, and after a while some more complicated patterns; but, he emphasised again and again until I was sick of hearing it, it was my feet that mattered.

As Sir Richard and I practised in our dirt circle, we were often watched. Bernard, come to collect his daily rations from the hall, would lounge against the side of the building, grinning as I swiped at Richard and missed or was tumbled into the dust. And most days little yellow Godifa would stand solemn-faced by the edge of the practice ground and gaze at us as I sweated, and skipped, grunted and lunged on the exercise yard. She never said a word and always by the end of the session, at noon, when Richard and I would go and drink a pint of ale together in the buttery, she was gone.

I enjoyed the after-exercise drink as much as the sword-work itself. Sir Richard was taciturn at first, though perfectly amiable. But gradually I began to learn a little about him. He was more than just an ordinary knight, I discovered. He was a Poor Fellow-Soldier of Christ and the Temple of Solomon: one of the famous Knights Templar. They were the elite forces of Christendom, trained for many years in all forms of arms to become perfect killing machines for the glory of God. I was being taught to use a sword, it slowly dawned on me, by one of the best soldiers in the world. The previous year, Sir Richard told me, he had been one of the few Templar Knights to escape the massacre at Hattin, when the infidel Saladin had smashed a Christian army and murdered hundreds of Christian knights who had been taken prisoner. Later that year, Saladin had captured Jerusalem itself and the Pope had ordered a new expedition to free the Holy City from the hordes of Islam. Sir Richard had been sent back to his homeland to preach Holy War to the English and help King Henry raise forces for the great battles to come in Outremer.

He had ridden out with Murdac's men that spring morning on a whim, feeling a need for some exercise and excitement; he had believed he was going out on a jaunt to punish a rabble of outlaws and the last thing he expected was to be grievously wounded and taken prisoner for ransom.

'But God always has a plan, Alan,' he said to me when I asked if he cursed his fate. And I remembered that he, like all the Templars, was a monk as well as a soldier.

The autumn approached and, with Sir Richard's help, I grew quick with a sword. I was making musical progress, too, with Bernard; and with his encouragement I was beginning to compose my own songs. They were embarrassing little ditties but Bernard was kind – on occasion he could be scathing, but he never made adverse comments about my attempts at composition, never. So I made love songs, picturing Robin's beautiful lady Marie-Anne in my mind and pretending that I was her lover.

At first, I found it quite difficult to play the vielle. Bernard was introducing me to some of the simpler songs he had written. But even for an easy *canso*, the fingering on the strings had to be precise and the changes of position executed swiftly. One day Bernard lost his temper and shouted at me: 'On that stretch of mud over there, with a heavy sword and shield in your hands, you seem to move your feet quite daintily for that knightly oaf – all I'm asking for is that you move your fingers half as neatly for my music.' In a flash of inspiration, I realised he was jealous of Sir Richard, and the time we spent together. I was touched. It made me realise, perhaps for the first time, that I had real friends in this wilderness.

A week later, Robin returned to Thangbrand's.

Chapter Six

The Lord of Sherwood arrived at Thangbrand's just after dawn on a bright September day, accompanied by half a dozen grim archers led by their captain Owain, and a string of thirty unladen packhorses. The whole community turned out to greet him and he and his brother Hugh embraced as if it had been five years rather than five months since they had seen each other. I felt rather shy around Robin; the few days we had spent in each other's company seemed a long time ago and I wondered if he had changed, and even whether he would remember the callow boy he had sung with, and fought beside, and then left behind in the spring. So I hovered on the edge of the scrum of outlaws surrounding their returning master like eager hounds round a huntsman.

He saw me through the throng and pushed his way towards me. 'Alan,' he said, 'I have missed your music,' and I felt a great rush of warmth for the man. I immediately forgave him for leaving me at Thangbrand's but felt an almost ungovernable urge to blurt out that I had missed him too. Thankfully, I controlled myself. 'How are you keeping?' he asked, clasping my shoulders with both hands and boring into my head with his silver eyes. 'I hope Bernard has not led you astray from your studies with drink and loose women?' He smiled at me. I grinned back.

'Bernard is . . .' I began. 'Bernard is . . . well, he's a great musician,' I said foolishly. He laughed and said: 'Well, I hope he can spare you from your music-making for a day or so. I have need of your famous light fingers. Pack a warm cloak and a deep hood, and get saddled up. We're going to an ale house in Nottingham – just you and I – and leaving within the hour.' Then he turned away to speak to Thangbrand.

I found this news, in my boyish way, tremendously exciting – and also slightly unnerving. The last time I had been in Nottingham, I'd been arrested as a thief, and nearly lost my arm. And a tavern seemed a strange destination as we had plenty of ale, and wine too, at Thangbrand's. But just to be going on a journey alone with Robin made me feel special. Privileged. My master had picked out me as his travelling companion; we were going on an adventure together. I collected cloak and hood, strapped on my sword, and saddled a brown pony, the rouncey that Hugh had taught me to ride on. The horse was a placid creature, not worth much in terms of silver, but he had a lot of stamina, and could run all day and all night, if necessary. And he knew me and would not throw me off and cause me to be shamed in front of Robin.

Within the hour we were on the road, jogging along, apparently in no particular hurry, and Robin explained what was to be required of me. It all sounded simple enough, I was relieved to hear: an easy job for a cut-purse, and something I had done a hundred times before.

'We are going to The Trip To Jerusalem, the new ale house just below the castle in Nottingham. You know it?' said Robin as we trotted along in the September sunshine. I knew it: it was a lively place with good ale, hacked out of the sandstone rock that the castle was built on, and much frequented by armed pilgrims headed for the Holy Land and Sir Ralph Murdac's off-duty men-at-arms. When I had been in Nottingham, I tended to avoid the place, not because it lacked conviviality, but because of the military clientele. But I knew it, right enough.

'There is a man who drinks there every night,' continued Robin. 'Name of David. A sot. And he carries a key in a pouch at his waist all times. I want you to steal that pouch, that key, without him noticing. Can you do it?'

'As easy as kiss my hand,' I said. 'That's the simple part. But the difficult part is getting away afterwards. He will surely miss the purse sooner or later after I've lifted it; if luck is against us, perhaps only a few moments afterwards. Then there will the hue and cry, and we will be out in the streets of Nottingham after curfew, two thieves with no home to hide in and every man's hand against us. They'll catch us, sir. No doubt about it.'

'They won't. Trust me for that. We will not stop long in Nottingham; we shall be out of the gates and on the road before your victim knows what he is missing.'

'But the gates are locked at sundown, and none may pass till dawn, by order of the sheriff.'

'Trust me, Alan. I know another kind of key, a golden one, which will open any gate guarded by a poor man. But we must make haste now. We must be at The Trip an hour after sundown.'

We put spurs to our mounts and raised dust for many long miles until, by late afternoon, our horses lathered, our hoods pulled well forward, we were passing through the open gates of Nottingham and into the familiar crowded streets of my larcenous childhood.

We tied up our horses at a rail outside The Trip and, ordering a flagon of ale, we took our places at a rough table in the corner of the dimly lit place. My aching back – I was not used to such long rides – rested against the cool sandstone of the wall as I sipped my ale and looked around me.

The room was moderately full of drinkers; there were perhaps a dozen, seated at small tables or on benches around the wall. A large communal table dominated the place, at which simple food, soup or bread and cheese, was served by a full-fleshed wench with forearms as plump as my own legs. A tall, thin, dark man stood sipping a mug of ale and leaning against the wall by the fire. He looked a little foreign; sinister even. I saw him look at Robin, then stare round the room and then glance over to Robin again. He seemed unnaturally interested in us. I wondered if he were a spy, or an informer, for the sheriff, and a ripple of fear went through my body. We sat sipping quietly in the corner, saying little, minding our business. I hunched down and pulled my hood further forward to cover my face. When I looked up again, the dark man was still looking at us. He caught Robin's eye and then indicated, with a very slight inclination of his head a hugely fat man seated at the communal table, half-stupefied with drink, his head lolling. Robin nodded almost imperceptibly at the dark man, and I felt a surge of relief rush into my stomach. The dark man finished his mug of ale, put it down on a nearby table and walked out of the door.

Robin put his head close to mine and said very quietly, 'You see our mark?'

I nodded.

'You are the master, in this situation,' he said in a voice only a little above a whisper. 'This is your work. How do you want to do it?' I turned to look at him in utter astonishment. My cheeks flushed with pride. Robin Hood, Lord of Outlaws, was asking my advice on the execution of a crime. I quickly collected my wits and said: 'Distraction. I need you to make a distraction while I'm taking the purse.'

'Very good,' said Robin. 'What do you suggest?'

Again I was surprised and flattered by his confidence in my opinions. It was a novel sensation taking charge in the presence of my master. And, I found, a pleasurable one. Reflecting on this later, I realise that Robin knew exactly how to cut a purse – he had after all been living, thriving even, outside the law for many years. He was merely testing me. But at the time, his deference to my views gave my soul a great lift.

'I will sit beside him on his left hand side, the side the pouch is on,' I whispered. 'You sit opposite, on the other side of the table. Take your cloak off and put it beside you on the table. Pretend to be drunk. We order food and drink, and sit for a while, we order more, and when a fresh pot of ale arrives, you drunkenly spill it all over the mark. Then, crying aloud how sorry you are, damning your own clumsiness, you come round on to his side of the table and begin to mop at his clothes with your cloak. Do it roughly, loudly crying your shame at having wetted such a fine gentleman. He will ask you to stop pawing at him, but you must insist that he must be dried and that you must dry him to make amends. Play the drunken fool to the hilt, but make sure, make certain-sure that his left-hand side is covered by your cloak, as you mop away at his clothes. That's very important.'

'I understand,' said Robin gravely. 'And while the cloak covers his left side, you cut loose the pouch?'

'And in the confusion – let us hope that he becomes angry at your clumsy ministrations and makes a fuss; you may also raise your voice, become angry yourself – I shall leave the inn and wait for you in the alley by the horses. Leave as soon as you can after me. Then we ride.'

'A good plan, Alan,' Robin said. 'A very good plan. Are you ready?' I nodded. Robin rose, and strode towards the communal table, weaving slightly and shouting for the pot boy to bring more ale, quickly, d'ye hear, and some bread and cheese, not too mouldy, you dog! I followed after him with lowered eyes, like a servant embarrassed by his drunken master, and slid into my place beside the mark.

'That,' said Robin, trying hard, and failing to control his laughter, 'was the most fun I have had in an age.' We were trotting up the road leading north out of Nottingham, Robin having bribed the gatekeeper handsomely to let us out, curfew notwithstanding. I was almost helpless with laughter, too, and having difficulty staying on the back of my rouncey. Robin had a natural talent for play-acting, and clearly he had enjoyed the role of drunken boor to an almost indecent extent. He had roared for more ale, spilled it, apologised to the mark, mopped him and cursed himself with huge enthusiasm. His placing of the folds of the cloak had been inch-perfect and my hands were under it with my little knife as he dabbed at the poor mark's face with the far edge of the garment, covering the man's eyes as I slipped the pouch into my tunic and walked quickly towards the outdoor privy and away into the night. Then he joined me only moments later, roaring backwards to the inside of the room about innocent mistakes, anyone

can spill a drink, and some folk should not think themselves too good to mix with honest men.

We tried to pull ourselves together, but every time I
caught Robin's eye we would both begin giggling, louder
and louder, until we were howling with mirth again. Finally,
tears streaming down our cheeks, we managed to drive the
horses into a canter, the road lit only by starlight and a
sliver of moon, and put some miles between Nottingham
and ourselves.

Dawn found us riding up the slope of a small hill towards
a squat stone tower, about halfway between Nottingham
and Thangbrand's. I had no idea where we were going and
for the past hour exhaustion had been hanging heavily on
my shoulders. But a day and a night in the saddle seemed
to have had no effect on Robin. His back was still straight
and he rode with a jaunty grace that I tried my hardest
to imitate. At the top of the hill, with the sun bright and
cheerful over the eastern horizon, we pulled up at a copse
at the summit of the hill and my mouth fell open in surprise.
For waiting for us there was Owain the Bowman, his six
men and the train of packhorses.

The key in the pouch, I discovered, opened an iron
door in the strongly built tower and once it had been flung
back, and Owain and Robin had entered with lit torches,
I realised why our jaunt into Nottingham had been so
important to Robin's plans.

For any bowman, it was a storehouse of riches. Though
it contained no silver, no gold or jewels, it did contain
stack upon stack of the best-quality arrows, newly
fletched and arranged in bundles of thirty around two
leather discs which prevented the goosefeather flights
from being crushed against each other. There were also
seasoned yew bowstaves in thick bundles, and swords,

shields, lances, even a few elderly chain-mail hauberks standing on T-shaped stands.

'We didn't bring enough packhorses,' said Owain.

'What is this place?' I asked Robin, staring around at this cornucopia of arms, enough to equip a small army.

'This is one of our King Henry's armouries. He is amassing weapons for a great pilgrimage to free the Holy Land from the infidel. Our good friend David, who by now I hope will only just be discovering that he has lost his key, is the King's Armourer, charged with collecting stores in the north for the great adventure. The King doesn't trust Ralph Murdac with these weapons, otherwise they would be locked up tight in Nottingham Castle. So David, a loyal King's man, if a little bibulous, has their charge.'

'*Had* their charge,' I said.

'We'd better hurry, sir,' said Owain. 'The armourer will have raised the alarm by now.' And so we did.

An hour later, with thirty packhorses tottering under monstrous loads, we were back on the road north towards Thangbrand's. The armoury was only half empty. Robin left the door open and carefully hung the key on a nail on the wall. With a piece of chalk he wrote the words 'Thank you, Sire,' on the grey stone beneath it.

Robin was in high spirits as we trotted along on a narrow path through the trees but suddenly he stopped and raised a hand. We all paused, the bowmen taking the bridles of the heavy-laden packhorses to keep the beasts quiet and still. There was a clatter of hooves on the path and I saw the bright yellow thatch and giant frame of Little John approaching at speed round a bend in the road. He was mounted on a huge sweat-lathered horse, and

100

accompanied by two men-at-arms that I had seen at Thangbrand's but didn't know well.

Robin waited impassively, silently as John reined his sweating horse in savagely and they stared at each other as the big horse steamed gently in the late summer sunshine.

'It's the Peverils,' said John, after he'd caught his breath. 'They are raiding our villages again.'

'Where are they, and how many?' asked Robin.

'They've sacked Thornings Cross; pillaged the church there, killed a few. Now they are heading north, back to their nests in Hope Valley. About twenty of the bastards.'

'Geraint, Simon, take this train back to Thangbrand's,' Robin was addressing the two men-at-arms who had arrived with John. I was amazed that he knew their names, as I did not. 'You go with them, Alan.'

'I would prefer to come with you, sir,' I said.

'Do as you're told,' snapped Robin. Our mutual hilarity, the camaraderie of our purse-lifting adventure in Nottingham was gone. Robin had assumed his battle demeanour: grim, decisive, a captain not to be questioned.

'John, lead the way, Owain, you and your bowmen are with me.'

And he was gone, riding hard up the road after Little John, and followed by Owain and his six grim archers. The two men-at-arms looked at me dumbly. And I said: 'You heard him; take this train to Thangbrand's. I have other business.' And I spurred after my disappearing master.

I knew who the Peverils were: a big old sprawling clan of petty bandits and reivers who operated in the north of England, most of the time staying out of the area under Robin's control. The family claimed to be descended from William the Bastard, though from the wrong side of the blanket, and one branch had once owned an impregnable fortress at Castleton. But because of their evil ways, they had been dispossessed by King Henry thirty odd years ago, and now they made their living by robbery and murder and ransom. In fact, if the truth be told, they were not much different to Robin's band. There had been some talk of them at Thangbrand's: the Peverils were reckoned to be cruel but cowardly and until now they had usually respected the places where Robin's writ had run.

I caught up Robin and his men within half a mile or so, and just followed behind them trying to keep up as they galloped hell-for-leather across the county. I once saw Robin look round and notice me. He frowned but never slackened his pace. I stayed at the end of the tail of men and speeding horses and ate dust for a good fifteen miles, sometimes on small dirt tracks through the woodland, sometimes across meadows, commons and fields, until we pulled up on a gentle rise overlooking a hamlet huddled in the crook of a small stream. A thick cloud of smoke hung over the place, and I could see that at least two cottages were still burning. The place had been totally destroyed: houses torched, cattle and sheep driven off; men murdered and women and children raped. Even the old cross that gave the hamlet its name had been pulled down. As we trotted down the slope into the village, I heard the sound of a woman wailing, and saw her soon afterwards. She was kneeling on the ground in front of a smouldering hovel, with the bloodied corpse of a young boy, maybe six years old, in her arms, rocking back and forward and keening to herself, a thin, high, wordless sound of sorrow. The boy's head lolled with every rock of her body. We drew up on our horses and Robin dismounted and went over to kneel beside the woman. He put a hand on her shoulder and she started suddenly but stopped that dreadful noise and, through swollen red eyes, she stared at Robin, dumb with grief.

As I looked around the village I saw signs of an evil I could hardly contemplate: the broken, chopped bodies of half a dozen peasants were scattered about the muddy street. The corpse of a priest lay a few yards away, an arm outflung in death. I noticed that some of his fingers were missing, hacked off, no doubt, for the rings they had borne. A girl, her throat slit and gaping like an extra mouth, was propped up sideways against the tumbled stones of the ancient stone cross in the centre of the hamlet. Her skirts had been tucked up around her chest and her naked lap was a mess of caked blood. I saw that someone had taken a knife to her white buttocks and I looked away quickly.

'It seems they are all dead but her, sir,' said Owain, indicating the grief-stricken woman. He and some of the men had briefly ridden around the tiny village looking for wounded survivors. The woman holding her dead son stared up at Owain on his horse and then at Robin kneeling beside her. He was offering her his wine flask. She took a sip and then a gulp and then began to sob quietly, her eyes closed, her chin sunk on her neck.

'Which way have they gone?' Robin asked her. She carried on crying, ignoring his question. 'Which way?' he asked again. She looked at him bewildered and then she indicated the northern road out of the village with a bloody finger. 'We will be back to help later,' Robin said, 'but now we need to catch the men who did this. And make them pay.'

'We paid you,' the woman said in a low voice. Robin flinched, but he kept her gaze. 'For protection,' the woman continued. 'Your men said that if we paid, you would protect

103

us from . . .' the woman's free arm waved at the scene of carnage in the muddy street. Robin stood up. 'I failed you,' he said. The woman stared at him. 'But I will catch them,' Robin continued, 'and I swear I'll make them regret that they did this.' She nodded: 'Catch them,' she said, her voice rough. 'And kill them, kill them all.' Robin nodded and put the wine flask into her hand. We saddled up and Robin detailed one archer to ride ahead as a scout. He looked blankly at me. 'I told you to go to Thangbrand's,' he said, but without much emotion. I shrugged.

'Don't ever disobey me again,' he said, and his eyes flashed like a knife drawn in the night. I nodded, too dispirited to be truly frightened, and we rode out of the defiled village and took the northern road.

That night we camped, cold and fireless in a high wood of beech trees. Matthew, the archer-scout, had reported back to Robin. The Peverils were less than half a mile away, feasting on stolen roast mutton round a great blaze in a hollow below and to the north of our beech wood. They had not bothered to set any sentries, Matthew reported, and were drinking plundered casks of ale round the fire, and singing. They also had a captured woman with them and were taking turns to rape her.

The night air was cold but Robin had forbidden us a fire. We were to march down upon the Peveril camp, leaving the horses behind, and attack them on foot just before dawn. They were twenty-four men. We were nine. But they would be in a drunken sleep, unaware of our presence until we struck. We were cold and we were angry – the men had been shocked by what had been done at Thornings Cross – and, best of all, we were led by Robin. The enemy would all die, of that I was certain.

I was on the edge of sleep, wrapped up in my cloak and hood, sitting between two roots with my back to the trunk of a comfortable tree when Robin came over to me.

'In the morning, take care that you don't get yourself killed,' he said quietly. 'Hang back when we go in, these are very dangerous men.' I shook my head. 'Do not disobey me further,' Robin said, his voice chilling.

'I can fight,' I said. 'I've learnt a thing or two at Thangbrand's.' I wanted very much to pay them out for what they had done at Thornings Cross.

'You haven't learnt nearly enough,' said Robin. 'I want you to hang back, come in when the fighting is nearly over. And even then be careful.' I said nothing, feeling strangely sullen, mulish.

'Look,' he said, his voice dropping so that no one but I could hear him, 'you are more valuable to me than a common archer. Truly. Bernard says you have real talent. I don't want you dead in some forgotten skirmish, I need you alive.'

I continued to sulk. Did he think I was afraid? Had he forgotten that I had already killed a man in battle?

'You are just like your father,' said Robin. 'He was a headstrong man, who did not like to be given orders.'

'Will you tell me what you knew of him?' I asked, wanting to change the subject. 'He never spoke to me about his life before he came to Nottinghamshire, met my mother and fell in love with her.'

'Really? How strange that I should know more about him than his son,' he said, and settled down beside me, back to the tree. 'Well, he was a good man, I think, and kind to me, and a truly wonderful singer. But you know that already. He came to my father's court at Edwinstowe when I was just a boy of nine or ten. He was a *trouvère* . . .'

I sat up straighter against the tree, my interest quickening. Robin went on: ' . . . and when he came to Edwinstowe during the winter, my father invited him to spend Christmas with us. We had little entertainment in that district and his music made the castle seem warmer and brighter during the short, cold days and long, frozen nights of that season.'

'Where had he come from?' I asked. I found it difficult to imagine my ragged father, the field-toiling villager, as a silk-clad *trouvère*, keeping his Christmas at a great lord's castle.

'He had come from France. His father was known as the Seigneur d'Alle, a minor landowner, and Henri d'Alle, as the second son, was destined for the Church. As I remember, he joined the choir of the great cathedral they were beginning to build in honour of Our Lady in Paris. But something happened. He never spoke about it but I believe he fell foul of Bishop Heribert, a cousin of our own Sir Ralph Murdac, as it happens, and a powerful man in the Church. Heribert was, from what I have heard, a thoroughly corrupt priest, but at the time he was in sole charge of the cathedral music at Notre Dame. There was a rumour of stolen gold plates and candlesticks and your father was blamed. They told him that if he admitted that he had stolen the gold, he would be forgiven and, after a penance, allowed to remain in the Church. He refused absolutely. I am certain that he was innocent, by the way, and so maybe he was right to refuse to admit guilt. But, he was a stubborn man, and by refusing, he was forced to leave the Church and France itself and take to the road in England as a *trouvère*, entertaining the nobility with music at their castles. He never forgave the Church for discarding him; at times he was even openly hostile to its priests.'

Robin paused, hesitating for a moment's thought, and then he continued. 'At Edwinstowe, I had a priest-tutor sent by the Archbishop of York. He was a brutal man, and he used to beat me often. He's dead now, of course, but he plagued me somewhat when I was a boy. Your father spoke to him. I do not know what he said to the man, but that Christmas, while your father was there with us, there were no more beatings. And I am grateful to him. I feel I owe him, for that brief respite.'

He fell silent. Then he said: 'So, you see, I feel that I owe you a little because of the help your father gave to me that Christmas, and of course the joy that his music gave me. And so I ask you to promise me, be careful in the morning. Hang back.'

'What they did today, the Peverils, at the village, I want to avenge that,' I said, hoping to please him with talk of vengeance.

He sighed. 'They deserve to die, they deserve to suffer. But, if I am honest, what we are doing tomorrow is in my own interest, too. For years the Peverils have respected me and my demesne. They acknowledge me as Lord of Sherwood. Now they have broken our pact and shown a lack of respect and I must teach them a lesson, them and others like them, that when I stretch out my hand to protect a village, a family, a man, they are protected. I must demonstrate that I will defend my realm. My safety, and my freedom, and my future all depend upon this. If men do not fear me, why should they not inform the sheriff of my whereabouts? Why should they pay me for protection, pay me to give them justice, if they think I can deliver neither?'

'Is it not a simple matter of right and wrong?' I said. 'These are evil folk and they must be punished.'

107

'There is that. But right and wrong is rarely simple. The world is full of evil folk. Some people would even say that what I do is evil. But if I were to rush about the earth punishing all the bad men that I found, I would have no rest. And, if I spent my entire life punishing evil deeds, I would not increase the amount of happiness in this world in the slightest. The world has an endless supply of evil. All I can do is to try to provide protection for those who ask it from me, for those whom I love and who serve me. And in order to protect myself and my friends, men must fear me, and to make men fear me, I must kill the Peverils tomorrow. And you, my young friend, must hang back.'

I could see his teeth grinning at me through the darkness as he rose to his feet. And I smiled back at him. After he had left, I pulled my cloak tighter and tried to sleep, but his words haunted me. Was the world really a place with an endless supply of evil? Yes, we were all sinners, that was true. But what of Christ and his promise of forgiveness and eternal life?

We attacked the next morning, in the grey light just before dawn. It was less a battle than a slaughter. Robin's men advanced on silent feet, took up positions behind trees less than thirty paces away, and loosed arrow after arrow into the sleeping forms on the ground by the remains of the large campfire. The first victims' screams awakened some of the Peverils but few in their drink-befuddled state managed to get all the way to their feet, and those who did were cut swiftly down with a relentless barrage of arrows. Then we charged, and the survivors were hacked apart as John, Robin and the six bowmen stormed through the camp wielding axe and sword in a welter of swinging steel, screaming men and spraying blood. I had meant to hang back as Robin had asked but, when he blew his trumpet for the attack and the men charged, I ran with them, the blood running hot in my veins.

I was in no danger, though, as I faced no opponents. All the enemy were dead within a dozen heartbeats from when the first arrow shaft was loosed. Except two.

Sir John Peveril had an arrow in his shoulder and one through his heel and he swung a heavy falchion, a thick bladed sword, in menacing sweeps at the three bowmen who surrounded him. 'I want him alive,' shouted Robin, and Little John, who was behind him, stepped forward and swung his great axe, cracking the back of his skull with the flat of the axe-head.

Sir John dropped immediately and lay still.

The other survivor was a mere boy, no more than ten years old, I reckoned. He had not received a scratch, the archers being reluctant to target such an insignificant foe. He was quickly disarmed of his rusty, short sword and trussed up like a Christmas goose.

Sir John Peveril, meanwhile, had been spreadeagled and tied down securely to four pegs driven deep into the ground. Robin made sure that the pegs were at least a foot deep in the soil and that they were immoveable. Then the men stripped Sir John's clothes from his body and woke him by taking turns to piss in his face. As the man awoke, roaring, spluttering and cursing, he looked down at his naked body, strapped to the woodland floor, and his eyes widened with terror. He lifted his head and made out Robin in the first rays of the sun, standing above him like the Angel of Death, and his control dissolved. His whole body began to shake with terror.

'Rob . . . Robert, please,' he stammered through slack lips. 'I'll pay you, I'll pay you anything you like. Just cut

109

me loose. I swear, I swear, I will go away. I will leave, I will leave England . . .'

Robin looked away from the dribbling, piss-drenched coward, pegged and helpless on the ground in front of him. I followed his gaze. He was looking off to his left at a pale object on the ground. It was the naked body of a young girl, dead, bruised face turned to the sky; the waist and legs sheeted in black blood. Robin turned back to Sir John. His face was a cold mask of indifference.

'Pick a limb,' he said.

'What? What?' spluttered Sir John.

'Pick a limb,' said Robin, in a voice of ice.

'Yes, right, of course, Robert. I deserve to lose a limb. But can we talk about this . . . I can make reparations . . . I can pay back . . .'

'Pick a limb – or you'll lose them all,' said Robin, implacable. He nodded to Little John who was standing by, his great axe held casually in one hand.

'God fuck you, Robert Odo, and all those you love. May all the demons of Hell carry you now to the rotting pit . . . ' Little John took a step closer. Sir John shouted: 'The left, God damn you all, the left arm. I pick the left arm.'

Robin nodded. He turned to Little John and said: 'Let him keep the left arm; remove the others. And I want three tight tourniquets on each limb before you cut. I don't want the bastard bleeding to death.'

I would like to forget the sound of Little John's skilful axe as he carried out Robin's orders, three hideous wet crunches; and the screams of Sir John before they gagged him; and the sight of his unconscious torso, with a single white arm still attached, the fingers clutching deep into the soil to ride the agony, but I never shall, if I live for

110

another fifty years. I could not watch it all and Robin, perhaps as a kindness, ordered me to check that all the rest of the enemy were dead. One was not, but he was badly wounded and unconscious with two arrows in his belly, his eyes fluttering and rolling. As I sawed down on his windpipe with my sword to send him onward, I heard the last meaty hack of John's great axe-blade and a great sigh of held breath expelled from our bowmen. None had been killed and only two had slight injuries. It had been a great victory, but the punishment meted out to Sir John had dimmed the men's spirits; they had had their vengeance.

We set the boy free, unharmed, leaving him to tend to the mutilated half-man that was his captain and to pass on the message to all the other Peverils that this was Robin's work. Then we wrapped up the corpse of the girl and, loading it on to a horse, we left that grim hollow and our dead enemies where they lay.

Robin delivered the corpse back to the woman at Thornings Cross, and gave her silver, which had been re-covered from the Peverils. Owain had been wrong in his report that all the villagers were dead; several had run into the woods when the Peverils had charged into their village and had thereby saved their lives. All the inhabitants were in the tiny churchyard as we rode off, mid-afternoon, digging graves for their friends and family: a group of miserable peasants, survivors, toiling in the shadow of the church, dwarfed by mounds of fresh earth.

It was after dark when we returned to Thangbrand's and I felt drained of all energy both in body and spirit. When Robin came to say goodbye to me the next day – he was returning to his cave hideout in the north – I could not look him in the face. I had slept badly, suffering nightmares

111

in which Sir John Peveril was pulling his truncated form towards me over the floor using only his remaining arm.

Robin took me by the chin and lifted my face so that I was forced to look into his bright silver eyes. 'Do not judge me, Alan, until you know the burden I am carrying. And even then, do not judge any man, lest you be judged. Isn't that what you Christians preach?'

I said nothing. 'Come,' said Robin, 'let us part friends.' And he smiled at me. I stared into his silver eyes and knew that as horrified as I was by his cruelty, I could not hate him. I smiled back, but it was a pale, watery grimace. 'That's better,' he said. And he clasped my arm once and was gone.

Chapter Seven

Autumn was approaching; the days were growing shorter now and Sherwood, glorious with leaf-hues of copper and gold, was often filled in the early morning with a freezing mist. I began to wear my padded aketon almost daily and, when I visited Bernard for my music lessons, the first thing he'd do would be to ask me to make a fire to warm our fingers. With Robin absent, my adventure in Nottingham and the awful mutilation of Sir John Peveril seemed to belong to another world, like a dream – or a nightmare. I had returned to life at Thangbrand's as if nothing had happened.

Sir Richard was leaving us. Murdac had flatly refused to ransom him, even though it was his clear duty to do so, as Sir Richard had been serving him when he was captured. By rights, Robin could have executed him. He didn't, though; Robin sent him a message saying he was free to go and that it had been an honour to have him for so long as a guest. We held a feast to mark the knight's departure from Thangbrand's, for he was much liked and respected by the outlaws, and I performed for the first time as an apprentice *trouvère*, thinking of my father as I sang.

I am afraid it was a dreadful song, unworthy of his memory, delivered without accompaniment, about a knight who having travelled the world and done great deeds and won great renown was finally returning to his hearth to hang up his sword and husband his lands. I have tried very hard to forget it, but I recall rhyming plough with slow, and I think that gives you its flavour. My poor efforts were kindly applauded by the company – and then Bernard sang. It was one of the finest performances I ever saw him give: he started with a bawdy, stomach-clutchingly funny song about a rabbit knight that wants to mate with a lady rabbit, with much amusement about finding himself in the wrong hole; then Bernard, judging the amount of wine and ale that had been taken perfectly, gave them a classic song of doomed love, Lancelot and Guinevere. Those rough outlaws were weeping by the time he bowed the last exquisitely beautiful chord. And then, again judging his audience perfectly, he gave them a stirring battle song to lift their spirits: the tale of Roland dying heroically at Roncesvalles, a ring of slain Moors at his feet and his horn clutched to his heart. They cheered Bernard to the rafters at that. And then everyone, including me, drank themselves unconscious.

The next day, Sir Richard made a solemn vow that he would not reveal any information about Thangbrand's to the sheriff – after Murdac had betrayed him I doubt he would have done so anyway. He was then blindfolded and led back through the narrow, secret paths of Sherwood to the Great North Road.

Just before he left, he gave me a gift. It was a poniard, a beautiful foot-long piece of razor-sharp, polished Spanish steel, three quarters of an inch wide at the cross-piece and tapering to a wicked needle point designed to be thrust through chain mail, splitting the links with sideways pressure, and on into the body of an opponent. 'This is a fine, strong blade,' he said as he presented it to me. 'And it has saved my life many times. Keep it about your person, Alan. It may one day save your life, too.'

I thanked him as they tied on the blindfold and I helped him into his saddle. 'I am sorry that I will not be able to teach you how to use it,' he said. As they spurred away, over his shoulder he shouted: 'Don't forget to move your feet!'

The very next day Tuck arrived at Thangbrand's bringing supplies, half a dozen young men and boys for Thangbrand to train, and news. I was very pleased to see him and he greeted me with a great bear hug. 'You've grown,' he said. 'And put on a little flesh.' He grabbed my upper arm, kneading the muscle that had arrived after many hours of sword practice with Sir Richard. 'You're one to talk about flesh,' I said, prodding him in his great belly. He aimed a gentle cuff at my head which I dodged easily.

As we sat down in the hall over a mug of ale and a cold roast chicken, Tuck's face turned grave: ' I have bad news, Alan,' he said. 'It's your mother.'

My heart lay like a stone in my chest. And he told me she was dead, killed by Murdac's men along with many, many others in a raid on the village. 'Sir Ralph told his men that he wanted to make an example of the village, as a warning to others not to harbour outlaws,' said Tuck.

They had ridden in at dawn and started killing without ceremony; the grey-mailed horsemen chopping into men, women and children; attaching ropes to hovels and pulling

115

them apart; burning anything that they couldn't pull down. The men had fought, rake and spade against sword and mace, and they had died. Many ran into the greenwood to hide. An image of Thornings Cross, despoiled by the Peverils, came into my head. What difference was there, in truth, between the forces of the sheriff and a clan of robbers, I asked myself.

I was clutching the hilt of my Spanish poniard. 'I must go there,' I said, white-faced. But Tuck held my arm. 'The village is gone, Alan. There is nothing left but ash and sorrow. Your mother is with God, now. I buried her myself and said the holy words over her body. She rests with the angels.'

'If only I had been there . . .' Tuck put a brawny arm around my shoulders. 'If you had been there you would be dead. No, Alan, God has other plans for you. Your path lies with us.'

He had other news but I listened to it through a haze of grief, as in a waking dream coming in and out of understanding of his words. Robin had been causing havoc in Barnsdale, Tuck told me, raiding cattle and sheep from Yorkshire landowners. He had been pursued by Sir Roger of Doncaster, who had nearly trapped him twice. But Robin linked up with his men and turning on his pursuer he had trounced him in a fight. Little John had been wounded – but not badly. Sir Roger had barely escaped with his life. Tuck's story lifted my heart a little, despite the aching pain of my mother's death.

'What news of Marie-Anne?' I asked timidly. Tuck gave me a strange look. 'Robin's betrothed, the Countess of Locksley,' he said formally, 'is at Winchester with Queen Eleanor, and unlikely to stir for a while.' Then he changed the subject.

116

The Queen, I knew, was as good as a prisoner in Winchester, a hundred and fifty miles to the south. Henry, her husband and, by the grace of God, our King, no longer trusted her as she had supported their son Duke Richard in his wars in France against the King, and although she was allowed a royal retinue, including ladies in waiting such as the lovely Marie-Anne, and all the comforts that befitted her rank, she and her ladies were under strict supervision by the Constable of Winchester, a bastard of King Stephen's known as Sir Ralph FitzStephen.

The chance of my ever seeing Marie-Anne again seemed impossibly remote. I fought back a fresh wave of misery and tried to pay attention to Tuck's news from the north. '. . . he's nearly got all the men he needs,' said Tuck. 'They are all housed in and around a series of great caves in the north of Sherwood; perfectly well hidden and with enough room to house a small army. And, in perhaps a six-month, he'll actually have a small army . . .' But I couldn't concentrate on the news of Robin; my mother's lined face, worn down by a lifetime of brutal work and private sorrow, rose before my eyes and tears spilled down my cheeks.

Tuck did not stay long at Thangbrand's. He delivered his ragged charges for training and collected the chest containing Robin's Share, swelled by a summer of plundering travellers in Sherwood. Then he left, accompanied by a dozen of the more competent men-at-arms, some mounted, some on foot carrying bowstaves. I thanked him for bringing me the tidings of my mother and told him that I now had a double reason to seek revenge on Sir Ralph Murdac: the deaths of both my mother and my father. 'Revenge is for fools,' said Tuck. 'Christ teaches forgiveness.' I must have looked bewildered because he

117

continued: 'Always remember that God has a plan, my son. We sinners may not know what it is but He does,' and he pulled me towards him and hugged me. As I buried my face in his rough monk's robe, with its earthy scent of sweat and woodsmoke, I remembered that Sir Richard had used the same words. Then Tuck blessed me and rode away with his silver and his soldiers into the depths of Sherwood.

With his departure, the cavalry school at Thangbrand's was suddenly short of recruits and Guy, having proved his quality at the quintain, was absorbed into its ranks. I was still training with Thangbrand as a foot soldier but, thanks to Sir Richard's help, I was now demonstrating his hackneyed sword moves to the new arrivals. Bernard was impressed with my progress at music; I had a natural ear, he said, and I was now composing with increasing confidence: indeed, one set of verses that I created at this time, about the threshing of corn and the winnowing of chaff, is still being sung to this day. I heard local peasants singing it just the other day as they worked; the words have changed slightly but it is still my simple tune. When I asked one of them about the song, he said it was traditional. That made me smile and remember Bernard's waspish comment: 'I don't know why you waste your time writing chants for grubby peasants. Life is about love, boy, love, it's the only fitting subject for a *trouvère*.'

But I didn't know anything about love, except for a strange yearning to see Marie-Anne again. Lust, on the other hand, was something I was beginning to know a great deal about; indeed I felt it daily as a growing pressure in my loins. Tuck had warned me about the sin of onanism; it would make me go blind if I indulged myself, he said. The other boys at Thangbrand's, particularly Guy, jeered at this notion but I liked and respected Tuck and, for his sake, I tried very hard to abstain.

There were a dozen or so women at Thangbrand's: fat Freya, of course, and the wives and daughters of the men-at-arms. Little yellow Godifa, of course, if you could count her as a woman. And there was Cat – gorgeous Cat – about seventeen summers old, with creamy skin, generous breasts, red hair and startling green eyes. And she was available. She was available to anyone for a silver penny. She had haunted the fringes of my thoughts since I had first set eyes on her rutting against the wall with the outlaw on the first night after I joined Robin's band. I knew she had sometimes lingered by the battleground to watch me at sword practice with Sir Richard but I had never had the courage to speak to her. And yet I lusted after her, I lusted almost day and night. Particularly at night. When I could no longer control myself, under my blankets, amid my snoring companions in the hall, it was she who appeared in my mind, naked and beckoning. The problem, as I saw it, was that I didn't have a single penny or anything valuable that I could exchange for her favours. I did, however, know where to get them.

As well as Cat's lubricious charms, the great ruby that I'd seen in Thangbrand and Freya's chamber had also been at the back of my mind. Although Thangbrand's ferocity had terrified me, as time went by, my curiosity about the contents of that metal box buried in the floor was growing. What was in there apart from that great jewel? I decided to find out.

My chance came soon enough. Winter was knocking on the door at Thangbrand's and with it Slaughter Day. On this day, all the farm pigs – there were about half a dozen – which had been fattened in the wood all autumn would be killed, cut up and preserved in salt for the winter. We did not have enough feed to keep them through the cold months and so if left alive they would lose weight until they were skin and bone, or even dead, by spring. So we killed them.

Slaughter Day was something of a celebration at Thangbrand's: there was a lot of work to be done, penning, killing, scalding the flesh to remove the bristles; dismembering the carcasses and packing the meat in casks of salts. But it was also a feast because a lot of the meat could not be salted and so it was eaten in a variety of forms. Sausages were made from thoroughly cleaned intestines; the heads were boiled in great vats to make brawn; the air was filled with the delicious scent of roasting pork as the off-cuts, and odds and ends of pork, not worth salting, were cooked and eaten hot. More or less everyone was involved in the work, which was supervised by Freya and Thangbrand. But I slipped away at the height of the blood-letting, muttering that I had an errand to run for Bernard, who, of course, was not the slightest bit interested in gorging on pig meat with the rest of us, not when he had his own private barrel of wine and his beloved vielle at home. Bernard claimed that the squealing of the swine hurt his sensitive musical ears.

With everyone either at the pig-pens, the slaughter yard or in the kitchen, a separate building because of the risk of fire, I slipped unnoticed into the hall and crept into Thangbrand and Freya's chamber. My heart was fluttering like a trapped bird, though I knew the chance of someone catching me was slim, and my mouth was dry. It was a sensation I knew well from my days as a thief in Nottingham; I liked it. And I had an excuse ready: Bernard had lent Freya a comb, I would say, and I had been asked by him to retrieve it.

120

The door to the chamber creaked appallingly as I pushed it open. I called out to Freya to say that it was only me, knowing well that she was elbow-deep in pig's blood at the slaughter yard, and went inside. Although it was full daylight outside, I could barely see in the gloom of their bedchamber. It had no window and the only illumination came from spears of light that bored through tiny holes in the wattle-and-daub wall and from under the eaves. There was little furniture in the room: a big curtained double bed, a chest for clothes, a table and two chairs. I went straight to the corner where I'd seen Freya on her knees a few weeks before and put my hand to the earth floor where I thought the box had been hidden. I found nothing under my groping fingers, just smooth earth. I brushed my fingertips back and forwards, in wider and wider sweeps: nothing. I couldn't understand it; had they moved the hiding place? It was likely, Thangbrand knowing that I had seen it. And then I heard someone coming, footsteps outside and the door creaking . . . and in a blind panic, forgetting my comb story, I scuttled under the bed and curled in a tight ball at the far side by the wall. Visions of Ralph, the rapist who had been beaten and castrated, flooded into my mind. And the informer whose tongue had been sliced off outside the church. And Sir John Peveril. If I was caught stealing . . . it didn't bear thinking about.

From under the bed I could see the boots of two men. The door creaked shut. Then a man was kneeling by the foot of the bed. I couldn't breathe. I thought my lungs would explode with terror. It was Hugh; I could just make out his long, thin shape and, O merciful God, he was facing away from me tugging at something in the floor. Through my naked, shivering fear, I had a cold clear

121

thought: they *hadn't* moved the hiding place! Hugh pulled out something from the ground – it looked like a small bag. There was a chink of silver as he passed it to the other man. And then he spoke: 'So it is agreed, then. Tell your master to be careful. Tell him to speak to no one about this. Tell him . . .' The other man interrupted rudely: 'He knows this business better than you.' There was an awkward silence for a few heartbeats, and then the boots moved, the door creaked and they left.

I let out my breath in a long shuddering gasp but lay curled under the bed for a few moments longer, pondering what I had heard. Hugh had been paying one of his spies: that was plain. These shadowy men drifted into Thangbrand's at all hours of the day and night; they would talk only to Hugh; eat, rest for a few hours and disappear again. But there was something about the exchange that struck me as a little odd. Who was the spy's master if not Hugh? I could not think and, as I brought my beating heart back under control, I dismissed it from my mind. Then I was out from under the bed and on my knees by the patch of earthen floor where Hugh had found his bag of silver. In the gloom of the bedchamber, it was hard to see anything that looked like a hiding place. My panic started to rise and I wanted desperately to be gone from that room. Frantically sweeping my fingertips over the surface of the floor, I could feel nothing but the hard earth, and then, to my soaring joy, my fingers brushed against a cold, hard circular shape buried in the ground. It was a metal ring, embedded in the earth, and I levered it vertical with my fingernails and pulled.

It was a trapdoor to a tiny cavern of riches. Inside the hiding place was a metal box. I pulled it out of its grave and into an area which was slightly better illuminated by a chink on the thatch. And my mouth fell open. It containing such things as I had never seen before: fat bags of coin, tiny jewelled pins, fine worked silver cups, golden crucifixes encrusted with precious stones, a string of great luminescent pearls and many, many precious stones from emeralds the size of a pea, to that glorious ruby that I had seen Freya holding, a gout of crystallised hearts-blood the size of a sparrow's egg. My jaw hung slack. It was more wealth than I had known existed in the world, enough wealth to buy an earldom. And, I couldn't help myself, I slipped the ruby into my pouch, along with a handful of silver pennies that were loose in the bottom of the box. It was madness, pure suicidal madness. I had seen how Freya had gloated over that ruby – there was no way that she would not immediately miss it. The moment she found out, we would all be searched, the ruby would be found and I would be brutally punished, maybe even killed.

I pulled the ruby back out of my pouch and held it in my hand. In the half-dark room it was no more than a cold hard lump in my hand. And then I held it up to one of the tiny beams of light that criss-crossed the darkness, and it leapt into life: its crimson heart ignited, and the stone began to glow with a malevolent beauty. I swear that the jewel began to feel hot in my hands as if one of the thin beams of light had given it life. I knew I could not put it back into Freya's box. But something stirred in my mind, the germ of a thought, the beginning of a plan, and I shoved the jewel back into my pouch, replaced the box's top, put the box in its hiding place, lowered the lid, brushed earth over it and crept out back into the harsh winter sunlight and the squealing of doomed swine.

* * *

I gave Cat my virginity that afternoon in one of the corn stores, along with a silver penny, of course. It wasn't what I had expected at all. Cat knelt before me and lifted my tunic and undid the woollen strings which tied my hose to my under-belt. She untied the string on my baggy linen drawers, too, and my undergarments fell to a crumpled heap around my ankles. My prick was as hard as steel, a pearl of dew glistening on the end, and she grasped the shaft and began gently to lick my swinging ball sack, and up and down the taut, engorged flesh of my most private part. I could feel an expanding bubble of heat in my loins, just above my arse, and I knew I would explode soon if I did not get her somehow to stop her delicious ministrations. But, oh Sweet Jesus, it was a heavenly feeling. Ripples of pleasure were running up and down my cock. I could feel muscles deep inside tensing like drawn bowstrings and begged, in broken tones, for pity's sake, for her to stop. She looked up at me, with a knowing, lust-drenched smile, fully conscious of her power over me, and she then lifted off her chemise and showed me her naked body underneath. She was superb: creamy white skin, startlingly pale in contrast to her brown face, neck and hands; her breasts bobbing like ripe pink fruit, with tantalising, wide rose-coloured nipples, slightly hardened at the tip in the cold air. He waist was narrow, so small I could have enclosed it with my two hands, but her body flared out again to round, curving luscious hips and a little triangular badge of fluff in the centre. She lay back on the straw and opened her legs. I tumbled forward on all fours, hardly able to breathe, and crawled over her, my stiff prick twitching like a dog's nose when it scents quarry. After a few moments of glorious, slippery fumbling, with her help, I managed to slide my manhood inside her tight hole . . . and almost immediately, in a matter of three heartbeats, I was pulsing out hot jets of my man's essence. It was glorious, for a moment, but only for a moment. Cat was furious. 'Not inside me, you fool,' she said, pushing me roughly off her naked body. The few moments of mindless pleasure I had experienced were wiped away, like a wet sponge cleaning a slate. I felt ashamed of my ineptitude, at the speed of my ejaculation. Cat was cursing me for a stupid boy as she fumbled herself into her chemise and wrapped a cloak over that. 'If I start growing a baby, and I have to go and see Brigid to get rid of it, you'll be the one paying the fee,' she spat at me. I nodded dumbly, just wanting her to be gone. I felt empty, foolish, a boy who had been trying to play the man and who had been caught out; and then there was the guilt. What would Tuck say if he knew that I had been consorting with whores? Cat spat a final volley of insults at me and stalked out of the corn store. So much for the act of love, I thought, as I wiped myself down with a scrap of cloth, pulled up my drawers, re-tied my hose and straightened my tunic. Is this really what Bernard is always extolling with his beautiful songs of illicit love? It seemed absurd.

I told nobody but Bernard, who was delighted and who insisted on drinking a toast to my manhood. He said he would write a song one day about raising a *posse comitatus* to recapture my lost virginity. Cat, it seemed, told everybody about my callow first attempt at the act of love. At the evening meal, Guy set the hall a-roar by taking a mouthful of ale and then swiftly squirting it out on the table as he jested long and loudly about the speed of my ejaculation. Will actually pissed himself laughing – and Guy naturally pretended that he had followed my example of involuntary emission. I should have felt deep hatred towards him. Normally his teasing antics would drive me to near-violent fury. And I did feel anger, at some level, but it was overlaid with sort detached pity for him: as if I were God himself looking down on an unfortunate mortal from a comfortable cloud. I knew exactly how I would serve him very soon. He did not.

It was several days before the theft of the ruby was discovered. The first I heard of it was a thin, high-pitched repetitive screeching, almost like a blast on a whistle, coming from the hall. I was on the practice ground with Will, going through the usual evolutions with sword and shield. We both ran immediately to the hall and the source of the awful noise. It was Freya, of course; she was in her chamber, kneeling on the floor with the contents of the jewel box scattered around her. She had ripped her plump face with her fingernails and blood streamed down her cheeks; now she was tugging at her thin grey hair and pulling it out in great greasy strands. All the time she kept up that appalling squealing, which only paused as she gulped a fresh lungful of air: *Eeeeeeeeeeeeeee, ah, eeeeeeeeeeeeeeeeee, ah, eeeeeeeeeeeeeeeeeeee. . .*

We all stood there staring at her, crowded into the chamber, in a half circle around this soft mound of screaming womanhood, kneeling on the earth floor amid the accumulated loot of a lifetime. She was terrifying, a blood-drenched howling madwoman, immobilising all with the eldritch horror of that awful, awful noise.

Then Thangbrand shouldered his way through the throng and hit his wife a huge open-handed wallop around the face. Freya was hurled across the chamber against the wall and mercifully she stopped howling.

126

She curled herself into a great grey foetal ball and lay there sobbing and shivering while Thangbrand herded the rest of us out of the chamber and into the hall. I caught his livid eye as I left the room, and his gaze projected such an animal ferocity towards me that I involuntarily took a step backwards.

Hugh gathered everyone together in the hall at noon. His thin, tall figure in its black tunic and hose was even more schoolmasterly than usual. He cleared his throat: 'It seems there is a thief among us,' he said. Somebody sniggered – about half the men in the hall were on the run from the law for playing fast and loose with other people's property. 'Quiet,' he snapped, his eyes roaming the hall and extinguishing any merriment with their bleak gaze. 'There is one here who steals from his comrades. We will find him out now and he will be punished. Everyone is to form up in one long line – now, do it now. Form a line with your left hand on the shoulder of the man or woman in front.'

The puzzled outlaws shuffled into a great line, snaking up and down the hall. Then, at Hugh's command, we all felt in the pouches and pockets of the person in front. 'You are looking for a jewel, a great and precious jewel,' said Hugh. I felt totally calm. The man-at-arms behind me ran his hands over my body in a cursory search and rummaged in my waist-pouch. He found nothing, of course. It might have been foolish to steal the ruby but I wasn't stupid enough to keep it on my person. Nothing was found.

The outlaws, despite Hugh's severe gaze, refused to take the situation seriously. 'I reckon you might need to be searched a bit more thoroughly,' said one broad-shouldered ruffian to Cat. 'Plenty of places you might have hid that jewel ain't been properly investigated yet. I'd better take

127

a look.' Cat waggled her behind and giggled: 'No extra charge to you, my big beauty!'

Thangbrand, hand clenched tightly on his sword, was striding about the hall, the embodiment of bottled fury. He kept glancing over at me. In a low voice, shaking with rage, he said: 'Search their chests; and start with his.' And he thrust out a finger directly at me. There was nothing in my chest, of course, except dirty clothes, as was soon proved. But Thangbrand continued to glare at me while the search was widened. The outlaws started hauling out the chests of their friends from against the wall of the hall where they were normally kept and pawing through their trinkets, keepsakes, smelly old hose and crusty drawers. No ruby was found. Instead, an infectious air of suppressed hilarity passed through the assembled men and women, with outlaws trying on each other's clothing and cavorting around the hall to jeers and cheers. Then suddenly, Will Scarlet gave a great yell of triumph and everybody stopped and stared at him. Held above his head, glinting bloodily in the sunlight, was the great ruby.

'Where did you find it, boy?' asked Hugh. Will's eyes opened wide. It was almost comical: he had belatedly realised what his find meant. He said nothing but he was staring straight at Guy, who was standing near the open door. 'Where did you find it, boy?' said Hugh once again, with iron in his voice. 'In whose chest did you find it?' Will was still staring at Guy and then with shaking hands he lifted his finger and pointed straight at him. Guy's face went white. He said: 'No, no . . .' The hall was frozen in shock. Thangbrand's son? How could Guy steal from his father? Thangbrand's face was crimson with fury. In the silence, the rattling scrape of his sword being drawn. Then, blade in hand, Thangbrand stalked towards his grey-faced son. Guy was terrified: he lifted both hands out in front of him, fingers outstretched, as if to push away the silent accusation; to insist upon his innocence. But Thangbrand was still advancing, naked sword in his fist. Then, suddenly, Guy's nerve snapped and he turned, quick as a rat, and dashed out through the open door of the hall and away into the sunshine.

Chapter Eight

After a long life, in which I have committed many sins, I look back on that moment in Thangbrand's hall with mixed but powerful feelings. I did a terrible thing by hiding the ruby in Guy's chest; and I fully meant to cause the harm that it did – breaking for ever the bond of love that had existed between Guy and his father Thangbrand. And Thangbrand, in his rough way, did love Guy. He loved him even after the discovery of the jewel in his chest. If Guy had not run, if he had kept his nerve and denied the theft and stood his ground, he might have been punished but Thangbrand would never have killed his own son.

I have asked God for forgiveness for what I did to Thangbrand and to Freya, who had been kind to me in their own way. But I have not asked forgiveness for what I did to Guy; and I never shall. He was a vicious bully and a boor, and he proved that day a coward too; he made my life miserable at a time when I was weak and vulnerable. And I hated him for it. In my mind, he was my enemy from the first few days at Thangbrand's when he beat me and threatened me. There were further insults and far greater injuries, and I could never forgive his sneering at Bernard's music, but it was after that first beating a few days after I arrived at Thangbrand's that I started to consider how I might engineer his downfall. My lovely wife, who is with God and his angels now, used to tell me I was ruthless, without pity; Tuck once told me I was a 'cold' man, but neither of those descriptions is quite true. I feel pity and I have shown mercy. But Guy was my enemy, a hated foe who had wronged me – and he was stronger than I. And if I defeated him by guile, so what? I defeated him, that is all that counts. Frère Tuck would not agree; but Robin would have understood: he would have called it vengeance, and considered it his duty.

By the time we in the hall had recovered from the shock of his exposure as a 'thief', and had tumbled out of the hall into the weak winter sunshine, Guy was long gone into the greenwood. Hugh organised a pursuit of sorts, but it was half-hearted: a handful of mounted men riding into the woodland and coming back an hour or so later saying they had seen nothing. The truth is that nobody really wanted to catch him. As far as everyone knew, he had harmed nobody but his father. Even Thangbrand's fury had abated somewhat; the ruby had been recovered, Freya had been put to bed with a jug of warmed wine and the prospect of meting out rough justice to his own son was not one that the old Saxon warrior relished. So Guy was gone. Good riddance, said most folk. I kept my mouth shut.

Life returned to normal at Thangbrand's. The weather had turned cold, with the first flurries of snow whipping through the skeletal branches of the trees. It didn't settle into drifts on the practice ground but Thangbrand decided anyway to suspend battle exercises for the winter. He seemed to have lost heart after the departure of Guy and grew morose and sullen, remaining in his chamber sometimes for days at a time, only emerging to answer calls of nature and bark orders for food to be delivered to the room. Freya too seemed dazed, stunned. She would sit silently by the fire all day spinning wool into yarn, unspeaking, almost unmoving, intent on her spindle.

I, on the other hand, was feeling rather cheerful. Christmas was fast approaching, the season of feasting and storytelling, of drinking and music and merrymaking. There were rumours that Robin would be coming south from his great cave hideout and would spend Christmas with us at Thangbrand's. And I was looking forward to seeing my master again – it seemed an age since our adventure at The Trip to Jerusalem – and perhaps impressing him with my musical prowess.

Christmas with my mother had always been a meagre affair but here in Sherwood with the outlaws, with Robin – and without Guy to torment me – I was expecting to wallow in song, good food and joyful companionship.

Without battle practice taking up half the day, the fighting men and I had time on our hands and we spent it preparing for the twelve days of celebrations for our Lord's Birth. Supervised by Hugh, we cut timber into logs for the great pile by the side of the hall, helped the alewives brew great vats of beer, hindered the cooks, who were preparing the pies and roast meat for the feasting, and decorated the buildings with holly and mistletoe.

Despite the Christmas preparations, I found I had more time for music with Bernard. We would sit in his little cottage away from the noise of the hall, drink wine and play music together all night, sometimes with little blonde

132

Godifa, whom we called Goody, listening quietly and shyly joining in the choruses in her lovely, clear little voice. Sometimes it was just the two of us, Bernard playing on his vielle and me accompanying him on an elegant wooden flute that he had carved for me. He taught me almost his entire repertoire from ridiculous smutty ditties to the great heart-bursting bitter-sweet romances. Sometimes we just talked. As well as music, Bernard loved wine and he loved to talk – about the women he had loved, about courtly life in France, and how he hated this outlaw existence, as he put it, 'pissing away the remains of my youth in this wilderness, surrounded by tone-deaf oafs who couldn't tell fine music from a monk's fart'.

He was rarely dull, except when he was very drunk, when he would go on and on about love, its wonders, its pains. And even then he would soon realise his pomposity and make mock of himself. I liked his company a great deal and I began to stay at his cottage more and more, wrapping myself up in a cloak and sleeping on a pile of hay in the corner of the room when the fire died down and the wine and the music and the talk were finished. It was too much trouble, late at night, to stumble back to the hall and find a place among the snoring outlaws. Occasionally Hugh would give me a scolding for ignoring my evening chores. But, in truth, there were plenty of people to lend a hand and I was seldom missed when I stayed over at the cottage. Bernard didn't seem to mind at all that I had, in effect, moved in with him. And my laziness was to save my life.

In the mornings, I would brush the hay from my clothes, splash my face with water and hurry the half mile or so back to Thangbrand's to begin my morning chores. Then I'd be back by midday to begin another round of music and talk that would last half the night. Sometimes Goody would curl up at Bernard's, too, when she had been staying up with us past midnight. We were a happy little group: Goody always eager to please, delighted to run errands for Bernard and myself. Bernard was drunk almost permanently – but he could take a huge amount of alcohol and still appear sober, and still play his vielle with wonderful delicate skill. I had not so hard a head – though I had turned fourteen that summer and counted myself a man – and I would mix my wine with plenty of spring water, as the Greeks and Romans used to do, Bernard told me.

On the eve of Christmas, we performed together in front of the whole community: as well as half a dozen pieces for flute and vielle, I played two of my own compositions, solo; Bernard performed an epic poem of King Arthur that he had set to music. He finished our performance with a haunting vielle tune, a swooping series of bitter-sweet chords that made the hairs on your neck stand, to which I sang the tale of a woman mourning her lover who had been killed in battle. It was a triumph; even Thangbrand applauded and smiled for the first time in weeks. Hugh made a pretty speech and described Bernard as a shining ornament to our fellowship. 'He makes me sound like some trinket, a golden earring or something,' muttered Bernard to me under his breath.

Hugh also led the prayers at midnight on that Christmas eve, as he was a monk-trained clerk, and deeply religious, and as we had no priest. I had hoped that Robin would be there but it seemed that he had been delayed in the north, and Tuck with him. Outside the warm hall we all trooped, at midnight, our breath steaming in the silver moonlight and, as the plump flakes of feathery snow began to fall, we gave thanks for the birth of Our Saviour. It was deathly cold, too cold to linger and after muttering a hurried Pater Noster and one Ave Maria, we all trooped back into the warmth of the hall. This was the only religious element during the whole of Yuletide but, by then, I was used to the unchristian ways of Robin's band. Prayer, though, keeps the Devil away and afterwards I wondered if perhaps, just perhaps, we had been more attentive to our souls on that Christmas night, we might have kept the horror that was about to fall on us at bay.

After those few brief prayers, the drinking began in earnest – all night and into the days and nights that followed. Christmas became something of a blur: huge barrels of ale, heated with red-hot pokers, with honey and spices added, were left open by the fire in the centre of the hall, where they stayed pleasantly warm. Men and women filled great flagons from them and guzzled until the liquid ran down their cheeks. One fool actually fell into one of the butts, and had to be hauled out spluttering, laughing and streaming with ale before he drowned. The outlaws staggered about roaring and laughing and chasing the women folk; some having the courtesy to go outside to piss or to puke, others just adding to the slurry on the rush-strewn floor.

The long table in the hall, normally dismantled every day after the noon meal, was left standing for the twelve days. The more sober outlaws gorged on the food that the servants brought to the table: roasted pork, fresh and salted, steaming platters of beef and haunches of venison, hot loaves from the bake-house; pigeon pies, boiled salted lampreys, spit-roasted goose; cheeses . . . At the end of each day the servants, those who were sober, cleared away empty platters and scraps and two strong men piled the unconscious revellers at the side of the hall out of the way

135

of passing boots. Then the storytelling would begin. The men told fabulous tales of giants and wizards and monsters; of the dog-headed men of the Far East, and of the monopods, men who had only one giant foot each, under which they would shelter from the rain or sun by lying on their backs and using their single giant foot as a roof. Then there were the lissom girls who lived in the great oceans and who had a fish tail instead of a pair of legs. According to some of the outlaws, there was even a monster lurking nearby in Sherwood – a werewolf. This was an evil man who could turn himself into a beast and who hunted other men and ate their flesh. Though I knew this was just idle fireside talk designed to frighten the listener, a shiver ran down my spine and, just then, as the tale was being told, out in the forest, a wolf howl sounded and one of the men, an evil-faced rascal named Edmund, leant forward, looked me in the eye and said: 'That's him. That's the man-wolf. And tonight he's hungry for human blood.' His brother, Edward, who was sitting beside me suddenly grabbed my shoulder and I jerked with surprise, hurling the contents of my ale pot over myself. The outlaws fell about laughing, absolutely rolling on the filthy floor in uncontrolled merriment. I couldn't see anything funny at all. Then my neighbour, the one who had startled me, slapped me on the back and someone brought me another pot of ale, and the stories continued.

There were three fights that I knew about that Yuletide, and only one of those fatal; a stupid row over who should enjoy Cat's favours that ended in a stabbing. While they were arguing, I led Cat quietly out to the stables and, while two outlaws fought to the death over the rights to her body, I took possession of her in a far more satisfactory way than our first fumbling time

136

together. Well, I enjoyed it more. She was just happy to receive her silver penny.

The dead man was hauled away and stacked to freeze by the woodpile outside. The snow was thick on the ground by now and he would be buried when the earth thawed enough, and the men were sober enough, to dig a grave: it might be many weeks. Thangbrand judged it a fair fight, another barrel of ale was fetched, a toast was drunk to the dead man's memory and the feasting carried on.

Even Bernard was disgusted after the sixth day – and he had been roaring and gorging and puking with the best of them – so we filled a sack with food from the long table and rolled a barrel of wine out to his cottage and continued our own celebrations there. God be praised, that decision saved our lives.

For two days we drank and sang and told dirty stories, sometimes with the more respectable guests from the hall, invited by Bernard, sometimes with only Goody as an audience. Hugh came for a brief visit with a gift of a whole roasted pig, but he seemed distracted and uneasy and he left after a short while without getting drunk. We carried on carousing without him. Then, early one morning, at the beginning of January, I was wrenched out of my vinous slumber by Goody, who was vigorously shaking my shoulder. I stared blearily at her. It was not long after dawn, far too early to be up and about after the revels of the night before. Then I noticed that she was whey-faced and crying, the tears rolling down her grubby cheeks cutting pallid channels in the grime.

'Those horsemen, those men, they are killing everyone . . . it's horrible, horrible. And the hall is burning,' she was babbling and pulling wildly at my clothes. 'All of them: Mother, Father, Hugh . . . everybody . . . they're

137

burning . . .' She burst into a frenzy of sobbing and instinctively I opened my arms and the child fell into them. Then she pushed herself away, drummed her fists on my chest and shouted: 'Come *now*, you *must* come now.' I was still dazed from wine and sleep and then I smelt it: a thread of scent that made my blood run cold. Woodsmoke on the wind, and a waft of charred flesh.

With growing dread and cold-swollen fingers, I buckled on my belt, with the poniard and waist pouch attached, and tugged on my boots. My sword, I remembered, was in the hall. I could hear Bernard snoring like a trumpet in his chamber and decided that to wake him before I knew what was going on would be a waste of time. So out we went into the cold morning. Goody led the way, down the familiar path through the snow to Thangbrand's, tugging my hand to make me hurry. I was reluctant; I could sense that I was walking into catastrophe. The smell of smoke was growing stronger and I could hear faint indistinguishable cries in the morning air.

'Come on! Come on!' pleaded Goody, trying to pull me bodily towards the settlement. I could see a thick cloud of smoke hanging over the place where the hall was. Then I stopped and crouched down to Goody's height. I looked into her wide, frightened blue eyes: 'I want you to stay very close to me and, whatever happens, to keep very, very quiet.' She nodded dumbly. 'We have to get off the path,' I said and, with Goody following, we waded into the snow at right angles to the path and into the welcoming shadow of the treeline. It took nearly half of an hour to circle around the settlement, with the snow sometimes up to our knees, so that we could approach from the south, via the main track. Then, hiding in the trees, with Goody held tightly under one arm, and the snow falling gently, we looked through the main gate, which had been ripped from its great hinges, and gazed upon a scene from a nightmare.

The courtyard was strewn with bodies, lying in strange poses, arms and legs out-flung, scattered like dolls that a child has discarded. But they were not dolls: even from the treeline, a hundred paces away I could see the gaping wounds, red spattered tunics and hose, great swathes of bloody slush across the battle practice ground where we had all so often moved mechanically to Thangbrand's commands. Mailed horsemen now picked their way among the mangled dead. These men wore the colours of Sir Ralph Murdac – black and red – their swords and spear tips dyed in gore, a strange colour-echo of the sheriff's markings on their shields.

And there was the man himself. Astride a great black charger, bare-headed, his handsome face alight with battle joy. He was issuing orders to the mounted men and they formed up at the edge of the practice ground and faced the hall. The door of the hall, three inches thick of solid oak, was shut tight, but a ring of dead men – ours – was sprawled about it. The thatch above was well alight, sheets of smoke rolling from under the eaves and forging upwards to join a great black column that poured up to heaven. The outhouses were burning too; the horses in the stables hamstrung, slaughtered and roasting in the flames. Here and there patches of thatch of the hall roof would burst spontaneously into flames, even the wattle-and-daub walls were smouldering. And then I realised: the closed door, Sir Ralph's men forming up in a conroi, ready to charge ... Of course, there were too few bodies! Only a dozen or so and our company was fifty souls at least. Not everyone was dead. Thangbrand, Hugh, all the fighting men, they were still inside the hall. Soon they would sally out and . . . I felt a flicker of hope. And then it was gone. Murdac's men ordered their dressing. More horsemen joined them. A second conroi was forming up on the other side of the courtyard. They were waiting for the sally. Waiting to slaughter the outlaws when they rushed from the burning hall. I could imagine the horror of the scenes inside the hall, the choking smoke, burning cinders falling from the roof, the knowledge that death awaited outside, the bitter despair, women and children weeping, shielding their heads with cloaks wetted in ale, Thangbrand giving orders, calm and brave, the men hitching up their belts, gripping their swords, wiping the sweat and tears away from smoke-shot eyes and waiting, waiting for the order to charge . . .

When the sally finally came, to my surprise, and to that of the sheriff's men, it didn't come out of the smouldering oak door but from the end of the hall, where Thangbrand and Freya had their chamber. The whole end of the hall fell away in one piece with a huge crash and out came the outlaws in a boiling rush. A ring of snarling, shouting swordsmen, clothes singed, faces blackened, surrounding our women and children. They held together well, twenty or thirty folk, jogging as a compact group toward the ruined gates, slipping in the slush, coughing smoke and screaming defiance and trying not to stumble over the dead on the ground. And then Murdac's cavalry charged.

The steel-clad horsemen smashed into the ring of charred outlaws like an iron fist punching through a rotten reed basket. Immediately the cohesion of the circle was gone. Outlaws were fleeing in all directions, pursued by the men on horseback. It was sheer bloody slaughter. Some folk ran for the palisade, leaping up the wooden walls and trying to scramble over to escape and find safety in the forest. Very few made it. The horsemen murdered them, skewering backs as they clambered, pinning bodies to the wood with their spears. Those of our people still on the practice ground were swiftly cut down. The horsemen riding by at the trot, hacking down at heads and shoulders with their swords as they swept past, crushing skulls with mace and axe, and wheeling to ride and slash and bludgeon again.

There was little resistance as the horsemen, almost casually, carved our little band – men, women, even children – into bloody carnage. I saw Cat, beautiful, wanton, sinful Cat, with her red hair flowing free, running from a horseman, who caught her and caved in her skull with his mace, hard-ridged iron smashing through springing red hair, to leave her staggering, blood-washed, her head grotesquely deformed, before she dropped and never rose again. A knot of men and women, no more than a dozen, reformed by the gateway, clustered around Thangbrand, who stood above a cowering Freya wielding a great two-handed sword and bellowing his war cry at the circling horsemen. Outlaws, those who were still on their feet, some with horrendous wounds, gashed arms and sliced open faces, pressed around him, kneeling at his feet and looking outwards in a loose circle, clutching shields, if they had them, or holding out swords and spears, defying the enemy with a desperate courage. For a few seconds it resembled what it was supposed to be: the hedgehog, an ancient defensive manoeuvre against cavalry that Thangbrand had drummed into our heads over many hours on that very practice ground. But only for a few seconds. The second conroi of cavalry poured over the hedgehog like a great waterfall of horses and men, of sharp hooves and swinging swords, washing it away in a welter of blood. I saw Thangbrand take a spear to his throat that hurled him to the ground and then the outlaws were scattered again, the horsemen everywhere, scarlet-dappled swords rising and falling on running figures, blood splashing the horses' flanks and fetlocks as they reared and trampled among the dying and the dead.

I was clutching Goody, my cloak wrapped around us both, and I covered her eyes with my hand as her father coughed out his last bloody breath on that gore-slicked stretch of mud and snow. 'We must go,' I whispered to her. 'They will be searching for survivors soon and, if they find us, they will kill us.' Goody said nothing. She just looked at me, her blue eyes huge in that deathly white face, and she nodded. She was a brave girl, that one. I urged her on and we began pelting back through the trees to Bernard's cottage.

I pulled him from his bed, as he cursed me to Hell and beyond, thrust his shoes into his arms, and I made him understand by shouting and slapping at his boozy sleep-sodden face that we must run, now, no time for explanations. I grabbed a loaf and the remains of cold leg of pork, a tangle of cloaks and hoods from a nail behind the door and, as we tumbled out of the cottage into the bright light, I looked round and my heart jumped into my throat as I saw the first of the cavalrymen – half a dozen grim, blood-splattered riders – come trotting up the path from the hall. We sprinted for the thick cover of the trees, Bernard ahead holding tight to Goody's arm, some-times even pulling her off her feet as we fled. I followed behind, arms full of clothing and food, stumbling, sliding through the snow that seemed to suck at my boots. I imag-ined I could feel the thudding pulse of hoofbeats behind me and the wind before the slice of an unseen sword into my face. We ran, hearts pounding, breath sawing in our throats and burst through the undergrowth into the safety of the forest. Still we ran, lungs bursting with effort, away from the cottage and its clearing and deeper, deeper into Sherwood. At last we stopped and burrowed under a huge ancient holly tree, the spiky leaves scratching our faces as we scrambled deep inside its cover and came to rest, breathless, and curled round the thick trunk of the tree. There was no sound but our laboured breathing. We could see almost nothing through the thick green-black foliage. But if we could not see, we could not be seen.

The ground was dry beneath that wonderful old holly tree, and we bundled ourselves into cloaks and hoods and waited for our hearts to return to their normal pace. Twice in two hours we heard a horseman passing close by, the hooves of his beast visible through the spiny walls of our den. We ate up the bread and pork and munched on handfuls of snow, eyeing each other glumly but not daring to say a word. I loosened the poniard in its sheath on my belt. The snow fell fast and thickly, creating a heavy white blanket over the tree; and we could see even less of the outside world. The cold began to gnaw at my fingers and I shoved them under my armpits. We shifted our bodies, cuddling together like puppies with the cloaks shared among us. Goody seemed to be in shock, with red scratches criss-crossing her bone-white face; Bernard looked grey and haggard, his nose glowed red from booze and cold and, though he was not yet thirty, I could see the old man he would become. I peered out again through the leaves and wondered if anyone else had survived the massacre and whether we ourselves would live through the day. And then, after

143

perhaps another hour, when in spite of the cold and the terror I had grown a little dull, even sleepy, I heard a drumming of horses' hooves and the jingling of equipment that set my heart racing. The noises quietened and I could make out, through the curtain of holly, the legs and hooves of a large force of cavalry stopped not ten yards from our hideout.

Then a voice spoke, loud and so terrifyingly close that it might have been in my ear: 'You are to take this sector, captain.' The voice was speaking French, and was tinged with feverish excitement and a slight lisp. 'And I want every tree, every bush, every leaf searched. I want all of these vermin dead, do you understand me. If you take them alive, hang them. Every single one of them. They are outlaws and their lives are forfeit. I want not one to escape and breed their poison in my county.'

I knew that voice, I'd last heard it in Nottingham, when I was quaking in the grip of a man-at-arms and its owner was calling me 'filth'. It belonged to Sir Ralph Murdac.

Chapter Nine

Huddled with Goody and Bernard, rigid with terror, under the flimsy protection of the holly tree, I listened to Sir Ralph Murdac just a few feet away as he gave orders to his mounted men-at-arms for our murder. I could see the blood-splattered hooves of his horse just a few feet from my nose but, penetrating the fear, his lisping French tones grated on my soul and I felt a lick of hot rage. As I lay there, I could image his handsome, scornful face as he commanded his minions to hunt us down and extinguish our lives. I remembered the pain of his riding whip as it lashed my face. I could even smell his perfume over the stench of hot horse, battle sweat and blood, a revolting waft of lavender, and, frightened as I was, angry as I was, I felt the beginnings of an itch in my nose and an almost overwhelming urge to sneeze.

The slightest noise would have meant death for all of us, and yet the sneeze was growing inexorably, making my nose twitch and my eyes feel as if they had been rubbed with onion juice. I could do nothing to stop it; I stuffed the bundled hem of my cloak into my face, and my face into the leaf mould on the floor of the forest and then it came roaring out: an eyeball-bulging explosive whoosh that convulsed my whole body. Inside my head it sounded deafening, but when I lifted my head I heard . . . nothing. Murdac was silent, listening, I assumed, to confirm what he had heard. A horse shifted its weight, steel accoutrements clinking. My heart was in my mouth, every muscle tense. I was determined to run if we were detected. I would not stay to be hanged like my father. In the silence, a horse farted loudly and a man laughed and said something in an undertone to his mate. Murdac called the men to order and continued giving orders in his sibilant French whine. I felt my body relax and looked round at Goody and Bernard who were staring at me in unbelieving horror. Their expressions were so comical that I felt like laughing. Instead, I sneezed again.

It was far louder than the first sneeze, which had been almost totally muffled by my cloak. And we didn't wait to see if we had been detected. As fast as a frightened rabbit, Bernard was squirming out from under the holly branches, followed by Goody and myself. We burst from under the back of the tree and sprinted away into the wood. Behind us there were shouts and trumpets and the thunder of hooves and we raced towards the thickest part of the forest, our faces whipped by branches, arms and legs scratched by grasping twigs.

They were slow to come after us, no doubt surprised by our sudden appearance. But a race between a man on horseback and a man on two feet is no race at all. Except, that is, in thick woodland. We were off the path in ancient wilderness, dodging through the small gaps between trees, wading through thick snow, scrambling under fallen

146

boughs, through brambles and ropes of ivy, all three of us hurtling, ploughing through the thick snow, spurred by panic, in roughly the same direction, Bernard in the lead, myself in the rear. We could hear the horsemen behind us but, as I snatched a backward glance through the thick undergrowth, I could see we were getting farther and farther way from the half a dozen riders following us. They had their swords out and were chopping wildly at low slung branches and trailing fronds to hack a clear path for their mounts, but they could only proceed at a walking pace, twin plumes of smoke shooting from the horses' nostrils. I looked behind me again and we were a good fifty yards clear, almost out of sight. Hope swelled – but then I looked to my friends and I saw that they were both in trouble. Bernard was staggering with exhaustion from the unaccustomed exercise, Goody was trembling with cold. She looked ready to drop. I ran forward to them and, with a fast backward glance to check we were unseen, dragged them away at right angles to the direction we'd been running, deep, deep into the thick snowy undergrowth, ploughing through the freezing white crust and sinking up to our knees. After thirty yards of stumbling through the drifts, we all tumbled into a ditch and lay there gulping air, hearts hammering; ears straining for the sound of horsemen.

Nothing. Sherwood seemed empty of all life. A white wilderness. But our track through the snow was clear to see, leading straight to our damp, slush-splashed, panting huddle. We couldn't stay there more than a few moments to catch our breath. I looked up at the grey sky; it had begun to snow again, but there were only two or three hours of daylight left in that short winter day. If we could stay out of reach of the horsemen until nightfall we would be safe. Probably. So I loaded Goody on to Bernard's back and pulled a dead branch from a fir tree, the crack as it broke off echoing loudly through the forest. We all paused, listening in terror. Then, when we heard nothing but the eerie silence of the snow-blanketed wood, Bernard whispered: 'Which way?'

I paused to consider. Robin was God knows where in the north, Thangbrand's was a smoking ruin by now, my mother was dead, my village had been destroyed, but, from nowhere, an image of Marie-Anne came into my head. She, I knew, was at Winchester, far away from Murdac and his murderous horsemen. And she could put us in contact with Robin. 'We march south,' I said, trying to sound decisive, and I stuck out an arm in the direction that I guessed led towards Winchester. And Bernard turned without a word, Goody gripping on to his back like a monkey, and began to tramp through the snow. I walked backwards behind them, brushing at the marks in the snow with the branch, trying to erase our footprints as best as I could, and blessing the falling snow that would, given enough time, cover our tracks.

All that frozen grey afternoon, as the snow fell steadily, we tramped through the woodland. Sometimes we carried Goody on our backs, sometimes she walked by herself. She never complained as we trudged through the silent white landscape. I was sure our tracks must have been covered by the snow and, after an hour of quiet progress, I dared to hope that the horsemen had abandoned the chase. The only living thing we saw was the low, lean form of a wolf, a grey shadow running through the wood on a course parallel to our own. January in Sherwood, I remembered, was known as Wolf Month; there were tales of babies snatched from their cradles by starving wolves in January, even one tale of a wolf leaping out from ambush on a mounted man and biting a chunk of flesh out of the horse's rump before disappearing back into the forest.

I picked up a broken branch and hurled it in the direction of the grey slinking beast, and it shambled away, disappearing into the gloom of the twighlit wood. On we marched, legs numb from cold. We were drenched and exhausted. As night began to fall, I knew we must find a safe place to rest: Goody's fingers and nose were blue with cold and Bernard's face was a sickly yellow colour. Suddenly, from directly ahead, there was the shocking blast of a trumpet. Galvanised with fear, we dived down a snowy bank and cowered beneath the white roots of a beech tree, as two horsemen in Murdac's black-and-red livery galloped past. I was certain that they hadn't seen us as they thundered by, but what worried me was that they had come from in front of us, not from behind. In despair, I discovered that I had completely lost my sense of direction and, in the gloom of coming nightfall, we must have been walking in circles. I realised with dread that I had no idea where we were or in which direction we should be heading. As we crouched under the bank, beneath the lattice of snow-covered roots, trying to muffle the noise of our teeth chattering, I tried to work out which way we should be heading. But my brain was clouded with the cold. And as the snow continued to fall, it dawned on me that the threat of Murdac's horsemen notwithstanding, if we did not find warmth and shelter soon we might not survive the night.

After another quarter of an hour of trudging through the snow, in the last of the light, we came upon the perfect place to camp. I don't mean to blaspheme, but there are times in my life when I feel as if the Lord God Almighty

149

has ordered the world just for my benefit. As we stumbled through the snow, numb with cold, terror and fatigue, we came into a small clearing in the forest, at the centre of which was a huge, ancient oak tree, several yards across, which had been hollowed by time and rot into a half-open tube, with space for three to sleep inside. We were not the first to have used this as a resting place: scraping away the snow near the entrance, we found the remains of a fireplace, with large blackened stones placed to reflect the heat and muddy cinders. And inside the hollow trunk, neatly stacked, was a small pile of dry kindling and a dozen seasoned oak branches, snapped into logs. We knew it was a risk, and that the light would be visible for hundreds of yards in all directions, but we needed the warmth of a fire. So I made a blaze with the flint and steel in my pouch, we huddled in our tree shelter and waited for our limbs to unfreeze. We had no food – we had left the remains of pork and bread under the holly tree that morning – but as the warmth filled the round wooden space, my mood began to lift. Goody, who had not said a word since she had seen her mother and father cut down at Thangbrand's, snuggled up to my side and began to weep quietly. I cuddled her skinny body to me and stroked her fine golden hair until she fell asleep. Bernard, on the other hand, seemed to become more irritable and twitchy than relaxed as the heat flowed back into his body. He appeared to have forgotten our hideous adventures and soon he was recovered enough to complain about our lack of wine. 'There was an almost full wineskin by the cottage door; why on earth didn't you grab that as we were leaving?' he asked me testily. I said nothing. My stomach growled and my mouth was dry but we had nothing to eat, let alone Bernard's precious wine, so I chewed a few handfuls of snow and just sat, gazing into the fire, allowing my clothes to dry out, and thinking about that terrible day. Had anyone survived except us? Were there others scattered in the forest, dying of their wounds in the cold? Thangbrand was dead, I'd seen that horror; and Freya, no doubt, had been butchered with the rest. But where was Hugh? Had he managed to escape?

Suddenly I sat up straight with a jerk. I had been dozing. Bernard appeared to be asleep, lying stretched out along the curve of the inside of the tree. Goody was cocooned in a cloak at my feet. What had awakened me? It was danger of some kind or another. The fire was dying down, but the moon was bright and nearly full. I threw another log on to the hearth and, as I watched the sparks burst and the flames revive, I saw, at the far edge of the clearing, in the bright moonlight, the figure of a man. And he was walking towards us.

My hand leapt to my belt and settled on the comforting handle of my poniard. And I gave Bernard's sleeping form a kick. The man walked across the clearing directly towards our fire. He was skeletally thin, with a lean, hollow face, covered almost to the eyes with a grey beard. His greasy grey hair fell to his shoulders. His lips were twisted into a smile of greeting, and I caught a glimpse of small sharp yellow teeth. As he came closer, I could see that he was dressed in what appeared to be a cape of wolf pelts, and a wolf-pelt kilt, his feet bound in grey rags. I could see his naked chest and prominent ribs beneath the cape – by God, he must have been cold – and his skin, filthy and covered with scratches and half-healed cuts. He carried a heavy wooden club over one shoulder and, as he arrived at the other side of the fire, I could see he was shivering. He raised his free hand in greeting.

151

'Good evening, masters,' he said. He spoke haltingly as if he was not used to human speech, but there was something familiar about him. 'Of your mercy, allow a poor man a place by your fire . . . and a morsel of your meat, if you have some.' I looked at Bernard, who merely shrugged, and moved his legs to allow the man to come around to our side of the fire into the shelter of the oak tree.

'We have no food,' I said. 'But you are welcome to the comfort of our fire.' He came into the shelter of the oak tree, put down his club, squatted down and held his hands out towards the fire. His arms, too, were painfully thin and covered with old scabs and fresh scratches. I eyed him suspiciously. I couldn't rid myself of the idea that we had met before. Nottingham, perhaps?

After a few minutes silence, in which Bernard appeared to have fallen back to sleep, the man said: 'May I ask, master, what brings you young folk into the forest on such a cold night – and without food or horses?'

'That is our business,' I said stiffly. 'Not yours.' I didn't want to tell him anything about ourselves. There was something about him, a feral quality, that put me on my guard. And I silently vowed that I would not fall asleep while he was in our company.

'It *is* your business, master, and I'm your guest. I'm sorry for my impudence, and I beg your pardon.' He looked shy and embarrassed as he said this, and I felt a little guilty for being so gruff with him. But I was still not easy having him with us inside the hollow tree. And I was more and more certain that we had met before. 'I'm going to sleep now, master, by your leave,' the man said. And I nodded at him and tried to smile encouragingly to make up for my earlier discourtesy. He looked at me a little longer than was quite comfortable and I noticed his eyes, a light brown

152

almost yellow colour, and then he curled up in his wolf-skin cape, for all the world like a large skinny dog, and went to sleep.

Bernard was snoring lightly by now and Goody hadn't moved a muscle since the strange man had come into our camp. She was still wrapped from nose to toe in a cloak and lying unmoving at my feet. I put another log on the fire, gathered my cloak around my shoulders and determined to stay awake.

Sometimes a man's will is just not enough. It was warm in our little tree shelter. The fire stones reflected heat into the wooden chamber and the sound of Bernard's gentle breathing had a soothing effect. The horror and then terror of that long day no doubt also had their impact and soon I felt my eyelids drooping. I got up, walked around in the cold outside the shelter; scrubbed my face with snow. But when I sat down again my head began to droop once more. And I slipped into a strange dream world.

I was riding behind Robin in a cavalcade of soldiers. I galloped at his left shoulder, the position of honour. Before me, above me, his banner fluttered bravely in the wind: a grey wolf's head on a white field. I gazed at the stylised image of the wolf's mask on the flag as it rippled in the breeze and then, suddenly, the image changed and the animal face came alive, the black and grey brush-strokes on white linen became real fur, sharp pointed ears and snarling teeth and the animal was glaring at me. And then, with a roar it leapt, straight out of the banner, straight towards me. And I awoke with a start.

The strange man was standing over the sleeping form of Bernard holding his club in one hand. As my eyes opened, the weapon swept down and cracked into the *trouvère*'s head. I shouted something wordless and fumbled

153

at my belt for my poniard. He turned and I was shocked by the transformation from the meek man humbly begging my pardon a few short hours ago. He had become a fiend, a beast: his yellow eyes glittered in that grey-bearded muzzle of a face, his mouth was slightly open and a thread of drool hung from his lips. 'Meat,' he said, almost in a whisper, 'fresh meat. And it just walked into my house, without a by-your-leave, and made itself a fire. A fire to cook itself on.' He laughed, a dry maniac cackle. I knew then that the Devil had entered him and he was mad. He advanced towards me in a crouch, the club held in both hands, the thick end swaying from side to side. 'Come to me,' he said. 'Come for supper.' And he laughed again. My hand was wet on the handle of the poniard; I stood erect and watched the movement of the club. It was hypnotic, and it was only by using considerable force on myself that I wrenched my gaze upwards to his eyes. I was scared, trembling with hideous ancestral fears, but I knew enough to wait, and watch those terrible yellow eyes for an indication of his attack.

Goody woke up and pushed her head out of the cloak. She was lying on the floor between me and the wildman. He stared at her. 'Pretty, so pretty,' he crooned. 'So sweet and juicy. Welcome to my kitchen, little miss.' He sucked the thread of saliva back into his mouth and swallowed it, smacking his lips. I took a pace forward, poniard extended in my right hand, so I was standing over Goody, but in doing so I stumbled slightly and was unbalanced. And then he moved – as fast as lightning. He feinted to my head with the club, a straight jab with the blunt end, and, when I pulled my head back out of range, he changed the stroke and the hard wood came crashing down on my right wrist. The poniard dropped to the floor and skittered away to the wall of the tree shelter. Then he leapt at me and, with Goody's cloak tangling my feet, we both crashed to the floor.

He was amazingly strong for such a thin man; perhaps it was the strength of madness, for as we rolled on the ground he kept me pinned easily and he was trying to bite me, on the face and throat. I kept him away but with only the greatest difficulty. I could smell his breath, a strange faecal odour, and his yellow eyes blazed like candles in his snarling face. Fear was my friend – I locked my hands around his neck and, made more powerful by my terror, I held on for grim life, while he thrashed and kicked and scratched at my face and body. But he was too much for me, and he broke my grip and rolled on top of me, red mouth gaping, drooling and searching for the big veins in my neck. And I could only keep his sharp teeth from my life by pushing weakly on his sweat-slicked chest and shoulders. My grip was slipping and his face closing into my soft flesh. I screamed: 'Goody, get the poniard!' And with a heave that took all of my remaining might, I flipped him off my body and managed to pin one of his arms with my knee as he writhed on his back on the ground. I grabbed his free right arm with my left and for a second stared down at the hideous face of this beast-man. His eyes left mine and suddenly looked beyond me, above me to my right, and then I felt the rush of air past my face and two thin girlish arms, locked around the handle in a double grip, plunged the poniard hard down punching through his left eye and beyond into his tortured brain. The beast jerked once, twice, and then was still: the body limp, the arms spread wide in the shape of a crucifix . . . the head nailed to the earth floor by a foot of cold Spanish steel.

I fell back panting with exertion. Goody rushed into

155

my arms and I held her rocking slightly and gazing at the dead man – for truly in death he was no longer an animal. Just a man, dead. His wolf kilt had ridden up over his hips during the fight and I noticed that between his legs there was . . . nothing. Just a dark ugly scar. It was then that I recognised him: it was Ralph, the rapist who had been beaten, mutilated and exiled from Thangbrand's in my first few weeks there. Well, *requiescat in pace*, I thought. May God forgive you for your many terrible sins.

I held Goody in my arms for a long while, staring at the dead man while she cried silently into my chest. Then I wrapped her up in a cloak, checked on Bernard – he was unconscious but breathing easily – revived the fire and then tended to myself. My right arm was swollen and sore but only bruised. I rubbed it with snow to reduce the swelling and the cold numbed the pain to some extent. Then I wrenched the poniard out of Ralph's skull and cleaned it on his kilt before dragging the corpse out of the hollow tree across the clearing and into the treeline. I had no strength to dig a grave or even find stones to cover the body. So I just left it there, thirty yards from our camp, out of sight in the trees. As I walked back to the warmth of the fire I heard the first of the howls. A lonely sound, mournful in the silent forest – and I hurried my steps back to Goody and Bernard.

I dozed until dawn, with Goody clasped in my arms, and the wolves making their ghastly night music in the forest around us; and at first gleam, I scrubbed my face with snow and searched our wooden hideout in the dim morning light for anything that could help us. I found an old iron pot and set it by the fire filled with snow. But, apart from that, I found nothing but some scraps of cloth, mouldy and stinking and a few old bones that looked disturbingly human. I gathered the bones and took them to where I had left Ralph's body at the edge of the clearing. But the body was gone. The place had been churned up by the feet of dozens of wolves and there was a little blood on the snow and a few scraps of fur but nothing else. It was Wolf Month in Sherwood and these starving animals would eat old boots if they were left outside a cottage at night.

Bernard was still unconscious, with a great knot on his temple from Ralph's club. But, as far as I could tell, his skull was not cracked and I believed he would wake up in time. Goody was sleeping again and, given what she had been through in the past day and night – watching her parents' deaths and then taking the life of a monster herself – I was happy for her to be unconscious, too. I realised that we were not going to go anywhere that day. I couldn't carry Bernard and Goody and I reasoned that it would be better to stay warm in the tree shelter than to go wandering about the woods without knowing where we were or where we were going. So I set about gathering more firewood, breaking off dead branches and hauling them into our shelter. I grew hungry as I worked and once or twice I heard the wailing of wolves and hurried back with my armful of wood to the safety of the camp.

I built up a good fire and a stockpile of wood for the night and managed to get a few hours uneasy sleep. Hunger was gnawing at my belly – it had been a day and a night since we had eaten that meagre meal of pork scraps and dry bread under the holly tree. I even began to envy Bernard, who was still unconscious and therefore oblivious to hunger pains. He was pale but his heart was beating regularly. I covered him with his cloak and let him lie.

Goody woke in the mid-afternoon, asked about food and accepted a drink of warmed water instead. I felt slightly in awe of her – ten years old and handling this situation like a grown woman, like a seasoned soldier, in fact. I still could not get used to the idea that she had coolly dispatched a madman with a single strike of my poniard. But then she was the daughter of a warrior and had grown up among outlaws. Violent death at Thangbrand's was hardly an uncommon occurrence.

As the dusk settled around the clearing, the wolves began their mournful chant. First one and then a second joined the chorus. Then three and four. The pack was being summoned and, as if I were a wolf myself, the hair stood up on the back of my neck.

'It's really quite beautiful, isn't it?' said Bernard. 'Almost in harmony but not quite. And so sad . . .'

I was so pleased to have him back with us that I rushed over and embraced him. 'Don't smother me, boy,' he said testily. 'And stop that ridiculous snivelling.' He was exaggerating, of course. There was merely a suspicion of dampness about my eyes. But I was very happy to have him back in the land of the living. He groaned and sat up feeling the knot on his head. 'So what happened?' he asked. 'My head is killing me but I feel I haven't had a drink for a lifetime.' And so I told him, the words tumbling out: the wolf-like man, the club to his sleeping head, the fight and Goody's life-saving poniard strike, and about the madman's body being eaten by wolves.

Bernard nodded and then winced at the head movement. 'You are a very brave girl,' he said to Goody, who blushed. 'So what is our plan?' he asked me.

Together we considered our situation: night was falling but it was no longer snowing; we had no food, but we did

158

have warmth and shelter; then there was the possibility of Murdac's men still looking for us; and the possibility of other survivors needing our help. Should we stay put? Or push on south and hope to find some cottage where we could beg for help? And then there were the wolves . . . Our discussions had been punctuated by a rising volume of howls, and they were close by. In the treeline at the edge of the clearing, from time to time, I caught a glimpse of eyes glinting in the darkness, catching the reflection of the firelight. Here and there a grey form moved in the trees.

Bernard stopped my talk with an upheld hand. 'I think it's clear that we must stay here tonight, if we all want to remain in one piece.' He gestured at the dark wood where three separate sets of animal eyes could now be seen. He was right. The howling had stopped. The wolf pack was assembled on our doorstep, and we were going nowhere.

We built up the fire and for half a dozen hours of that long night nothing much happened. We dozed and drank hot water and watched the eyes come and go in the tree line. Then, long past midnight, a slinking shadow detached itself from the dark wood and a wolf trotted across the white clearing before disappearing into the forest on the other side. He was a big animal, but lean, and he eyed us malevolently as he crossed in front of our pathetic shelter. Then, in ones and twos, made bold by the first wolf's crossing, other animals came out of the darkness and began to approach our camp. We piled more branches on the fire and, at first, the animals moved away from the roaring heat. But gradually, they came back. Eventually, one wolf sat on his haunches a mere dozen feet away. He yawned massively and I could clearly see his huge tongue and his teeth glinting in the light of a great full moon.

159

We stared at the hulking animal in silence. It yawned again, curling back black lips to reveal the big, razor sharp killing teeth. I pulled a branch from the fire, and waved it to fan the glowing end into flames. Then I hurled it straight at the wolf. It dodged easily and moved away a few paces – but then returned to exactly the same spot. And his brothers came out to join him, more than a score of lean grey beasts.

'Don't waste wood like that,' said Bernard. 'We are probably going to need it.' I looked at the woodpile at one side of the tree shelter and I knew with a sinking heart that he was right. Though dawn could not be all that far away, we had barely enough wood even to keep a small fire burning for the rest of the night. I cursed myself for not collecting more. The wolves gathered in a loose ring around the edge of the firelight, looking like the fiends of Hell, all big teeth and eyes and savage hunger. After the haunting beauty of their howls earlier that evening, they were strangely silent. But they didn't sit still – some peeled off to investigate behind our hollow tree, others changed position to observe us from the left or the right with their evil yellow eyes. Bernard and I had armed ourselves with clubs; Bernard had a stout tree branch and I had Ralph's weapon. We stood on either side of the fire in the entrance to the tree shelter waiting for the attack which we knew would come. But the wolves appeared to be in no hurry. Goody stood directly behind the fire, feeding it from time to time, as sparingly as she could, from the dwindling pile of firewood, and standing ready with the poniard. The wolves were now running back and forward across the clearing in front of the fire, staying well clear of our clubs, and the fire, but coming nearer with each crossing. Occasionally one would run towards us, a little probing

160

run within yards of us, loping closer and closer, until we reacted and stepped out to swipe at the beast with the club. Then the animal would dodge, and angle away into the darkness. They seemed to be testing us, trying our strength, perhaps trying to scare us into running away from our shelter and the safety of the fire. But we had nowhere to run to and, with the hollow tree at our backs and the fire between us, Bernard and I were in the best positions we could imagine in the circumstances.

But I admit that I was scared. If they got in among us, those great beasts could tear us to bloody ribbons in a snarling instant. I tried not to think what those pointed white teeth would feel like plunging into my flesh, ripping, tearing me open. But if I was frightened by the wolves, they showed little fear of us. The probing runs continued, the animals always staying just out of danger and then when Bernard and I had grown thoroughly weary of this game, one beast came sauntering towards me and then suddenly made a great leap for my throat.

He almost caught me unawares; I had been so lulled by dozens of similar advances, which had always ended in a swift retreat, that I was unprepared for the assault when it came. But, thank God, I reacted just in time as the huge grey shape launched itself at me. I stepped back a pace and swung the club in a short vicious arc, catching the beast full on the side of the snout while it was in the air. He tumbled sideways, yelping in pain, but, landing like a cat, he simply slunk round behind the mass of his brothers, licking at his nose and seeming more embarrassed than hurt. That first move, however, had broken the deadlock.

Another wolf was coming at me fast, lolloping forward and then leaping up towards my face, a blur of snarling

161

malice, and yet another was trotting up behind him; and out of the corner of my eye I saw a big grey form leaping at Bernard at the same time. I swatted hard and caught the first beast on the body with a crunch of ribs. Reversing the swing I caught the second wolf a glancing blow on the shoulder, and they both scrabbled yowling away out of range. Bernard had his wolf's teeth fixed into the tree branch, which he was holding like a quarterstaff, horizontally in both hands. The *trouvère* suddenly shoved his staff away from him, dropping it and the attached animal in the snow, and stooping and grabbing a burning branch from the fire, he thrust it into the surprised animal's face. There was a sizzle and a yelp and the beast retreated but Bernard's blood was up. He seized another brand from the fire and screaming with rage and whirling two flaming boughs around his head he charged the whole pack. It was a suicidal move, to leave the security of our position, but it worked. The wolves scattered before him, leaping nimbly out of the way of his flailing, half-burnt bludgeons.

They were not daunted for long. I saw a big black wolf circling behind him as he whirled and swiped ineffectually at its pack brothers, but then I too leapt out beyond the protection of the fire, took three paces to reach the animal, and smashed Ralph's club down on to the centre of its spine. There was a sickening crack and the dark beast, back legs paralysed and howling in rage and agony, pulled itself out of the circle of firelight on its front paws. Bernard and I retreated quickly back to our positions either side of the fire, and as we did so the animals returned, only slightly chastened, and resumed prowling on the edge of the circle of firelight – which I suddenly noticed had grown appreciably smaller.

'Please don't do that again,' said Goody from behind

us. 'Please don't leave me here alone to be eaten by them.'

I looked back at her and then at Bernard. He was breathless after his mad rampage and laughing silently to himself. 'Don't worry, my sweet,' he gasped. 'We are all in this together, I believe. If they get one of us they get us all.' I frowned. I did not consider Bernard's remarks to be helpful. 'Not long till dawn, Goody,' I said. 'And remember, they are just as frightened of us as we are of them.' It was a ludicrous thing to say and, in the midst of our terror and exhaustion, we all began to laugh. Bernard was leaning on a half-burnt branch-club, tears streaming down his face as he hooted and screamed with mirth. The wolves truly seemed to be unnerved by the strange noises their prey were making and moved uneasily in and out of the firelight. But not for long. And soon the attack began once more. This time in earnest.

The same pattern developed as before – the wolves would make little short runs at us, in twos and threes; we would swing and they would dance lightly out of the way of the clubs. It was exhausting. Once in a while, Bernard or I would catch a beast with a satisfying crunch. But rarely, and our arms were growing tired, mortally tired from the constant swinging of the heavy clubs. We had a bigger problem than our near exhaustion, though. Firewood.

The fire was growing low and I looked back at Goody in reproach. It was her job to keep the blaze high. But she just mutely pointed at the woodpile and I saw our death in the pathetic handful of sticks that were left. 'Not long till dawn,' said Bernard. We had been saying that to each other for several hours now. But what difference dawn would make, I knew not.

The last of the wood went on to the fire: we looked at

163

each other. Goody was clutching my poniard and crouching at the back of the shelter. The wolves were attacking in relays almost continuously by now. As one would make a run, we would swing at it, but while we were engaged with the first animal another was snapping at our legs. Swing at that one and another was leaping, biting at your face. We rarely hit our targets. It was like a game, a deadly game, of charging beast and flashing jaws and the sweep of the heavy club; and the fire settled lower and lower. Our arms grew weaker and weaker and yet there could be no respite. I knew that if I lowered my guard for a second, a wolf would be through the gap and ripping into Goody's flesh, followed by a wave of snarling, snapping ferocity that would tear us all to bloody ribbons. One animal, leaner than the rest, was skulking by the right side of the tree wall. I could see it from the corner of my eye and, when the other animals gave me a moment's pause, I jabbed the club at it, forcing the beast back into the shadows. But then a grey shape launched at me from the front and, as I bashed it hard on the hindquarters, the second animal leapt back out of the shadows and sank its teeth into my right forearm. I shrieked in horror and pain; I could feel the animal's dreadful weight dragging me down, down to the floor where I knew I would be immediately overrun by the pack. But almost at once, Goody – beautiful, brave Goody – was at my side and she lunged with the poniard at the beast's body. It squealed as the point scored its side and released my arm and, on my knees, with my blood streaming through the frozen air, I swung the club left-handed at another grey form that was flying at my head. By God's mercy, the pack pulled back then and I could see half a dozen still forms on the snow as I clambered back to my feet, panting, fingers dripping blood.

164

The fire was almost out now but a greyness had began to fill the clearing. But as I leaned on my club, breathless, exhausted, I saw that there were still fifteen or so animals slavering in a half ring around the tree. Was this my end? Was my fate to be worn down by these monsters, and then torn apart and devoured? I lifted the club with great difficulty and swung feebly at one of the beasts as he feinted towards me. His brothers did not move. Their great pink tongues lolled from their jaws and they seemed to be laughing at our feeble attempts to fight them off. Goody was wrapping a piece of torn shirt about my wounded arm when, as if by a silent signal, all the wolves advanced together. I waved my club, biting my lip from the searing pain in my arm. Bernard managed to hit one great wolf a smart crack on the skull and the animal howled and scuttled out of range. And then, suddenly, all together, the animals froze and turned to face the far end of the clearing. It was almost comical: the animals, for an instant, all absolutely still in the attitudes of attack as if they had been turned to stone. I turned to look in the direction they were all staring and my heart leapt as, out of the tree-line, raced the two biggest dogs I have ever seen. As big as bull calves, coats red and grey, with massive square heads and terrible jaws that could bite through a grown man's leg, two huge hounds came bounding across the clearing. Crossing it in a couple of heartbeats, they piled straight into the wolves. Though they were outnumbered nearly eight to one, it was no contest. One of the huge hounds seized a young wolf's head in its massive jaws and crunched straight through into its skull. The other ducked and plunged its fangs into a wolf belly and ripped out a trail of red and yellow intestines before turning to snap gorily at another cringing grey form. Men were spilling into the

165

clearing, too. Some on horseback, some on foot. The wolves were now in full retreat, tearing away across the snow, pursued by the two giant hounds. One horseman, holding a strung war bow, galloped into view, leapt from his mount and, without pausing for breath, drew and loosed an arrow that skewered a running wolf through the body and left it kicking and yelping in the snow. It was Robin, I saw, with a surge of joy. And beside him was Tuck, firing arrow after arrow at the disappearing pack, and the huge shape of Little John and half a dozen other much-missed friends.

'About bloody time,' muttered Bernard. And he dropped his branch and collapsed in a heap in the wolf-churned frozen mush.

Chapter Ten

I fell to my knees in the snow, dropping the club and finally allowing my bone-weary arms to dangle from the shoulders. Robin was here. I didn't know why and how he had appeared in the nick of time to save us from certain death, and in my soaring relief, I didn't care.

Tuck came over and lifted me to my feet. He enfolded me in his brawny arms and I felt his great warmth and strength flow into me. He tended to my arm, cleaning it quickly and wrapping it in a fresh bandage. Robin greeted me, stared into my face with his great silver eyes, and congratulated me on my survival. He looked pleased to see me and I felt the familiar glow of affection for him. Then he thanked me for rescuing Godifa. 'It was she who saved me,' I said, my voice unsteady with relief. And I told all of them how she had slain Ralph, the wildman, and helped to fight off the wolves with my poniard. Goody just stood there with her head hanging, looking more guilty than heroic, but the men all made a great fuss of her, telling her that she was her father's daughter, and that he would have been proud of her, which made her choke back a sob.

Best of all, Robin's men had brought food. John spread thick woollen blankets on the snow, and we fell on the cold meat, cheese and bread that they provided from their saddlebags. Bernard discovered a skin of wine and appeared to be trying to drink it all in one huge draught. Tuck had looked at the bump on his head and allowed that he probably wouldn't die immediately. In fact, the wine and food revived Bernard sufficiently that, sitting on a crumb-strewn blanket in that snowy clearing, he even began to compose what would later be known as 'The Death Song of the Sherwood Werewolf', an eldritch melody mimicking the howls of wild wolves, that tells of the beast that lurks in the hearts of all men. I could hear him humming under his breath between gulps of wine. He performed it some weeks later, in a cosy fire-lit cave when I was surrounded by dozens of Robin's warriors, and even in that stout company, it chilled my soul.

There was one incident that struck me as a little strange, though. Robin had brought a prisoner with him, a common soldier of middle age or even slightly older, with a hangdog, frightened expression on his saggy face, and a painful-looking wound in his shoulder from an arrow that prevented him from lifting his right arm to defend himself. Robin told me that he had encountered a small group of Murdac's men while he was searching for survivors of the massacre at Thangbrand's. They had quickly destroyed this handful of enemy soldiers but, unusually, instead of dispatching all the surviving warriors cleanly and quickly, Robin had insisted on keeping this man alive. Looking at him, and remembering Sir John Peveril, I suppressed a shudder. Seated on a horse, with his legs bound underneath the animal's belly and his good hand tied to the pommel, he was a forlorn figure. I went over to speak to him, but Robin stopped me with a hand on my shoulder. 'Don't talk to him, Alan; in fact, don't even look at him,' he said. 'Just make believe he doesn't exist, that he's a ghost.'

I stared at him. Was he contemplating another ghastly mutilation? But I dared not disobey, so I avoided the poor man. May God have mercy on my soul.

My recollection of the rescue fades at this point. Perhaps it was the shock of the past few days that robbed me of my memories, perhaps the wolf bite or my total exhaustion. Perhaps it is just the price of living such a long time: I am old now, by any standard. And the details of some parts of my life have become blurred and some moments disappear from the mind altogether. But some memories are clear as a crystal mountain stream, and one of those was my first council of war with Robin's men at the Caves.

We must have packed up our belongings in the clearing, though I don't remember it, and mounted the horses. And Tuck must have called his great wolfhounds to heel: they were Gog and Magog, he told me later, and he insisted that they were still puppies. A friend had given them to him and he was training them for war, he said. But puppies or not, I never found myself entirely comfortable in their presence, knowing that these huge canines could rip one of my arms off with no more effort than it would take me to pull a drumstick off a capon.

Doubtless we rode away through the forest for many hours, though I can recall not one thing of the journey. And, presumably, when we reached Robin's secret base, half a dozen great caves deep in Sherwood, my wounded arm was attended to and I was allocated a place to sleep.

I must also have spent some days recovering from my recent ordeal but this too has slipped my memory: my recollections revive at a long table loaded with food and drink, three or four days after the fight with the wolf pack. Robin was seated at the head, flanked by Hugh and Little John. The benches down the sides of the table were filled with outlaw soldiers eating a midday meal of roast venison off solid gold plates that bounced the light from outside the cave on to the low ceiling. I had never seen such splendour before and I was shocked by the casual way that the men banged these precious plates about and scraped them with their knives. Right at the bottom of the table, Will Scarlet and I sat sharing a boiled capon with onion sauce. Tuck was absent; he almost never joined in the councils of Robin, saying, only half in jest, that it offended his Christian soul to hear the wicked plots of evil men.

Bernard took no part in our deliberations either; he and Goody were in a separate cave where they were polishing 'The Death Song of the Sherwood Werewolf', Goody providing a spine-chilling howl-like accompaniment. She had made an astounding recovery since her adventure and seemed to be her bright and cheerful self once again, although she liked to keep either Bernard or myself close by her at all times and I did hear her sobbing quietly beneath the covers once or twice, when the pain in my bitten arm prevented sleep.

Hugh and Will Scarlet, I discovered, had survived the massacre at Thangbrand's by pure chance. Early on the morning of the attack by Murdac's men, Will had been squatting at the long trench, partially covered with wooden boards, which served us as a latrine. He had seen the first mounted troops pour through the gates at dawn and, without even tying up his hose, he had sprinted straight

170

into the forest and had hidden in a tree for a day and a night. Robin's men, riding south to join Thangbrand for the end of the Yuletide celebrations, had come across Will in the charred ruins of the old Saxon's hall, crouched on the ground, knees hugged to his chest, rocking back and forward and weeping uncontrollably. To me, now, he seemed a changed boy: friendly, seeking my favour. The days of our mutual animosity, it seemed, were long gone. However, every time he smiled at me, and I saw the gap in his front teeth that I had put there with my sly iron nail, I did wonder if he had truly forgiven me, or whether, one day, when I was least expecting it, he might seek vengeance.

Hugh, too, had been relieving himself around the back of Thangbrand's hall when the enemy horsemen struck. He said he had bellowed a warning into the sleeping hall, grabbed a sword and raced for the stables, intending to fight on horseback. But, by the time he was mounted, the outlaws were barricaded inside the hall and all of Thangbrand's men outside it were dead. So he too fled into the forest and, riding north at a breakneck pace, he came across Robin's men by nightfall.

Robin called his council to order by banging a jewelled silver cup loudly on the wooden table. A hush fell over the company; I couldn't help but feel a wave of excitement. I was being included, for the first time, in the deliberation of the greatest outlaw in England. I felt that I was one of his trusted lieutenants. My face felt hot, sweaty and my pulse was racing with excitement.

'Gentlemen,' said Robin. 'Before we begin. Let us make a toast to Thangbrand, a good friend and a great warrior. And I vow, here and now, upon my honour, that his death shall be avenged. Gentlemen: Thangbrand the

171

Widowmaker.' We all murmured the dead man's name and drank. Robin emptied the jewelled cup and set it down. It may have been the closeness of the packed cave but I began to feel slightly uncomfortable. My head began to ache, a pulse pounding in it like a great drum.

Robin said: 'Which brings us to the next point: I believe we were betrayed at Thangbrand's. Somebody led Murdac and his men to the farm. The question is – who?'

Hugh said: 'It could have been anyone. A local peasant, a villager dissatisfied with Robin's justice . . .'

'They are all too fearful,' interrupted Little John. 'God's greasy locks, we put enough effort into terrifying them. Who would betray us and risk pain and death for himself and his family?'

'There is one candidate,' said Hugh slowly. 'Wolfram – or, as he now calls himself, Guy. He stole a great jewel from Thangbrand and fled the farm in fear of the wrath of his father.'

'Would he betray his own parents?' asked Robin. 'Stealing – well, yes. But leading troops to his mother and father's door, setting them up to be butchered . . . I don't know. Make enquiries, would you, Hugh. I want to know quickly. And, if it is Guy, I want him dead. But not so quickly.'

Robin continued: 'The next problem is what to do about Murdac. For many years we had a perfectly good working arrangement with our high sheriff: I didn't molest his men, I allowed his servants to carry out their duties in peace, and he left what is my preserve untroubled. That arrangement is at an end. He has murdered my friends and stolen my property. He has ceased to show the proper respect for my operations and he has demonstrated, in a most barbaric fashion, that he does not fear my vengeance. So,

172

gentlemen, any ideas? What shall we do about Sir Ralph Murdac, liegeman of our noble King Henry and constable of the royal castle of Nottingham?'

There was a silence for several heartbeats and then one of the outlaws, a big stupid man called Much, the son of a rich Nottingham miller who had been forced into outlawry after murdering a man in a tavern brawl, muttered: 'Why don't we kill the bastard?'

Robin smiled at him but without using his eyes and said: 'I'm listening . . .'

Much was clearly embarrassed to have the limelight – he ducked his large head and muttered: 'Get a few men into Nottingham Castle, I know it well, I used to deliver flour there . . . wait in dark passage in the keep, Murdac comes along, knife to the throat, no more problem.' His words were greeted with the silence of incredulity. He stumbled on: 'Or maybe a good archer on the battlements could . . . a long shot, but with one arrow . . .'

'Stop your mouth, you fool,' interrupted Little John. 'We'd never get in there. Do you know there are more than three hundred men-at-arms in the castle? And what about afterwards? How would the men get out alive in the uproar that would follow? No, no, no. We must wait till he ventures out of his lair and then cut him down in Sherwood; we take him on our ground, not on his.'

Hugh cut in: 'Do we really desire his death?' There was another stunned silence. 'I mean, is it not better merely to teach him a lesson? If we can take our revenge, and teach him a lesson at the same time, he may be more malleable. More amenable to making another arrangement with us, that would be to our mutual advantage.' My head was still pounding. I took a sip of ale from a silver goblet and, as I looked at the beautiful vessel, it swam in and out of focus. I tried desperately to concentrate and listen to the arguments.

'What about his family?' said Will Scarlet, from his seat beside me.

'We're not going to be killing women and children,' said Robin. 'Whatever people may say, we are not monsters.' He looked round the table to be sure that all present had taken this point. Will blushed: 'I wasn't thinking of Sir Ralph's wife and little ones, sir – his wife died last year, and his children are in Scotland – merely of his cousin William Murdac, the tax collector. Do you know him? He lives out towards Southwell?'

'That's possible,' said Robin.

'Possible? He's perfect!' Hugh pounded the table with his fist. The blow echoed through my skull. 'That man is hated, loathed by everyone – his zeal in collecting the Saladin Tithe has bordered on madness, and I doubt he handed over all the silver to his cousin. What tax collector does? We know that Murdac himself squirrels a good bit of silver away that is never passed on to the King. His cousin's coffers are probably overflowing, too.'

Robin's brother pushed his chair back and stood at the table, fists balled and resting on the wood. He radiated certainty. 'His manor is fairly remote, I visited there once years ago,' he continued, his voice booming painfully in my ears in the confines of the cave. 'He has only a handful of men-at-arms living permanently in the place. And,' he said with a flourish, like a gambler playing the winning card, 'he's unmarried. No wife and bairns to worry about.' Hugh sat back down again looking at Robin in triumph.

'Yes. Good. Well done, Will,' Robin said, nodding down the table at the red-head, whose face split into an enormous gappy grin. To Little John, Robin said: 'Can you

174

handle this one?' John nodded. Hugh frowned. And Robin added: 'I want this William of Southwell's head brought back here. I will have it delivered to Murdac with a personal message. Take Will Scarlet with you, as he knows the place.' The big man nodded again. Robin turned to Hugh: 'Peace, brother, I want you to organise something else for me, more important than a punishment raid . . .' Hugh nodded, but he seemed reluctant.

'All right. Next,' said Robin. 'I want Selwyn's Farm set up as a new training school, and I want guards posted day and night on all the roads approaching it. I do not want a repeat of Thangbrand's.' Then to Hugh: 'You still have people inside the castle? Good. Make sure they give us plenty of warning when any force larger than, say, fifty men rides out of Nottingham . . .'

The conference continued. But I began to feel seriously ill. My bitten arm was throbbing – it had not healed well despite being bound in a bandage soaked in Holy Water by Tuck. My head was banging and my vision came in and out of focus. I watched blearily as Robin listened to his men's views, made a decision and moved on to the next point. He was unfailingly polite, even when the most ridiculous schemes were proposed, saying merely: 'I don't think that idea is the best we've had today.' He didn't need to be cruel: John was always ready to lambast a fool and Hugh's analysis of an idiotic proposition was merciless, as I knew well from my days as his pupil.

Even though I was trying hard to concentrate, I found my attention wandering. The words blurred and I began, through my dizziness and pain, to ponder the relationships between these men. They all seemed to have well-defined roles within the band: Hugh, it seemed, controlled the money, and the intelligence side of the operation; he had

175

a subtle mind, a philosophical approach to their business. John was the enforcer of Robin's will, and responsible for training the men in the use of arms. Robin was the judge: he made decisions, gave orders, balanced the two competing forces of mind and body represented by his brother and John. And Tuck? Tuck was an enigma. What was he even doing associating with this rough company?

The conference came to a conclusion and, after dismissing the men, Robin remained at the table with Hugh, talking quietly with the clerk. I watched the two men talking. Hugh's face was alight with pleasure as he listened to Robin's quiet instructions. In that light they looked so alike, though Hugh's face was longer and older and, in some way, sadder. But it was clear that Hugh worshipped his younger brother; his face had a look of total devotion as he listened. Robin put a hand on Hugh's shoulder and they both rose from the table, Hugh hurrying off out of the cave, happy and purposeful. I didn't see him again for weeks.

Robin came over to me as I loitered by the mouth of the cave, hoping that he would give me a mission as well or some difficult task to perform. He looked hard into my face, concerned. 'You are not well,' he said. 'Let me see your wound.' He led me back to the long table, my legs wobbling beneath me, and sat me down. As he gently unwrapped the layers of bandage, I noticed the smell for the first time, a waft of corruption, the stench of rotting meat. As he loosened the last layers of blood-and-pus-soaked cloth, he broke the half-formed scabs over the puncture marks made by the wolf's teeth, and I screamed as a white agony rioted up my arm and howled into my brain. Then I knew no more.

*   *   *

176

I dreamed of women. And the wild wood. I was lying on my back in the sun-dappled forest, and I could hear singing: it was 'The Maiden's Song'. The singer was a girl of almost impossible beauty: lithe and slim as a young willow tree, with a white shift that clung to her young body and small sweet breasts. As she sang, she danced, weaving in and out of the trees as if they were her dancing partners. I scrambled to my feet and began to run after her, crying for her to wait for me. As I blundered through the woodland with the girl always just out of reach, the sky began to grow dark and I burst out of the forest into a wide stretch of empty moorland and stopped. My eye was drawn to a huge grey stone, almost man-height but canted over at an angle like a partially uprooted tree. The white girl danced on by the stone but her steps were slower, more solemn. She beckoned me but I could not move and, with a pretty shrug, she continued to dance around the grey rock, caressing it. Then she stepped astride the stone, mounting it as one might a horse, the massive grey rock thrusting out between her thighs. And the rock transformed into a great grey stallion, pawing the air with great plate-sized hooves. The girl gave a great howling cry and she and her mount took off into the sky. They flew above the clearing, wild shrieks bursting from the girl as they swooped above my head. And then, softly as a falling feather, they returned to earth and the horse became a stone again. The girl rolled smoothly off its back and lay curled at its base, seemingly asleep. As I watched her, her pale face began to flush with colour and she clutched her belly and started to moan. Again I tried to move, to go to her aid, but I could not. It was dawn and when I looked down at my feet, I saw that they had become the roots of trees. I looked again at the white girl: and saw that she was no longer a girl. She was lying on her back, naked, in a pool of blood that rippled and changed and became the folds of a red blanket under her body. Her breasts grew and filled and hung pendulously either side of her chest; her belly swelled too and now was massive, ripe; and then, as I stared at her, her vulva opened like an enormous flower and, with a long scream from the woman, a huge bloody baby squeezed out from between her legs. I held out my right arm to her, but found it almost impossible to lift – I saw that it had become a thin branch, ending in gnarled twigs where my fingers had been. The limb burst into flames and pain shot through my arm. The flames began to spread higher, burning slowly up towards my shoulder.

In the shadow of the great rock, the dream woman was holding her baby, both of them wrapped in the scarlet blanket. She looked across at me and smiled and immediately I felt calmer; it was a smile from across the ages, an eternal comforting smile. The flames in my wooden arm were suddenly extinguished, as if the limb had been plunged into a bucket of water, and the scorch marks receded, pulling back into a single black line across my forearm. I looked back at the mother and saw that she was changing again. The scarlet cloak began to darken, to brown, then black; the woman began to alter her shape, her back became more curved, her breasts shrivelled. Teeth dropped from her mouth like the petals from a dead flower and the flesh of the face collapsed in on itself. The baby on her knee began to darken and shift its shape. A dark fuzz appeared on its skin, thickening into fur and a long black tail sprouted from its backside. I was looking at a crone with a black cat blinking on her knee. She looked again at me and smiled: a toothless grimace in a walnut face. She held out one hand, extended a bony finger and

178

beckoned: and I screamed, filled with a nameless masculine terror.

When I awoke, I was lying on a straw pallet in a dark hut, naked under a thick blanket that smelled of smoke and ancient sweat. The only light was provided by a small fire in the centre of the room. A blackened iron pot hung from a chain over the fire, and a woman was tending the pot, and humming to herself under her breath. By her profile, I knew she was the woman from the dream, all of them somehow, the maiden, the mother and the crone, all in one. Bundles of dried herbs hung from the ceiling and in the corners of the hut were stacked mounds of rubbish: old swords and shields covered in cobwebs, the antlers of a great deer, dusty old cloth bundles and what looked like a human skeleton. The woman saw that I was awake and, ladling some broth from the iron pot into the bowl, she brought it over to my pallet.

'How do you feel?' she asked in a curious lilting accent. I mumbled that I felt better and then realised I was starving and began gulping down the thick soup. She watched me eat and I stared back at her while I slurped and swallowed like a greedy child. I studied her with care. She had an ordinary oval face, about twenty years old, I guessed, but careworn with the beginnings of the lines that would stay with her for the rest of her lifetime. She had long brown hair pulled back and tied up like a horse's tail at the back of her head. No hood nor wimple; and she appeared to be wearing only a shapeless brown sack of a dress. Around her neck, on a leather thong, she wore a curious symbol, shaped like the wishbone of a chicken or the letter Y. I looked into her face again and saw that she had the kindest nut-brown eyes, and, though she was only a handful of years older than me, I realised that she reminded me of my own mother.

When I had finished eating she took the bowl and gave me a goblet containing an infusion of herbs to drink, slightly bitter but refreshing. 'Let me see that arm,' she said, beginning to untie the clean white linen bandage. 'We thought for a while that you must lose the limb, it was so badly infected, but, by the blessing of the Mother, and what little skill I have, it seems to be mending well.'

She undid the final twist of the bandage and I cried out in shock. There were four deep punctures in the flesh of my arm, deep red wounds with black edges rimmed with yellow pus, and in each pit crawled a couple of fat, pink maggots. She smiled: 'Don't be alarmed,' she said. 'They're doing you good. They eat the bad flesh and leave the wholesome meat alone. You owe your arm to my fat little beauties.' With infinite care she picked off the maggots one by one and dropped them in a small wooden box. Then she gently washed the wound with a yellowish liquid and packed each puncture with a mass of cobwebs, before binding the whole arm again in a fresh bandage. 'You must sleep now,' she said. 'Rest will bring healing . . .' And before she had finished speaking, I was fast asleep.

When I next awoke, Robin was there. 'Brigid says you are healing well,' he said with a grin.

I stared at him. 'Who?'

'Brigid, the priestess; the one who healed you. The Irish woman who has no doubt been feeding you eye of newt and dried bat's penis for the past week.' He was smiling. 'Though I must say you look well on it.' And I did feel well. There was yet another clean white bandage on my arm and it gave a little twinge when I flexed the muscles but apart from that I felt fine. A little weak perhaps, but fine. Actually, I felt rather good.

'Well, you've spent long enough as a slug-a-bed. What you need is some fresh air, exercise.' Robin grinned at me. 'I know you like to steal so let's go and take a few of the King's deer.'

That afternoon and for many days afterwards I hunted deer with Robin. Though I was weak at first, my full strength returned after a day or so and I found I was happy. In fact, I had never been happier. We would ride into the forest to a place where the huntsmen had seen small herds of red deer and then we would proceed on foot; stalking the animals through the dense woodland, armed with war bows. These man-killers made from yew had a much greater range than the light ash hunting bows most people used, but I could not draw one to even half its full extent with my wounded arm – to be honest, I never really mastered the great bow, even after spending years with some of the finest archers in the world. But I could stalk like a born forester, moving silently through the wood, watching every step to avoid treading on a stick that might snap under my feet and scare the game. We would approach the deer, moving painfully slowly with the wind in our faces to prevent the animals from scenting us, pausing for a few heartbeats between each step and remaining still as statues to check we were undetected. When we had worked our way close enough to the hart or hind, say, a distance of fifty yards, or even closer if the trees were dense enough, then Robin, or occasionally one of his men, would loose an arrow, aiming a hand's breadth below the shoulder to rake the heart and lungs. Robin was a magnificent shot, but there was always a helter-skelter chase after the animal had been hit and had begun its death run. We crashed through the undergrowth following the trail of bright red blood splashes until we would come across the heaving, exhausted, dying beast. Then the huntsmen would dispatch it with their spears.

If the animal was a stag, with a set of impressive antlers, the men would cut the horns free from the body and pack them up with special care, while the carcass, belly contents removed, was heaved on to the back of a horse for the journey home. I noticed that the death of each deer seemed to affect Robin strangely. Each time we killed, he would bow his head and offer a silent prayer over the animal before the huntsmen could gralloch the beast. And more often than not, Robin almost seemed to have a tear in his eye after the kill. It was strange behaviour, knowing as I did what he was capable of doing to his fellow man. But his sadness over a dead animal never seemed to dampen his enthusiasm for the chase.

My time was my own at Robin's Caves; I had no formal lessons, and few chores. When I wasn't hunting with Robin, I enjoyed a few practice sword bouts with Little John. He had returned after his mission to Southwell with a heavy, dripping sack, which he had dumped at Robin's feet. I excused myself and left the cave while they examined the contents, but I heard that Robin had a severed head delivered to Murdac during one of his feasts with a parchment note stuffed in the mouth.

Little John seemed impressed with my sword skill, though when we fenced – both of us with borrowed blades, as mine, I presumed, had melted in the fire at Thangbrand's and John always used an enormous double-bladed axe in battle – I knew he was going easy on me and, try as I

182

might, I could never penetrate his guard. I was a little scared of him, truth be told; he had held himself apart from me in our previous encounters but our fencing sessions at the Caves brought us together and I sensed that he wanted to be friendly. And, despite his huge size, his toughness and his appallingly blasphemous oaths, I liked him.

One day, as we sat at the big table, caring for our weapons after a muddy practice session in the forest, with the wind moaning outside the main cave and the rain dripping from the entrance, John told me the story of how he had come to join Robin as an outlaw.

'I was in the service of his father, you know, old Baron Edwinstowe,' he told me as he scrubbed at a rusty patch on his chain-mail armour. 'I was master-at-arms at the castle, as my father was before me, God rest his soul, and it was my duty to teach young Robin to fight. He was about your age, maybe a little younger, and full of sin and impudence in those days.' He chuckled at the memory. 'But he was a good-looking boy and there was fire in him – and courage, too. I like a brave man, always have, always will.' He paused in his tale and used a small fruit knife to scrape away at an obstinate patch of red rust on his massive hauberk. Then he continued: 'We started our training the right way, with the quarterstaff. The Baron objected, saying it was a peasant's weapon. A mere piece of wood. But I insisted – there is great skill in wielding a staff; it doesn't cost anything to make, and, when you are desperate, a solid piece of wood can save your life.' I thought of Ralph's club and the night of the wolves and silently agreed.

'He was quick, and strong and he learnt fast. And he had grit. We used to practise on the castle drawbridge. The two of us on the drawbridge above the moat with half the castle servants hanging over the battlements and watching. I'd knock him in the water nine times out of ten, but he always crawled out of the mud and filth and picked up his staff again. Like I said, he was a gutsy boy. After a month or so, he could sometimes knock me in the drink – and then I felt he was ready to move on to cold steel.

'The thing is, though we knocked each other about something fierce with the quarterstaves, he always had more bruises than he should when we stripped off to wash after a bout, and he sometimes had bruises on the face, too. I asked him about it once and he just shook his head and pretended that I had given them to him at our last session. 'You are a cruel and brutal man, John Nailor,' he would say, in jest. 'You don't know your own strength.' He was lying, of course, and I knew it. But if he didn't want to tell me, there wasn't much I could do . . .'

John stopped, took a huge pull on his tankard of ale, and dropped the hauberk in a wooden bucket. He added a double handful of sand and some water and vinegar and began to stir the mixture vigorously with a thick stick. 'The thing was, I liked the boy,' he said, speaking loudly over the grinding of the sand against the chain-mail. 'You could put him down but he always got up again. And he never complained. Never. But I was curious about who could be knocking him about. Who would dare? He was the youngest son of a Norman baron, descended from the great Bishop Odo, who came over with the Conquerer. His eldest brother William was away with his father attending the King for most of the year. Hugh, who was only a year or two younger than William, held the post of chamberlain for the de Brewister family in Lincolnshire. It couldn't be either of his big brothers who were beating him. It couldn't be any of the servants or men-at arms.

In fact, when I thought about it, I knew it could only be one man, but I couldn't believe him capable of giving Robin such vicious punishment. He was Father Walter, a priest, a man of God, who had been sent by the Archbishop of York to serve as a tutor to young Robin.' He stopped grinding the chain mail against the slop of sand, pulled the sopping hauberk out, peered at it, noticed a remaining patch of rust and dropped it back into the bucket. He took another pull from his tankard, and then went back to stirring the noisy bucket in regular grinding circles.

'One day, when Robin came out to battle practice with me, he was in obvious pain from his ribs. He kept insisting it was nothing but I forced him to lift his shirt and show me his side. His whole torso was a mass of bruises, and at least three ribs were cracked. So I went to have a word with Father Walter.

'He was a tall, lean man with a long curved nose that looked like a beak, and a mournful, pious expression. I pushed open the door of his room at the top of the castle and found him at prayer, kneeling on the cold stone flags of the floor before a large open window and clasping a large wooden crucifix in front of his body. He had been praying out loud and I caught the end of it: " . . . forgive this miserable sinner his weakness; remove the snares of temptation from his path and make his will to resist strong. Keep me from the fires of everlasting damnation. I ask in the name of Our Lord Jesus Christ, the one and only Son of God, Amen."

'He rose stiffly from his knees and turned to me: "How may I help you, my son?" he asked calmly. I stood uncertain, in the doorway. "It's about the boy Robert," I said and I told him that in my opinion he was being too hard on him. I mentioned the bruises and the broken ribs and

185

I suggested, in a polite and friendly way, that he should go a little easier on him in future.

'Father Walter drew himself up to his full height, and he was not much shorter than me, though very thin. "You insolent ox, you dare to speak to me about the chastisement of a sinner?" He was shouting at me, bellowing like the wrath of God, and I admit I was taken aback. "Calm yourself, Father, I'm only suggesting that—" But he overrode me. "You lumpen dolt, you think a few marks on the body are important. He is a fiend of Hell sent to tempt good men from the path of righteousness and I will beat him bloody, if I choose, to remove the foul stain of pride from his soul." He ranted on and I could feel my temper beginning to rise. His noise had summoned a couple of serving maids who watched our debate, mouths agape, through the open door. "Christ's crusty drawers, Father, there's chastisement and there is beating blood out of a young boy on a daily basis and—" He interrupted me again, shouting: "You dare to question my actions? Get on your knees before me and beg my forgiveness or I will consign your soul to the furthermost pit and your flesh will be seared for eternity by rivers of fire!"

'Then I lost possession of myself,' John said, with a wry sideways smile at me, and he finally stopped grinding away at his bucket. 'I've never had much admiration for priests and I don't care to be threatened by anyone. So I grabbed that ranting bully, hustled him bodily across the room and held him out of the window upside down, by one ankle. That shut him up. He just dangled there, me holding him by one skinny leg, the skirts of his robe flapping around his head and fifty foot of air between his tonsure and the stone of the castle courtyard. A crowd formed below, though none of them thought to fetch a blanket to catch him in. Perhaps they hated him, too.

'I said, as calmly as I could, "If you ever lay a finger on the boy again, I will end your miserable life. And to Hell with my eternal soul. Do you understand me?" He nodded furiously; his face was red, engorged with blood, but I swear I have never seen a man look more frightened. So I hauled him inside and set him down on his cot. He was speechless with terror. I don't think anyone had ever stood up to him in his life. So I took my leave, and he sat on his cot shaking with fear and staring at me with outraged eyes. It was the last sight I had of him alive.

'The next morning, I waited for Robin in the courtyard – we were supposed to be working on sword and dagger combinations, if I remember right. It was just after dawn but there was no sign of him. So I went looking for him, thinking he must have overslept. His chamber was at the top of the castle as well. As I walked past the priest's room, I glanced inside. It was bad – Christ's bulging haemorrhoids – it's a sight I'll never forget. And I've seen a few things, lad. Done them, too.

'The priest was naked and tied to the bed. A gag was stuffed into his mouth. His entire body was covered with burns – red-raw oozing burns with blackened flesh around the edges. Around the bed were the stubs of a dozen candles and the burnt-out remains of two wooden torches that would usually have been stuck in a becket to light a dark passageway. The air was filled with a smell like that of burning pork. It looked as if every inch of skin had felt the touch of a naked flame, over what must have been several hours. I shudder even now to think about the agony that man must have endured before he was finally given

187

release by having his throat cut from ear to ear. And, as a final insult, his own wooden crucifix had been crudely shoved up his arse, right up to the cross bar.

'I stared at the dead man; and I knew who had done this. But, just to confirm, I looked quickly into Robin's chamber. There was no sign of the boy, his bed had not been slept in and his clothes and weapons were gone. Then it struck me. I would be blamed for this. Yesterday, I had publicly argued with the priest and threatened to kill him – and today he was found dead. It wouldn't be long before they came looking for me.

'I gathered a few belongings, saddled a horse and was riding out of the main gate by the time the screaming had started in the upper floors of the castle. I ran into Robin about noon. He was sitting by the side of the southern road, calmly eating bread and cheese. As I looked at him sitting there, as innocent as a spring lamb, I found it hard to believe that he had spent the greater part of the night torturing a priest. He hailed me as I approached and I dismounted and sat down next to him. There was a faint smell of burnt pork about him, but otherwise he seemed unchanged. We ate for a while in silence, then I said: "Well, you've killed a man of God, for which they will hang you if you are caught. And if they don't blame you, they'll blame me. So what are we going to do now?"

'"Don't worry, John,' said Robin, 'I've got it all worked out. I think . . . I think I'm going to have to get myself an earldom."

'I laughed in disbelief, thinking he must be mad. After all, the boy was penniless, friendless and on the run from the law for murdering a priest. But Robin calmly went on, as if he were talking about what tunic he would like to wear that day: "And, for what I want to achieve, I need to become much feared, and then very powerful, and then extremely rich.' He looked at me with those weird grey eyes, and I realised he was perfectly serious. Then he said: "I'm going to need your help, John."'

Chapter Eleven

Alan, my little grandson, has a fever. It came as the new leaves were appearing on the apple trees; as the first flushes of green life burst out after the bleak months of winter. His mother, Marie, my daughter-in-law and housekeeper, is beside herself with worry; she fears he will die as her husband did. She does not sleep, but sits beside Alan's cot trying to feed him thin gruel and mopping at his forehead with a damp cloth. When he sleeps, she prays. She spends hours on her knees at the village church, beseeching the Virgin Mary to save her boy's life, and wearying the ears of the Holy Trinity. But it seems to be doing no good. The boy is losing weight fast, he sweats and tosses the bedclothes off in his fever. He mumbles and shouts and thrashes his arms about – I fear he will soon be with God.

Father Gilbert, the priest of this parish, has recommended fasting and prayer to persuade the Almighty to save the life of the boy. I cannot object, I will gladly go without food if it will save my grandson; when I pray to Our Saviour, Lord Jesus Christ, I ask him to take my life instead of his. Marie says the sickness is a punishment. She says that my past sins, amassed in my days as an outlaw, are the cause of the boy's suffering. Heaven's revenge, she calls it. She may be right; certainly I have many a black stain on my soul from those days of robbery, killing and blasphemy, but I find it hard to believe that Our Merciful Father would kill a lively, innocent boy for the long-ago misdeeds of one tired old man.

If Alan does not soon begin to recover, I have decided that I will sacrifice more than my worthless old carcass. I will place my very soul in jeopardy. I will pay a visit to Brigid. She still lives, and not far away, though she is even older and more shrivelled than me these days. And even as I know her to be a witch and a woman of depraved and devilish practices, I know, too, her power, and I will go to her and beg her help. For Alan's sake.

At Robin's Caves, as my arm grew strong again and the marks of the wolf's teeth faded to four pink glossy dimples, I saw less of Bernard than I had at Thangbrand's; he was withdrawn after our adventure in the woods and he had begun to neglect his toilet and grow a scraggly, patchy beard. The iridescent cockerel was gone; he began to look more like the other outlaws and he spent much of his time drinking and making music alone in one of the many rock chambers that made up Robin's sprawling hideout. The acoustics in his cave, he told me, were extraordinary; and certainly the music he made there had a booming, earthy quality all of its own. Robin's Caves, men said, had been carved out of the bedrock by magical dwarfs, and they could close tight, according to legend, when the spirits of the woodland wished, leaving no sign that they had ever been there. In fact, they were merely very difficult to find, deep as they were in an uninhabited part of Sherwood, and I shall never reveal their whereabouts. I swore an oath never to tell and, although my lord Robin is dead, I shall not break my word to him.

The Caves were roomy, though; at a pinch, they could shelter a couple of hundred men. It was rare, of course, for there to be so many at the camp at one time. Robin sent out a constant stream of armed patrols, each twenty men strong and under the command of a trusted 'captain', to scout the surrounding area for enemy troops, and to lay ambushes for rich travellers. He did it, I think, to keep the men hard and busy and out of trouble; for if they were allowed to stay around the Caves, they tended to sit about drinking and gambling and would soon get into fights among themselves. Discipline, though, was as harsh as it had been at Thangbrand's. The rules were simple: show respect to Robin and his officers; obey his orders without question; don't steal from your comrades; and don't even think of touching the chest of silver in the back of the cave that held Robin's Share. If you transgressed, the penalty was a horrible death.

I was happy there. The men accepted me as Bernard's assistant *trouvère*, and Robin's protégé. I sang for the men at night, either with Bernard, or, increasingly, on my own. I hunted almost daily with Robin, gorged myself on venison, enjoyed philosophical discussions with Tuck, when he was there, which was seldom for he preferred to stay alone at his monk's cell by the ferry. What had been a temporary place of exile from Kirklees Priory had become his permanent home. Some said the prior was glad to be rid of him. It certainly suited Tuck. Occasionally, I practised my sword-play with John, although he was busy training the recruits that seemed to appear by magic at the cave, always hungry, always ragged, and mostly grateful for a chance to serve Robin in battle.

Goody became a great favourite of the outlaws and their womenfolk. She was spoiled by almost everyone in the camp and she ran about the place making smart remarks to grizzled old warriors and being applauded for her wit and spirit. They had heard the story of her courage against the werewolf, as I heard the wildman Ralph being commonly called, and they loved her for it. And she was quite at home in their company, having grown up at Thangbrand's. However, her clothes grew ragged and unkempt and face and hair soon became filthy. In that rough company, her new look fitted like a hand in a glove.

I mentioned the wildness of her appearance to Robin one day when we were out hunting and he nodded. 'She needs a mother,' he said. We had stalked a herd of deer that afternoon but they had been spooked by something and had galloped away; now we were walking slowly back to the top of a hill where we had left the horses. 'I shall have to send her away somewhere. You too.' He looked at me sideways. I was shocked. 'Send me away? Why, sir?' The prospect appalled me. I had settled in well to life in the Caves, I was happy there; I felt I had earned Robin's trust, maybe even his friendship.

'I can't have you wasting your youth here with us,' Robin went on. 'Singing crude ballads for drunks every night. You've got much too much music in you for that, you know. Bernard has done a fine job in teaching you.'

'But where will you send me?' I asked.

'Somewhere civilised,' he said, and then he changed the subject.

'You're a fairly pious fellow, Alan, aren't you?' I knew he had seen me making my prayers before bed in the main cave every night. But he did not say it in a mocking way; he seemed genuinely interested.

'I believe that the Lord Jesus Christ is my saviour and the saviour of all mankind,' I said. He grunted. 'Do you not believe in Our Lord, sir?' I asked, knowing the answer.

'Used to,' he said. 'I used to believe with all my heart. But now I think that the Church stands between God and Man, and its shadow blocks out the light of God's goodness. I think the way to God is not through the corrupt and prideful Church.'

He fell silent, thinking, and perhaps conserving his breath as we walked up that steep hill. Then, as we neared the top, he said: 'It seems to me that God is everywhere, God is all around, God is this . . .' He swept his hand in a wide curve around him, indicating a swathe of woodland. It looked particularly beautiful that spring day. We had reached the top of the hill and we looked over a rolling stretch of lush greenery. Below us, twenty yards or so away, our horses were tied in the shade of a magnificent spreading hornbeam, bright green with new leaves. Below the tree, a purple carpet of bluebells, like a rippling sea that flowed away seemingly endlessly through the forest. It was a golden afternoon; a light wind rustled the new leaves, and a pair of larks swooped and played in the branches. Just as Robin spoke, a stag stepped out of the trees ahead of us. Its noble head was crowned with a huge set of spreading antlers; its liquid eyes surveyed us from beneath impossibly long eyelashes. We froze. Robin and I were alone, the hunt servants were still struggling up the hill out of sight behind us with our equipment. Robin had a strung bow in his hand and a linen bag full of arrows at his belt. But he didn't move. The great red animal stared at us and we looked back in wonder. It was a perfect spec-

194

imen, in its prime: head alert, mounted on a long proud neck, glossy muscular haunches and long clean legs ending in neat black hooves. It stood four-square, and shook its antlers in our direction as a challenge; every inch the king of the forest. I looked at Robin out of the side of my eye, expecting him to raise his bow. But he didn't move. Eventually, after a final long regal look at us, the great deer trotted back out of sight into the woodland. And I found I had been holding my breath.

'Was that beautiful creature not a fine example of God's presence?' asked Robin. 'God made that animal, and there is much godliness in that splendid beast. I need no priest or bishop to tell me that.' He was speaking the vilest heresy – I knew that none could come to Salvation without the Church, but part of me, a wicked corner of my soul, could not but agree with him.

There was one distressing note in my life at Robin's Caves. It was the captive soldier that Robin had taken just before he had rescued us from the wolves. He was kept in a small wooden cage, a short way from the main cave, which was just high enough for him to stand and long enough for him to lie down straight. I stumbled upon him one day when I went out to stretch my legs. He was filthy, confined as he was and open to the weather, and near starving, too, as he was fed only slops that a pig would refuse. Everyone in Robin's band just ignored him but I couldn't get him out of my mind. His name was Piers, he told me, and, feeling sorry for him, I would steal food from the kitchens and bring it to him from time to time, and talk to him like a human being.

He was not an intelligent man. Just a local Nottingham boy, an orphan who had been forced to beg and steal for his bread in the town and had even been outlawed for a time and had hidden out in Sherwood. When he told me this, I felt a bond of kinship with him. But then a cold realisation crept into my stomach. And I knew why he was being kept here, a prisoner with no ransom value. He had once been part of Robin's band and then he had run away from his comrades to rejoin lawful society. With a shock, I knew I was looking at a corpse. Quite apart from the fact that he had participated in the slaughter at Thangbrand's, he had, as Robin would see it, betrayed the band. He was, as Robin had said, a ghost; a dead man breathing.

I kept my face calm as he told me how he had joined the city watch and then, after a few years, and after much sweat and many a hard knock, had made the leap into the ranks of Sir Ralph Murdac's elite cavalry. It was something of which he was very proud. He was, as I have said, a very stupid man. He had no wife, nor children, and little conversation besides constant complaints about his conditions. His wound had been healed by Brigid, though he was not grateful, and called her a witch, but without room to exercise, and little food, his muscles were wasting away. In truth, he was a miserable fellow. But my heart was filled with pity for him nonetheless and I prayed that his end would be swift and painless. My friendship with Robin would be sorely stretched, maybe even to breaking point, if I had to witness another punishment of the like meted out to Sir John Peveril.

The only other person who spoke to Piers was Tuck. Once, when I came to see the poor man, I found Tuck in earnest conversation with him. And another time, when I approached the cage, I heard Tuck saying prayers for the poor man's soul. But though I felt pity for the caged soldier, a part of me, a shameful part, began to hate him just a little, too. I hated him because he was weak, and stupid, and helpless – and because I could not help him. But mostly I hated Piers because he was the cause of a great rift between the two men I most liked and admired.

I had been exercising my sword arm, which was by now fully healed, with some of the men in the woods outside the caves, when a great thunderstorm had gathered almost without warning and drenched us. As we all streamed back into the main cave, dripping and cursing, I saw Tuck and Robin standing almost nose to nose. The atmosphere in the cave crackled like lightning. Tuck, flanked by his great wolfhounds Gog and Magog, was shouting: ' . . . don't tell me you are seriously going to go through with this bloodthirsty pantomime.'

'I have told you my reasons,' Robin replied in a voice as cold as charity. The great dogs, sensing their master's hostility to Robin, began to growl deep in their throats, a terrifying rumble that was almost as loud as the thunder outside the cave.

'You think this . . . this barbaric, blasphemous, pagan display will bring you power over these people, that you will be seen as some kind of incarnation of a god? You are chancing your immortal soul with this nonsense, you are risking—'

Robin, his face like a stone, interrupted him. 'Do not speak to me about my soul, priest!' The dogs' growling had reached a higher pitch, their lips pulled back to display their huge white teeth. I remembered what they had done to the wolf pack, and shuddered. Robin ignored the animals completely. As I stood there, stomach churning with anxiety, I heard a creak behind my ear and turned to see Much, the miller's son, with a bow in his big hands, an

197

arrow nocked, and the string at full draw. It was pointing at the dogs. I looked around the great hall of the cave and I saw half a dozen other men, either with bow strings drawn and aimed at Tuck, or clutching their sword handles ready to sweep out their blades and cut the monk down.

The two men stared at each other, faces inches apart, neither giving any quarter in this dispute, and then Robin broke the locked gaze and looked around the cave. He had a curious expression on his handsome face; just for a second he looked like a guilty schoolboy. In that intense, private communion with Tuck, he had seemed unaware that bloody violence was only a heartbeat away. Now, as he realised that the cave was poised to break out into war, a flash of irritation rippled across his face.

'Oh, for pity's sake, Much, put that bow down,' he snapped. 'And the rest of you, put up your swords. Now! We are all friends here.' Then he looked back at Tuck and gave him a half smile. The monk shook his head, almost smiling too, and fondled the heads of his great animal bodyguards, quieting them. The tension was draining out of the cave and the men began to move about, unbuckling their war gear, starting to clean their muddy swords, and drying the rain from their faces with rough woollen blankets. Tuck said quietly to Robin: 'I can't stay here, I can't be part of this . . .' And Robin said simply: 'I know.'

Tuck plucked up a bundle of his belongings from a corner of the cave, whistled up his dogs and, without a word of goodbye, he strode out of the cave and into the rain.

Easter was approaching and with it the beginning of the new year. And we had wonderful news: Marie-Anne would be traveling up from Winchester to pay a visit to Robin at the Caves. I had dreamed of her on many a cold night, her beautiful Madonna face framed in blue and white, and now that she was coming, I could barely contain my excitement. I even went so far as to bathe my whole body in a freezing stream, rubbing my skin with a mixture of ashes and fat and scrubbing it clean with fine sand from the stream bed. I washed my clothes, too, though they were a sorry threadbare collection of rags after so long in the wild. There was new cloth to be had, bales and bales of the dark green wool that Robin's men wore as a badge of their allegiance to their master. One day I begged for a length of cloth from Robin to make myself a new surcoat and he took me to a chamber far at the back of one of the smaller caves where the stores were kept. Robin showed me a roll of fine green wool and told me to help myself to as much as I wanted. I was grateful but Robin brushed aside my thanks and left me to cut my cloth.

There were two other men in the chamber, engaged in a curious task. Using the same dark green cloth, Lincoln green I have heard it called since, they were cutting thin ribbons of material, less than half an inch thick but of extraordinary length – about ten yards long. When I asked the men what they were doing, I was told: 'We're making summoning thread.' And when I asked what that was they just chuckled and said I'd find out in good time.

Marie-Anne arrived with almost no fanfare and a small retinue of a dozen soldiers from Gascony, liegemen of Queen Eleanor, her mistress. But she had an immediate effect on the camp. She kissed me affectionately on the cheek, admired my new exercise-given manly physique, asked after my singing – which to be honest, I had rather neglected since coming to Robin's Caves – and left me

199

more in love with her than ever. She was introduced to Goody, took one look at her dirty face and raggedy clothes and ordered a great cauldron of water heated and an area to be closed off with curtains. After Goody had been forced to wash – she had to be dragged screaming into the hot water and forcibly scrubbed – Marie-Anne soothed her sulks by getting an outlaw tailor to make her a new silk dress and tying ribbons in her hair. Within a day or so, Goody was her willing slave.

Robin seemed immeasurably happier now that she was by his side at last. It was a strange, unpleasant sensation to see them together. I found that I resented Robin for having her love. My master had aroused many emotions in my heart in the year I had known him: awe, fear, disgust; but also respect, affection, maybe even a kind of love. Now I felt angry with him for spending so much time alone with a woman for whom I would have done anything. They asked me to sing with them one evening, soon after Marie-Anne's arrival, but I could not bear the thought of the three of us being together and so I pretended that I had a head cold and was not in good voice. I could see that Marie-Anne was hurt by my boorish refusal; Robin too seemed puzzled.

I knew I was being childish, and berated myself for my stupid behaviour, but I could not help myself. When I saw them together I could see that they truly loved each other, and it burned my soul like cold fire. At dinner she would sit by his side and while Robin engaged in rough banter with the other outlaws, I often saw him taking her hand in his below the table. Marie-Anne's presence seemed to have had changed Robin's demeanour; he was more light-hearted, even boyish around her. In fact, everyone seemed more cheerful with Marie-Anne in the camp; the laughter around the Caves was louder, the men went about their tasks with merriment and snatches of song. I was the only one who was out of sorts.

Fortunately, there was plenty to occupy my hands while I brooded on life and love: Robin was planning a great gathering for Easter and all the men and women of Sherwood who served him, or who did not care to offend him, were to be summoned to a great feast in the heart of Sherwood to mark the beginning of the new year. Little John had set me and several other outlaws to making a great plank table in the shape of a ring, enough to seat five hundred folk for the Easter meal. As well as a great deal of gorging at the gathering, there would be games and contests, gift-giving, singing and dancing, and displays of martial prowess.

Hugh returned to the Caves the day after Marie-Anne's arrival, and he brought with him a large ox-drawn cart that was filled with wicker baskets. The baskets contained hundreds of doves and were each marked with a letter crudely painted on the wicker lids. I greeted Hugh, who seemed very pleased with himself, and asked him what the doves were for: 'Are we going to eat them at the feast?' I asked. He looked shocked. 'Certainly not,' he said. 'These are home-loving doves, very special, and they'll be used for the summoning.' I was mystified and he explained.

'These doves know where their home is, where their mate and nest is, and they can find it even when they are hundreds of miles away. The Caliphs of Baghdad use them to send messages by attaching tiny written notes to the birds' feet. But as few people hereabouts can read, we use them to communicate a simpler message.'

I had no idea then what a Caliph was, and I had never

201

heard of Baghdad, but I was intrigued by the idea of communicating with birds. Hugh continued: 'We transport the birds far from home and then release them with a long thin green banner attached to their legs. The birds can then be seen for miles as they fly home, the banner flapping beneath them. A home-loving bird with a green banner is a message; it means simply: "Robin of Sherwood summons you". And all who would serve Robin are then required to arm themselves and travel in exactly the opposite direction that the birds are flying.'

I must have looked confused because Hugh frowned and snapped, 'It's very simple, boy, just pay attention,' exactly as he had when he was my schoolmaster. Then he pulled out a dagger from his belt and began to draw in the bare dirt at my feet. He stabbed the dagger into the ground six times, making a rough circle of marks. 'Each one of these is a farmhouse, with a dovecote, that Robin uses as a safe place. Here, for example,' he stabbed one of the marks in the circle, 'is Thangbrand's. May he rest in peace. Here,' he stabbed again at another mark, 'is Selwyn's Farm; this,' he stabbed again, 'is Kirklees Priory.' He looked to see if I had grasped it; and indeed an understanding of the elegance of the system was dawning on me. He stabbed the point of the dagger in the centre of the circle. 'We are here at Robin's Caves, but we have doves with us that make their homes in all these places.' He indicated the marks in the dirt circle. 'When we release the doves, they fly home trailing the green banners.' He drew lines from the central point to all the outlying marks on the circle, making a star shape. 'A loyal man who sees the dove on the wing knows he must march in exactly the opposite direction to the dove's flight and he will meet up with our patrols who will guide him – and scores of his fellows – into the camp. Simple, eh?'

It was. And I was impressed. 'But don't the banners get tangled up in the tree branches, trapping the doves?'

He nodded. 'Some do, and they are usually pulled down by farmers who sometimes eat the dove. Some men bring the dove back to Robin, and he is careful to reward those who do. Some of the doves are taken by hawks. It's not perfect, but it does work. It summons Robin's people from distances of up to fifty miles in all directions.'

A few days later I saw the system in action. Hugh and myself and several outlaws took the cartload of doves to the vast clearing in the woods where we would be feasting in a few days time and after attaching each dove to a banner, which took a surprisingly short time – the birds lay quietly in my grasp as I tied on the green material round one pink foot with a simple knot – we released them and watched as they soared up into the sky, circled the clearing until they found their direction, and then headed off, north, south, east and west, trailing the thin green banners behind them. 'In a few days,' said Hugh, 'there'll be a multitude here.'

And he was right. Two days later the patrols started to bring in the people of Sherwood. There was a motley collection of humanity: mostly they were outlaws, outcasts and runaway serfs, who scratched a living in Sherwood but were not members of Robin's band. Many of them wore the same Y-shaped amulet as Brigid around their necks, but not all. Some wanted to serve Robin as men-at-arms or bowmen; some just wanted a decent meal and a drink. But there were others too: well-fed yeoman farmers with quarterstaves in one meaty hand, men for whom

Robin had done a favour at some time; villagers looking for justice or a small loan or help against an oppressive lord of the manor; apprentices from the towns, who had slipped away from their masters for an illicit holiday; small merchants looking to sell their wares, and, strangest of all, two brothers who lived deep in Sherwood and who shunned all settlements. This strange pair, who dressed entirely in animal skins, were not outlaws in the way that we were, because they had never lived within the law. Both wore the Y-shaped amulet; they were pagans, who worshipped the old gods of the forest: Cernunnos, the horned deer god and his consort the Triple Goddess, who was maiden, mother and crone all at once, the deity that Brigid, the Irish wise woman, served. They avoided settlements with their Churches and law courts, unless it was absolutely necessary. I was intrigued and made friends with them: a grizzled old hunter called Ket the Trow and his brother who was known as Hob o' the Hill, who was a charcoal burner, and who reeked of pungent smoke. Neither of them stood taller than my shoulder and I had not finished my growing yet. But they were superb mimics and could imitate all the birds of the forest with great accuracy and could hunt and track better than anyone else in Sherwood. They were devoted to Brigid and Hob especially seemed to be impressed with the little row of dimples that was my memento of the night of the wolves. 'A wolf bite is very dangerous,' said Ket, while Hob nodded wisely beside him. 'Our uncle was bitten by a wolf, and he died a week later.'

'He fell out of a tree, while picking mistletoe, and landed on his head,' said Hob, looking at Ket with disapproval.

'Yes,' said Ket, 'but why was he picking mistletoe? To make a cure for a wolf bite gone bad.'

Robin's Caves were transformed by the crowds, who began arriving on the Easter Saturday morning and were clearly in the mood to make merry, and this quiet area of woodland became as busy and muddy and colourful and noisy as the Nottingham Fair. Anyone who arrived clutching a summoning dove was duly paid a silver penny by Robin, thanked and relieved of the bird, which was put back in the appropriate basket. Some of the visiting folk had brought tents; others quickly threw up crude huts made from turf and tree branches, to shelter them at night, and then they hurried to one of the larger caves where Little John was serving out great tankards of ale, free to all who asked him. Pedlars with trays of gimcrack goods, brightly coloured ribbons and whistles, lucky tokens and sweetmeats, roamed about crying, 'What do you lack?' in an attempt to sell their wares. There were dog fights and wrestling matches, foot races and a tug of war. An archery contest was held, which Robin won, to absolutely no one's surprise. He even beat Owain, the Welsh captain of his bowmen, who had first taught him the use of the war bow. Queen Eleanor's Gascon cavalry gave a demonstration of their prowess, galloping about and spearing cabbages nailed to poles at head height. Bernard judged a children's singing contest and then got drunk and sang bawdy songs for hours to an audience of equally drunken revellers. A travelling storyteller, a wise old man named Wygga, with a grey pointed beard and a mischievous grin, kept scores of people entertained with his marvellous tales of long-ago battles. I sat at his feet for hours, entranced by the bold deeds of King Arthur and his knights, and vowed to remember his fabulous stories and to make up my own songs about them one day.

On Easter Sunday, a great feast was given at noon. Everyone sat on rough benches at the huge hollow circular table that I had helped to construct from sawn planks in a clearing near the caves. We were about five hundred souls in all. Eighteen red deer and a dozen wild boar were roasted on spits and stripped to the bone by the hungry hordes. A hundred chickens, and two hundred loaves of bread were brought out to the great round table with great vats of pottage. The wine and the beer flowed like rivers; and all of it was provided as Robin's gift. Everyone ate their fill and became drunk and joyful. It was wonderful; some of the poorer folk looked as if they had not had a decent meal in weeks, and the great round table was suffused with a spirit of raucous harmony, with people from all parts of the country mingling in peace. There was only one thing that troubled me. I mentioned my fears to Hugh, who was sitting beside me toying with a sallet, a bowl of cold boiled vegetables and herbs, and sinking great drafts of wine. 'With all these people here, surely this place is secret no longer. Will not Sir Ralph Murdac know where to find us?'

Hugh shook his head. 'We're too strong now,' he said, slurring his words ever so slightly. 'There must be three hundred fighting men here at this moment eating Robin's meat. Murdac would have to strip Nottingham bare to even match our numbers. No. If he wanted to take us he would have to gather a real army, a thousand men or more, and we would get wind of that long before he was ready to move.'

I was comforted by this thought, and set to my plate of roast wild boar in a sauce of preserved brambles with enthusiasm. As I chewed, another thought struck me, and I looked sideways at Robin's brother. 'Hugh,' I said, emboldened by his booze-suffused face to ask him a personal question. 'Why are you an outlaw? Surely a man of your skills could find a place in a noble household? Perhaps you could even serve the King, keeping him safe from his enemies, the way you do for Robin.'

Hugh sighed, and I could smell the sweet fumes of wine on his breath. 'You don't have any family, Alan, do you?' he asked. I shook my head. 'They are a blessing and a burden,' he said in his schoolmasterly way, as if beginning a lecture. 'A family is like a great castle; a source of much power and strength – but it is a prison, too.' I poured him another goblet of wine and he nodded his thanks before continuing: 'Our father died shortly after Robin was declared outlaw. Some said it was of a broken heart. The old baron loved Robin best of all his three boys, though he was the youngest. He never much cared for William and me, and had the old bastard lived he would have probably persuaded the King to give Robin a pardon, I think. But the Archbishop of York, the saintly Roger de Pont L'Eveque, insisted that Robin be punished to the full extent of the law for having foully murdered one of his servants. And, as Robin would not come in from the forest to face judgement, he was declared outlaw by the Archbishop. Soon after that, the old baron had a seizure and died, and William, our eldest brother, took over his lands. Then Archbishop Roger died. But, by then, Robin had a list of serious crimes to his name a yard long, and Ralph Murdac was after his blood.

'Neither Robin nor I are close to William, though he is only two years older than me. He is everything that Robin is not: pious, mean, timid, cautious and respectful of authority. He's something of a shit-weasel, to be honest.' I was slightly shocked to hear Hugh talk of his older brother in this way. And he seemed to sense this through the wine.

'To William's credit,' Hugh continued, 'he has made Robin a standing offer: surrender to him and he will intercede with the law, and try to get leniency. Robin's not interested, of course; he'd much rather negotiate from a position of strength, which is why he does all this.' He made a sweeping gesture with his hands at the hundreds of happy, red-glowing faces at the tables to our left and right. 'Robin would rather have a private army at his back, a couple of hundred loyal men-at-arms, and a dozen barrels of silver to spend when he asks for a royal pardon. And he's right, too.' He took a deep swig of wine. 'He's always right, you see, always. Not like me. I'm always wrong. Always in the wrong.' His drunkenness was entering the self-pitying stage.

'So how did you come to be with Robin in the forest?' I pushed him.

'Because of a woman, of course,' said Hugh. And he laughed, his head hanging loose between his shoulders, chuckling and chortling until his noises began to sound more like sobs. Then cuffing his face with his sleeve, he turned his bleary eyes to me and asked: 'Have you ever been in love, Alan?' He didn't wait for an answer. 'You *trouvères* seem to think that love is an amusing game, something to pass the time. But it is not.' He lifted his bleary eyes to mine. 'Love is pain,' he said with a perfectly blank expression. 'Love is an agony that banishes sleep and turns bread to ashes in your mouth. I have loved, and I know what I'm talking about.'

He paused there and stared at me but I said nothing. I wanted him to continue but I felt the belligerence in his tone, the truculence of the self-pitying drunk, and I knew enough to stay silent.

'I was in love,' he said, after little a while, 'with the most beautiful woman in the world. Most beautiful girl in the world. Jeanne was her name and she was the daughter of Richard de Brewister. Oh God, she was beautiful!' He took another sip of wine and straightened his shoulders, trying to sober himself. 'I was Lord de Brewister's chamberlain. I ran his household, kept his accounts – oh, five or six years ago now – and it was there that I fell in love with Jeanne. She loved me, too. And when Jeanne became with child, I wanted to marry her but Sir Richard wouldn't hear of our union. He had set his sights higher, on an Earl or a Duke, not the second son of a minor baron, a mere clerk. He sent me away, in disgrace; the unfeeling bastard, he sent me back to William. And he sent her to a nunnery, where she was to bear the child, in secret. It was a boy. But I heard . . . I was told . . . that God took them both during the birth.'

He had broken down and was weeping openly now, the tears running down his long face, and I was embarrassed for him. When he had been my stern teacher at Thangbrand's, I had never seen him drunk, never seen him so vulnerable. I wanted to get away from him, to flee from his humiliation but, instead, I put my arm clumsily around his shoulders, and he seemed to draw some comfort from it. So I asked what happened next.

'I was so unhappy after she died, I couldn't settle. Back at Edwinstowe, I was just a hearth knight, the younger brother of the lord. I would never inherit anything, I'd never be allowed to marry, I would just live out my life in his shadow, existing on his generosity, on the scraps from his table. I was desperate. I thought about taking Holy Orders – I have always tried to love God with all my heart, and to serve Him, but William wouldn't allow it. He wanted me close at hand, a grateful dependent, living on his largesse, for ever. I think deep down he hates me. But then Robin summoned me. He reached out from the forest to save me.'

Hugh made an effort to compose himself. He sniffed and dabbed at his red eyes with a linen napkin. Then he blew his nose with a loud trumpeting sound. 'Robin needed me, you see. His band had really grown; from just him and a few friends waylaying travellers in Sherwood to the whole complicated circus you see today: with safe houses, and informers, and his travelling court, delivering his justice to the people. He's just like a king, in fact, deciding the fate of hundreds, maybe thousands of people, he's got a decent treasury, he makes loans to distressed knights, to merchants, he practically has his own army . . . And he asked *me* to help him. It wasn't much of a decision, really. Poor dependent hearth knight, a gentle beggar really, or chief minister to a king, albeit an outlaw king.'

The feasting went on long into the afternoon and early evening, with jugglers and acrobats and fire-eaters entertaining the diners long after they were full to bursting. And, as a full moon began to rise in the night sky, I staggered away from the table, my stomach tight as a drum, and went back to the cave to find my warm straw bed. I left Hugh snoring at the table, his long balding head resting on his arms.

I awoke after only a few hours. The big moon was high in the sky outside the cave but it was not the moonlight that had awakened me. Some of the men were moving about in the cave, quietly, almost stealthily, dressing in warm clothes and moving in ones and twos out of the entrance and into the night. All was quiet except the soft rustling of fur cloaks and woollen surcoats as the men dressed and made their way out into the bright moonlit night. I was curious. Where were they going at this hour? Many outlaws were still curled up and snoring, oblivious, but I decided to follow the men and see what I could see. So I jumped up, pulled on a big hooded cloak with wide sleeves over my shirt and followed them.

There must have been half a hundred men and women walking away from the cave and the crude huts of the visitors and into the wood. It was an eerie sight after that boisterous day, but everyone was silent, almost reverent as they walked away from the hearth fires and into the dark, wild wood. Gripped by a sense of excitement, I pulled the hood of the cloak well forward over my face, and followed the silent crowd. I felt part of some great and solemn secret as I walked along behind two outlaws I knew slightly, through the trees along an old path much overgrown with creepers and brambles, the path indicated by small candles set into the forks of trees at regular intervals. Once we were deep in the wood, I caught up with the two men and they greeted me with nods but no words and somehow I knew instinctively that I should not sully the night with my questions. We walked for the best part of an hour in silence following the path of candlelight ahead and then, all of a sudden, we came out of the woodland to the edge of a piece of wild moorland, and I could not suppress a gasp of surprise. It was the moorland of my feverish nightmare at Brigid's, with the great grey stone exactly as I had dreamed it, the slanting shape of the ancient rock pointing at the same angle to the sky. But there were the shapes of about fifty dark-robed figures, hooded and solemn, surrounding the ancient stone before which was burning a great fire; and strapped to that great granite rock, naked, gagged, illuminated by the flickering flames and with his eyes huge with terror was the prisoner Piers.

Chapter Twelve

As I stared at Piers, a drum began to beat; a slow heavy regular booming that sounded like the heartbeat of a giant beast. I was glad of my cloak's deep hood, and I pulled it even further forward, for I did not want to catch the poor wretch's eye. Or look anyone full in the face. It was shame, I suppose. I knew now why Robin had preserved this enemy soldier, this traitorous former outlaw, and my blood ran cold as I realised the blasphemous cruelty that was to be perpetrated this night. But for some reason I could not move; could not protest. I did nothing but watch with mounting horror as the ungodly ritual unfolded. And when it was over, when I was tormented by the voice of my conscience, I excused myself with the thought that I could have done nothing to save his life in a crowd of fifty blood-lusting pagans; that to try to disrupt that Satanic ceremony could have led to my own death and would have served no purpose. But the truth is darker than that. I did nothing but watch because a part of me, a rotten corrupted corner of my soul, wanted to see the ritual played out. I have told myself that it was witchcraft, that I was rendered immobile by magic that night, but the truth is that, like all the other participants, I was curious and some part of me wanted Piers's lifeblood to be spilt for the ancient gods.

The big drum's deep booming was joined by another lighter but still thumping pulse, and then yet another drum, a half beat before the first two. All together, that awful combined rhythm sounded the death of the terrified man tied to that ancient rock: *ba-boom-boom; ba-boom-boom; ba-boom-boom* . . . In spite of myself, I found that I was moving in time to the beat of the drums, swaying from side to side, my conscience dulled, made drunk by the rhythmic pounding. As I looked about me, I saw that all the other men and women there were swaying, too. Then they began to sing: a grave anthem with a haunting melody that I had never heard before. It had a majestic beauty, though, a hymn to the Earth Goddess from whom all life springs, the source of all fertility. I did not know the words but the song was powerful, irresistible, and I too was caught up in the joy of the music and, as the hymn came to an end, with a series of rising notes and a shout, I found myself chanting along with the crowd 'Hail the Mother . . . Hail the Mother . . . Hail!'

At that last great cry of 'Hail!' a figure stepped out of the circle of worshippers into the central space by the fire. It was a woman dressed in a long black woollen robe embroidered with stars and hares and crescent moons. Her face, partially obscured by the hood of her robe, was painted pure white and she carried a small round iron pot in one hand and a bunch of mistletoe in the other. She stepped gracefully over to the fire before the great stone. She raised the pot and the mistletoe and, seemingly looking straight at me, she said in a loud clear voice: 'Are you ready to come into the presence of the Goddess, the Mother of the World?' And the crowd answered, shouting with one terrible voice: 'We are ready, Mother, we are ready!'

The priestess knelt before the fire and, after muttering a prayer, she threw a handful of herbs into the fire, making it flare up with a green-blue light. Then, with her eyes closed, she passed the iron pot slowly three times through the flames. She stood, opened her eyes and, walking slowly round the circle of onlookers, she dipped the mistletoe in the iron pot and flicked a spray of water over the celebrants, crying: 'By fire and water, thou art cleansed.' As she moved round the circle dipping and splashing the congregation, I dreaded her coming to me. It was only Brigid, I knew, in that weirdly embroidered robe with her face terrifyingly whitened with chalk. It was only the kindly woman who had healed my arm. But a horror was growing within me; I was sure that a nameless evil was among us and, as she approached with water pot and mistletoe, I kept my face down to the earth and a shudder went through me as I felt the cold water splatter on my cloak.

When the priestess had completed the purification of the congregation, she stepped into the circle of light by the fire and, eyes flashing and with a great cry of: 'Behold the Mother!' she stepped out of the robe in one quick movement and stood there, quite naked, her arms outstretched. Her body was painted with a jumble of mad symbols, the images running one into another: on her lower belly were three intersecting crescent moons in a bright white entwined star shape. They could only dimly be made out behind the red and blue and yellow stripes and swirls that seemed to grow up her body to her chest. Her full breasts had been painted red, with black zig-zag lines seeming to shoot from her nipples; her outstretched arms had been painted with green serpents, speckled with bright yellow dots; it looked as if the snakes were coiled around her arms and were squirming towards her heart. Where there was room, the rest of her body was covered with symbols depicting the animals of the hunt: stags and hares, dogs and hawks – a wild boar growled silently from her hips through a great pair of tusks. She stood still, allowing us to admire the designs on her naked body. And in spite of my revulsion at this pagan display, I felt my loins move. She had a beautiful body, in the full flush of womanhood: round perfect breasts, still pert and bountiful, a slim waist, flaring to smooth generous hips, and the dark bush nestling in the crotch of her long slim legs. I could feel my prick stiffening in my drawers.

I tore my gaze away from her nakedness and looked, as if as a punishment for my lust, beyond her to Piers, bound to the rock. He too seemed mesmerised by her nakedness; his eyes were huge and dark and I guessed that he had been drugged. Then I noticed, in the far edge of the firelight, behind the great stone, the form of a wild deer. A great spread of antlers and the muzzle of a noble beast were just visible in the moving shadows. It couldn't be real; no hart would come this close to such a gathering. There were gasps of wonder from the congregation as they caught sight of the beast and a murmur went up like the whisper of wind through a willow tree: 'Cernunnos, Cernunnos, Cernunnos . . .' And out from behind the grey stone stepped a creature, the like of which I had never set eyes on before.

It walked on two legs, like a man, but the body was much smaller, hunched over and covered with tanned brown leather almost to the ground. Huge wide antlers sprouted from its head and over its face it wore a wooden deer mask. But the way it moved was unmistakably like a deer, the nervous movement of the head, the sudden starts and then that incredible stillness that overcomes an animal when it is watching for danger. As it began to make its way around the circle of celebrants, I was struck by how uncannily real it was; something about the delicate steps, the angle of the head. And then I knew what – or rather who – it was. It was Hob o' the Hill – I had seen him imitate the deer and several other beasts for our amusement the day before. Now he was playing the part of an ancient forest god. When the man-deer had walked the circle, with a leap, the creature disappeared behind the rock exactly as a stag will bound away into the forest when it sees the hunter.

I turned to watch the priestess and saw that now she was armed with a tiny bow and arrow, like a child's plaything, and, as I looked, she fired a shaft into the darkness behind the rock. A great wail went up from the congregation, and the cry of 'Cernunnos, Cernunnos . . .' began again growing from a whisper into a full-blooded chant. From behind the rock stepped a man, naked but for a deerskin kilt around his loins. His face was painted brown, the eyes circled in white to make them appear huge, and on his head was mounted the same great spread of antlers that Hob had worn before him. His hand was clutched to his heart, from which an arrow protruded between his fingers, a very thin trickle of blood, as if from a light scratch, running down his naked chest. It was Robin, I realised with a sinking feeling of inevitability. And as the cry of 'Cernunnos' reached a peak of frenzy, he collapsed gracefully in front of the stone and lay still, the arrow in his heart pointing to the sky. As I stared down at his body, amid the whirl of conflicting emotions, something struck me as strange about his brown-painted face; it was his mouth. Every now and then it seemed to give a faint twitch. In this solemn moment, at the height of this powerful ritual, which was clearly an offence to all that was Christian and decent, Robin's corpse looked as if it were trying not to laugh.

The congregation fell silent – nobody but me seemed to have noticed Robin's facial contortions – and into the quiet, into the firelight in front of Robin's dead body, stepped Brigid, now robed again, but with the hood thrown back and a fierce, determined expression on her face. She was holding an iron mace in her right hand, and a rope noose, and the iron pot in her left; around her neck, on a thin leather string, was a large black flint knife that glittered in the firelight with ancient malice. She walked to the great stone. Piers, gagged and bound, was staring up at her with pleading eyes. Their eyes met, I'm sure, for an instant but there was no mercy in her and raising the mace she cried: 'In the name of the Mother . . .' and smashed the heavy iron ball into the side of that poor wretch's head.

He slumped immediately, lolling at the neck, and I felt nothing but a sense of great relief. 'Dead or unconscious,' I thought, 'he feels nothing now.' And then I realised that, in my mind, I had already accepted the inevitability of his death – and my guilt began to flow like the blood that ran down Piers's cheek.

Brigid looped the noose around his unstrung head and, crying 'In the name of the Mother', once again in a shrill voice, she pulled hard on the end of the rope, tightening the hemp until it cut deep into the soft skin of his neck. Piers made no movement except when Brigid tugged a few times on the rope and I thought: 'Thank God, he is at peace now.' I was wrong.

218

The priestess removed the noose and, tilting the head to one side and positioning the iron pot carefully beneath, she raised the black knife and screamed: 'His life for the Mother,' and sliced hard through the limp neck, cutting his pale throat right to the bones of the spine. There was huge spurt of blood and a great collective sigh from the congregation; his still beating heart forced the gore to jet crazily from his body and then slow to a pulsing flow that ran down his bare white shoulder to drain into the little iron pot. I closed my eyes and offered up a prayer to our Lord Jesus Christ for his wretched soul. And for mine.

Dipping her fingers in the blood running from the victim's neck, Brigid knelt by Robin's side and carefully drew the shape of the letter Y on my master's chest as he lay on the ground in his death-pose. Then she held out her bloody hands to the circle of watchers and cried: 'Arise, Cernunnos, arise Lord of the Wood . . .' and the gathering echoed her cries, quiet at first and then growing louder and louder. 'Arise, Cernunnos, arise Lord of the Wood . . .' and Robin, as if awakening from a deep sleep, climbed unsteadily to his feet and raised his arms above his head, the shape of his body echoing the bloody Y on his chest and the two great antlers above his head.

The chant had changed to 'Hail, Cernunnos, hail, Cernunnos . . .' growing louder and louder until it was nearly deafening, and the drums began again, beating in time to the chant and growing more frenzied with each beat. Finally, suddenly, Robin lowered his bare arms and the noise ceased immediately. An eerie quiet spread over that stretch of God-cursed moor, Piers's body hung limp, bound to the rock, the last drops of blood dripping into the iron pot. And Robin said, his voice unnaturally loud in the quiet: 'Those who would receive the blessing of Cernunnos, step forward, and kneel before him.'

A woman stepped from the crowd and knelt before Robin. He reached a finger into the pot of Piers's blood and, stooping, drew the bloody stag sign, the sign of the Y, on her forehead. She shuddered with ecstasy as his fingers touched her head and she turned away, grabbing a man from the congregation and dragging him away from the firelight, tearing at her clothes in her haste to begin coupling. Another outlaw stepped forward and knelt before Robin and was marked with the sacrificial gore . . . but I had had my fill of blood and play-acting and unnecessary death and as more people surged forward to receive Robin's blessing, I melted back into the darkness and, with a heavy, guilty heart, I began to make my way back to the cave. Behind me I could hear the howls of men and women, strangers to each other but inflamed by this night of blood, engaging in frenzied sexual excess. I knew I would not be missed.

I left Robin's Caves the next day. Not, I must say, because I had found the courage to leave such a wicked crew of murderous heathens. No, because Robin sent me away. He summoned me the morning after the sacrifice. He looked weary and there were still traces of brown paint on his face. I made no mention of the brutal ceremony I had witnessed the night before, though I had to bite my tongue. As I had been well hooded, and had left without receiving Robin's bloody pagan benediction, I believed that my master would not know that I had attended his foul rite, but if I started to talk about it, to ask questions, I knew my disgust would gush out like Piers's lifeblood.

'I'm sending you to Winchester,' Robin said to me; he

seemed to sense my disapproval and his voice was cold. 'Your singing is good, though Bernard says you don't practise enough; and John tells me you can handle a sword well. But I don't need another swordsman, I need a *trouvère*, like your father, a man who can travel from castle to castle and deliver messages for me and pay his way at any gentle home he enters with good music and good manners. So I think it is time that you acquired a little more polish and knowledge of the world. And the court of Queen Eleanor at Winchester can provide that. The Countess of Locksley will take you there and steer you safely through the halls of the mighty.'

At these words, my disapproval evaporated. I said: 'Thank you, sir,' and I meant it. I would be travelling with Marie-Anne to visit the Queen! And I would live at court with the noblest folk in the land. Me, a grubby parentless cut-purse from Nottingham, rubbing shoulders with lords and ladies, even royalty! I was lost in an elaborate fantasy in which the King pardoned me, called me his good and faithful friend and made me a Gentleman of the Privy or something when I realised that Robin was still speaking.

' . . . Godifa needs to grow up a lady, which she won't do here. And Bernard – well, Bernard is falling apart in these surroundings.' He paused. 'Are you listening, Alan?' I nodded. 'Marie-Anne has her Gascons, of course, but I want you to keep a special eye on her for me. Will you swear to keep her safe on the long road? He fixed me solemnly with his great silver eyes.

'Oh yes, sir,' I said. 'It will be my honour.' I could have hugged him. All thoughts of Cernunnos and human sacrifice had flown from my head. He had that effect on many people; whatever wrongs he did it was impossible to stay angry with him for any length of time. That was his true power, I believe, not his ranks of bowmen and cavalry.

We set off at noon. But before we departed, Robin presented each of us with a gift. Marie-Anne received a gorgeous necklace of a hundred fat pearls, with two matching pearl-cluster earrings. To Bernard he returned his apple-wood vielle, retrieved from the cottage at Thangbrand's. Our cosy former home had not been razed by the sheriff's marauding horsemen, though the place had been ransacked. Miraculously, though, the precious vielle had not been stolen – perhaps Murdac's men were not musical – and was rescued by one of Robin's long-range patrols, which had buried the dead and gathered up anything of value.

To Goody he presented Freya's ruby. My jaw fell; I had never expected to see that great blood-red jewel again. I had assumed it was lost in the fire. But Robin's men had been told exactly where to look by Hugh and they had dug it out of the charred floor. As he handed her the ruby, Robin said: 'This stone once belonged to your mother and so I give it to you, for you to remember her by. But have a care with it. I feel in my bones that it is not a lucky jewel. Guard it well.' He had had it mounted in a clasp on a fine golden chain and I had to admit it looked magnificent. But Goody, curtseying and thanking Robin prettily, turned to Marie-Anne and offered it to her. 'Won't you take it, Marie-Anne?' she asked. 'It is too fine a jewel for a little girl; I might lose it or it might be stolen from me but I think it would look fine on you.'

Marie-Anne accepted the great jewel. 'It is beautiful,' she said. 'I will keep it safe for you until you are fully grown, and perhaps, on special occasions, I may be permitted to wear it?' Goody smiled at her. And they both fell to examining the gorgeous red stone.

To me, Robin presented a flute, a beautiful ivory instrument, chased with gold. I suspected that it had once been owned by a musical clergyman, who had had the misfortune to bring it with him on his travels through Sherwood, but I kept silent. I put it to my mouth, holding it vertically, as I blew into the mouthpiece. The notes were as sweet and rich as butter and I thanked Robin once again for his kindness. 'We also found this at Thangbrand's,' he said. 'Buried in the ruins of the hall.' And he handed me a long object wrapped in an old blanket. It was my sword, my old friend; the wooden handle a little charred and with a few scorch marks on the battered scabbard, but it was my blade. The blade with which I had killed my first man. My own shabby Excalibur. My eyes were misting with emotion, so I bowed low to hide my face.

Just before we left, Hugh drew me aside. 'Robin has asked me to speak to you about this matter,' he said, gravely; he looked quite ill, no doubt suffering from yesterday's wine. 'While you are in Winchester, he wants you to be our eyes and ears in the castle. Just gather what information you can about the people there, who's talking to whom; who's not talking to someone else. Any plans the King may have, any news from France, anything concerning Robin or any of us, in fact.' I nodded. It sounded exciting, Robin was giving me a grave responsibility: I was to be a spy. I grinned at him. 'I thought that might appeal to your larcenous spirit,' said Hugh, smiling back at me. 'See if you can purloin the Queen's private correspondence, or something.' I laughed at this absurd idea. Then I realised Hugh was quite serious. He continued: 'There is a man in Winchester called Thomas – you can find him at a tavern, the sign of the Saracen's Head. He has only one eye and he's probably the ugliest man in Christendom but you must identify yourself to him by saying: "I am a friend of the woodland folk." He will say: "I prefer town people." Give him any message you want to relay to us here. Got it? Thomas, Saracen's Head, woodland folk, town people. Got it?' I nodded again and he said: 'Good lad.' Then he gave me a fat purse full of silver pennies, more money than I had ever owned in my life. 'Expenses,' he said. And then he frowned and, in his best schoolmasterly voice, added: 'And it's not to be spent on ale while you lark about in taverns, nor on saucy Winchester wenches, either.'

He was one to talk about drink; and I had no thoughts of saucy Winchester wenches. I would be riding south with a perfect specimen of womanhood, who drove all thoughts of others out of my head. We set off, two by two, on horseback with mules behind us carrying our possessions. Four Gascon cavalrymen rode at the head of the column, and four at the rear, and four rode up and down the column as we jogged along. The road was busy with revellers from Robin's great feast making their way slowly back to their lives. Many looked the worse for wear, but, at first, there was a carnival atmosphere as we made our way down the highway. I rode next to my Marie-Anne, taking my role of bodyguard very seriously; Bernard and Goody rode behind. Bernard looked like a rotten cheese; badly hung-over, eyes bloodshot, his face saggy and grey. Goody, on the other hand, was in irrepressible high spirits. She felt we were going on an exciting adventure with a glittering prize at the end of the journey. And she kept pestering Bernard with questions about what a royal court was like and how we should be treated when we arrived. Most of the time he merely grunted in reply.

In the late afternoon, the weather turned cold and a storm began to brew in the south. The merry revellers seemed to have disappeared and I couldn't shake the feeling in my gut that we were riding into trouble.

As we trotted along, wrapped in our warmest clothes against the chill wind, I began to ask my lady about her life when she was away from Robin's band. 'As you know,' she said, 'I am a royal ward. I became one when my father, the Earl of Locksley, died several years ago. Ranulph de Glanville sent some of his men with a letter from the King, claiming me as his ward. The Locksley lands are rich and wide, and the King wishes to have control over who marries me and becomes the new Earl. They said it was for my own protection, of course, but they lied. It is to enrich the King. Whoever wishes to marry me – and I pray with all my heart that it will be my Robin – must pay the King a fat price for that honour. I sometimes feel like a prize cow at market, up for auction to the highest bidder.' She laughed but her mirth had a touch of bitterness in it. 'Even so, Robin cannot buy me at the cow auction. King Henry would never allow me be married to an outlaw. He would always look for some advantageous match; or I might well become a way to reward a faithful servant. And that would certainly rule out Robin.'

She sounded so sad that I felt a pang of guilt about my jealousy. I said quietly, though the words choked in my throat: 'You must love him very much.'

'Very much. And I know that he loves me. I have always loved him, since we first met ten years ago. He came to stay at my father's house when I was just a girl – but I loved him from the first day. He was kind, he was funny and handsome. He made time to listen to my foolish prattling. He did not love me then, the way that he does now; how could he? I was just a child, barely out of my mother's apron strings. But he was kind to me. And that is the quality that I find most attractive in a man.

'As we grew older, his feelings changed towards me and he became more ardent. He would ride over to visit me from his home in Edwinstowe and bring fresh flowers and ripe fruit, and tell me wonderful stories about our future together, how we would be so happily married and live in a great castle and have dozens of children, and laugh and love all the days of our lives until one day, we would die together, of extreme old age, at exactly the same moment, hand in hand.' She smiled at me, a sad, mocking smile, as if to say, 'Ah, the folly of youth'. Then, after a pause while we negotiated our horses around a muddy pothole in the road, she continued.

'But when Robin was declared outlaw, everything changed. My father, who was ill by then, would not allow him to enter the castle. When I told my father I loved Robin, he threatened to raise his tenants, arm them, and hunt Robin down. Not that he could have managed it, the drunken old fool. My mother was useless; she just told me to listen to my father.

'But Robin still came to visit me, even though he risked capture and death every time we met. We would take secret rides together in Sherwood: once, it was on my seventeenth birthday, he organised a midnight banquet for me deep in the forest, even attended by some of my friends. There was a long table laid out, garlanded with wild flowers and laid with rich exotic food in a clearing in the middle of nowhere; with musicians, jugglers and servants pouring wine and bringing platter upon platter of roasted meats.

226

Heaven knows where they cooked the food. And, that night, he asked me to marry him.

'I said yes, of course, but we both knew it could never be while he was an outlaw. So we became betrothed in secret. Robin wanted us to lie together, to seal the bargain with our bodies. But I would not. I had vowed to my mother that I would keep my maidenhood until marriage. Robin was disappointed, very disappointed, but he respected my wishes. And I have kept my vow, despite what some in Robin's band might think.' She gave me a sideways glance, and I blushed. Like almost all the other outlaws, I had assumed that Robin and she were as intimate as any other couple, married or unmarried. I could see that Marie-Anne was blushing, too, and so I prompted her to continue the story.

'My father died soon after,' Marie-Anne said. 'He grew thinner and thinner until there was almost nothing left of him. By the end, I could have picked him up with one hand. And it wasn't long until my mother followed him. I think she died of loneliness; I mean that I think she willed herself to die, to be with him. She had always said she could not bear to be parted from him. And I pray they are together now in Heaven.'

I mumbled something about my being sure of it. A rabbit darted from under our horses' hooves and away into the woodland and we took a minute or two to control the startled mounts. Then Marie-Anne picked up her story again.

'The day after my father's death, while the whole household was in mourning, a local knight called Roger of Bakewell came to pay his respects. After my father had been laid to rest in the churchyard, Sir Roger took me aside and tried to kiss me; his breath smelled of onions. When I refused, he told me that he would marry me, that he had made an arrangement with my father and paid him

227

half a pound of silver to seal the bargain for my hand. I was shocked, but I believed he spoke the truth. My father might well have done such a thing. He would have considered it the right thing to do, to ensure that I had a strong husband to protect me and safeguard the earldom.

'But, you know Alan, from that day on I never spoke to the man Roger ever again. In fact, for ever afterwards he always tried his hardest to avoid me. Once, in Nottingham, after I had become a royal ward, I bumped into him in the market place. He was mounted and I was afoot. The minute he saw me, he wheeled his horse and galloped – literally galloped – through the market throng to get away from me. The brief glimpse that I had of his face showed me that he was terrified. Terrified of me.

'Of course, I discovered later that Robin had paid him a visit. And he had taken big John Nailor with him. The story goes that they broke into his castle at night, broke into his bedchamber, and while John stood over the man with his great axe, Robin made him eat half a pound of silver, a hundred and twenty silver pennies, one penny at a time. Robin explained to Sir Roger, very quietly and reasonably, that he had now been repaid the money he was owed for my hand, and that if he ever tried to press his suit with me again, there would be very unpleasant consequences. "She is under my protection," he told Sir Roger. "And anyone who troubles her will feel my displeasure."'

I still was laughing at the image of a proud knight being forced to eat a big bag of metal, when Marie-Anne said: 'It can make for a lonely existence, though, being under Robin's protection. Men are wary even of speaking to me. And that is why I am so enjoying talking to you, my handsome bodyguard.' She smiled at me. I stopped laughing and imagined I could feel a cold wind blowing on my neck. I wondered what Robin would do to me if he knew some of the thoughts I had had about Marie-Anne.

She seemed to be reading my mind. 'I am promised to Robin,' she said, 'and my heart will always belong to him. But that doesn't mean you and I can't be good friends.'

I gave her a sickly smile. Hugh had been right the day of the great feast when he wept into his wine. Love could, quite often, mean pain for someone.

Chapter Thirteen

Although it loomed over the city like a great stone fist, Winchester Castle looked wonderful to me. I have never been quite so glad to see a symbol of Norman power in my life. I had grown up in and around Nottingham town but I had never been *inside* its castle – indeed, had I entered it, I'd have been terrified, as being inside that fortress meant facing torture and death for a thief such as me. But, as our mud-splattered, blue-nosed party approached Winchester on the Andover road, I realised how much I had changed in the year I had been with Robin's band. I caught a first glimpse of the castle as we topped a small rise, and I merely thought: 'Praise be to God: hot food, hot water to wash in, and a chance to put on some dry clothes.'

Then my eye was drawn to the soaring majesty of the city's long cathedral, famous for housing the holy shrine of St Swithin, the saint who brings the rain – and I scowled. It had taken us more than a week to travel the two hundred or so miles from Robin's Caves to Winchester, and it had hardly stopped raining since we set out. The roads had become quagmires, mere channels of mud through which the horses had picked their way with their hooves sucked down by the sludge at every step. Wherever possible we rode off the road, on the verges which were higher and less muddy, or on open fields. But it was easy to get lost and the Gascon men-at-arms were uncomfortable when we left the highway. So we splashed through mud for most of the way, stopping at manors and farms held by friends of Robin and Marie-Anne or at religious houses at night where the monks would give us a slim meal, a doubtful look and a cot in the dormitory to sleep in. Every morning, though, we awoke at grey dawn and rode out again into the ever-falling rain.

Marie-Anne, God bless her, had remained cheerful for the whole journey and while I was huddled in my cloak, cursing the rain that ran down my neck and shivering as the wind blew against my sodden hose, she told stories to Goody and described the wonderful time we would have at Winchester; the parties, the games, the mock 'courts of love', which Queen Eleanor had introduced from her native Aquitaine, in which poets and troubadours would compete by performing their love poetry. The songs were judged by Eleanor and her ladies-in-waiting and the winner awarded a kiss. Bernard pricked up his ears at the sound of this. He had been sullen and quiet for most of the journey, wrapped, like me, in damp woollen misery, but when Marie-Anne mentioned these 'courts of love' he seemed transformed and asked her endless questions. What sort of songs did the Queen like? How far could a musician go, politically, in the satirical *sirvantes*? Were her ladies-in-waiting pretty? When he had at last finished pestering her, he was a different man.

'It seems we are going somewhere that is quite civilised,'

231

he said to me, almost cheerfully. 'And now we will have some proper music. You'd better pull up your hose and start practising that fancy flute, Alan. You'll be expected to perform at some point and I do not want you to disgrace me in front of the Queen.' He smirked at me and began to sing; the song, one of his favourite *cansos* in French, was muffled by his soaking hood and almost completely drowned out by the hiss of the rain as it drove down into the mud around us.

We entered the city of Winchester through the north gate, and were briefly challenged by the guard but, when the Gascon captain shouted 'Comptess Lock-ess-lee', the big wooden barrier was swung open and we trotted through and into the busy streets of the city. The city seemed to be more crowded than Nottingham; the houses huddling closer together, the streets narrower, meaner. The other thing that struck me most forcibly after a week travelling in the countryside was the smell. The city reeked of a thousand foul odours: of shit and rotting meat, of decaying rubbish and human sweat. I covered my nose and mouth with my damp sleeve; and then just ahead of me a house-holder hurled a chamber-pot of piss from a window into the street. It narrowly missed the rump of Bernard's horse and he turned and snarled at the woman in French and she hurriedly apologised and slammed her shutters. The contents of the chamber-pot joined the trickle of foul slurry that oozed down the centre of the street and we steered our horses to the side of the road to avoid that noisome stream, picking our way around piles of rotting refuse, dead dogs and filthy beggars, crouching in their rags in door-ways and crying for alms. Rats scurried away from our horses' hooves and I thought longingly of Sherwood and the wild, clean woodland.

We clattered over the drawbridge of the castle at about noon and into a great courtyard, where we were greeted by servants who took our horses and ushered us into the wing of the castle that housed Queen Eleanor and her retinue. I was shocked at the great size of the place; just the courtyard was three times the size of the hall at Thangbrand's and many doorways led off from it to a maze of chambers and corridors, lesser halls and, of course, the great hall where Queen Eleanor would dine with the constable of the castle, and her nominal captor, Sir Ralph FitzStephen. In truth, Eleanor was not as confined as closely as she had been in previous years, when she had been totally cut off from the outside world, and denied any company save for her maid Amaria. In fact, at one time, Eleanor's quarters had been so spartan that she and Amaria had had to share a bed. Now, although the King still kept her closely guarded for fear that she would encourage support for their son Duke Richard, with whom he was at war in France, she was permitted all the comforts that she was entitled to by her rank, including a sizable retinue.

However, the King was old and sick, and worn out by the years of constant warfare with his sons over their inheritances. When he died, and some whispered that it might be soon, Richard would become king and his beloved mother Eleanor would be an even more powerful woman. So Ralph FitzStephen stepped lightly around his royal prisoner and while she was not allowed to leave the castle, he turned a blind eye to the frequent messengers she dispatched to and received from France and Aquitaine.

Of course, I knew none of this at the time. I was in awe of the huge stone building that we had just entered and bewildered by the number of rooms that made up the royal apartments. Most people in England lived in one room, mother, father, children, and their livestock all in one small smoky space a few yards long; at Winchester there were more rooms than I had ever seen under one roof, with high ceilings and the walls hung with tapestries or painted with dramatic scenes of the chase or images from the Bible or pictures of the Virgin Mary. We were informed by the servants that the Queen was resting, but that the bathhouse would be ready in no time at all and that there were fresh clothes and food laid out in a chamber that had been set aside for Bernard and me. Goody had been swept up by the women of the household and taken away, and Marie-Anne had disappeared off to her own apartments, but we were all to meet up at dusk. So Bernard and I stripped off our sodden travelling clothes and made our way to the bath house. There, in great padded wooden tubs filled with steaming water, by the side of a roaring fire, we let the pains of the journey dissolve. It felt wonderful: servants in relays brought jugs of boiling water and topped up the bath, while another scrubbed my fast-thawing back. Bernard seemed to be burning with excitement despite his weariness; he was singing to himself almost constantly, clearly composing something, a love song, I believe, and muttering 'No, no, no . . . Ah, but how about . . .' I tried to listen to his new song but in no time I drifted off to sleep in the warm water.

We were summoned to the royal presence that evening. Washed, brushed and dressed in clean tunic and hose of rich green silk, courtesy of Marie-Anne, we were ushered into the lesser hall that Eleanor used as her private meeting place. It was still a large room, with dressed stone walls, brightly painted with what I guessed were scenes of famous landscapes from Aquitaine, and a high arched wooden ceiling. Though it was spring, two large braziers burned in the centre of the room making it pleasantly warm, and about a score of men and women, beautifully dressed, stood around the hall drinking wine, laughing and talking to each other. We entered the room, Marie-Anne leading a clean and well-brushed Goody by the hand, with Bernard and myself following. Bernard looked like a royal prince; while I had slept away the afternoon, he had found a barber in the castle and his hair, now glossy and clean, had been trimmed to a neat bowl shape; his face was shaven and he had even found time to weave coloured ribbons of red and yellow into the seams of his green silk tunic, giving him a merry, festive air. He smelled of rose oil and some other heady spice. He was the cockerel once again, bright and shiny and happy. He stood straighter, he looked totally at home in this huge and daunting castle; I suspected that he was even sober. In comparison, I felt dowdy, provincial and nervous and I was glad he had asked me to carry his vielle, which had been polished until it shone like a mirror; it gave me something to hide behind.

As we entered the hall, the crowd parted to reveal a great chair at the far end of the room, in which sat an elderly woman in a splendid golden satin gown embroidered with jewels and pearls. She must have been in her mid-sixties, an age far greater than most people achieve, nearly ten years older than I am now, but her face was lean, alert, and barely lined, and her eyes were bright as a sparrow's under an ornate white horned headdress bound with golden wire. She was Eleanor, she was the Queen, and I realised with a shock that despite her advanced age, she was still beautiful.

She smiled when she saw Marie-Anne and stood up and beckoned her forward. 'Welcome home, my child,' she said in French. She had a warm voice, with a deep smoky burr that gave it a pleasant sensual quality. Marie-Anne curtseyed prettily and then moved forward to embrace her. Eleanor took Marie-Anne's chin in her left hand and stared intently into her eyes. 'So you have returned from that den of thieves intact?' she said. Marie-Anne seemed to blush, and replied: 'Yes, your highness, as you see, I am quite unharmed.' ▾

'Hmmm. And how is that dreadful Odo boy?' she asked.

'He is well, highness,' Marie-Anne replied, 'and he sends you his respectful greetings and this gift.' At this she handed over a heavy gold ring adorned with a great emerald, the size of a quail's egg. Eleanor took it, in an already much-beringed hand, and turned it to catch the light from a torch burning in a becket set into the wall. Then she laughed: a dark, intimate chuckle.

'He is a terrible fellow; I gave this ring personally to the Bishop of Hereford as a parting gift the year before last.' She sounded that raspy deep laugh again. 'He really is naughty . . . but amusing, very amusing! No wonder you are so in love with the rascal.'

Then she turned to look at us. 'And you have brought some friends with you, how delightful . . .'

'This is Bernard de Sezanne, the noted *trouvère*, sadly exiled from his native lands,' said Marie-Anne, and Bernard bowed low and, looking at Eleanor, began to speak a stream of gibberish. It sounded like French but it wasn't; it was like hearing somebody speak in a dream when you can't quite grasp what they are saying. Eleanor, on the other hand, seemed delighted by his words. She beamed at him and replied in the same dialect, clearly

236

asking him a question. Bernard replied in the negative but added something and then bowed again. Belatedly, I realised that they had been speaking in langue d'oc, or *plena lenga romana*, the tongue spoken in Aquitaine and many of the southern lands of Europe. I had heard the Gascons speaking it to each other, although they had always addressed me in bad French. I found that I could almost make out the sense of the words, if I concentrated; it was similar to French, but much of the meaning escaped me. But it was Eleanor's native language, the language of the troubadours.

Then Marie-Anne spoke again, in French: 'May I present Godifa, an orphan of good family from Nottinghamshire, who is under my protection, and Alan Dale, an honest Englishman and the personal jongleur to Bernard de Sezanne.' This was news to me. I'd never in a thousand years have described myself as honest, but I felt proud to be called a jongleur, which was a professional entertainer, a man who often combined singing other people's musical compositions with dancing, juggling, even telling amusing stories. It was ranked lower than a *trouvère*, who would, of course, 'find' or compose his own music. But to be the personal jongleur to Bernard sounded a lot better than the bag-carrier and bottle-bringer that I actually was. I stood a little straighter and then bowed low to Eleanor who regarded me with a faint smile.

'Now come, child,' the Queen said to Marie-Anne, 'and tell me of your adventures in the wild wood. And, in a little while, Monsieur de Sezanne will entertain us with some of his famous music.' She smiled at Bernard and he bowed again. Then she sat down and Marie-Anne pulled up a stool and the two women were soon deep in conversation; the rest of us, it would seem, had been dismissed.

I looked around the gathering at the elegant knights and ladies, talking merrily, flirting and ignoring us. Bernard took the vielle from me, muttering something about checking the tuning. He wandered off into a corner and began fiddling with the pegs in the head of the instrument. Goody, completely unselfconsciously, sat down on the floor by Marie-Anne's knee to listen to the conversation between the Queen and her protégée. I was left alone. And I had absolutely no idea what to do. A servant passed with a tray of hot honeyed wine and I grabbed a cup and hid my face in the sweet red liquid, taking tiny sips as I surveyed the company.

The men were dressed in a bewildering variety of styles from the dark woollen robes of clergymen to the bright silks of courtiers, with here and there a knight in chain mail. Even in my smart new green silk tunic, I felt out of place. I had a nagging fear in some part of my mind that one of these fine ladies and gentlemen would see me for what I really was: a grubby thief from Nottingham, and everyone would point and laugh, before I was dragged away to be hanged as an impostor.

One of the soldiers in the party throng, a big man with a bushy black beard, was dressed particularly severely in mail from head to foot, over which he wore a pure white surcoat with a large red cross on the breast. He was talking to two other men, both knights wearing identical gorgeous surcoats of scarlet and gold. As I looked at the knight in white, he must have felt my gaze and he turned away from the two men and looked directly at me. To my surprise, his strong black-bearded face split into a huge white grin

and he shouted: 'Alan! By the Cross, it's Alan Dale!' and
he strode over to me holding out his arms in welcome. It
was Sir Richard at Lea, whom I had last seen at
Thangbrand's, and in this crowd of elegant strangers, I was
as glad to see him as I was surprised.

'Where did you spring from?' he asked, embracing me.
'Don't tell me you've been pardoned?'

I blushed. 'I came with the Countess of Locksley,' I said
shyly, and Sir Richard looked at Marie-Anne in close
conversation with the Queen and nodded and said: 'I see,
still with Robin, then?' And, as I murmured agreement,
he said, 'Let me have a look at you,' and he grinned at
me. 'I don't believe I've ever seen you in clean clothes
before.' He kneaded my shoulders and arms and said: 'And
you've put on some muscle; still practising with the sword?'
I nodded again. 'Good man, you've a talent in that direction; let me introduce you to some friends of mine, good
fighting men both,' and he led me over to the two men
in scarlet and gold. 'This is Sir Robert of Thurnham, and
his brother Sir Stephen; I'm trying to convince them to
take the Cross and come on the Great Pilgrimage with
the King next year. We will need a good many Christian
warriors to win back Jerusalem from the infidels, as His
Holiness the Pope commands. Perhaps you too can be
persuaded? I offer certain salvation for your immortal soul?'
He looked me in the face, his sincerity blazing out of his
bright brown eyes.

I shook my head and said: 'I'm sworn to Robin,' but I
felt a little ashamed. It would have been a wonderful thing
to be a warrior for Christ, to cleanse my soul of its many
sins in battle against the Muslim devils. Sir Richard turned
to the two men, who were looking slightly surprised by
his offer to me. 'Young Alan here is a very decent

swordsman; he'd make a fine companion for us. I know . . . because I trained him personally.' The brothers looked impressed; clearly they knew of Sir Richard's great skill on the battlefield. My big bearded friend looked at the poniard hanging at my belt. 'Learnt how to use that yet?' he asked, pointing at the blade.

'Not really,' I replied, 'but it has already saved my life twice.' I didn't mention that both times the poniard had been wielded by a little girl.

He nodded: 'Told you so! How about a little practice? Show you a few moves. Might even convince you to come out East. Tomorrow at dawn in the courtyard?'

'I would be honoured,' I grinned at him. 'But doubtless I won't be upright for long.'

Sir Richard just snorted. 'Nonsense. You'll probably have me rolling in the dust; if, that is, you can remember how to move your feet.' We stood there beaming at each other like idiots and then Sir Robert of Thurnham coughed and said: 'If I may make so bold, sir, whom did you say you served?'

This was tricky. I had never officially been declared outlaw; there was no price on my head, as I was beneath the notice of the powers that be. But Robin was certainly beyond the pale and, by association, so were all who served him. But in this southern part of the country? Under the protection of the Countess of Locksley, ward of Queen Eleanor; I was surely safe. So I lifted my chin, looked Thurnham in the eye, and said proudly: 'I serve Robert Odo of Edwinstowe.'

His brother Stephen choked in surprise: 'You mean Robin Hood, the notorious outlaw?'

Sir Richard started laughing. 'Keep that under your helmet, Stephen, if you don't mind. And you, young

240

Alan, should probably keep it to yourself, too.' He grinned at the brothers: 'Alan is a good friend of mine. We met when Robin captured me last year; that slimy toad Murdac of Nottingham refused to pay my ransom, but Robin was a gentleman about the whole business. How's that old scoundrel Thangbrand?' he said looking keenly at me.

'He is dead, sir,' I said. Sir Richard frowned, and I looked at the floor, suddenly overwhelmed with images of the burning hall and the blood-drenched snow.

Robert of Thurnham took a step towards me. 'Many a knight has spent a little time outside the law and yet was an honest man at heart,' he said. 'But tell me, it is said that Robin Hood is training an army up in Sherwood; how would you rate them as an effective fighting force?' I was glad that the conversation had moved on from Thangbrand and flattered that this knight should ask my opinion on a military matter, but I didn't feel comfortable discussing Robin's affairs with a stranger.

Sir Richard answered for me. 'It's damned good, if the skirmish I saw is anything to go by: Robin knows how to use archers and cavalry in combination. Few commanders do. I have to say it was a very efficient force, serfs and outlaws to a man, of course, but damned good.'

Stephen sniffed, and began to say: 'Surely, mere bandits—' But he was interrupted by the blast of a herald's trumpet. We all turned and I saw Bernard striding into the centre of the room, grasping his vielle in one hand.

I have never heard Bernard play so well as he did that evening in front of the Queen. It reminded me of his performance the first time I saw him at Thangbrand's; the simplicity of the notes, and the purity of his voice.

241

He began with a *canso*, a love song, in langue d'oc, which, of course, I didn't completely understand. But it was beautiful nonetheless: his fingering on the vielle was absolutely precise, his phrasing exquisite. I felt a lump in my throat, and I vowed then and there to master that gorgeous liquid language so that I might attempt one day to produce music of such splendour. Queen Eleanor, I swear, had tears in her eyes.

He performed several other songs, some in French that won applause from the assembled ranks of knights and ladies, even one in English, to more muted applause as it was still viewed as a slightly uncouth tongue, not quite the thing for refined company. Sir Richard cheered lustily, but then he was an Englishman to the bone. When Bernard had finished, the Queen presented him with a purse of gold, described his music as sublime and invited him to attend her and her ladies in her garden the following day.

My music teacher was walking on clouds. Afterwards, with a smile a foot wide on his glowing face, he said: 'I'm made, Alan – no more squalid caves, no more oafish outlaws.' He danced a few steps around our shared chamber. 'The Queen, may she live a thousand years, loves my music, and I am made. I shall never go back to that damp forest, I shall live the life of a prince, a *trouvère* to royalty.' He went on and on in this vein. But the odd thing was, though he had had a cup or two of wine, he was not drunk. He just sat upright in our huge shared bed – it was, by the way, the finest bed I had ever slept in by a long chalk, with a feather bolster, fine linen sheets, and goose-down filled pillows – and glowed with happiness. I was exhausted and, while he remembered every note aloud, and pointed out to me the moments of particular musical genius, I fell into a delightful and dreamless slumber.

We settled comfortably into life at the castle over the next few weeks. As spring turned to early summer, I practised my sword and dagger work with Sir Richard in the castle courtyard each day at dawn and became, if not Christendom's most accomplished warrior, then at least proficient in the use of those arms. On one memorable occasion I did even manage to tumble Sir Richard into the dirt by back-heeling his legs as we were chest to chest, swords and daggers locked. To my joy, and I pray God will forgive me for the sin of Pride, Robert of Thurnham was watching when I performed this feat. He congratulated me and said that if I ever needed employment as a man-at-arms he would welcome me into his service.

I liked Sir Robert, though I was a little wary of him; although he came from Kent, our conversations seemed to turn a little too often to Robin's force in Nottinghamshire: how many men did he have? What proportion of them were cavalry? How many archers? And so on. I turned aside his enquiries as best I could by claiming ignorance, and to his credit, after a while, he seemed to realise how uncomfortable his questions made me feel. One day he said to me: 'Alan, I do not wish you to betray any confidences; but, believe me, I do not hold any ill will towards your master. As you may know, I have now taken the Cross and a good company of archers, such as those commanded by Robert Odo, could be indispensable in the Holy Land against the fierce mounted bowmen of Saladin. But, I beg you, you must tell me to mind my business, if it makes you uneasy to talk of such matters.'

Bernard was as happy as I have ever seen him. He attended the Queen almost daily, performing in the sweet-smelling garden at the back of the castle for her ladies, including Marie-Anne. They made music there and played childish games, such as hoodman blind with the ladies, blindfolded, running around and trying to catch young gentlemen by the sound of their voices. Bernard soon embarked upon several love affairs with the Queen's attendants and quite often I would awake in the night to find him gone from our shared bed. The next day he would be tired but smug. I attended these garden jollities several times, at Bernard's invitation, sometimes accompanying him and playing my gilded ivory flute to feminine acclaim. But I found the company of perfumed ladies, day after day, a little stifling and often escaped to talk about manly military affairs with the Gascon guard, who were also teaching me to speak langue d'oc. In later years, when I performed my own music in that lovely, rippling southern tongue, I acquired a reputation for using ripe, earthy language in my love songs, inadvertently using words for dalliance and lust that I had picked up from the Gascons. Strangely, the crude soldiers' phrases that I used were applauded as fresh sounding and original, in a style of music that was often ridden with flowery conventions and clichés.

Marie-Anne had set about the process of 'taming' Goody, as she put it, with real determination. My little friend was being taught to spin wool into thread, an endless task that seemed occupy all the time when she was not using her hands for another purpose; to embroider, to sing (though Bernard had given her a thorough grounding at Thangbrand's); to act demurely; to walk gracefully; to serve wine in an elegant manner and a thousand other skills that a gentlewoman needed to attract a husband of knightly status. Occasionally, she rebelled, sneaking out of the castle to roam the city with a pack of grubby Winchester boys, causing mischief, even fighting other urchins, and returning with a torn gown and dirty, bruised face to the scolding of her keepers. I saw little of her at that time, but I sensed that she was happy; and so, I realised one day, was I.

There was just one dark cloud on the horizon: my promise to gather information and report back to Robin. The problem was that I did not, particularly, have anything to report. The first time I went to the Saracen's Head, which was not far from the castle on St Peter Street, it was a cold and rainy night. I met Thomas there and after the ritual question and response of the woodland folk and the town people, he told me to tell him what I had learnt in the past few weeks since we had arrived. So I told him about Bernard's triumph, and Goody's adventures, and I offered him all the best and latest gossip of the court: how so-and-so was sleeping with so-and-so; that this courtier was in favour with the Queen and that courtier was in disgrace.

Thomas was a truly ugly man. Apart from having only one eye, the other being just a mass of pink and red scar tissue, he had a great round head adorned with several huge smooth bumps the size of acorns on his forehead and crown, a flat, brutish nose and a sparse mangy-looking head of curly black hair. He resembled a troll or some other outlandish monster bent on the destruction of mankind. In fact, he was a decent man, if a little sardonic – and devoted to Robin. When I had finished giving him a particularly juicy story about two of Eleanor's young male clerks who had been caught naked in each other's arms

245

and had been banished back to France in ignominy, he cocked his big, misshapen head on one side, staring at me out of his one dark eye and said: 'All very interesting, no doubt. But the pot-boy here could tell me tales of the filthy frolics of young clerks. What else have you got for me? What news of the King? Or of Duke Richard?' My face fell. I knew that they were both in France and at daggers drawn, but no more beyond that. Thomas realised that he had hurt my feelings and quickly added: 'But you are new at this game; never fear, we will make you a spy as great as Joshua in no time.' And he clapped me on the back and ordered another pot of ale for me.

When I had recovered from my embarrassment, he leaned forward and said: 'What you need to do, Joshua, is to get close to Fulcold, the chamberlain. You have met him? Good. Now you need to gain his trust. And, eventually, through him to get a look at the Queen's private letters. Hugh tells me you can read and write, that you are *litteratus*?' I nodded. He continued: 'That will be very helpful. Go to Fulcold and offer to help him in his duties, now that he is short of two clerks, he will be overworked; flatter him, say that you wish to learn how a clever man organises the affairs of the greatest lady in Christendom.'

He took a small sip of ale. 'Don't push things,' he said. 'Don't ask too many questions. Be helpful, be hard-working. Never complain if he asks you to undertake a difficult or dull task. And watch for your chance.' He was getting to his feet, preparing to leave.

'Robin wants to know what Eleanor is saying to Richard in her letters to him, and how he is answering. But don't do anything too dangerous, young Joshua, don't risk getting caught. Robin says you are very valuable to him and that he is quite fond of you. I'm under strict instructions not

246

to let anything happen to you.' He gave me a smile and lightly punched my shoulder. Then he went on: 'I'll meet you here at the same time, on the same day of next month, and you can tell me how you've been getting on. If you need to see me before then, leave a message for me here. And give your name as Greenwood. Understood?' I nodded, we clasped forearms, and he disappeared quickly out of the ale house and into the black, wet night.

Chapter Fourteen

I presented myself to Fulcold the next day, flattered him and gave him a present of a little yellow songbird in a small wicker cage that I bought in the town. Master Fulcold liked it well enough, and he told me that I might assist his team of clerks who kept the rolls of the Queen's accounts and learn how a great household was managed.

He was a strange little man, immensely fat, shy and sentimental. He adored music and loved the idea that the jongleur of such a noted *trouvère* as Bernard de Sezanne was working under his auspices. When there was not much work for me to do, which was quite often, he had me play my gilded flute for the entertainment of the clerks.

As well as recording the Queen's accounts on great rolls of parchment, the clerks of the royal household were mainly concerned with Eleanor's correspondence – and she wrote and received letters constantly. Every morning, the Queen would rise at dawn, wash, break her fast and attend the service of Prime at the Cathedral. After that she would attend to her correspondence. She wrote to everybody, from her beloved son Richard, the Duke of Aquitaine, and Philip Augustus, the King of France, to humble knights in Poitou or Germany. And they wrote to her. But these exchanges had to be discreet as she was in theory a prisoner and the King had given orders that she was to be kept incommunicado. But the King was unwell; likely to die, many said, and if he did, Richard would inherit the throne of England.

So, every morning, the Queen would stride about her chamber dictating letters to Fulcold, who would scribble notes on parchment, which would be taken away to be turned into a fair copy by his clerks. However, as a novice, I was not permitted to do this work, not because Fulcold did not trust me, but because the parchment or vellum – the finely stretched skin of a calf or young sheep that we wrote on – was very valuable and I might make mistakes or ink blots and ruin a fine piece of writing material.

This was frustrating: Thomas would have loved to have knowledge of everything that the Queen wrote, but I dared not push the clerks too far and, when I did casually question them about the Queen's letters, they seemed to have a blind spot as to their content, almost as if they were merely copying the words without truly taking in their meaning. So here I was, able to physically see the letters she was sending out, but unable to read their messages. I dreaded my next meeting with the one-eyed man.

Then two events occurred that were to change my mood – and the course of my life. My duties with Fulcold were light and on sunny afternoons I was still occasionally performing with Bernard in the castle gardens for the ladies. One day, after we had played together and been lavishly praised, Bernard suggested that I should make my debut as a solo *trouvère* in front of the court. The ladies thought it was a wonderful idea and the Queen suggested that I perform at a feast that was taking place in a week or so, at the beginning of July, to honour some important visitors to the castle. I would be performing in front of Sir Ralph FitzStephen, the constable, for the first time and so I was determined to make a good impression. The second event occurred when one of the clerks fell ill and Fulcold asked me to help with the making of palimpsests. As I have said, parchment was very expensive, even for a Queen, and so many of the letters that were sent to Eleanor were scrubbed clean and reused. Fulcold gave me this task and this is how I finally learnt a secret worthy of Thomas.

It was a painstaking process: the used parchment was clamped to a wooden board, where it would first be gently washed with fresh cows' milk and then scrubbed with oat bran, which would remove most of the dried ink from its previous use. However, if the writer had pressed hard on the animal skin, some of the ink would be more deeply ingrained in the parchment and this could only be removed by scraping with a pumice stone, a grey crumbly rock that was so light it would float on water. This was a delicate task; the parchment was very thin and scraping too hard with the pumice could tear holes in the material. If you scraped the parchment too gently, of course, the resulting palimpsest would still be covered with the original writing.

'You will be careful, my dear boy, won't you?' said a worried Fulcold as he assigned me a stack of parchments, some of which had already been partially cleaned.

I took special care with the parchments he gave me that day and the chamberlain was pleased with my work. Of course, I also read each document thoroughly before I cleaned it. I did so well that this became my regular employment in Fulcold's establishment and I was pleased with

myself: if I could not yet read the Queen's outgoing correspondence, I could at least read what people were saying
to her. Some letters were very intimate. Eleanor, it seemed,
had an insatiable curiosity about a noblewoman named
Alice, the daughter of the King of France, who it was
rumoured had been King Henry's mistress. She received
several letters that I saw in the same small cramped hand
describing, in extraordinary detail, the life of this unfortunate princess, who was now betrothed to Richard: what
she ate, what she wore each day, even the number of times
she visited the privy.

Mostly the letters contained dull fare, information that
would not be of the slightest interest to Robin, I judged.
For example, one letter revealed that the Count de
Something had a young and beautiful daughter and the
writer wondered whether Eleanor would help to arrange
a suitable marriage. The Abbey of Quelquepart invited
Eleanor to become a patron, their church needed a new
roof and perhaps the Queen would like to contribute ...

Then, at the beginning of July, I came across a letter
that drove all this trivia from my mind. Irritatingly, it was
a parchment that had already been partially cleaned but
I could still make out some parts of the missive. It was a
letter dated the eleventh day of February of this year, and
it was from Sir Ralph Murdac.

He was coming to Winchester; in fact, he was the special
guest for whom I would be performing the next day. My
heart gave a jump but almost immediately I steadied myself.
He could not possibly know me: we had met only once
face to face, more than a year ago in Nottingham, when
I was a bruised, snotty thief apprehended for stealing a
pie. He may have seen me briefly again, or at least my
back, when I was fleeing through the snow from his

251

horsemen, but surely he would not remember me, surely he could not connect that ragamuffin, that peasant 'filth', with the polished *trouvère* playing (I dared to hope) exquisitely at a royal court. It was impossible, I concluded, and then I even began to relish the thought of performing before Murdac, inspired to greatness by my hatred for him.

But other parts of Murdac's parchment were much more disturbing. After an illegible patch, the letter continued '. . . it would be a most suitable match, I believe; the Countess of Locksley has much property but she needs a strong man to manage both her and her lands. I am that man and I mean to press my suit with her during my sojourn at the castle with the greatest vigour; who knows what magic a sweet word and a lavish gift may work on a young girl? I trust I may have your support in this venture, though I note that you mentioned in your last letter that she has formed some sort of attachment to Robert Odo of Edwinstowe. I must warn you, and I shall certainly inform the Countess, that this Robert Odo is a scoundrel, a scofflaw and that the moment the loyal forces of the King lay hands on him he will be hanged as a common felon. He has made a great nuisance of himself in Nottinghamshire, indeed all over the north of England, but his run of luck is nearly at an end. I know his every move before he makes it and I shall soon have him in my grasp and, I swear by Almighty God that I will punish him for his misdeeds to the full and fatal extent of the law.'

I read the letter through twice and then, thinking furiously, I washed it and began to scrub the parchment with pumice. That diminutive French popinjay, that lavender-scented swine, wanted to possess my beautiful Marie-Anne. The thought of his sweaty little paws on her body in the marriage bed, on her white neck, her breasts. Never. I'd see him dead first. I'd walk right up to the bastard at the feast and smash the vielle over his head. I'd plunge my poniard into his black heart. To Hell with the consequences. I was scrubbing so hard that I tore the parchment, and Fulcold came clucking over. Seeing the tear, he relieved me of my duties and sent me to lie down in my chamber and recover my temper.

I warned Marie-Anne that evening but, to my surprise, she seemed unconcerned. 'There are many men who would marry me for my lands,' she said. 'Some would even try to force me to marry them. But I am safe here under the protection of the Queen. Don't fret, Alan, I am safe while I am at Winchester.' I was to remember her words well a few days later.

I spent most of the next day getting ready for my perform-ance at the feast. I would be using Bernard's vielle and I was worried that my technique was a little rusty, so Bernard helped me to prepare for the evening, running me through scales and suggesting small refinements to my bowing. I was to play four pieces only – unless my audience demanded more: firstly, a simple song that I had written in praise of the Queen's beauty, comparing her to an eagle, as she had been in a famous prophecy, and admiring her haughty looks and towering personality. I was certain that it would go down well. Next, a *canso* about a young squire who is in love with a lady he has never even seen; he is in love with her reported beauty and the stories he has been told about her goodness. Then I would perform a *sirvantes*, a witty satirical ditty about corrupt churchmen and their dull-witted servants, which I had written while in Sherwood and which had them rolling on the floor when I performed it at Robin's Caves. Then finally, Bernard and

I would play a *tenson*, a two-part musical debate in which I would suggest with my verses that a man could love only one woman, while Bernard would argue, in each alternate verse, that it was possible for a man to love two women or even more if they were all of comparable beauty and virtue. At the end of the *tenson*, we would ask Queen Eleanor to judge which of us had proved our point more convincingly and which of us should be declared winner of the musical debate.

We practised for most of the morning, then I bathed, changed into my best clothes and we waited in an ante-room off the great hall where the guests were dining noisily. Bernard was sober and fidgety, he kept plucking at the ribbons entwined into his green silk tunic. I was nervous but I kept thinking of Sir Ralph Murdac and trying to use my hatred of him to banish my nerves. Then Fulcold was at my shoulder; it was time to go in.

We made our way into the great hall of Winchester Castle to a blast of trumpets. Bernard walked over to the wall at the side of the great hall – it was to be my perform-ance, after all, he was only going to accompany me in the *tenson*. Then, with an unnaturally loud voice, completely different to his usual gentle tones, Fulcold announced: 'My lords, ladies and gentlemen, for your pleasure, I give you the renowned and talented *trouvère* Alan Dale.' I bowed low, lifted the vielle to my arm and ran my eyes over my audience.

The guests were seated at a long table in the shape of a T in the centre of the great hall of Winchester Castle. At the high table, the cross piece of the T, sat Queen Eleanor, splendid in a jewelled gown of gold cloth, Sir Ralph FitzStephen, stern in black, Marie-Anne, the bloody red ruby glinting at her neck and Sir Ralph Murdac:

handsome, glossy but seated on a fat cushion to disguise his lack of height. All the courtiers sat on either side of the long table that formed the down stroke of the T. I stood at the far end of the low table, concentrating my gaze on the most important guests at the top table. I struck the first chord of the vielle and began to play. I sang the first verse and then my voice began to tremble, for half way down the lower table, as I warbled on about the royal eagle and her joyous third nesting, was a grease-slicked face bulging with roast mutton that I'd hoped I would never see again. It was Guy. He looked almost as surprised as I was.

Somehow I managed to finish the song, though it can't have been delivered with much finesse. There was a polite, muted scatter of applause and then, as in a dream where everything is moving with exaggerated slowness, Guy stood up, splendid in a clean surcoat of green and yellow, extended an accusing finger and shouted, as if from very far away: 'That man is an impostor! Arrest him!' Everything speeded up again and I heard him yelling, loudly now: 'He is an outlaw, a thief, a henchman of Robin Hood.' And just as Guy had done on that day when he had been accused of stealing the ruby, I panicked. I dropped the vielle and bow and rushed for the door.

Chapter Fifteen

Panic is a great enemy. As I discovered that day at Winchester. I have been told that the word comes from an ancient god of the Greeks called Pan, a terrifying flute-playing demon with the hind legs and horns of a goat, and the body of a naked man. But, to this day, whenever I ponder the unreasoning terror inspired by that long-dead Greek spirit, I cannot help but think of Robin, dressed as Cernunnos for that awful sacrifice, with his blood-daubed naked chest and antlers.

An all-encompassing, choking fear grew in my heart this spring, not quite a panic but very close to it, as the fever rose in young Alan, my grandson. He is the last of my line, the last of me in this world. As the days passed, he grew thinner, more like a skeleton, unable to keep down food or drink, silent and still, edging closer and closer to death. And I admit I was teetering on the lip of madness as I galloped through the woods on my mare, my old bones rattling, searching out a wooden cottage deep in Sherwood that I had not visited for almost half a century.

Brigid knew me immediately, despite the span of years, my time-worn face and ashen hair, and welcomed me, and asked to look at my right arm. But I thrust a live new-born lamb into her bosom and brushing aside the civilities, begged her on my knees to make a charm to help my boy. She placed a hand on my head, and immediately I felt calmer, soothed by her fingers running through my sparse locks. 'Of course I will help you, Alan,' she said. 'And the Mother will not suffer your boy to die.' She sounded so confident, so sure in her powers, that I felt a great weight fall from my shoulders. I let out a deep breath and my bunched muscles loosened a little as she busied herself at an old oak table, slitting the lamb's throat and draining its blood into a bowl, grinding dried roots, mixing dusty powders and muttering charms to herself. I looked around the cottage. It had hardly changed in forty-odd years: the same bunches of dried herbs hung from the ceiling, the cobwebs in the dark corners were even thicker, even the skeleton was still hanging on the far wall. And yet, for all its witchery, the place felt homely. A place of goodness and healing. I began to relax as Brigid worked. The power of that ancient Greek demon began to wane.

At Winchester Castle, though, I was held firmly in the dizzying grip of that Greek deity. I dropped the vielle, something for which Bernard was very angry about long afterwards, and rushed for the door of the hall. I had not got five yards before half a dozen men-at-arms had grabbed me. Running was proof of my guilt in their eyes, you see. If I had held fast, said nothing and thought, I might have been able to talk my way out of it. But my instinct to run, ingrained after years of thievery in Nottingham, was too strong.

The men-at arms dragged me back to the spot where I had been playing, and despite my cries of innocence, appeals to the Queen and desperate struggles, they trussed me with a rope, and gagged me. The room had dissolved into uproar. The Queen was on her feet demanding loudly to know the name of the man who had interrupted her entertainment. Guy was shouting that he had known me at Thangbrand's and that I had been one of the worst of that gang of cut-throats. The other guests were demanding to know who I was, who Guy was, and what the fuss was all about. Marie-Anne sat still, staring at me, the colour gone from her face, the ruby a bold red against her blood-less neck. It was Sir Ralph Murdac who restored order to the hall by shouting 'Silence!' again and again and again, until there was quiet.

'Who are you, sir?' said the Queen to Guy, her voice unnaturally loud in the sudden hush.

'I am Guy of Gisborne, your highness, a humble soldier in the service of Sir Ralph Murdac.'

Oh yes, I thought, despite your proclaimed 'humility' you've picked up a territorial title in your travels, you turd. I'd heard of the manor of Gisborne, a moderately rich farm not far from Nottingham, whose lord had died a few years ago. Presumably Sir Ralph had given it to Guy for ser-vices rendered. What those might be, I could only guess, but I was sure it must be connected to giving up infor-mation about Robin.

'You vouch for this man, then?' said the Queen, turning to Sir Ralph. The little man smiled and ducked his black head. 'He has been most useful to me,' he said in his lisping voice. 'And before he entered my service he was indeed a member of Robert Odo's band of felons.'

'Then continue,' the Queen said to Guy, who, puffed

with self-importance, then related to the assembly how he had grown up at his father's farm in Sherwood, and how his father had been tricked into harbouring outlaws from Robin's band. Alan Dale was one of them, he told the audience, a particularly vicious thief from Nottingham, much given to murder and blasphemy. 'Bernard of Sezanne is also an outlaw,' he continued, 'and . . . and . . . the Countess of Locksley is affianced to Robin Hood.'

'Impossible,' interjected Sir Ralph Murdac coldly, frowning at Guy. 'You are mistaken. The Lady Marie-Anne is a woman of the highest nobility, and a close personal friend of mine – she could not possibly consort with bandits. You are mistaken.'

'And Bernard of Sezanne is a noble gentleman of Champagne,' chimed in the Queen, 'and he is my servant, my personal *trouvère*. You are clearly mistaken about him, too.'

'But . . . but . . .' stuttered Guy. He was interrupted by our host, Ralph FitzStephen. He had held his silence until this moment but now he wanted to stamp his authority on the extraordinary proceedings in his hall. 'The accusations against the Countess of Locksley and . . . and Bernard of Sezanne are, of course, ridiculous and will be ignored. But the allegations against this Dale person are serious,' he said, 'and must be investigated. Take him down to the dungeon and hold him securely until the truth can be ascertained.' And with that I was dragged from the room and marched through the castle, down, down to the lowest level where I was bundled through a cell door to sprawl on a pile of foul-smelling straw. The door closed behind me with a clang.

*   *   *

259

I lay in the blackness of that stinking cell, with its damp stone walls and ice-cold floor, and listened to the scurry of rats. My gag had come loose, thank God, but my arms were still tightly tied behind my back. And they were a cause of considerable discomfort in the following few hours. Although they were nothing compared with what came later. To take my mind off my bound wrists, I considered my situation: to the good, I had powerful friends in Winchester. Queen Eleanor had known about Marie-Anne's visit to Robin, and presumably she had condoned it; and she also knew that we – Bernard and I – had been members of Robin's band, and that had not troubled her when she accepted Bernard into her service. Marie-Anne, of course, was quite safe from the accusations of a jumped-up soldier and I knew she would try to come to my aid. To the bad, Eleanor was a prisoner herself, though a privileged one, and she might be powerless to help. Sir Ralph FitzStephen had authority over the castle and he would definitely not turn a blind eye to charges of outlaws running loose around his halls. But, worst of all, Murdac would no doubt want to put me to the test to get information about Robin. That meant pain, a great deal of pain.

To control my bounding fears, I played the scene in the great hall over and over in my mind: Guy's spiteful face and out-thrust finger as he denounced me; Marie-Anne's look of fear and shock; the Queen's anger; Murdac's ostentatiously gallant protection of Marie-Anne; Guy's confusion at his master's rejection of his accusations.

We had all assumed at Robin's Caves that it was Guy who had been responsible for leading Murdac's men to Thangbrand's; that Guy had been the traitor, who, it would seem, had been rewarded with the manor of Gisborne. But, as I lay there on the damp straw, in the permanent midnight of that cell, thinking about his treachery, and imagining the bloody vengeance I would take, I realised something was wrong. Something was burrowing at the back of my mind; something about the letter that Murdac had written to the Queen. I remembered it clearly: . . . *his run of luck is nearly at an end. I know his every move before he makes it, and I shall soon have him in my grasp* . . .

'I know his every move before he makes it'; that implied that Murdac had someone in the camp who was a traitor, who was informing him of Robin's plans. Had that been Guy? It would appear so. But why, what was Guy's motive? Until I had spatchcocked him with the ruby, he was a fairly contented, if obnoxious, young man. And then, like the click of a latch opening a door, I knew Guy could not be the traitor. The letter was dated the eleventh of February, which was two months *after* Guy had left Thangbrand's. And it followed that, if Guy was not the traitor in the camp, someone else was.

That thought gave me a chill of horror; somebody, one of my dear friends, was betraying our every move to Murdac. It could be anyone: Much, the miller's son, Owain the Bowman, Will Scarlet, Hugh, Little John, even dear old Brother Tuck. Anyone.

But I was pleased with my conclusion; I would have something crucial to confide to Thomas when I saw him again. If I saw him again. Suddenly my spirits plunged once more. Would they hang me as an outlaw before I got a chance to talk to the ugly one-eyed brute? Where were my friends? I had been lying in this black pit for hours and nobody had come to visit me. My bladder was full and aching. I was determined not to wet myself but the prospect of sweet release, even if it meant warm wet hose, was almost too tempting. I bit my lip and held fast.

I dozed for a while and the next thing I knew the cell door was opening, blinding me with the yellow light of torches, and there was Murdac and his God-forgotten lackey, Guy. They stood silhouetted in the doorway for an instant, Guy towering over Sir Ralph, and then they entered that stinking room, followed by two men-at-arms. I sneezed violently; even above the dungeon stench I recognised Murdac's revolting lavender scent. He came close to me and stared down at my curled form on the filthy floor. I sneezed again. Under Guy's supervision, the men-at-arms lit torches and set them in beckets in the wall. Ominously, one of the men-at-arms set up a brazier, filled it with cordwood and oil-soaked wool and set it alight with a flint and steel. I knew it was not to keep me warm during the long, cold night. Another man-at-arms attached my bound arms, with a rope, to a hook in the ceiling and adjusted the length so that I was partially suspended from my wrists, which were still bound behind me. The strain on my arms was enormous, but by leaning far forward and standing on my tiptoes, I could make it just bearable. Then the soldier cut my new clothes from my body with his dagger, leaving me as naked as the day I was born. I was filled with shame at my nudity and kept my eyes on the straw below me. But worse than the shame was the fear. Rising like a river in spate was sheer skin-tightening terror. Somewhere in the corner, in the foul shadows of the dark cell, the Greek demon Pan was taking shape. And he was silently laughing. As I tried to control my dread, I was aware that Murdac was watching me, studying me with his extraordinary pale blue eyes.

The brazier was burning merrily by now, and Guy set three stout iron pokers in the blaze. He caught my eye and grinned unpleasantly. 'Are you scared, Alan? I think you are. You always were a coward!' he jeered. Then he pulled on a pair of stout leather gloves. I tore my gaze away from the heating irons and looked down again at the straw-strewn floor. I knew what was coming, I knew it would be bad beyond my imagining and I found that I was shivering with fear. I bit my tongue and determined that I would hold out against the pain, transport myself to a better place with my mind, refuse to tell Murdac anything. Nothing, particularly nothing about my suspicions about there being a traitor in the camp. That was something I had to bury deep in my brain; so deep that even I did not remember it. Then Ralph Murdac spoke, his sibilant French whine filling the damp stone cell, somehow defiling even that repugnant place.

'I remember you. Yes, yes, I do.' He sounded pleased, excited to have placed me in his memory. 'You are the insolent thief from the market in Nottingham. You sneezed on me, you foul creature. And you escaped, did you not? I think I recall someone telling me. You ran off into the forest to join Robert Odo and those scum. Well, well, and now I have you again. How gratifying, how very gratifying.' He laughed, a thin, dry chuckle and Guy immediately joined in the mirth, with a false sounding cackle, too loud. Murdac gave him a sharp look and snapped, 'Hold your noise,' and Guy cut short his guffaw in mid-breath.

My shoulder joints were on fire, but I gritted my teeth and said nothing. 'So you have been with the outlaw Robert Odo's men this past year?' said Murdac, as if he were making conversation. I said nothing. Murdac nodded to Guy who walked over to me and punched me as hard as he could, swinging his fist up into my unresisting naked stomach. The blow winded me, but worse, it was more than my bladder could take and, involuntarily, I released a hot stream of urine down the inside of my leg. The liquid spattered and dribbled into a pool at my feet. Guy laughed and punched me again, a hard driving blow with his shoulder behind it, but then stepped back with a curse of disgust as he realised he had trodden in a pool of my piss. 'You *will* answer my questions, filth,' continued Murdac in the same dispassionate voice, as if he was merely stating a fact. I kept my silence, but my mind was whirling. The bastard was right. In time, I would talk, I knew that, when the hot irons made the pain unbearable, I would talk. But I had to work out how to order my knowledge, so that I gave out the least important information first. They might grow tired of interrogating me – if I could hold out long enough, perhaps the Constable or the Queen would intervene. Anything might happen, I just had to hold tight and stay silent.

Guy walked away from my bent naked body towards the brazier, and my eyes followed him. By now, the tips of the irons were glowing a deep orange-red. He shoved one deeper into the fire and pulled out another, tracing small circles in the air with its gaudy point.

Murdac slowly repeated: 'Did you join Robert Odo's band of murderers?'

Again I held my tongue and Guy moved forward with the glowing iron in his right hand. 'This will make you sing, little *trouvère*,' he sneered, and he laid the burning metal against the naked skin of my ribs on my left side. A white whip of pain shot through my whole being. I jerked my body away from Guy and screamed – a long howl of agony and fear that echoed round the stone room long after I had controlled myself and snapped my mouth shut.

'Did you join Robert Odo's band?' asked Murdac again. 'It's a very simple question.' And I shook my head, teeth clamped hard on my lips to stop myself from speaking. Guy touched me again on the ribs with the iron with a fresh burst of indescribable pain and once again I screamed until the sinews in my jaws were cracking.

Guy returned the first iron poker to the flames and pulled a second from the crackling blaze. The tip glowed the colour of ripe cherries. He came and stood close to me; I could feel the heat from the metal on my chest. He whispered into my ear: 'Keep silent, Alan. We can do this all night, if you do. I do hope you will keep silent, for my sake.' And he giggled. Then Murdac spoke again, his siblant voice cutting through the pain in my ribs. 'Did you join Robert Odo's band?' I said nothing but tensed my body and cringed away from Guy, who was still beside me with a yard of red-hot iron in his gloved fist. He paused for a few heartbeats and I held my breath and then, deliberately, he rubbed the iron lightly up and down against my right side, smearing the skin like a man spreading butter on a piece of bread. I howled like a madman while the skin blistered and burnt, and a gout of steam and a foul smell of cooking meat attacked my nostrils. He pressed the burning metal harder against my raw body and I bellowed: 'Fuck you! Fuck you! Fuck you both . . .'

Guy stepped back, and replaced the iron in the fire. He looked enquiringly at Murdac, who nodded. Guy grabbed a handful of my hair and pulled my face up and brought his close in so that our noses were inches apart. 'No, no, no, Alan,' he said, leering at me. 'It is not us, it is you

265

who is going to be fucked.' And he made a gesture of command to the men-at-arms.

Two soldiers grabbed me and wrenched apart my legs, holding them steady in a steel grip. Guy took another bright-hot poker from the brazier and moved behind me. Murdac said: 'For the last time, Alan, did you join Robert Odo's band? Answer my questions and this pain will stop, I swear it. It is entirely up to you. Just answer my question; who will it hurt if you talk a little? I already know the answers. Just answer my questions and the pain will stop.' I bit my lip and shook my head. Then my buttocks were roughly pulled apart by the soldiers, and I could feel the immense heat of the iron against my shrinking ball bag, and the strip of sensitive skin between it and my arse, the glowing iron not touching, thank God, but radiating with a huge malevolent intensity at my most intimate areas. Then the molten tip of the poker just grazed the soft skin on inside of my right buttock cheek and, though the pain was less than the burns to my ribs, I screamed long and loud enough to wake the dead: 'Yes, yes, by God, I joined his band. Yes, I joined it.' I was babbling, shrieking with terror and pain, all self-control suddenly lost. 'Stop, please, stop. Don't do it. Don't burn me there, I beg you.'

Murdac smiled, Guy actually laughed, and I felt a great, joyous relief as the heat of the poker faded away from my private regions. My buttocks were released from that terrible grip and I clenched them tight shut, bunching the muscles as tight as a fist, as if that could protect me. Suddenly, I was engulfed in a black wave of shame, a cold, sinking sadness at my own want of courage. I wanted to die, for the earth to swallow me up. I had been stripped so easily of my last shreds of dignity by that obscene threat. I *was* a coward; I was the traitor in Robin's camp, if anyone was. Then, as quickly as it was born, I pushed that thought away. That was one secret I would never give up, even if I suffered this night all the torments of damnation.

Murdac was asking another question: 'Where is Robert Odo now?' I said nothing. I gritted my teeth. The little man sighed; he looked genuinely disappointed. Then he nodded at Guy who plucked a fresh poker from the brazier and came towards me. As the soldiers once again laid hold of my backside and pulled the cheeks apart, I found myself babbling: 'He's at the Caves, at the Caves, dear God please . . .' and then I stopped in sheer surprise as the cell door opened with a thunderous crash, and through my tears of pain and humiliation, I made out a commanding figure in the doorway. Stepping forward into the light came Robert of Thurnham, clad in grey mail, his long sword at his hip.

'Gentlemen,' he said loudly. 'Please excuse my intrusion. But the screams of this fellow are disturbing the Queen's rest. She commands that the interrogation cease forthwith, to be recommenced tomorrow at a more suitable hour.' He walked forward, drawing his sword, and cut through the rope that held my arms up behind me. I collapsed in a shaking heap in the dirty straw on the floor of the cell, my poor burnt ribs and the burn on my arse cheek chanting a melody of anguish. But, for the moment, it was over. I stole a glance at Sir Ralph and saw in his pale eyes a monstrous anger that he was trying to conceal. Guy seemed merely irritated by the turn of events. Murdac looked at me, curled baby-like on the floor, and said: 'Till tomorrow, then,' and suddenly Sir Robert was ushering him and Guy and the men-at-arms out of the cell. 'Don't get too comfortable, Alan, we'll be back soon,' sang out Guy as he was leaving the cell. The knight paused at the doorway to give me a final glance and, in the flickering light of the brazier, as I shivered on the filthy floor, drowning in self-hatred, he silently mouthed a single word at me: 'Courage!'

I must have passed out, or maybe my mind just retreated into blackness from the horror of that night, for, when I next came to my senses, Marie-Anne was at my side. At first I thought I was dreaming. There were tears on her cheek and, as she cut through the ropes at my wrists with a small knife, she was murmuring: 'Oh Alan, Alan, what have they done to you?' She had brought an old monk's robe to cover my nakedness and had dressed me and begun to chafe my swollen wrists before I really came to my senses. I had lost all feeling in my hands, and the shooting pains as she massaged them back to life was almost as bad as the irons. Almost.

When she saw that I had recovered a measure of feeling in my limbs she said: 'Come, Alan, we must go quickly. Before the guards return. I have bribed them to let me have a few minutes with the prisoner. I think they believe I have a *tendresse* for you.' And Marie-Anne actually blushed. 'Come, this way,' she said and taking my arm we stumbled together out of that stinking cell and into the dim light of the passage outside.

She led me through a part of the castle that I hadn't known existed. Down corridors, and up stairs, through twisting cob-webbed ways, until we paused finally in the shelter of a little annex at the head of a narrow passage that sloped downwards. I peered round the corner and saw that at the end of the passage there was a small wooden door in the castle wall. 'Thomas is waiting outside, beyond that door,' whispered Marie-Anne. That was the good news, but I could see that, on this side of it, there was a very large problem. Two problems to be precise.

Seated on two wooden stools, playing dice by the light of a guttering candle, were two strapping men-at-arms with swords at their waists. One of them I recognised as the man who had brought the brazier into my torture cell, and held my arse cheeks apart while my dignity was ripped away. The other I did not know, but there was a good chance after the fuss in the hall the day before, that he would know me. Marie-Anne whispered: 'Maybe, if I could distract them . . .' But I shook my head. I could feel a tide of purple rage rising from my bowels up into my chest. I had been tied up, stripped, burnt and humiliated; tortured and forced to speak against my will. But now my hands were free. My head felt dizzy with what I knew I was going to do, but a great wild joy was growing inside me. 'Thank you, Marie-Anne,' I whispered, 'I thank you with all my heart for what you have done, but I must do this myself.' And pulling the deep hood on the monk's robe forward to cover my face, I stepped out into the passage way and walked confidently towards the soldiers, hands held together in front of me in the attitude of prayer.

My steps were light, but my heart felt huge in my chest and I was aware of every inch of my body, from my poor burnt ribs, and the blistering inside my bum cheeks, to the sweat on the skin of my fingertips. I felt as if I were buzzing like a swarm of bees with dark, joyous fury.

As I approached the two men-at arms, they rose from their seats; one of the men scooping the dice and hastily putting them away in his pouch so that a man of God, as they assumed me to be, would not know that they had been gambling.

'Can we help you, Brother?' asked the man on the left,

the taller of the two, the man who had been in the torture cell. I walked right up to him and tilted my head back as if to peer shortsightedly up at his face, and then as fast as a snake I went up on to my toes, whipped my head forward and smashed it into the bridge of his nose in a short hard arc. It was a colossal blow, with all the anger at my recent humiliation ringing through it and, coming from what appeared to be a monk, it was totally unexpected. I could feel the crunch of bone and gristle as my forehead powered into his face and and he dropped like a stone at my feet. Then I turned, the blood roaring in my veins, and launched myself at the second man, grabbing him by the shoulders and trying for a second massive headbutt, as effective as the first. His mouth was wide in total surprise, but he moved his head sideways just before my strike and all I achieved was a glancing blow as my forehead raked across his cheekbone. Then we were both on the stone floor, grappling like madmen. My rage found an outlet and I knew I was screaming incoherently as I pounded again and again at his head with both my fists in turn. But he was stronger than me and, like myself, he was no stranger to street fighting. As we rolled on the hard floor he caught my forearms, crushing them in his meaty hands, ending the rain of blows that had left his face bloody and bruised. So I brought my knee up into the fork of his legs, my kneecap driving hard into the pelvic bone and, catching him by surprise, I mashed his balls between that bony mortar and pestle. He screamed in agony, doubled up and tried to protect his ruptured privates with his hands, which meant releasing my arms. So I grabbed a hank of his long, greasy hair and smashed his head down as hard as I could against the stone floor. He was only mildly stunned, but it was enough and I took his head with both hands by the

270

ears and smashed it twice more against the flagstones. His eyes rolled back in their sockets and suddenly I was on my hands and knees, panting, my burnt ribs bleeding, and looking down at two battered, unconscious men. Neither had had time to even draw their swords. I staggered to my feet, waved goodbye to Marie-Anne who was goggling at me with her pretty mouth wide open, unbolted and pulled open the door and stepped out into the cool night air – and tumbled straight into the arms of Thomas.

He glanced at the unmoving bodies of the men-at arms with a look of disbelief, closed the wooden door tightly behind me and said: 'Can you walk?' And, half supporting me, he led me down the steep path from the castle and into the dark narrow streets of Winchester itself.

For two days I hid in a back room of the Saracen's Head, nursing my wounds with a concoction of goose-fat and herbs, waiting for the one-eyed man's return. Thomas had collected my poniard and sword from the castle and returned them to me before disappearing off to gather information from his contacts. I wore my weapons night and day – even when I slept. Something had changed in me since that terrible night of fire and pain. I was harder; something of the boy had been burnt out of me. But I also knew myself better. I knew that I would have told them anything if Robert of Thurnham had not intervened when he did. So I vowed I would not be taken alive again to undergo more of that treatment. I would die first. On the morning of the third day, Thomas came with news.

We sat at the rough table in the common room of the tavern, eating bread and cheese. He was silent for a few moments and then he sighed and said, 'First things first: the King is dead. God rest his soul. He died ten days ago

271

at Chinon and his body is being taken to lie at rest in the abbey at Fontevraud. Duke Richard will take the throne now, when he decides to return to England. But that could be months away.'

I was shocked. I had known the King was ill but for my whole life Henry, God's anointed ruler, had been a fixture of my world. I could hardly comprehend that he should be no more.

'The castle is like a kicked ants' nest,' said Thomas, 'with messengers coming back and forth. Eleanor has been formally released by FitzStephen, though she is staying at Winchester for a few more days.' He paused, sighed and said: 'But I have worse news than the King's death.' He breathed out heavily again. 'The lady Marie-Anne has been taken. Sir Ralph Murdac and his men snatched her while she was out hawking with her ladies yesterday morning. We think that little black-haired shit-weasel is, as we speak, hurrying to Nottingham with our master's lady. And when he gets there he will marry her.'

'But she would never consent,' I said. Thomas laughed, a cackle entirely without mirth. 'Consent? She'll have no choice. Murdac has enough priests in his pocket to marry them whether she consents or no. He wants the Locksley lands and, with the King dead, well, there is no power to stop him. If they are married by the time Richard is crowned, he will not separate them. Murdac will be a powerful man and Richard may wish for his support. If she continues to refuse the marriage, he will force her, maybe even have his men rape her. Her honour would then be destroyed and no one would have her. Even Robin might feel differently if he knew she had been Sir Ralph's and half a dozen of his randy soldiers' bed-partners, whether she was willing or not.'

'I'll murder the bastard.' I felt the scabs on my burnt torso split. 'I'll cut his fucking head off.' I was panting heavily, somehow standing over Thomas and my sword was in my hand. I said: 'I must go to Robin now, and we must ride to Nottingham immediately!'

Thomas was infuriatingly calm: 'Yes, we must go to Robin. But we need to think a little first. Murdac would rather have a willing bride than one whom he has violated. So we probably have a little time. Sit down before you do yourself an injury. We need to think about your traitor. My friends are bringing horses and provisions for the journey, but until they arrive, calm yourself and tell me who the traitor might be. Think! Who is he, Alan? Start from the beginning.'

I forced myself to sit down and breathe calmly for a few moments; I could feel hot streams of fresh blood running down my sides. Then I began to think.

'After the massacre at Thangbrand's, we thought the traitor must be Guy. But Murdac's letter to the Queen boasting of an informant was dated February, and so it cannot be him. Guy left Thangbrand's in December.

'Next: I think the massacre was designed to kill or capture Robin, who was supposed to be there at Christmas time but who was, in the event, delayed, and therefore the informant must have been someone who believed that Robin would be there at Christmas. Who knew so much about Robin's movements?'

'Someone close to him,' said Thomas.

'I think it must be one of four people,' I said, 'his lieutenants, his inner circle: Little John, Hugh, Will Scarlet or . . . Tuck. So, who would want to see Robin destroyed? Little John . . . well, it was Robin's fault that he was made an outlaw. He had a comfortable billet at Edwinstowe as

273

master-at-arms, Robin ruined all that when he murdered the priest. Robin forced him to become an outlaw.'

'I just can't see it,' cut in Thomas. 'John would die for Robin. He loves him like a brother.'

'Which brings us to Hugh. I don't believe he would betray his own brother. Robin saved him from a life of ignominy as a penniless hearth knight. Now he has power, money and he worships Robin, too. Just watch them together. So I don't think it could be him, either.'

'Will Scarlet, then?' said Thomas. I thought for a moment.

'He was a great friend of Guy's as well as his cousin.' I said. 'And Guy could have made contact with him after he joined up with Murdac. He could have been passing on messages, for money or the hope of a pardon. But I can't believe it. Will's just not . . . well, not bright enough to be an agent of the enemy, to burrow into Robin's confidences, to trap him.'

'So that leaves Tuck,' said Thomas, with a leaden formality. And I grimaced.

'I don't want it to be Tuck,' I said. 'I love the man; he's been so good to me. But, in all honesty, I can easily think of a reason why he might wish Robin ill.'

I didn't know quite how to put this. So I said to Thomas: 'Are you a good Christian?'

The ugly man smiled. 'A Christian, yes, but not a very good one. Ah, now I see what you are driving at. Robin and his midnight woodland frolics: "Arise Cernunnos!" and all that pagan bollocks. I know Robin experiments with the old religion. Witchcraft, some call it. I heard he even sacrificed some poor sod, nearly cut his head off. But I don't think he really believes in any of that nonsense. He just does it to add to his mystique with the country

274

folk. To give himself an aura of supernatural power. Do you think that would give Tuck cause to betray him?'

'I heard them arguing about it. It nearly came to bloodshed,' I said. We both fell silent for a while and then our musings were interrupted by a loud banging at the door. I stood up with a start and half drew my sword. 'Steady, Joshua – that will just be Simon with the horses,' said Thomas.

Simon had brought four horses for me and Thomas, all fully provisioned with grain for the animals and food and drink for us. The plan was for us to ride without stopping for Robin's Caves but, in the event, the weather was so bad, constant rain and gales, and we made such poor progress through the mud, that we were forced to stop about halfway at an abbey near Lichfield, through sheer exhaustion. That day's journey had been a nightmare for me. My scabbed sides and the burn on my arse gave me a great deal of trouble as I bounced about on the back of a horse at Thomas's relentless mile-eating pace. In the end, despite my desire to get to Robin as soon as possible, I felt utter relief when we trotted through the gates of the abbey, sore, hungry and sopping wet. The monks asked no questions of us. We were fed a bowl of hot bean stew, our horses were rubbed down and after the brief, sparcely attended service of Compline in the gloom of the abbey church, I sank into an exhausted sleep in a narrow cot in the travellers' dormitory. The next morning, still damp but much refreshed, though my burnt sides were still hurting like sin, we set out on fresh horses, determined that we would be with Robin by nightfall. And by late afternoon, our nags worn near to death, we were stopped by one of Robin's patrols ten miles south of the Caves, and brought to see the man himself.

Robin, looking almost as haggard as Thomas and I, was seated at a table with a very thin man in a dark robe – a Jew, I realised with a shock like a face full of ice-cold water. He was the man I had seen in The Trip To Jerusalem, the man who had identified David the armourer for Robin and me to rob. The Jews of Nottingham, few as they were, were much despised. We called them Christ-killers and accused them of secretly kidnapping babies and using them in foul rituals. For a second, I wondered if Robin was involved in some Satanic business with this man; I would believe anything of him after witnessing that unholy blood-rite at Easter. But then I realised that their meeting was of a much more mercantile nature. As we approached the table, Robin pushed two heavy money bags towards the lean Jew and made a note on a scroll. All was made clear. This was a part of Robin's business that I had not encountered before: usury. He lent money, ill-gotten gains from robberies, to the Jews of Nottingham and they lent it out to Christians at a steep rate of interest. Robin provided the initial funds, I had heard, but he also offered the Jews a measure of protection. If a man would not pay, Robin would send some of his hard men to visit, to make the point, forcibly, that a debt, even to a Jew, must be honoured.

Robin looked up and saw us for the first time. He smiled wanly. He looked as if he had not slept for days. 'Thomas, Alan,' he said. 'Greetings. You know Reuben, of course?' We both bowed stiffly to the Jew, who smiled back at us. He had a dark, lined, leathery, but immensely likeable face; black hair and a short, neatly trimmed beard. His twinkling brown eyes radiated goodness and, God knows why, but I immediately trusted him. 'Am I correct in thinking that I am addressing Alan Dale, the famous *trou-vère?*' Reuben said, rising to his feet and making a bow in return to ours. I blushed; I knew he was teasing me but it was done with such good humour that I did not mind. 'Not famous yet,' I said, 'but I am hoping, one day, to become at least competent.'

'Such modesty,' Reuben said with another smile, 'a rare and valuable quality these days in the young.' He bowed to Thomas, who grunted something unintelligible. 'Sadly, my friends, I must now leave you,' said Reuben, and he scooped the heavy money sacks from the table as if they were filled with air. I realised that he must be very strong for such a lean man. He bowed low to Robin, who stood and returned the bow, as if to an equal, and then the Jew walked out of the cave, packed the silver in his saddle-bags, mounted his horse in one lithe movement, and cantered away into the dripping night.

At Robin's invitation, we sat at the table. He looked at our mud-splattered, exhausted faces and said: 'You've come to tell me about Marie-Anne.' His voice seemed strained, his whole body drooped with misery. We nodded. 'I know about that,' he said. 'Reuben told me. We are riding for Nottingham at dawn. But . . . but there's some-thing else, isn't there?' I nodded again and, haltingly, I outlined my theory about the traitor in the camp. Robin listened in silence. As I finally came to a stop, he sighed, a long deep shuddering exhalation. 'I see,' he said. 'Well, thank you for bringing this to me, Alan. It's something I've suspected for some time, since Thangbrand's in fact. And I think I may know who our man is.' He sighed again. 'I must ask you two, on your honour, not to speak to anyone of this.' He stared at Thomas and then at me, his silver eyes boring into my head. 'Say nothing about this

277

to anybody,' he repeated. We both nodded. And he continued: 'But first we must recover Marie-Anne; so get some food, get some sleep and be ready to ride at dawn. It's good to have you back, Alan,' and he smiled at me, his silver eyes glowing in the candlelight. It was a brief glimpse of that golden, carefree smile of yore, shining like a beacon through his misery. At once I felt the old familiar glow of affection for him.

'It's good to be back,' I said and smiled back at him.

Then Robin looked a little more closely at me. 'You are hurt,' he said, the concern strong in his voice. I stared at him. How did he know? I thought I had hidden the discomfort of my torture wounds perfectly. 'I will get someone to fetch Brigid,' he said. 'And don't trouble yourself too much over this business about the traitor, Alan. All will be well.'

An hour or so later, Brigid took me to a small cave away from the main camp and, by the light of a single candle, she bade me strip so that she could examine my wounds. After anointing them with dark, musty smelling tinctures and binding the worst burn on my right side ribs with a cold moss poultice, she made me bend over while she examined the burn inside my buttock. I was unwilling but she told me not to be childish and, reluctantly, I obeyed. As I leant forward, hands on knees, and could feel her hot breath on the back of my legs, an image of her naked painted body at the pagan sacrifice sprang into my mind. Oh God, and, as if I had not had enough humiliation, I could feel an uncontrollable stirring in my private parts as her long fingers gently daubed something cool on the small burn between my cheeks.

'All finished,' Brigid said brusquely, and she stood up. I straightened and hurriedly fumbled for my drawers in an

278

attempt to hide my fully erect member. These days I would be proud, overjoyed even, to sport such a tumescent organ; but in those youthful years I seemed to have a swelling in my drawers at least half the time, and I thought it a cause for shame. Brigid just laughed and, looking directly at my wayward organ as I desperately tried to cover myself, she said: 'You should have stayed longer at the spring ceremony of the Goddess, rather than slipping away like a thief that night. Instead of wasting your sap mooning over Marie-Anne, you might have made some pretty young girl very happy.'

I was speechless with embarrassment. I'd thought that hardly anyone had known I was there at that pagan blood-festival, as I had my hood pulled forward, and had shunned the firelight. But, evidently, my participation was common knowledge. I felt humiliated; twice in a handful of days had I been as easily stripped of my tender dignity as a dead rabbit of its fur, and so, stung, I snapped: 'I'd had my fill of the murder of innocents and had no mind to watch more blood-drenched blasphemy.'

'Innocents murdered, you say.' Brigid was totally calm. 'Blasphemy, too.' She gazed at me but her kind brown eyes now seemed harder than oak. 'That man who was the sacrifice—'

'His name was Piers,' I interjected hotly.

'The sacrifice,' she said emphatically, refusing to acknowledge his humanity by naming him, 'would not have been allowed to live by your master. Robert of Sherwood would have had him killed for his disloyalty. Instead, he gave him to me. And now he is with the Earth Mother, cared for by Her as lovingly as She cares for all her children, living and dead.'

'Robin would never have taken part in that foul

witchcraft, that Devil worship, but for you.' I was almost shouting now. 'He would have given the man a clean death and a Christian burial.' Even as I said it, I knew I was only partially speaking the truth.

'The Lord of the Wood is not a follower of your nailed God, Alan. He is no Christian,' Brigid said. 'He has the spirit of Cernunnos inside him, whether he believes it or not.' I was shocked by her words, hearing them spoken out loud. But she spoke honestly: Robin was no Christian.

'He's no God-damned pagan either,' I yelled. Brigid was as cool as a January dawn, while I knew I was behaving like a furious, impotent child. I dropped my eyes from her brown gaze and took a deep breath.

She laid a hand on my bare arm, I looked up again and she smiled at me. I could feel my temper begin to wane. 'I think that none of us can know what another truly believes,' she said. 'And Robin is even more compli-cated than most in that way. I believe he is constantly looking for the Divine, constantly looking for God, in whatever shape or form he – or she . . .' she smiled at me again, and I smiled ruefully back, 'might take. And I hope that, one day, he may be successful in his quest and find true happiness.'

'Amen,' I said.

I slept badly, dreaming of Marie-Anne being violated by a long queue of laughing soldiers. The queue stretched all the way around the walls of Nottingham, like a snake. And then the queue indeed transformed into a real snake, a great red and black muscular reptile that tightened its coils around the castle and squeezed and squeezed until the stone fortress erupted like a penis bursting with lust, ejaculating a steam of men and women into the sky in a great hot jet . . .

Thomas awakened me an hour before dawn. I opened my eyes and stared into his hideous one-eyed face and I couldn't suppress a start of fear. The pain in my ribs was almost gone, only a dull ache reminded me of my humiliation. 'Better get ready,' said Thomas, 'we've a long ride ahead of us today.'

I stumbled around in the half-dark, chewing on a crust of old bread while I rooted out my aketon. I knew the thick padding of the jacket would be too warm later on in that July day, but I was prepared to suffer the discomfort of heat for the sake of extra protection. Over the aketon I strapped my sword and poniard. I put on a hood over my head and over that a bowl-shaped steel helmet that I buckled under my chin. Then I went to see about the horses.

The storms of the previous days had scrubbed the sky clear of clouds and sun was straining to rise above the treetops as we rode out of Robin's Caves, and headed south towards Nottingham. We were fifty or so well-mounted horsemen, most of us, although not me, armed with twelve-foot ash-wood lances with Robin's wolf's head device fluttering just below the razor-sharp steel tip. Robin rode at our head, with Hugh just behind. At the rear of the column rode Little John, a battered ancient horned helmet on his straw-coloured head, his huge war axe strapped to his back, leading a string of pack mules laden with baggage: food, barrels of beer, extra weapons, even a few crates of the home-loving doves. I caught Will Scarlet's eye as he rode in the centre of the body of horsemen. He grinned nervously at me. Was that the guilt of betrayal I saw in his eyes? Or was I imagining it? Did I want him to be the traitor? Tuck had not been seen for many weeks, Thomas had told me that morning when he bad me farewell; not since his argument with Robin at Easter. I prayed that it was not the big monk who was responsible for the betrayal. No, it couldn't be Tuck. As we thudded through the forest, the hot yellow sun rising on our left flank, I wondered again if the traitor was riding among us. And whether we were all galloping blindly into a trap.

Chapter Sixteen

We did not, thank God, charge directly into Sir Ralph Murdac's lair. Instead, Robin led us south to the fortified manor of Linden Lea, some miles outside Nottingham. The manor stood in a long valley, forested on the eastern side and with steep hillsides to the west. North of the manor house was a vast field of ripening corn. South of the manor was meadowland, with a fair-sized stream running along the bottom of the valley, following the main track to Nottingham. The stream filled the deep moat that circled the manor house and the settlement was further defended by a fifteen-foot-high palisade of stout wooden tree-trunks with sharpened ends inside the moat and surrounding the hall and its half a dozen outbuildings. Standing legs astride at the door of the hall, as our caval-cade clattered over the wooden drawbridge in the golden light of a perfect summer afternoon, was its master, Sir Richard at Lea himself.

We were given a royal welcome by Sir Richard, who had evidently been prepared for our arrival: hot meat and bread, wine and ale aplenty had been laid out on trestle tables in the courtyard. But before I had a chance either to wash the dust from my throat or grab a morsel of food, Robin called me aside for a private conversation. There were certain things he wanted me to do while it was still light, he said; chores, you might say. I was to keep what I was doing very quiet and tell no one, not even my closest companions. I was to ask him no questions; just do what I was told. Of course, I agreed and set to my tasks; but it wasn't until dusk that I was free to scrounge around for something to eat and drink.

With everyone fed and watered, Robin summoned all fifty of us, plus Sir Richard and his servants, into the hall of the manor for a war conference. I had seen him talking to one of Hugh's shadowy messengers before the meeting and I knew he must have fresh intelligence about Marie-Anne. When everyone was in the hall, everyone, including even the sentries, who would normally patrol the walkway behind the wooden palisade, I slipped out through a back door to complete a final task that Robin had asked me to perform. When I re-entered the hall, Robin was saying: '. . . and it seems that Murdac has hired a force of Flemish mercenaries, about two hundred crossbowmen and about the same number of cavalry, we believe, to help him erad-icate the foul scourge of banditry in Sherwood Forest.' There was a loud ironic cheer from the crowd of outlaws. 'Mercifully, they are not at Nottingham yet. Our inform-ants say that they are travelling up from Dover and they are not expected for at least a week or ten days. By the time they arrive, we'll be long gone, safe and snug in the forest. We will never have the pleasure of their company because . . . we are going to Nottingham tomorrow night.' His eyes glinted savagely in the light of a dozen good beeswax candles. 'We are going to rescue my lady and we are going to bring her back here; and we will slaughter anyone who stands in our way. Anyone. Is that understood?' There was a roar of approval. 'Right,' Robin continued, 'everybody is to rest until then. You have been allocated your quarters. Get some sleep; look to your weapons. We depart at moonrise tomorrow night. Hugh, John, Sir Richard, if I could trouble you for a minute to go over the details. You too, Alan,' he said, beckoning me from the back of the hall.

We gathered round Robin as he spread out a roughly drawn plan of the castle on an old oak money chest. 'She is being held in this tower, part of the wall defences, in the north-west corner of the castle. Not far from this gatehouse here.' He stabbed a finger into the parchment. 'Apparently Murdac wants to keep her imprisonment a secret and so she is not being held in the keep, but separately, discreetly in a wall tower, guarded only by his most trusted men. And that is very good news for us. Tomorrow night we will ride up to the gatehouse dressed in Murdac's colours – you have enough captured surcoats, Hugh?' Hugh nodded. 'So, we're wearing his colours, and we claim to be Murdac's men who have been in France for several years serving Henry, and who are now, after the King's death, returning to our master. Understood?'

Sir Richard, Hugh and John all nodded. But I notice John looked a little worried. 'So they let us in . . . and then what?' the big man asked, frowning.

Robin gave him a hard stare. 'We kill every single mother's son in that gatehouse, as quickly and as quietly as we can. Then we scoop up Marie-Anne, and we are away before anyone notices. If the alarm is raised, we can hold that gatehouse against all comers for hours, and we only need, at most, a quarter of an hour to find Marie-Anne and get her away safely. Then, when she's gone, we're all in the saddle and off in as many different directions as we can think of. Rendezvous at the Caves.'

'That's your plan!' said John, the scorn thick in his voice. 'You call that a plan? Christ's blistered fingers, it's the worst idea I've heard all year. For a start . . .'

'Hush, John, hush,' said Robin. 'It will work, I promise. You just have to trust me.' John looked unconvinced, he shook his head and continued more quietly: 'But it's sheer lunacy . . .'

'Just trust me, will you,' said Robin with just a touch of iron in his voice. 'You do trust me, don't you, John?' The big man shrugged, but he stayed quiet.

'Well,' said Sir Richard, 'as I shall not be joining you on this . . . escapade . . . I don't feel it's right for me to make any comment, except to say that I wish you Godspeed. And now I will bid you goodnight.' And with an uncertain smile he strode off in the direction of his private chamber.

'I'll leave the fine tuning to you, Hugh, weapons, horses, that sort of thing,' said Robin, 'and now I think we should all get some rest.' John walked away shaking his big yellow head and Hugh went out to the stables to talk to one of his couriers, leaving me and Robin staring at the sketch of the castle.

Robin turned to me: 'Want to know what we're *really* going to do?' He said it very quietly, but with a grin of pure devilment. 'Me and you, Alan, are going to get our lovely girl back all on our own. And we're going tonight, when the moon's up. Are the horses ready?'

'They're hidden in the wood, as you asked.' I couldn't help grinning back at him. I remembered the last time

286

Robin and I had been in Nottingham, the hilarious jaunt to steal the armourer's key.

'And the doves?' Robin said, his silver eyes shining.

'It's all done,' I replied happily. 'It's all done.'

At about midnight, when all the world was asleep, I led Robin out of the back gate of the manor and south-east towards the thick woodland where I had hidden the horses that afternoon. We were dressed for fast travel; no armour, just swords, daggers and a cloak against the chill of the night. We also took a spare saddled horse with us; if we returned at all, we would not be returning alone. Regardless of the danger, I was bursting with pride and excitement to be riding with Robin on this mission: we were two knights errant, straight from the tales of King Arthur, riding through the night to rescue a damsel in distress.

Two hours later and we were crouching in a damp ditch, up to our ankles in slimy refuse, looking up at the imposing bulk of Nottingham Castle wall and trying not to breathe. Quite apart from not wanting to make any noise, the stench of a hundred years of dumped excrement and general household rubbish in that ditch was suffocating. More than a hundred feet above us I could dimly make out the crenellations at the top of the wall. Robin gave a low whistle. Nothing happened. We waited for a few heartbeats. Robin whistled again and then suddenly I could see a head outlined against the moonlit sky and the battlements. There was a faint thump and a slither and a rope appeared, hanging from the top of the wall and knotted at one-foot intervals. Robin said: 'Up you go,' and I was climbing the wall like a monkey. The strain on my arms was tremendous, and my burnt ribs, though almost healed, were paining me a good deal, but there was no way I was going to admit my weakness to Robin. Finally, I made it to the top. With a great heave, I got my stomach over the wall, and a leg, and I collapsed on to the broad stone walkway, panting with effort. I heard a voice cry 'Hey,' and saw to my horror a man-at-arms in Murdac's red and black livery come striding towards me, sword in hand. I struggled to my feet and fumbled for my sword hilt but, before I could draw my weapon, a dark shadow rose out of the wall, from the lee of the battlements, and a hand was clasped hard round the soldier's mouth from behind. There was a glint of steel as the hooded figure shoved a thin blade hard into the base of the unfortunate guard's skull. He twitched once in the dark man's arms and then collapsed without a sound. The man threw back his hood and said: 'Are you all right, Alan?' and I saw it was Reuben, the Jew. I nodded, looked up and down the empty walkway and peered down into the gloom of the big castle courtyard. Everywhere was deserted. To my right was the great bulk of the castle keep, with one or two points of light showing from small windows, perhaps where a clerk sat up late over his rolls, but there was no movement. Everything was as quiet as the grave.

Moments later, Robin's head appeared over the parapet, followed lithely by the rest of him. Reuben cleaned his bloody knife on the soldier's surcoat and between us we rolled the dead man over the wall and down into the darkness. Robin clasped Reuben's arm and murmured: 'Lead on, old friend,' and we were hurrying along the walkway and down some steps into the entrance of a small guard tower, one of dozens built into the castle's curtain walls. Robin had his sword out, the naked blade winking in the moonlight, and I saw that Reuben had his knife in his hand, so I hastily drew my own sword, too. We plunged down a spiral staircase into the heart of the guard tower, my heart beating like a blacksmith's hammer, the pulse banging in my ears.

Down and down we went, in pitch darkness. And suddenly I blundered into the back of Reuben, who had paused before a wooden door. By the candlelight leaking out from the cracks in the door, I could see that it was occupied. We stood there in the gloom for a few moments, listening; me trying to control my pumping heart and ragged breathing; Robin and Reuben seemingly as calm as if they were on a summer's picnic in Sherwood. Reuben held up two fingers, indicating that there were two men inside, and Robin nodded. And waved his hand forward. Before I knew what was happening Reuben had pulled the string that lifted the latch on the wooden door and both he and Robin burst through. I followed as fast as I could but only in time to see Reuben hurling his heavy knife with extraordinary force and accuracy five yards across the room to smack into a man-at-arms who had apparently been dozing on a stool. The thick knife punched straight into the man's chest and into his heart, and the man coughed once, twice and dropped to the floor. Robin was almost as fast as Reuben's flying dagger; he took two quick paces forward and sliced the life out of the second soldier with a whip-like slash of his sword to the throat. There was a spray of blood and the man, who had been warming his hands by a brazier, swayed slightly for a moment or two, brimming blood from his gaping neck, and then collapsed to his knees, his face falling with an awful crunch and hiss into the glowing coals. He was clearly dead as he moved not a muscle as his blood bubbled and hissed and seethed around his scorching face.

It had all been over in less time than it takes to string

a bow. And not a word had been spoken, not a cry made. Robin lifted his victim clear of the flames and dragged him over to the second corpse. He reached down to the dead man's belt, unhooked a bunch of keys and strode over to a locked door in the corner of the room. In a couple of heartbeats, the door was open and Marie-Anne was in his arms. After a long embrace, Robin drew back and looked into her face. 'Did he hurt you?' he asked. I noticed that she looked pale and thin and her fine hunting gown was badly torn and covered in mud and filth, and what looked like blood. She hugged him close to her again and muffled by his cloak I heard her say: 'All is well now that you are here.'

As I looked at Marie-Anne clasped in Robin's arms, and saw the love that was so clearly between them, and how right they looked together, I felt something inside me shift. The resentment that I had felt towards them at the Caves was completely gone. She was still my beautiful Marie-Anne, I could see her beauty in a dispassionate way, even thin-faced and grimy as she was, but she had subtly changed. Something indefinable about her was different. I still loved her, but perhaps for the first time I saw her as a real woman, a woman with fears and joys, pains and pleasures, rather than a goddess, to be worshipped in a dream. She was not mine, I knew then, and she never would be.

We wasted little time: Robin hurried Marie-Anne out of the guard house and up the narrow spiral stairs. At the top, we paused to see that the wall was clear of sentries; then we were jogging along the wall and in no time Robin and Reuben were lowering Marie-Anne in a loop of rope to the ground. I followed, with Robin just feet above me, climbing hand over hand down the knotted rope. I saw

Reuben's head, once again, outlined against the greying sky; the rope was pulled up and we three were scrambling up the other side of the ditch and back to where we had left the horses.

Pride is the worst of my sins these days, but I cannot help but feel a glow of satisfaction that I was part of that night's work. It was a quintessential Robin exploit: precise, well-planned but with no frills and based on speed, good intelligence and audacity. But, above all, what made it typical of the way Robin operated was that it was successful. As the three of us trotted back up the track towards Linden Lea in the golden early morning light, we were greeted by the surprised sentries at the ramparts with a blast of trumpets. The noise woke the rest of the outlaw band who, tumbling out of the hall and the outbuildings, saw Marie-Anne was returned, and began to cheer us until the manor's encircling palisade seemed to tremble with the tumult. No one seemed to mind that Robin had deceived them the night before in pretending that the attack would be today. John handed me down from my horse and said: 'I knew that devious swine was up to something,' before nearly crushing me to death in a welcome bear-hug. Many, many people, friends and relative strangers, crowded round me to hear the story of the rescue, which I was not too modest to tell, although I may have exaggerated my role by a small amount. When breakfast was brought out and set on the trestle tables in the courtyard, Linden Lea took on a holiday air, with men shouting jests and insults to their friends, and raising mugs of ale to Marie-Anne's safe recovery. Sir Richard shook me vigorously by the hand and told me that he was proud of me. I felt lighter than air, a genuine hero and I was grinning so much my face began to hurt.

For a moment, the jollity was interrupted by another fanfare of trumpets and, looking out over the valley, I saw a great column of men and horses and baggage approaching down the track to the south that ran parallel to the stream. I was alarmed, at first, and then I saw Thomas's ugly old face out in front of the column, and Much Millerson beside him, and behind them a horde of familiar faces all dressed in dark green and armed to the teeth with war bows and swords, spears and axes: I was looking at the full strength of Robin's private army, almost three hundred men-at-arms and bowmen, each armed, trained and disciplined by Robin and his officers – and spoiling for a fight.

We welcomed them into the courtyard of Linden Lea; more food was fetched, someone broached a cask of wine, and all across the open space the newcomers were told the story of how Robin had rescued Marie-Anne from the jaws of the Nottingham beast. As stories will, it grew in the telling. And continued to grow in the years that followed. Robin had single-handedly slaughtered a hundred men, according to a version I heard a few years ago. He had hidden in the belly of a great deer to gain entrance to Murdac's feasting hall, according to another story. But the truth, I believed, was impressive enough.

After an hour or two of feasting, Robin had a plank set atop two big barrels and vaulting onto it he shouted for silence in the noisy courtyard. The men were not completely sober at this point and Robin had to call three times for quiet before he had their attention.

'My friends, we are well met here, and firstly it is right that we should thank our host, the generous provider of this shelter and this fine food and drink: Sir Richard at Lea.' The knight, who was standing next to me, took a modest bow and was lustily cheered by the outlaws. 'I would also like to thank all of you for joining me here in this beautiful valley, and I will tell you what we are here to achieve. There are many here with a price on our heads, myself included,' there was another loud cheer, and Robin took an ironic bow, 'and there are many here who have been forced to leave their families, their hearths and homes by so-called law-men, by bullies who claim power of life and death over you in the name of the King.' The mood in the courtyard had grown more sombre now and there were one or two angry growls. 'And there are many here who have been injured, humiliated and denied your natural rights as free Englishmen.'

'And free Welshmen,' someone shouted.

'That's right,' continued Robin. 'We are all free men here. And as free men, we join together; we come together in the wild places, away from towns and priests and Norman lords, and we come together because we have one thing in common. All of us have chosen to say no! No, I will not be subjugated by your unjust laws; No, I will not submit to your corrupt Church; No, I will not bow down to any local petty tyrant who demands my labour, the sweat from my brow, who takes the food out of the mouths of my babies. No! We are free men; and we are willing to prove the fact of our liberty with our swords, with our bows, and with our strong right arms. And we will never surrender our freedom. Never!'

Robin had bellowed the last word and the crowd began to cheer like men possessed. The noise rolled towards Robin in great waves of emotion. Our leader let the uproar continue for some time and then he raised his hands to call for quiet again.

'Tomorrow, my friends, tomorrow, we will have an

opportunity to show our mettle. Sir Ralph Murdac, the High Sheriff of Nottinghamshire, Derbyshire and the Royal Forests is coming here; that French cur is coming to this beautiful valley with his armed men, and his big horses. He is bringing his law to us, here, in this place. And, as we are outlaws, he means to kill us all. So what shall we do? Shall we run away and hide? Shall we crawl back into our holes in the forest and await, shivering with fear, to receive his *justice?*' Robin gave the last word an ironic twist. 'No, my brothers; look around you, and know our strength. We will not run. We will fight. And we will kill. And we will win.

'There is a new King coming to the throne; a just King; a noble King; a fair man and a mighty warrior; and, if we can win this fight today, if we can smash this man Murdac, bring down this so-called High Sheriff, I warrant that the King will grant us all full pardon for any crimes committed. Full royal pardons for all who fight with me. So I ask you now to remove your hoods and raise your voices to good King Richard: God Save the King! God Save the King! God Save the King!'

How they roared. Some of the men even had tears in their eyes. I looked at Sir Richard: his jaw was hanging open in amazement. 'I've never heard anything like it,' he said. 'He talks like a ranting priest, but he rants about the most extraordinary Godless, unnatural things: freedom from the Church? Freedom from our rightful lords, who have been set above us by God? What nonsense, what dangerous, heretical nonsense. But they loved it. They absolutely loved it.' He was staring around at the courtyard which was filled with cheering men, embracing each other, and shouting God Save the King! over and over.

Robin called the captains to him in the hall: Little John, Hugh, Owain the Bowman, Thomas and me. Sir Richard attended the meeting as a military adviser. Robin's first command was: 'Don't let the men drink too much, I need them with clear heads.' And then he plunged into his plans for the battle.

The valley of Linden Lea, a wide grassy expanse that might have been designed by God as a battlefield, ran roughly north–south, with the manor at the northern end, and the road to Nottingham running alongside a stream down the centre of the valley. To the east of the valley was thick woodland, to the west, rose steep bare hills with an ancient track running along the top. Robin's plan was simple: our infantry, about two hundred men-at-arms, and perhaps a third of our bowmen, say twenty-five archers, would form a line across the road about halfway up the valley. They would make a shield wall blocking the way. They were bait. Robin wanted Murdac to attack the outlaw infantry with his cavalry, and when he did, Robin's men would form up into an impregnable hedgehog, a ring of sharp spears and shields that no horse would charge.

'We think he can muster, in total, only about two hundred and fifty knights and mounted men-at-arms and about four hundred foot soldiers,' Robin told us.

'We're still badly outnumbered,' grumbled Little John. 'We have, what? Four score bowmen; two hundred men-at-arms and only fifty cavalry: three hundred and thirty men against six hundred and fifty. God's holy toenails, that's odds of two to one.'

'Their infantry are not good,' said Robin confidently, 'and we have, as you have pointed out, John, about eighty prime bowmen who can knock out a sparrow's eye at a hundred paces. We'll win; it will be a tough fight, but we'll surely win.' And he carried on with the briefing.

The bulk of the archers would be hidden in the woodland to the east. As the cavalry attacked the hedgehog, the archers would emerge from the wood and fire into the advancing conrois from their right flank, hopefully completely disrupting their charge and killing many men and horses. 'You are to command the woodland archers, Thomas,' Robin said. And the one-eyed man nodded. If the cavalry attacked the archers they could retreat into the wood and safety. Even if the cavalry reached the hedgehog largely intact, they would still not be able to break it, if it was well formed and well commanded. 'That's your job, John,' said Robin, for which he received a sarcastic: 'Thanks very much.' As their cavalry tried vainly to break into the ring of shields and spears, our own mounted force, hidden just behind the crest of the hills to the west, would swoop down and destroy the enemy horsemen from behind. 'That's you, Hugh, don't bring the horses down until they are committed to trying to break the hedgehog. Then come down and smash them. Understood?' Hugh said nothing.

With Murdac's mounted men in flight, Robin continued, our men would then combine and march on the ranks of their infantry. Seeing their defeated cavalry streaming back to the lines, followed by our victorious troops, they were likely to flee, and if not, they would be softened up by our archers emerging from the wood on the left before being charged by the combined outlaw infantry and cavalry.

I thought it was a brilliant plan. I could see it all in my mind's eye. The bloody field, enemy horsemen fleeing for their lives, the feeble cries of the enemy wounded, myself victorious after the battle . . . Hugh awoke me from my reverie. 'That's all very well, but what if Murdac's cavalry doesn't attack,' he said, with an edge of irritation in his voice. He was very put out that his brother hadn't included him in his plans for the rescue of Marie-Anne and had been sulking all day.

'If he doesn't attack, so be it. The shield wall slowly retreats, making its way back to the manor, then we settle down and wait. When Murdac brings his forces up to attack us in this well-fortified manor, we still have archers to his left rear, and our cavalry to his right rear. We have him between three fires. Any more questions?'

Nobody said anything and so Robin dismissed us to make the men ready. As the captains left to organise their men, Sir Richard said to Robin: 'It's time I was on my way.'

I was appalled; I had assumed that Sir Richard, that supreme warrior, that *preux chevalier*, would be fighting alongside us.

'I can't persuade you to join us?' Robin asked.

'As I told you before, it's not my fight,' said Sir Richard. 'Christians should not shed each other's blood when we need every good fighting man in the Holy Land. In turn, I ask you again, can I not persuade you to take the Cross? To join me in this great mission to free Jerusalem from the infidel?'

'It's not my fight,' said Robin. They smiled at each other and clasped hands. Then Robin turned away and I was left with Sir Richard. 'Are you really going to leave us?' I asked, trying to keep my voice steady.

He looked at me and said gravely: 'I'm sorry, Alan, but I must ride south to join Queen Eleanor. She is travelling the land and taking homage from the barons of England

297

on behalf of her son Richard. My brother knights of the Order and I are our future King's trusted counsellors – we ride with the Queen as an escort, but also we hope to persuade many of England's nobles to take part in the holy pilgrimage that Richard has sworn to undertake next year. I would like to help you but I am engaged in God's work, far, far more important than the outcome of this brawl.'

'But this is your family's land. This was your father's house. Will you not fight to protect it?' I asked.

'It is mine no longer,' said Sir Richard. 'Our Order demands a vow of poverty. When my father died, I made over this hall and these lands to the Poor Fellow-Soldiers of Christ and the Temple of Solomon. This place belongs to God, now. He will protect it. And have no fear, Alan, my friend, God will keep you safe through this battle, too, I am sure of it.' He smiled. 'That is . . . as long as . . .' he stopped again.

'What?' I asked. 'God will keep me safe as long as . . . as long as what?' There was a note of desperation in my voice that I wasn't proud of.

'God will keep you safe . . . as long as you remember to move your feet!' And with a grin and a gentle cuff to my head, he strode away to the stables. I didn't know whether to laugh or cry.

God might well have been keeping me safe, but I made my own preparations for surviving the battle. I sharp-ened both my sword and my poniard on a whetstone; I mended a rent in my aketon and padded the inside of my helmet with scraps of wool for extra protection. Around me the men were making similar preparations. I saw with a twinge of unease that Marie-Anne was busy cutting linen sheets into long strips to make bandages and I wondered how many of us would need them the next day.

My job during the fight was to act as a messenger for Robin. He would be with the infantry and I was to ride out to his captains – bowmen and horse, on either flank – and deliver his orders. It was a dangerous job that would depend on the speed of my horse to evade capture and death at the hands of the enemy. So I went to the stables and, on Robin's authority, I chose the best horse I could find for the job: a mettlesome grey gelding, young and feisty; in fact, the same horse I had ridden on the night of the rescue. I had found that I liked him, and he seemed to like me. I brushed him down myself until his grey coat gleamed, and made sure he was well fed that evening with a hot bran mash. Then I went up to the walkway that ran all the way round behind the palisade to watch the sun sinking over the hills to the west. There were a dozen fellows with me, idling, gossiping, spitting over the rampart into the moat, and, as we watched the great red orb slide down behind the bare hillside, a stir of movement rippled through the men on the ramparts. Somebody pointed and I looked due south to the end of the valley and saw horsemen; a line of mounted men trotting down the valley towards us. They looked to be too few, no more than four dozen men, perhaps a three score at most, and I felt my spirits lift. We had about the same numbers of cavalry. In that arm, at least, we were equal. Perhaps God was looking out for us after all. And then, to my left, there was a gasp and I looked again and saw, on the horizon in the gathering gloom, a skyline thick with black figures, hundreds and hundreds of them, horses and foot, wagons and pack animals. It was a proper army, a horde. That thin line of horsemen, I realised belatedly, stupidly, had just been the scouts. A mere skirmish line that was equal in numbers to our entire mounted force.

Sir Ralph Murdac had come to Linden Lea.

Chapter Seventeen

As the light fled from the valley of Linden Lea, Sir Ralph's vast host settled itself for the night, spreading out over the fertile land like a pot of spilled ink. They set up camp a mile from the manor, their cooking fires making dozens of pinpricks of light, winking in the blackness like the myriad eyes of an enormous beast that was waiting to devour us.

Robin's estimation of their strength had clearly missed the mark, or he had been misled; their numbers must have been at least three or four times our own. When I mentioned this to Little John, who had come to stand by me on the rampart in the dusk and survey the enemy host, he merely shrugged, and said: 'So we'll have to kill a few more of the bastards, then.' He seemed wholly unconcerned and that made me feel a great deal better. Looking at this giant of a man, standing with wide-spread legs, idly twisting his great double-bladed war axe in his ham-like hands, ancient horned helmet crammed on his straw-coloured head, I could not imagine him being defeated by any number of enemies – he looked like some invincible Saxon deity – and that gave me heart.

When it was fully dark, Robin called all of us together again. He addressed a packed courtyard, but his talk had none of the flamboyant rhetoric of his speech earlier that day. He simply said: 'The plan stands. It's a good plan. Yes, there are a few more of them than we thought, but don't be down-hearted, they'll die just as easily. Just obey orders, do the bloody work that you all do so well, and we'll be celebrating victory this time tomorrow.

'One more thing,' he said. 'If the battle goes awry, and I truly do not believe it will, I will give three long blasts on my horn.' His hand went briefly to the hunting horn at his belt. 'If you hear this horn ring out three times, you are to retreat, all of you, you are to break off the fight immediately and get your raggedy outlaw arses back here' – there was a faint ripple of laughter – 'any way you can, as fast as possible, get back here. I really don't think we will need to retreat. I believe we will beat them out there. But if you hear my horn, it's back to the manor. Once we're in here, if necessary, we can hold them for weeks.'

Then he ordered the archers, sixty men led by ugly old Thomas, to form up in silence, ready to take up their positions out in the forest. Each man had two full arrow bags at their waists, each holding thirty shafts fitted with mail-piercing razor-sharp bodkin heads. They left from a side gate in the palisade, crossing the moat on a bridge of planks, formed up in groups of ten on the other side, hardly visible in the darkness, and sprinted the hundred yards to the welcoming cover of the woodland. There was no sign of movement from the enemy as the little groups of bowmen scuttled through the darkness and into the trees. Confident of their superior numbers, Murdac's camp seemed happy to ignore us. Perhaps they thought we were running away.

Next, the cavalry under Hugh: fifty-two hard, well-disciplined men, clad in chain-mail and armed with twelve-foot spears, with horses trained to rear and stamp and kill, trotted out of the main gate and rode away towards the hills behind the manor house. Before he left, Will Scarlet sought me out and clasped my hand. He said: 'If I have ever wronged you, Alan, I ask for your forgiveness now. I would part as friends so that, if misfortune befalls either of us tomorrow, we will not die with any ill-feeling between us.' I was moved and, with a tear in my eye, I embraced him. 'There is nothing but friendship between us,' I said. And he grinned at me again before vaulting on to his horse and disappearing out of the gate. It was only after he left that I thought about what he had said. Had he wronged me? How had he wronged me? Was he the turn-coat? The thought curdled my good feelings at our parting like a splash of vinegar in a bowl of sweet milk.

With the archers and the cavalry gone, the manor seemed a half-deserted place. We ate a subdued meal in the hall and I spread my blankets by the banked logs of the central fire and tried to sleep. But the night was hot and I could not find rest. The men were talking in low tones, gathered in small groups of friends; some were drinking quietly, others were praying, or moving about the hall restlessly. And always, as a low accompaniment to the dull hum of nervous humanity, there was the constant scraping of whetstones on steel blades – *sheek, sheek, sheek* – as men sharpened their swords and spears obsessively to ward off the terrors of their imaginations. I thought of Bernard and Goody, safe in Winchester, with good food and wine and the protection of the royal household, and to my shame I envied them. When I closed my eyes, I saw the great grim host of Sir Ralph Murdac; and imagined that malevolent nobleman high above me on a great horse, swinging his bright sword and slicing its blade deep into my body.

I slept at last but was woken before dawn by men coughing and spitting and yawning and trampling on me as they passed by. I scrambled up and found a jug of water and ewer to make a quick toilet. I checked my burnt ribs and they seemed to be healing well: lines of pink scar tissue and the dark brown remains of the scabs. For some reason, this made me feel optimistic. When I had washed my body and face, I went outside to see the beginnings of a beautiful day. Up on the walkway behind the palisade, Robin and Little John were surveying the enemy and, as I came up to join them, I saw that the host was still there – seemingly even more numerous than the night before – the horses picketed in neat lines, the men scurrying about like ants. Robin was pointing at a large construction in the middle of their camp that was the focus of much bustling activity; a square frame made of thick wooden beams, with a vertical arm shaped like an enormous spoon pointing skywards and resting on a solid-looking crossbar padded with what looked like two great sacks of wool. John was saying: ‘ . . . I’ve seen likenesses of them but I never saw one in the flesh before. Do you think it will trouble us?’

‘What is it?’ I asked.

Robin replied: ‘It’s a mangonel, something the Romans invented many hundreds of years ago. It’s a giant catapult, which can throw great boulders hundreds of yards. I’ve never heard of one employed in England before but the French and Germans use them for reducing castle walls to rubble. Not very accurate, and it takes an age to set up and aim correctly. We'll be fine as long as we are mobile. And mobile we shall be. But, Alan, just to be on the safe side, don't discuss this machine with the men, all right. They might find it a little disconcerting.'

I nodded dumbly and continued to stare at the strange contraption. As I watched, a gang of soldiers attached ropes to the great bowl of the spoon and very slowly began to winch it down, away from us until it was level with the ground, where the men secured it with thick ropes tied to great metal nails hammered into the earth. I saw as the spoon was lowered that there was a great iron and stone counterweight on the far end of the throwing arm. Next, with a great deal of stumbling and shouting, the men wrestled a huge stone, the size of a full-grown pig, into the bowl of the spoon. After a brief consultation, everyone stood clear and one man pulled a lever that somehow released the ropes holding the bowl down. The great arm swung upwards and, with a clap that could be heard where we were standing half a mile away, the arm hit the crossbar and the stone flew from the bowl and sailed up in a low arc before splashing down with a tremendous thump into the stream in the middle of the valley a thousand feet from that devilish machine.

'It's too big to be very manoeuvreable,' said Robin.

John grunted. 'So it is,' he said. 'Which means, if we stay on the move, it should be fairly easy to avoid being squashed.'

'Do try to avoid it, just for my sake,' said Robin, in a mock pleading voice. John laughed and, ignoring the wooden steps that led up to the parapet, jumped straight down the ten foot from the palisade walkway to the court-yard floor and immediately began shouting orders to his men. Robin looked at me. 'Better get mounted, Alan, we've got a busy day ahead.'

With John at their head, more than two hundred outlaws, armed with sword and shield, helmet and spear and whatever oddments of armour they could scrape together, marched out of the front gate of the manor of Linden Lea. It was full morning and the sky was pure blue: it promised to be a very hot day. The beauty of the day lifted our hearts and the men began to sing: an ancient song that told of the battle of Mount Baddon in which King Arthur had defeated his enemies. Robin and myself, the only mounted men, rode at the centre of the chanting column. Behind us marched twenty-five archers, some of the best men with a bow that Robin possessed, led by Owain. Robin had left ten older men in the manor to guard Marie-Anne. They had all sworn that they would die before they would allow her to be captured. 'Make sure you do,' was Robin's reply, his eyes hard as granite.

We marched straight towards the enemy but stopped a hundred yards before the great boulder flung by the mangonel, which was stuck in the valley floor like a great raisin in a giant cake. The men formed two ranks of a hundred each, with the green wall of the forest about a hundred yards to our left, facing due south down the valley towards Murdac's army, which was a little more than three hundred yards away. Our front rank knelt, grounding their spears in the turf, held steady with the right hand, the left supporting a kite-shaped shield; the rank behind stood straight with spears pointing skyward. Owain's archers stood behind the second rank, and behind them sat Robin and I, our horses, my grey gelding and Robin's black stallion, munching the green grass as if there was nothing in the world that could be of concern to them. Then we waited. The sun beat down on our heads, and we waited some more, sweating quietly, for the enemy attack.

For an hour, we stood watching Murdac's men. A mass of cavalry had formed up to our front, in two loose ranks: about two hundred men. Equal numbers, I told myself. But I was lying. One horseman is worth at least three or four footmen. I could clearly see the red and black surcoats of Sir Ralph's killers. The square-topped steel helmets, and bright spear points winking in the bright sunlight as the knights of the first conroi jostled for a place in the long line. I was beginning to regret wearing my aketon; the padding might be useful in stopping a sword cut but it was as hot as the fires of Hell on this lovely summer's day. The metal on our accoutrements was becoming almost too hot to touch. The men began to fidget. I looked up into the perfect blue sky: far above a hawk was circling the field, watching the evolutions of men with a dispassionate avian eye. John turned to Robin and said: 'What are they waiting for? Here we stand, a mere two hundred footmen, as juicy a target as ever presented itself. Why don't they attack?'

'They think it's a trap,' said Robin.

'So they're not entirely stupid then,' growled John.

Robin raised his voice: 'Owain, go forward and give them a little tickle, will you.' Then he bellowed the order: 'Open ranks!' and with wonderful precision all the men moved as one, taking a step or two to the left or right, the line extending and leaving room for the archers to move through the rows of spearmen out in front of the line. Till then I had not appreciated how well trained Robin's infantry was. I had seen them at practice, at Thangbrand's and at Robin's Caves, marching and wheeling and going through their manoeuvres, but I had not realised how much like real soldiers these raggedy misfits had become. Owain's bowmen jogged fifty paces forward, lined up, pulled back the strings on their big bows and, on the command 'Loose!' sent a shower of arrows arcing forward to patter on to the line of enemy horsemen. It was at the extreme range of the bow, about two hundred and fifty yards, and the damage done was slight: one horse, skewered in the haunch by an arrow, reared and nearly threw its rider, barging into the next animal in the line and causing a ripple of movement all along the conroi. A knight pitched backwards in the saddle, a shaft protruding from his side. But that was all the harm we caused with that first salvo. The cavalry were too well armoured and the distance too great for much slaughter. Owain cried 'Loose!' once more and another thin curtain of steel-tipped shafts fell on the waiting line of men and horses. Again there was not much resulting carnage. Another poor animal began bucking and kicking from a wound I could not see. But the bowmen's provocation was having the desired result. A knight had ridden out in front of the line and was exhorting his men to valour. The first line of cavalry re-ordered itself and began to move forward at a walk.

Robin shouted: 'Owain!' and the archers turned and scrambled back towards the safety of our thin line of spearmen. When the bowmen were through, once again, the ranks closed smoothly. John shouted: 'Prepare to receive cavalry!' and the men at the ends of our line began to curl around to the rear until, in less time than it takes to put on a pair of boots, they had formed a tight circle, three ranks deep – Robin, myself and the bowmen in the centre of a steel ring of men-at-arms, fifteen paces across, spear points outward, shields raised, the front rank of outlaws kneeling, the second and third ranks standing behind them holding their spears poised to impale any horseman in range. This was the hedgehog, a formation that I had last seen at Thangbrand's – dying in the bloody snow. It was supposed to be impregnable to horsemen; the horses would not charge home into that glittering hedge of steel spear points. But at Thangbrand's, Murdac's cavalry had torn the hedgehog to bloody ruin. Would the same happen today?

As the first row of Murdac's cavalry moved forward at a walk, I had to admit that they were an impressive sight: each horse caparisoned in a black trapper that entirely covered its body, the material padded for the animal's protection, a red plume nodding atop each animal's head; the knight in a black surcoat with three red chevrons on the chest. By God, they must have been hot, but they looked magnificent. Each man held a twelve-foot lance vertically with a red pennant fluttering just beneath the glint of razor steel. The horses of the conroi walked in step, their riders knee to knee, the line perfectly straight, advancing in a slow black bar against us. Behind the first row of horse-soldiers, all of whom I had been told were knights, sworn to Sir Ralph's service, came the second; the sergeants, equally well-trained and just as lethal on the battlefield, but not of noble blood. They had only two red chevrons on their chests and carried no lances; they were armed with sword and mace.

The tactics of the conroi were brutally simple. The front rank of knights would charge into our body of infantry, a tight mass of heavy horseflesh and naked steel that would smash our formation apart with its weight and with the shock of the impact. As we were scattered, the second rank, the sergeants, would gallop in and slaughter the fleeing infantrymen. It was a devastating method of war, honed by the nobles of Europe over decades into a fine and murderous art.

The black knights began to trot and, at a signal, the lances came down in a ripple from left to right across the charging front line, each weapon couched, wedged under the armpit of the knight, pointed directly forward, seemingly thrusting ahead. Just then there was a shout from a man in our kneeling front rank and I looked left to the forest. Out of the thick trees stepped our bowmen, Thomas to the fore, sixty immensely strong men all in the same green woollen tunics, each holding a six-foot yew bow bent taut by a hemp string and ready for battle. They were ahead of us, in a loose group at the treeline, and two hundred yards from the first wave of trotting horsemen. The horsemen quickened their pace to a canter. 'Come on, come on, you bastards, shoot,' I heard John mutter and, as if at his command, the arrows began to fly.

The first cloud of grey streaks smashed into the black cavalry line like a shower of hail clattering against a barn door, yards of steel-tipped wood plunging deep into flesh all along the line and suddenly, like magic, a handful of saddles were emptied all along the row of charging knights. A second volley of arrows slammed home and the ranks were thinned again, a third volley and the ranks were looking seriously depleted; a fourth volley and all cohesion disappeared – instead of a neat row of black-clad warriors galloping to our destruction, there were clumps of horsemen desperately trying to control their wildly bucking horses, bumping into each other, shafts bristling from the bodies of horse and man like pins in a pincushion.

310

Another grey wave of arrows, and yet another, and there was no line left at all, just men and beasts spurting blood and struggling about at random, spread across a hundred yards of valley floor, in pain. Bodies dotted the green field, loose horses whinnied and galloped aimlessly about, unhorsed men staggered, retching, snapping off arrow shafts and trying to staunch deep puncture wounds with blood-drenched hands. Some mounted knights had turned back, galloping into the second line of sergeants behind them in their panic to escape the rain of death.

But the merciless arrows followed them, punching through the backs of their chain-mail hauberks, into their shoulders and necks and bringing more bloody chaos to the second line. Soon the whole body of cavalry was in retreat, terrified men and horses scrambling to escape that field of blood. And still the arrows fell, like the thunder-bolts of God's vengeance, smacking into horse and manflesh without the slightest discrimination. Two bloodied horsemen, brave men, actually made it to the front ranks of our hedgehog, but the horses baulked at our ranks of impregnable steel, and then I saw Owain sink a yard-long wooden shaft deep into the chest of the fore-most knight as he battled to control his shying horse. The second rider, realising that he was now alone, wheeled his mount and galloped away zigzagging his path to confuse the aim of our hedgehog archers who made bets, in loud excited voices, about who would be able to spit him first. Arrows whipped past to his left and right but, by some miracle, the man and his horse escaped back to his lines. And I wished him Godspeed. I had seen enough slaughter, I felt, to last me a lifetime. But that day of blood was only just beginning.

* * *

311

We cheered the woodland archers until we were hoarse; we had not lost a single man and the enemy's first attack had been decimated. And the archers responded with elaborate bows, pulling off their hoods and caps and bending from the waist until their long hair brushed the ground. They shouted rude jests at us about how few knights we had killed until, finally, Thomas got them in hand and ushered them back into the safety of the forest. Just in time. Out of bow range, a group of mounted sergeants were massing for what might have been a swifter and more lethal charge against our bowmen, a chance to revenge their fallen comrades.

But there was worse news than a handful of angry cavalry-men. Close by those milling horsemen, a large body of men, on foot, had marched out of a fold in the ground to the rear of Murdac's camp and were forming up to our front left. They were clad in sleeveless green and red surcoats, in a pattern of large squares, under which they wore padded aketons. Each man had a helmet, and a short sword strapped to his side. And each carried a great, black wooden instrument shaped like a large cross.

'God's crusted arsehole,' whispered John in disbelief, and he sounded genuinely shocked. 'It's the Flemings. It's the damned crossbowmen.' Robin was looking at this new body of men, about two hundred strong, with his head on one side and a strange expression on his face. 'This is going to make things a lot more interesting,' he said in a calm, ruminative voice. But when I caught his eye, I saw a flash of icy anger, a glimpse of a fury so terrible, that it gave me a real start of fear.

When the crossbowmen were formed up, to my surprise, instead of marching towards us, towards the hedgehog, they made a half turn and began to move in the direction

312

of the forest wall. Each man paused for half a minute at the edge of the woodland. Before he entered the curtain of green, each man slipped his crossbow string over a hook on his belt and, placing his foot in a stirrup at the end of the bow, by extending his leg, he pulled back the string on his powerful machine until it was caught by a ratchet and held in tension. He then loaded a foot-long wooden bolt, a quarrel, into the groove at the front of the weapon, and advanced into the forest ready for battle. In a quarter of an hour, the whole company had been swallowed by foliage and was completely lost to view. I knew what they were doing: they were going to hunt down our bowmen; arrow against quarrel, they would fight it out at close quarters in the greenwood – and there were at least two hundred well-trained mercenaries to our sixty men.

'Alan,' said Robin, urgently. 'Get yourself into the wood; find Thomas and tell him to pull back, a fighting retreat, pull back but slowly. I need those Flemings off the field for as long as he can keep them there. He's to pull back to the north, towards us, and, when he can't hold any longer, make a break and run for the manor house. Deliver the message and come straight back to me. I'll need you today. Understood?'

I felt a lump of fear in my throat but I managed to say as calmly as I could: 'Pull back, but slowly. Then they make a run for the manor. I come back here.'

'Good lad; off you go!'

I squeezed my grey gelding through the ranks of the hedgehog and galloped hell for leather for the treeline, angling the horse north, away from where the crossbowmen had entered the forest and towards the manor. As I got into the trees, I slipped from the saddle and tied the grey to a bush. As I recovered my breath and looked about me

313

I could see no one. But for the beating of my heart there was no sound at all. I felt as if I was alone in the world, and far from the rough companionship of the spearmen and the comforting presence of Robin and John, I realised I was afraid. I crossed myself, drew my sword and began to push my way through the thick undergrowth, forwards to where I had last seen our bowmen. There was not a sound in all the world except the faint rustle of leaves as I moved forward and the creak of branches moving above me in the slight breeze. I had the strange sensation that I was underwater, in this green and almost silent world. Where were our men? Where were the enemy? I stopped and listened again. Nothing. The wood was close around me and I could see no more than half a dozen yards in each direction. It reminded me of happier days, hunting red deer with Robin and, without realising it, I began to follow the methods of stalking I had learnt with him. Each foot placed in front of the other with deliberation and care so as not to break a twig or make any sound. Step, step, step, stop, stand absolutely still and listen. Then step, step, step, stop and listen. There was nothing here, I was sure of it. Where was everybody? I felt like a lonely soul in a green fairy otherworld, away from the blood and pain of the open battlefield, which lay, I knew, only two dozen or so yards to my right. The ancient trees, so closely packed that their branches intertwined, towered above me like the roof of a giant wooden cage, but the undergrowth was light, a few ferns and scrubby bushes. I pushed aside a trailing frond of ivy and ventured deeper into the gloom. Step, step, step, stop and listen.

And then I nearly jumped out of my skin: a huge blood-curdling scream, an impossibly loud soul-racked cry of agony, and only a dozen yards ahead a man in dark green suddenly appeared from behind a tree, staggering, with a thick black stalk protruding obscenely from his neck; and the quiet green world exploded into noise and movement. From behind me and to my left there came a sound I knew well: the *wheesht, wheesht, wheesht* of arrows passing close by, and then another bellow of pain from ahead. I could see dark figures to my front flitting from tree to tree, coming towards me, closer and closer, there was the whizz and thump of crossbow bolts striking wood near by. To my right, a loud groan, and the body of an archer fell from the branches of a venerable beech, dropping like a huge ripe plum to hit the forest floor with a sodden thump. And then I was smashed to the ground with a terrible force, half-pinned to the leaf mould by a great weight, someone had jumped me from behind; I squirmed in terror, sword gone, lashing out with my fists in blind panic but the man grabbed my flailing arms and wrestled me to still-ness and I found myself lying on my back gazing up into the one good eye of my friend Thomas. 'Quiet,' he hissed, and I struggled to control my panting breath. Then he hauled me behind the bulk of a great oak and we both rested our backs against the comforting solidity of the tree. The wood had returned to absolute silence again after the last violent flurry of battle. Thomas held up a finger to his lips.

When my breathing was calm, I leant forward and whis-pered in his ear the message from Robin. He put his face close to my ear and whispered: 'Pull back? As if we have any choice. We're being slaughtered like hogs here.'

I poked my head round the thick trunk of the tree and peered into the gloom of the forest. I could see nothing. A few yards away, lying half-buried in the leaf-mould where Thomas and I had briefly wrestled, was my sword. I got

315

to my feet in a crouch and made to step out and collect my weapon when Thomas roughly pulled me back behind the tree, and just in time. Two crossbow quarrels thunked in the bark of the tree exactly where my head had been moments earlier.

'Watch yourself, Joshua,' whispered Thomas, half-laughing at my expression of shock. 'You're not in Winchester Castle now. There's one of the bastards, just behind that elm yonder. When he next peeks out, I'll skewer him and you can collect your blade and then we'll pull back a mite. You watch him for me. Give me the signal. All right?'

Thomas stood tall, picked up his bow and selected a shaft from his linen arrow bag. He drew the string half way back and stood with his broad shoulders to the oak's rough bark, in cover but facing directly away from the enemy. At the level of his feet, I peered round the curve of the trunk through the green curls of a sprouting fern, exposing as little of my face as I could. There was nothing to be seen. The wood was eerily empty and silent, but, if I really strained my ears, once in a while I caught the scurrying rustle, like a rat in a barn, of a man moving fast through undergrowth. I felt the hairs on the back of my neck stand on end but, staying as still as stone, I watched the big elm Thomas had indicated. Presently, I saw a shape move against the outline of the tree. Just a flicker, but it immediately attracted my gaze. I waited a little longer. Then suddenly far ahead and hidden from view a rough voice shouted something in a language almost like English but that I could not make sense of. It was clearly an order from the Flemish captain for his men to push forward, for, as I watched, parts of the trees ahead detached from themselves and resolved into human figures. Men were peeling themselves away from the cover of the wood and cautiously beginning to move forward. I looked up at Thomas and nodded. In one smooth movement, he pulled the string back to his ear, turned round the side of the tree and loosed a yard-long ash shaft into the body of the Fleming a dozen yards away. The arrow passed straight through him, bursting out of his back and flashing away through the undergrowth. The man gave a small cry and sank to his knees, but in that time I scuttled forward, scooped up my sword and bounded away to safety behind a fallen beech tree before the man finally collapsed with a bubbling sigh to the ground. The other bowmen were loosing their shafts, too. And half a dozen crossbowmen were cursing in pain and stumbling and dropping to the floor. But the shadowy shapes were still advancing; I could see dim figures making short quick runs from tree to tree. I poked my nose out a little further, trying to see if any of our men were close by, but a dozen deadly black quarrels hissed above my head and clattered through the branches. They were winning. We were losing. It was time to go.

From the safety of my fallen beech tree, I waved at Thomas and he gave me a grin and a jokey salute. Then, gathering his bow and arrow bags, he suddenly sprinted a few paces, away from the big old oak and the fast-approaching Flemings, to the safety of another tree. I saw him conferring with another green-clad bowman and his friend, who in turn ran in a crouch back to another tree and another bowman to spread the message. I began to crawl away too. Not daring to lift my head, nor run upright, I snaked my way through the undergrowth on my elbows and knees, making for my horse. A part of me felt guilty at leaving the bowmen to their unequal fight but, I told myself, my duty was to Robin. Though I could not repress a feeling of relief to be escaping that silent slaughter in the treacherous murk of the greenwood.

Something of the terrible atmosphere in that deadly wood had affected my horse. He was trembling with fear and whinnied with pleasure at my return. That friendly noise was nearly the death of me.

I had the grey's reins in my fist, my sword was sheathed, and I was soothing him with my free hand when some instinct, some God-given warning, caused me to turn my head and at that moment, out from under the low-hanging branches stepped a tall lean figure in the green and red checked surcoat of a Flemish crossbowman. He was a big man of about thirty years, round-headed with greasy light brown hair. He was pointing his weapon directly at me, the stock snuggled into his right shoulder, string drawn back taut, the quarrel lying innocently in the groove to the front. I was staring at my own death. And the man smiled, revealing his yellow rotten teeth, an awful grimace of victory.

Chapter Eighteen

Training is a wonderful thing. Even a little goes a long way when you are in a tight corner. The dusty, sweaty hours that I had spent with Sir Richard in the courtyard at Thangbrand's and at Winchester Castle saved my life more than once that day. With a sword in my hand, much of the time I didn't need to think; one stroke naturally flowed from another, the muscles remembering the moves as if my arm had a mind of its own.

I stared at the crossbowman and, for a heartbeat, I was frozen in surprise. Then I moved. I dropped the reins, I grabbed at my sword hilt with one hand and my battered scabbard with the other. In one smooth movement my sword was free. The tall man, still grinning triumphantly, pulled the lever at the bottom of his crossbow, the string twanged, the bolt shot towards me in a grey flash and – he missed. I heard an equine scream from behind my head as the quarrel smacked into my poor grey gelding, a bare inch from my left shoulder, and then I was charging the Fleming, a wordless cry of rage in my throat. I feinted at

319

his head with my blade and he blocked it desperately with the crossbow. Steel cracked against wood but he stopped my swing, the blade a mere six inches from his face, and then I shifted my position and straightened my arm into the lunge, a move Sir Richard had made me practise no more than three or four hundred times. The tip of my sword punched forward, with the full weight of my shoulder behind it, smashing through his yellow teeth and on into the depths of his mouth; onward through his brain, my sword plunged, through the killing area where his brain joined the spine, until the tip came to rest six inches out of the back of his head. Hot blood sprayed from his ruined mouth, splattering my hand and sword arm, and suddenly I felt the dead weight of his body on the end of my steel, dragging it down, and, as he crashed to the floor as dead as a stone, I yanked my sword free of his distorted head, ripping sideways through the cheek and bringing with it a fresh gout of bright gore. It had taken no more than a dozen heartbeats, from his appearance to his death. And as I looked down at the corpse at my feet, the slashed mouth a gaping red hole of blood and fragments of teeth, and knelt to clean my sword on his surcoat, I felt nothing, no remorse, no pity but, instead, a surge of joy – and of pride. I had killed my enemy alone in single combat. He had tried to kill me, and yet I was the better man. I had boasted to Robin, all those months ago, that I would become a warrior one day. And I knew, at last, that I truly was one.

My lovely grey gelding had fallen to his knees. His eyes were rolling madly in his head. The quarrel was embedded in his side, a foot of steel-tipped oak buried up to the leather flights. He was sweating and shivering and, with every shuddering breath, bright pink bubbles formed at his mouth. I knew he was wounded hard in the lungs; that he would never run again. So, stroking his poor twitching head, I drew my poniard and cut deep into his throat, slicing through the big vein in his neck. He died under my hands. I stroked his long ears and he lay quietly, the blood running in a thick river down his wide grey chest.

I could not stay beside him long, however. Other crossbowmen might be close and my duty was to seek out Robin. So I left the humped body of my poor brave grey and crept further south to the edge of the forest and climbed to the topmost branches of a luxuriantly leafed tree to get a safe vantage point from which to survey the battlefield.

Things were not going well for Robin. The hedgehog was surrounded by a furious ring of enemy infantry; on all sides hundreds of black-clad sword- and spearmen were hacking and chopping at the small circle of our men, who were dying by inches, despite a valiant defence. Every so often the thick outer ring of enemies would withdraw, each man stepping back a dozen paces to glare, panting, at the outlaw foe who faced him, snarling, over the rim of his shield. Then, on command, Murdac's men would surge forward, to batter again at the hedgehog's thinning ranks.

We were fighting like the heroes of legend. I saw John, unencumbered by a shield, only protected by his hauberk and ancient helmet, swinging his great axe and cutting great holes in the enemy ranks with each gory swipe. He split a man straight through the centre of his head with one blow, and then stepped aside to dodge a spear thrust and lopped the spearman's arm off at the elbow. The bowmen were shooting their deadly missiles into the wall of enemies, each arrow passing through the first man and into the man behind. Robin was fighting like a

321

madman: as he hacked and lunged, a spray of fresh blood flew from his sword at each stroke. Then the enemy pulled back again a few yards, the gap between the lines strewn with bodies and the crawling shapes of broken men. I could hear the screams clearly, even in my tree a hundred yards away.

Away from the hedgehog, black-garbed cavalry men roamed the field; sergeants, I assumed, who had been routed in the first disastrous charge of Murdac's men. They seemed to circle around the great boiling mêlée in the centre of their field like great dark ravens, waiting for the hedgehog to burst apart, as it had done at Thangbrand's, so that they could ride down the fleeing men and cut them to bloody ribbons. There was no way that I could rejoin Robin and give aid in that desperate fight. Once I left the safety of my treetop eerie, on foot, out in the open field, I would be hunted down and slaughtered by the roaming horsemen before I got halfway to Robin's side. There appeared to be more cavalry, too, I saw, far back to the south in Murdac's lines. He must have had more than a thousand men in total. What madness had possessed Robin, I wondered, for him to invite battle at Linden Lea, when his forces were so overmatched? Was it arrogance? Or had he just made a fatal miscalculation? Then my eyes lifted away from the battle's bloody pulsing heart, to the hills at the far side of the valley – and I saw Hugh, faithful Hugh, riding to rescue his brother, at the head of his men.

Trotting in a great loose mass, a dust cloud in which appeared, fleetingly, horses' heads and glinting spears and dark green surcoats, under a flag decorated with a snarling wolf's head, our own horsemen swept down from the hillside where they had been concealed and spurred into the valley. The spear points dropped and with a drumming of galloping hooves they launched themselves towards the mass of dark-clad men clustered around the hedgehog.

They never arrived.

From the south, out of a fold in the valley floor, unseen by Hugh's men, a fresh conroi of cavalry trotted forward. Wearing the same green-and-red surcoats as the Flemish crossbowmen, but mounted on big horses and armed with long spears, half a hundred fresh mercenary horsemen galloped out of their hiding place and smashed straight into Hugh's exposed flanks and rear. There was chaos; our line of attack completely disrupted, and all but a handful of horsemen at the head of our charge were immediately engaged in a fight for their lives with the Flemish cavalry. Spears were soon abandoned in the close-quarter carnage, and horsemen wheeled and hacked at each other with sword and axe and mace. They were evenly matched, at first. But then the mounted sergeants, the remnants of the first disastrous cavalry charge, who had been roaming the field in ones and twos, flocked to join the cavalry battle and our horsemen began to die. A few, a pitiful few, managed to break through the enemy lines and, forcing their mounts through our weary ranks of spearmen, joined their comrades in the relative safety of the hedgehog. But many men in Lincoln green were cut down in their saddles, surrounded by two or even three black and green-and-red-clad killers on horseback. A few of our men, shamefully, turned their horses north and rode hard for the hills and safety.

I looked away from the battlefield, away from the blood-drenched mayhem of struggling, dying men on horse and on foot. I blocked my ears to the screams of the wounded. I could not bear to watch the final onslaught that would see the dark ranks of my enemies swamping that exhausted ring of my friends. I looked up at the deep blue sky, at the bright sun blazing above the western hills and a flight of swallows arching over that God-forgotten field of blood, high above the pain and gore and the stench of death. I closed my eyes against the bright sunlight, and listened to the wind in the treetops around me . . . and I realised that I could hear something else, too. A rustling sound, and a noise that was almost like a murmur. I imagined I could hear voices, I could hear voices, and then the drums began. *Ba-boom-boom; ba-boom-boom; ba-boom-boom* . . . I couldn't believe my ears. I shook my head but the noise was still there and growing stronger. *Ba-boom-boom; ba-boom-boom; ba-boom-boom* . . . I had heard that pagan sound before, months ago on a blood-soaked night near Robin's Caves.

I looked down at the ground, twenty yards beneath my feet and through the leaves I could make out the top of a man's head, shaved into a tonsure, the reddish-brown hair surrounding a sun-browned bald pate. It was a monk, and I saw then that he was carrying a war bow. And beside him sat his two great and terrible beasts: the wolfhounds Gog and Magog. My heart gave a great leap. It was Tuck.

With a shout of joy I shinned down the tree as fast as I could, nearly breaking my neck as I fell the last few yards. It was indeed Tuck, and he was not alone. There were a dozen shadowy figures in the gloom of the forest behind him. I welcomed him with an embrace, crushing his strong squat body to mine and smelling once again the homely earth scents of his brown robe. My mind was bubbling with questions. But before I could get them out, Tuck held up a hand. 'Answers later, Alan, we have work to do now.' The drums were still booming, slapping the air with their ancient call to battle, and I saw that the forest was thick with people, scores, hundreds even. A woman approached through the trees; she was clad in a long dark blue robe decorated with stars and crescent moons. Her forehead was painted in what looked like dried blood with the Y symbol. In her hands she held a thick black staff of hawthorn. It was Brigid. In my happiness, I embraced her too. She smiled at me, but a little oddly, blankly, without the comforting brown warmth that she had displayed when healing my bites and burns. She seemed filled with a cold hatred, a black fury, only just contained within her body, and I instinctively recoiled from her as if repelled by an invisible force. Over her shoulder, I saw more comforting figures. Little Ket the Trow, in a leather breastplate, holding an enormous club almost as tall as he was; his brother Hob grinning at me through the leaves of a low-slung branch; and many more: outlaws who were not members of Robin's band, travelling beggars, Sherwood villagers, wild men from the deep forest . . . They had all come to battle. The drums were booming, battering the inside of my head and then Tuck said in a calm, cool voice, 'Madam, I believe you must attack now, or it will be too late.' Brigid nodded, she paused, took a deep breath and threw back her head. And, with a wild, ululating scream that set the hairs all over my body standing on end, she hurled herself past me and burst out of the treeline and on to the field of battle. Behind her streamed hundreds of men, and even a few women, screaming just as wildly, many with the pagan Y painted on their foreheads, just as many without, but all armed with whatever they had brought: clubs, rusty swords, axes, mattocks, scythes – I even saw one old man with a grain threshing flail – and all of them crazed with the blood-lust of battle.

*   *   *

It was the home-loving doves, you see. On the afternoon before that secret ride to rescue Marie-Anne, Robin had asked me to release three baskets of doves, each with his thin green ribbon attached. Those birds had flown high in the late afternoon sunshine, while everyone else was in a war meeting with Robin, and then the birds had headed back to their dovecotes, trailing Robin's message: *Arm yourself, all you who would serve me, and come!* With those birds, he was summoning all of his woodland power. Every man in the whole of Sherwood who sought his favour, every man with a debt of gratitude he wished to discharge. I found out later that Brigid had also called all the men and women of her ancient religion together, from as far as North Yorkshire and the Welsh marches, luring them with the promise of the rich spoils of battle and the chance to strike a blow for the Mother Goddess. Tuck had seen the doves and had come, joining up with Brigid's cohorts: a Christian monk and a pagan priestess marching together. All for love of Robin. When I told the story to friends, years later, few believed me, but I swear it is true.

This rag-tag horde of outcasts, madmen and religious fools charged out of the treeline like a host of avenging ghouls, screaming their war cries. And Brigid raced ahead of them battering Murdac's men out of her path with the blackthorn staff that she wielded in both hands with savage, manic energy. Like twigs before a great river of humanity, all the black-clad troops before the charging horde were either swamped or swept away. In the forefront of that yelling, charging mass bounded Gog and Magog, silent and slavering. One of the great dogs leapt at an unfortunate man-at-arms in the rear ranks of the force surrounding the remains of the hedgehog, and with a snarl and a crunch had ripped off the lower part of his face. The man dropped his weapon and staggered back, hands groping at the bloody mash where his jaw had been. Then I saw a howling raggedy figure, stick thin, cut through both the man's legs with a single blow of a scythe. The other huge dog, no less savage, was biting through padded aketon sleeves, crunching through the arm bones of Murdac's men, crippling dozens in the course of that terrible onslaught. Brigid's men and women attacked with an almost inhuman frenzy, striking down soldier after soldier with mattock or club, finishing them on the ground with knives, and then tearing at their clothes, almost before they were dead, seeking out coins and other valuables hidden about their persons. Brigid herself seemed to have the strength of ten men, felling armoured foes with mighty blows of her thick staff and screaming paeans to the forest gods and encouragement to her followers. The scrum of enemies around the hedgehog dissolved, Murdac's troops, both horse and foot, wiped away by the ravaging army of raggedy pagans. Those who did not run immediately for their lives, were dragged down and slaughtered.

I followed the attack of the pagan horde in a more sedate manner, sword drawn nonetheless. But I encountered no enemies as I picked my way through the sea of corpses towards Robin. I could see clearly now the damage that the hedgehog had suffered; and it was a heart-rending sight. Great holes had been ripped in the once impenetrable circle of men and steel. More than half our men were down and those still in place were blood-spattered, weary beyond belief. I took my place beside Robin, silently waiting for orders, and surveyed the field that was, for the moment, ours.

Tuck had not charged with the pagans: he had gathered a score of bowmen, the remnants of Thomas's men,

I assumed, and they stood at the edge of the battlefield, by the treeline, calling targets to each other and shooting down the fleeing men-at-arms with dreadful accuracy. Murdac's attacking force was in retreat, panicked men racing south to the tents and horse lines. But the battle was not won. To the south-west, near the line of the hills, I could see a formed unit of black horsemen, standing still, watching the field. Due south was a full battle of unused infantry, a hundred men standing in a black square in the hot summer sun. To the south-east, scores of red and green clad crossbowmen were streaming out of the treeline. Although pushed out of the woodland by our howling pagans, they were retreating in good order and forming up to the rear of Murdac's line, beside the threatening box-like shape of the mangonel. I saw a group of dark horsemen, riding beneath a great black flag, cut deep with blood red chevrons, crossing to our front towards the Flemings. It was Murdac himself, his black head bare, and his closest companions; all still fresh, and completely untouched by the bloody hand of battle.

The enemy was not beaten. Far from it. To the cross-bowmen's right, Murdac and his picked knights stopped in front of yet another black square, another battle of marching spearmen, just coming into view from the far end of the valley, their weapons held aloft, spear points glittering in the bright sunlight. Sir Ralph checked his horse, circling in front of the marching men, shouting encouragement, and then he rode on to where the Flemings were straightening their ranks.

Robin, standing at the edge of his shattered formation, amid the dead and wounded of both sides, the ground a churned marsh of blood and mud, was watching the enemy as closely as I was. His shoulders were slumped, his face grey with fatigue. He had a cut on his cheekbone, but otherwise, to my relief, he appeared unharmed. Then he seemed to straighten up, to come to a decision, and I saw him reach to his belt with a bloody hand, tug at a strip of rawhide and release his horn. He stood straighter for a moment, took a big lungful of air, and blew. Three long blasts, and then again three. The notes echoing around the bloody field. It was retreat, the signal to return to the manor. 'Help the wounded, Alan,' he said to me in a toneless voice. Then with a final glance at the enemy lines, he turned, lifted a blood-drenched man to his feet, and the pair began to limp their way painfully back to Linden Lea.

We straggled back to the manor, hundreds of us, as the shadows lengthened and the sun grazed the top of the western hills: Hugh's tired horsemen, very few in number; the bloodied surviving spearmen of the hedgehog; bowmen hobbling and using their stout yew staves to make better speed; blood-spattered pagans, who stopped frequently to rifle the corpses of the dead. And there were so many dead, the field was littered with corpses, and wounded crying for water and aid. Most of us made it back to the manor unharmed, the unwounded helping the wounded; but a few fell prey to Murdac's circling horsemen; those men who had not heeded Robin's horn in time, and were cut down with axe or sword. I carried a spearman with a huge gash in his side on my back all the way home. But when I got to the courtyard of the manor and rolled him as gently as I could on to a pile of straw, I saw that he was already dead. As the last few men stumbled through the gate, almost unable to walk from tiredness, we slammed the great oak bar down and looked to our wounds.

*   *   *

Marie-Anne and the men who had remained in the manor had been busy. Food had been prepared, once again on great trestle tables in the sunny courtyard, and the wounded were given great jugs of weak ale to slake their thirst. The badly wounded were placed in the hall itself and tended by Marie-Anne, Tuck, Brigid and the servants. There were scores of them, bloodied and exhausted, crippled by spear and gashed by sword; a few jovial, proud of what they had achieved, others pale and silent, plainly just waiting to die. The most grievously wounded were helped onwards to their eternal rest by Robin's men. Robin himself went round the hall comforting the worst hurt and praising their valour. One man, a cheery rascal with a great hole in his shoulder, pulled a white dove trailing a scrap of green thread, from his ragged, blood-slimed jacket. Robin solemnly accepted it and scrabbled in his pouch to find a silver penny with which to reward the man. Most of the wounded, though, were more despairing; they drank greedily at the wine flasks that were passed around the hall and the sounds of pain increased as the sun finally sank behind the hills to the west. They all knew that Robin had thrown the dice and lost. Murdac's troops had surrounded the manor and, in the morning, he would overrun the place and we would all die.

The fall of night had ended hostilities and Robin had sent out emissaries to Murdac for a truce to gather our wounded from the field. Murdac agreed and all through the night parties of men walked in and out of the manor bearing stretchers. Soon the hall and all the outhouses were packed with wounded and dying men; the courtyard, too. The warm night was filled with the moans of the wounded and the sharp cries of those receiving medical attention. Tuck went round those near death offering the

330

last rites and he prayed with those who in extremis looked to Our Lord Jesus Christ to save their souls. Brigid did likewise with the pagan wounded. Marie-Anne was haggard with tiredness: she was trying to nurse all the wounded men, hundreds of them, with only the help of a few hall servants. John was organising the collection of wounded from the field; the dead we left where they lay.

Into this man-made Hell of death and blood, into this gore-splashed slaughterhouse, echoing with the awful screams of souls in pain, stepped Bernard de Sezanne. He was dressed in the finest yellow silk tunic, spotless and embroidered with images of vielles, flutes, harps and other musical figures. He was clean shaven and his hair had recently been trimmed. He held a scented handkerchief to his nose and he walked straight up to me, stepping delicately over the dead and dying on the floor of the courtyard without paying them the slightest heed, and, as I gawped at him stupidly, he said: 'Let me see your fingers, Alan, quick now.'

I was astonished; I could not believe this clean and scented apparition was real. It must be a figment of my battle-addled brain, but the figment insisted that I hold out my hands in front of me, like a schoolboy showing his mother that his grubby paws were clean. And I complied. Clean, they were not, crusted as they were with blood, earth and green tree lichen, but Bernard solemnly counted the fingers and professed himself relieved. 'All ten, that is a comfort,' he said. 'You may not be the greatest vielle player but you would have been a damned sight worse if one of these blood-thirsty villains had lopped off a thumb or two.' And then he embraced me and told me that he must see Robin at once.

I was bursting with questions: where had he come from?

331

What was he doing in the middle of a blood-sodden battle-field? But he hushed me and made me lead him over to Robin, who was helping a wounded man drink from a cup of wine.

'I have a message that I must deliver to you in private,' Bernard said to Robin. And my master, wordlessly, ushered him away to a private chamber at the end of the hall and the door was shut in my face.

They were inside for an hour or more, and after a while I was sent to fetch wine and fruit but forbidden to join their private counsels. Finally Robin and Bernard emerged, and Robin told me to find Bernard a jug of wine and a corner to sleep in, while he went back to caring for the wounded. Bernard would tell me nothing but that I should sleep easy, for all would be well. But sleep did not come. We shared the jug of wine, that is to say I managed to get a few sips down, while Bernard seemed, as usual, to have the thirst of ten men. Then I lay in the straw next to my musical mentor, listening to him snore, and trying to fathom what his coming could mean. Finally, I did fall into an uneasy sleep, only to be awakened before dawn, once again, by ugly old Thomas shaking me by the shoulder.

I sat up, my whole body stiff from the unaccustomed exertions of the battle the day before, and I was no more than half-awake when Thomas said: 'Robin wants to see you.' And so I left Bernard to his hoggish slumber and followed the one-eyed man through the courtyard to a corner of the hall.

Robin looked fresh, although I knew he had not slept. He handed me a pure white dove, and as I looked down at the gorgeous bird, and felt its fluttering heartbeat beneath my fingers, I noticed that it had a long red ribbon

332

tied to its pink left foot. 'Go to the palisade and release this,' he said.

'Just one?' I asked in surprise, 'What does it mean?'

Robin looked at me for a moment, and I saw a gleam of sadness in his silver eyes. 'It means simply: I accept.' And then he turned away to return to the wounded.

I walked to the palisade and climbed the steps to the walkway and, with a silent prayer to God the Father, his Son, and the Holy Ghost beseeching them all to come down from Heaven in their Glory and save us, I threw the bird up into the air. It flapped its perfect white wings, circled the manor, and then flew off to the West, disappearing over the hills and trailing its thin red message of acceptance behind it.

As I watched the bird fly to freedom, the sun came up in all its blinding majesty over the woods to my left, and I looked out on to the field of battle at the beginning of what was already looking like another beautiful day. During the night, Murdac's troops had completely surrounded the manor of Linden Lea; a thin black ring of men and horses and wagons on all sides, campfires already burning and skeins of grey smoke beginning to drift in the light wind. I saw crossbowmen, spearmen, and conrois of cavalry stirring among the various parts of the lines of tents and piled war gear. But they had suffered in yesterday's battle, too. They still outnumbered us, but this was not the invincible black horde that had marched on us the day before. Almost directly ahead, opposite the main gate, perhaps four hundred yards away, I could see the standard of Sir Ralph Murdac himself, the black flag with red chevrons, rippling in the breeze atop a large pavilion. And there was the man, riding across the front line, his face clearly visible under a simple helmet with a large triangular nosepiece.

I thought I could see something glinting redly at his throat, but I told myself it must be a trick of the light. He was heading towards the great box-like wooden structure of the mangonel, which had been moved much closer to the manor overnight.

Murdac arrived at the machine, consulted with the officers there, and with a chop of his hand to the men standing in groups around the weapon, the mangonel fired. The great spoon swept up and banged against the crossbar; a boulder the size of a small cow came screaming straight towards us and, with a deafening crash, it ripped a hole two yards wide in the palisade just a few feet from where I was standing. Half a dozen wounded men, who had been sheltering inside the wooden wall, were crushed to bloody pulp in an instant. The boulder rolled a few yards and came to rest almost in the centre of the courtyard.

I realised, with a sickening twist in my gut, that we had no protection against Murdac in this manor house. That infernal machine could strip away our feeble wooden defences at a whim, and then Murdac and his black cavalry would leap the moat and ride over our splintered walls and chop us all into offal. By noon, I reckoned with a sinking heart, we would almost certainly all be dead.

Chapter Nineteen

In many years of hard skirmishing, bloody battles and close escapes, I have never felt so close to despair as I did then when that great rock came smashing through the wooden palisade at Linden Lea. Except once. This spring, as my grandson Alan lay sick with a fever and near to death, I felt that the whole world would end with him. He is well now, God be praised, and his recovery was amazingly fast, or perhaps only amazing to an old man like me, whose cuts and bruises heal so slowly these days. I fed Alan the dark potion concocted by Brigid, when Marie, his mother, was sleeping, exhausted with worry, in the next room. It was a foul smelling brew and, no sooner had I got him to swallow it, than Alan's stomach threw it straight back at me. But I mopped up and tried again and finally I managed to get some of the noisome liquid to stay inside him. Then he slept.

The next day I dosed him again, as Brigid had instructed, with a half-strength mixture with plenty of water which had been boiled by moonlight and then allowed to cool.

The day after that he was awake and asking for gruel. Marie is beside herself with happiness and has vowed to light a candle to the Virgin every Sunday for the rest of her life in thanks for his recovery. I sent a side of bacon, three chickens, a dozen loaves of bread and a purse of silver to Brigid.

Every day that followed, young Alan grew stronger. Now, as I write this tale of death and destruction at Linden Lea, my grandson is playing outlaws and sheriffs in the woods outside the manor, with some of the local boys. And with his return to health, my melancholy has lifted. The days seem bright again; I go about my tasks with fresh vigour; I even laugh with Marie of an evening by the hearth fire when the day's tasks are done. I shall never tell Marie that I sought Brigid's help in saving Alan, but there is no shred of doubt in my mind: the witch cured him, and she cured me, too. Maybe Robin was right all those years ago: God is all around, in everything, and everyone, even in a witch. For the salvation of my boy could not have been an act of the Devil, whatever Father Gilbert, our parish priest, may say about Brigid's skill. And I shall pray for her soul, and count her a good friend, all the days that are left to me.

There were two things I had not yet realised about Robin, as that giant boulder smashed our hopes of safety behind the palisade at the manor of Linden Lea: first, he planned battles like a chess player, meticulously thinking ahead, anticipating the moves his enemy might make, and making his own preparations to counter them; and, secondly, he always had the Devil's own luck when it came to warfare.

That first missile from the mangonel must also have

been a devilishly lucky shot, for the next boulder rolled to a halt a good twenty yards short of the palisade. The next after that whistled over the top of the manor and churned through the field of corn behind. But, by then, we were all shaken in the courtyard and the atmosphere was close to panic. Robin was quick to take action – he ordered all the wounded to be taken into the hall of the manor, though there was scarcely room for the men already there, and they would not be offered much more protection from the great machine than in the courtyard; he also had three men move the boulder so that it partially filled the gap in the palisade; then he set us to strengthening the wooden walls, buttressing them with logs and planks. I believe he just wanted to keep the men busy and prevent them brooding on what the mangonel meant to our chances of survival. Certainly our strengthening work had no effect when the next great boulder struck. It smashed straight through the three-inch thick round wooden pallings, despite our reinforcing logs and planks, and continued on, rolling at the pace of a trotting pony, to rip out a bottom corner of the hall itself.

Between falling short and sailing clear over the manor, I calculated that about one missile in five hit our walls. And as the sun crawled up the dome of the heavens, it soon became clear that in less than an hour we would have no defences to speak of, just a litter of kindling and dying men, horribly mutilated and crushed by the massive flying stones. It was not only men who died under that cruel onslaught: one missile crashed into the stables, killing two horses and a mule outright and snapping the legs of two other mounts. The piggery also took a direct hit. Robin was here and there, all over the courtyard like a fiend, exhorting us to patch up the walls as

337

best we could, round up and slaughter the fear-maddened livestock, and carry the wounded into the hall, which itself had taken two full-on hits and had sunlight pouring through the thatched roof on to a scene of unspeakable pain and misery inside. I could see men looking out at the forest wall a mere hundred yards away, measuring the distance for a fast escape on foot. But it was hopeless as a way out of our torment, a full conroi of red and green horsemen was sitting by the treeline watching the gaps grow in the walls of the manor and anyone attempting on foot to run the hundred yards to the safety of the forest would have been cut down in a few bloody moments.

With almost all the front palisade gone, except for a few ragged sections of wooden fence, our defence looked like an old man's mouth, a few scattered teeth in a bed of bleeding gums. Then, God be praised, the mangonel ceased its vicious pounding. However, before we had time to enjoy the respite, I saw that Sir Ralph and his main force of black cavalry to our front was beginning to move. Beside him I could make out the face, under a plain round helmet, of Guy of Gisbourne, his yellow and green colours flapping from his lance. The cavalry force was perhaps a hundred and fifty men strong in three closely packed ranks, and it was approaching us at a slow walk; behind it marched a full battle of dark infantry.

Robin leapt on to a boulder in the centre of the court-yard and shouted to gain everyone's attention. 'Men,' he bellowed, 'comrades, brothers, I shall not sit here like a chicken in a roost, waiting for the fox to come to me. I will attack, I will sally out, right now . . . and I will kill that man.' He flung out an arm and pointed through the gaps of the fence at Sir Ralph Murdac, who was riding,

338

still at a walking pace, in the middle rank of his black-clad horsemen. 'Who will ride with me?'

There was a growl of assent, hardly enthusiastic, but the men knew they would die if they remained in the manor. 'Good,' said Robin. 'We will attack now, and when we have killed that man, when we have cut the head off the snake, the body will die. These mercenaries won't fight when they see their paymaster is dead. Two men to every horse, the rest to follow on foot, bowmen who still have arrows to give us covering fire on the flanks.'

We formed up behind the shattered remains of the main gate, a pitiful twenty surviving horses, two men to a horse, myself riding behind Robin. As I prepared to mount up behind my master, he turned in the saddle, looked down at me and said: 'Loyalty until death, eh? Well, you've kept your promise.'

I shrugged. 'I'm not planning to die just yet,' I said. 'Not until he is rotting worm-food.' And I nodded towards Sir Ralph Murdac and his advancing troops a bare hundred yards away.

Robin smiled. 'You wouldn't have said that a year ago.'

I said nothing, but scrambled up behind him and loosened my sword in its scabbard.

We few remaining outlaw cavalry were surrounded by a raggedy crowd of pagans and outlaws, all those who could walk or run, armed any-old-how with spears, swords, axes and farming tools. Tuck was there, flanked by his two great war dogs. Hugh was looking unhappy, mounted with a man-at-arms at his back. John, bareheaded and stripped to the waist in the heat, stood there, axe on one shoulder, his great muscled chest matted with blond hairs. A mere handful of bowmen, with no more than three or four arrows apiece, formed two groups to the left and the right. Robin roared: 'Come on, lads! Let's go!' The gate crashed down, bridging the moat, and with a wild, ragged yell from a hundred throats, we spurred forward, footmen and horse mingled together, to our certain doom.

As we galloped out, myself gripping tight to the wooden back of Robin's saddle, finding it middling hard to remain seated on the bounding haunches of his black stallion, I looked up from under the brim of my helmet to the hills in the west where something had caught my eye. And I beheld nothing less than our Salvation. A band of angels was coming to battle. For a minute I couldn't believe my eyes; but up on the ridge, arms glittering in the bright sunlight was a long, still line of horsemen in white, at least a hundred of them, each on a magnificent destrier draped in dazzling linen.

The line was motionless for a moment, then, at an unheard word of command, the white horsemen spilled over the edge of the hill and flowed like a great creamy wave down the side to join the battle. 'It's the Templars, the Templars,' I shouted in Robin's ear. 'Sir Richard has come, Sir Richard,' I bellowed to the men charging beside me and pointed to the hills where a hundred of the finest horse soldiers in Christendom were surging down the slope in a perfect line, charging to our rescue.

Sir Ralph Murdac's men, seemingly unaware of the threat to their rear, spurred on into the full gallop as we approached them, and the two unequal forces, the small scrappy band of Robin's men, two to a horse, and Murdac's rows of charging black horsemen met with a splintering crash of steel spearheads on wooden shields. We were more concentrated in a tight wedge of men and beasts, aimed like a living spear at Murdac himself, and for a few moments our force drove hard into their line, penetrating deeply;

Robin was cutting down men left and right in front of me, desperately trying to reach Murdac in the second rank. We drove forward, hacking, lunging, battering at men and animals, Robin spurring the horse brutally onwards, drawing blood on the stallion's dark sides. The black-clad line of Murdac's horsemen closed in on our flanks on both sides, and behind us, encircling us in a ring of hot horse-flesh, shouting men and swinging steel. But the High Sheriff was just yards away from us, with Guy at his shoulder. Murdac saw Robin and myself heading for him, I am sure of it – and, in an instant he had turned his horse towards us, pushing his way roughly through the ranks of his own men, his long sword drawn. Around his neck, bouncing on his black surcoat on its golden chain, was the great ruby. It seemed to flash angry red fire in the bright sunlight with every movement.

Robin hacked at a mailed horseman between us and Murdac and he disappeared into the dust of the mêlée. And then the sheriff was in front of us and he and Robin were blade to blade. A clash of steel, and their swords locked for an instant. They pulled apart, snarling at each other, circled their horses and both charged in at the same time. Another crack of their steel blades meeting. I swung my sword at his waist but missed. Murdac's horse reared and we were ducking the great hooves of his destrier as they sliced the air around our heads. Then the horse was down on four feet again and Robin spurred forward, driving hard to close again with Murdac. But a dark-clad horseman, bloody and out of control, blundered between the Lord of the Wood and the Lord of Nottingham, and as Robin smashed him aside with a great blow to his helmet, I saw that Murdac was further away than before, pushed by the inexorable press of sweating, straining men. Another horseman rode at us, his spear couched, aiming for Robin's side, but I beat the spear out of the line of attack, high and to the right – his horse cannoned into us, and as he passed me I gave him a great backhanded sword cut to his mailed arm and felt the bone crack beneath my steel. The blow overbalanced me and I felt myself sliding from the sweat-slippery haunches of Robin's horse. Only with a quick twist of my body, and a large helping of luck, did I land on my feet in the middle of that maelstrom of barging destriers and grunting hacking fiends. I was dimly aware that the long white line of Templar knights had crashed into Murdac's men, as the whole boiling mêlée gave a ripple at their impact. And from occasional glimpses through the crush of men, I could see that the white knights were doing great damage, plunging their lances deep into their enemies' unguarded backs, but I was much more concerned with my own survival.

A horseman's mace blow clanged off my helmet, stunning me momentarily, and the hooves of a war stallion slashed just past my face and then, thank God, I was out of the mass of whistling steel and whirling hooves. I drew my poniard with my left hand, sword gripped tight in my right, and prayed that I would live through the next quarter hour. Robin's footmen had caught up with the cavalry and charged into the milling throng, yelling 'Sherwood, Sherwood!' I saw a grimy-faced spearman stabbing up at a black-clad warrior on horseback. To no avail. The rider turned and chopped down with his sword, splitting his helmet through the middle. And then a great white rider, in a brilliant surcoat with its blood-red cross on the shoulder, cantered past me and speared the enemy horseman in the side, the lance punching through the chain-mail and leaving the man spiked on twelve feet of ash and screaming hideously. The white rider, his face completely masked by his flat-topped cylindrical helmet, dropped his lance, leaving it protruding, flopping, out of the dying man's side, and lifted a hand to me in salute before hauling out his great sword and wheeling away to rejoin the fray. As he galloped away in search of fresh prey, I heard his shouted, slightly muffled but familiar words drifting back to me: 'Don't forget to move your feeeeet . . .'

And move them I did. Murdac's infantry had joined the battle, too: a grim swordsman rushed at me with his weapon swinging. I blocked with my sword, stepped past him and back-cut with my long blade, slicing into his face just above the nose. He blundered away, blood spurting through his fingers as he clutched at his head. A man-at-arms ran at me, I parried with my sword without thinking, and stabbed my poniard down into the meat of his thigh. He screamed and hot blood sprayed my face and chest. I exchanged blows, sword and poniard against axe, with a man-at-arms in green and red. Our weapons locked together and I found my face only inches from his. I smashed my head forward, the brim of my steel helmet crashing into his nose, and he dropped at my feet. Another man charged in from my right waving a falchion, a heavy-bladed chopping sword, and I knelt under his clumsy swing and hacked my own blade deep into his waist, cutting through the padded coat he wore. He sank to his knees on the bloody grass before me, blood gushing from his side. I stepped back, twisting my steel free from the suck of the wound, and almost simultaneously fended off a weak axe blow to my head with the poniard in my left hand from the man whose nose I had smashed. I turned to face him, screaming a meaningless challenge, red blades in both hands, my face and body covered in other men's gore . . .

343

and, to my astonishment, he dropped his axe, turned and fled from the field. I was too surprised to follow him, too tired as well. Suddenly there were no more enemies about me, and I saw that the victory was in our grasp.

The Templars were masters of the field. The white robed warriors trotted about as if they had not a care in the world. The black cavalry and the Flemish mercenaries were in full retreat, galloping south with Murdac's standard in the fore. Robin, unhorsed, was five yards away from me fighting two men at once. His sword play was superb, almost too fast to see as he fended off blows from the two red-and-green men-at-arms. Then, before I could rush to his aid, he dispatched one man with a fast lunge to the throat, ducked a whistling haymaker from his other opponent and turned and stabbed him through his shoulder. I had been pleased with my own skills, but watching Robin, I was lost in admiration. That distraction nearly cost me my life.

A tall man charged into me from behind. I had no idea where he came from, but he took me completely unawares and I slipped in the muddy ground, churned by horses' hooves and slicked by many a brave man's blood. Before I knew it, I was on my back in the morass, half-blinded by sweat, blood and my helmet, which had been knocked forward; I had dropped my poniard and my sword was held unsteadily above me in a feeble attempt at self-protection, all my science gone, as I gasped breathless on the ground. Above me, the huge, grey-mailed swordsman was slashing at my arm – time slowed to a crawl, I could see the slow swing of his blade, I could see the expression of bitter rage on his face, I could feel the bite of the blade into the flesh of my right arm. And then, out of nowhere, came Robin's blocking sword-stroke, almost too late, but stopping the blade from slicing in deeply. Robin threw off the man's sword and, continuing the stroke, he ran his blade through his neck, into a gap between helmet and mail coat. The man reeled away, tottered a few steps and sank to his knees, coughing blood.

Blood was spurting from my wound, too, as I clutched at it, soaking the sleeve of my aketon, and there was Robin above me grinning and breathing heavily. He held out his right hand and pulled me to my shaky feet. The battle was over. Templar knights in blood-spattered robes, holding dripping swords, were rounding up prisoners at the point of their weapons; the last of Murdac's mounted men were disappearing south towards Nottingham Castle and safety; his defeated foot soldiers were running for the forest. The dead and wounded were thick on the ground, fertilising the soil with their blood. I looked around me in amazement. Unbelievably, our last helter-skelter charge, combined with the superb skill of the Templars had turned the tide. But the price had been high. To my left, I saw Thomas, lying in the stinking mud, one hand clutching his belly which was a mass of dark blood. His other arm buried beneath his body. His ugly face was pale, strained with agony. I hurried over to him and tried to pull his arm away to look at his wound, but he fought me off with surprising strength. 'Let me be, Joshua,' he mumbled. 'Just let me be.' He pulled the other arm from under him and I saw with a crash of cold shock that the hand had been severed. Through the dark clot of drying blood, a white bone protruded. He seemed unaware of the injury and scratched at his oozing belly with the stump. He moaned once and I cradled his great lumpy head in my lap. I felt a burning sensation behind my eyes, and a great aching sadness inside me, but no tears would come. I stared down at his horrible-kindly face, dry-eyed, as he died. I sat there for a long time with the big man's head on my thighs, my wounded arm like a line of fire, thinking of all the misery, pain and hatred in the world, as the blood dried to a thick crust on my hands.

It must have been mid-afternoon when Little John found me, hauled me bodily on to the back of a horse and walked me back the few hundred yards to the shattered ruins of the manor of Linden Lea. Sir Richard was there talking with Robin and I heard the Templar say as I rode through the battered gate on the back of a borrowed nag: 'So you will keep your side of the bargain, then?' And Robin saying in a weary voice: 'Yes, I'll keep it, as you kept yours.' Sir Richard waved at me and then cantered away to rejoin his surviving men, who had formed up outside the manor and were waiting to pursue Sir Ralph on the road to Nottingham.

Robin came over to me and insisted on bandaging my cut himself. Although he was as gentle as he could be, he chuckled as I let out an involuntary squeal of pain, and his half healed face-cut from the day before cracked as he smiled, leaking a few drops of blood down his grimy cheek. When he had finished washing my cut in wine and wrapping it in a clean bandage, he said: 'Between stealing pies, the Sherwood wolves and this inglorious shambles, it seems God really wants this hand, Alan. But I have denied it to him three times – and He shall never take it while I have strength.' He slapped me on the shoulder and went to deal with other more badly wounded folk.

And in truth we were in very bad shape: there was hardly a man who was not wounded in some way. Hugh was limping from a lance wound in his right leg. John had a gash on his left arm that looked as if a sword point

346

had scored up his naked forearm nearly to the bone. We had lost perhaps two score men in the final attack and their bodies were laid out in a neat row. The brothers Ket the Trow and Hob o' the Hill were dead, too, their tiny corpses lying together a little apart from the rest as they would receive a pagan burial. Only Tuck, indomitable Tuck, was unwounded. He was sitting on a barrel of ale, eating a great piece of cheese, with his two great hounds Gog and Magog at his side, guarding a prisoner. It was Guy of Gisbourne.

The boy – the man – who had tortured me, humiliated me, stripped me of my pride in that foul Winchester dungeon was slumped dejectedly, hands bound, between the two massive dogs. He was facing the death of a renegade from Robin's band with as much dignity as he could muster. One whole side of his face was swollen, I guessed from a great blow that must have rendered him unconscious, but before I could ponder his ill-luck in being captured rather than killed outright in battle, he caught sight of me, and with a cry of 'Alan, help me!' he tried to get to his feet. The two dogs growled, deep and terrible, like the vengeance of God, and Guy collapsed down again. I turned my back and walked away.

We washed ourselves and ate and drank and slept that hot afternoon at Linden Lea, and many of us, too many, died of our wounds. At dusk, Robin gathered together in the courtyard as many men as were able to walk. He stood over the forlorn figure of Guy of Gisbourne, who seemed to be trying to shrink into the earth at Robin's feet.

'We have fought, and we have won,' said Robin in his carrying battle voice. 'And many have died. And after victory comes justice. Here, before you, is a man who was once your comrade but today he rode with the enemy;

this man, who was once your friend, with whom you shared your daily bread, is a traitor. What shall we do with him?'

The courtyard rang with cries of: 'Boil him alive!' and 'Flay him!' and 'Hang, draw and quarter him'. A wag yelled: 'Tell him one of your jokes!' Robin held up a hand for silence. 'Very good,' he said. 'The punishment shall be—'

And then I was shouting: 'Wait, wait. I claim his life. I claim his life in single combat.' I don't know why I did so; I could have sat back and watched my enemy meet his deservedly cruel end – and even enjoyed it. But there was something about his pathetic air, the way he had appealed to me before, and perhaps my sense of guilt was stirring. If I had not engineered his expulsion from Thangbrand's with the stolen ruby, maybe he would have fought with us this day.

So I said it again: 'I claim his life. I will fight him and kill him in single combat, if the prisoner is willing.'

Robin looked at me oddly. 'Are you sure?' he said. 'What about your arm?'

'It will be fine,' I said, though I was far from sure. The cut was burning, my arm felt weak and I was trembling even as I loudly made the absurd boast: 'My sword requires his life.'

'Very well,' said Robin. 'The prisoner will face single combat with our brother Alan. Swords the only weapons. If he wins, he shall go free.' There was some grumbling from the crowd at this, although a good many seemed to consider a sword fight to the death a fine entertainment to crown such a bloody day. 'Does the prisoner accept the challenge?'

Guy had lifted his bruised head at this strange turn of events. He looked across at me, doubtless remembering

348

the many times he had beaten me on the practice ground at Thangbrand's. He half-smiled, a mere twitch of his dry lips, and said: 'I accept.'

Behind me I heard a deep voice whisper in my ear. 'By God's swollen loins, you are a fool, young Alan. But don't you worry; you'll easily slaughter him. And if by some mischance, he wins, I'll chop his head off myself.'

Both Guy and I stripped our tunics and shirts off to fight bare-chested in the warm evening. Robin had flaming torches brought out for light and I found myself facing my childhood enemy over the point of my sword inside a ring of jeering outlaws. As we circled each other, I felt the weight of my blade for the first time in months; my cut arm had weakened me more than I had supposed, and I was bone-weary from two days of battle. But then Guy spoke quietly, so that only I could hear him: 'I enjoyed hearing you sing in Winchester, little *trouvère*, or rather hearing you squeal.' He was looking at the burn scars on my naked ribs and, remembering the deep humiliation, the heat of the burning iron near my most intimate parts, I felt for the first time a flare of real anger. 'Good,' I thought, 'now I can kill you.' Whatever pity, whatever weakness I had felt before was swept away by his words. As we circled each other, naked steel in our hands, I felt my being fill with the strength that comes from pure hatred. I wanted his blood, I wanted his guts smeared all over my blade. I wanted him dying, begging for his life in front of me in the dust of the courtyard before my friends and comrades.

Then he sprang at me, and he was as fast as I remembered him; a lighting quick flurry of blows which I parried with my wounded sword arm. By God, he was strong, too, he was fighting for his life, and he had learnt a thing or two since our days at Thangbrand's. But, then, so had I.

He attacked hard down my right hand side, hammering backhanded blows against my blade. By luck more than skill, I managed to fend him off and we broke apart, both panting for breath. I looked down at the bandage on my forearm and noted with dismay that the bleeding had started again, and a large crimson patch was seeping across the white of the cloth. He came at me again, this time on the left, then left and right in succession. He was driving me back, the outlaws scattering behind me, back towards a surviving stretch of palisade, trying to corner me to a place where he could hammer me down.

And then he over-reached himself – he must have been tired too, for he mistimed his sword stroke and I was through his guard in a heartbeat, slashing him across his naked chest. A shallow cut but bloody, a foot long and an inch or so above his nipples. The crowd gave a great animal roar of approval. First blood to me. He looked down in complete surprise, as the gore welled and spilled down his bare chest and on to his belly. And then I was attacking. I used a combination of cuts and lunges that Sir Richard had taught me. Guy seemed bewildered by this change in my demeanour. In his heart, he still believed me to be the snotty thief that had been an easy target of his bullying only the year before. Or the cringing victim, screaming for mercy in that Winchester dungeon. But I was no longer that boy. I was a man, a full member of Robin's band, a warrior. He tried a desperate counter-attack to break my lunge-and-cut routine, but it was another mistake. I let his blade slide past my head and chopped down into the meat of his right bicep. He roared in pain and dropped his sword and I could have killed him there and then. The blood-drunk crowd was shrieking for his death. But I did not strike. I heard again his laughter at my humiliation, my agony of body and mind in that cell, and it was not in my head to give him a quick death.

I made him pick up the sword with his left hand and fight on. But after that cut to his arm, the battle was all mine. He was no swordsman with his left hand and in three passes I had sliced his chest again, slashed into his side, stabbed his calf muscle and, with a contemptuous flick of my wrist, made a deep cut on the unbruised side of his face. He was staggering and crying now. He could see his death in my eyes. His defence was at an end and he barely moved as I swung and sliced deep into the muscle of his left shoulder. By now, weak with loss of blood, he could barely lift the sword. And suddenly all my anger drained away. Here, in front of me, was a wreck of a man, bleeding from a half a dozen cuts, right arm useless, humiliated. I had had my revenge.

He stood there panting, his clean sword trailing in the dust, waiting for the death blow like a bullock at a slaughter-house. I felt disgust for myself; this was not how a true warrior behaved, to torment a beaten foe. I stepped away from him and looked round the ring of eager blood-lusting faces. The marks of recent battle and the firelight from the torches gave them an evil cast: they looked like a circle of demons glowing with a hideous desire. They began to chant: 'Death, death, death . . .' But I wanted no more part in their gory entertainment and said in a loud voice: 'I have finished. Let him go. The fight is over. Release him.' And I turned my back on that bleeding remnant of my child-hood and started to walk towards the manor house.

Then someone shouted my name and I whirled round fast. Guy had raised his sword in his left hand and he was charging at me across the torch-lit courtyard, a scream of humiliated rage in his throat. He swung the sword hard at my head but I ducked easily and lunged forward, spitting his already blood-slicked chest on my blade. His own momentum drove him forward on to my sword and he came to rest, inches from my body, his face close enough to kiss. I could see the light dying in his eyes and, feeling a last flicker of hatred, I leant forward and whispered in his ear. 'It was me who planted the ruby in your clothes chest, Wolfram. Take that knowledge with you to Hell.' He gurgled blood, a crimson stream running from his lips. I could see he was trying to speak, to curse me, and then he slumped at my feet, dead, on his back with my sword still stuck between his ribs, the hilt pointing to the heavens.

Chapter Twenty

The great hall of Nottingham Castle was filled with the scent of fresh flowers and fine beeswax candles. Sweet herbs strewn on the floor added their notes to the heady odours of a happy celebration. The brightly coloured robes of royalty and their noble entourages dazzled the eye, outshone only by the gorgeous tapestries woven with gold and silver thread that hung from the walls. I was as gaudily attired as anyone in this cacophony of colour in a pair of new green and yellow hose and a gorgeous scarlet robe, embroidered with silver thread, which reached almost to my ankles. My feet were encased in the lightest kidskin shoes, my head adorned with a soft, bright scarlet woollen hat that draped down one side of my face in what I believed was a magnificently aristocratic manner.

I was almost as pleased with my attire as I was to be witnessing the marriage of the Earl and Countess of Locksley. Robin and Marie-Anne, dressed respectively in sumptuous gowns of green and blue silk, were standing at the head of the hall being blessed by a solemn priest in black; a short, powerful man who bore a striking resemblance to one Brother Tuck, a notorious Welsh monk who was rumoured to have once consorted with outlaws.

None of us were outlaws now. Robin, as he had promised, had secured pardons for all those who survived the terrible battle of Linden Lea six weeks before. King Richard – we all called him that even though his coronation at Westminster Abbey would not take place for another week – had come to an arrangement with Robin, brokered by Sir Richard. Several large barrels of silver pennies had changed hands, some said as much as five thousand pounds' worth. Robin had done homage to the King, and in exchange for certain promises and assurances, Robin had been given a free pardon for himself and all his men. He had also been granted the hand of his lovely Marie-Anne and the Earldom of Locksley, to boot. As an Earl, he was now eminently respectable, a powerful magnate, and the King himself now sat beside his mother Eleanor, and his brother John, at the head of the hall in three great oaken chairs, witnessing the marriage of his newest vassal with a stern regal eye.

I was nearly overwhelmed to be in the presence of a King. He was magnificent: a tall, handsome man, haughty of face and about thirty years old with reddish-gold hair and blue eyes and an air of muscular directness. Clearly a man of action, he was known as a great soldier, a distingushed tactician and a man who adored poetry and music. Beside the King, fidgeting in his big chair, sat his far less impressive younger brother John, the youngest of King Henry's sons, who styled himself Lord of Ireland. In his early twenties, he was far shorter than his warlike older brother, and with a darker shade of reddish hair. As I watched Prince John, he picked irritably at the pommel of a great bejewelled dagger at his waist, his face screwed up in a childishly petulant expression. Queen Eleanor was the only member of that royal trio who looked genuinely pleased at the union of Robin and Marie-Anne. Her fine, well-aged face beamed at the happy couple as Tuck tied their hands together with a sacred strip of white silk and pronounced in a loud voice to the whole assembly that they were man and wife. I was happy too, my feelings for Marie-Anne having changed subtly since Robin, Reuben and I had rescued her from the wall tower. I would love her always, but my moon-calf adoration had transformed into the feeling of warmth that I used to have towards my own sisters. I was happy because she was happy.

Goody, who seemed to have grown about six inches in the few weeks since I had last seen her in Winchester, was looking angelic in a blue gown and white headdress to match Marie-Anne's, and she stood at her mistress's side bearing a huge bouquet of white roses. I had greeted her earlier that day with a big hug, but she had pushed me away and told me sternly that, as she was a real gentle-woman now, I might salute her with a respectful bow but no more. I had half a mind to put her over my knee and spank her but, in the end, perhaps wisely considering what I knew she could do to a man with a poniard, I decided to humour her. So I bowed low, grinning disrespectfully, and called her my lady.

Fulcold, resplendent in sky blue wool, attended the cere-mony as part of Eleanor's retinue. He had been delighted to see me again in good health, and we embraced as friends. Sir Richard was there too, with a dozen fellow knights, each in a pristine white surcoat. And Robert of Thurnham, my saviour in the cell at Winchester, now a trusted King's

355

man, gave me a friendly wave from the large group of royal retainers at the side of the hall.

Reuben had sent a fat pouch of gold as a wedding gift and a message that he was truly devastated that business in York prevented him from attending the celebrations. He was being tactful. As a Jew, he would not have been welcomed by many of the noble guests at this Christian ceremony. Robin's brother Lord William had sent his regrets too, but no reasons for his absence. He was being churlish, we all decided. Perhaps because, as a mere baron, his younger brother Earl Robert now outranked him.

Bernard of Sezanne was on fine form, cracking bad jokes, singing snatches of song and hardly drinking at all. With his royal mistress's permission, he and I would be performing later that evening at the wedding feast. All morning he had been wittering on to me about the great honour of performing before the King. He had made me physically sick with nerves, which were not helped by my memories of my last public performance in Winchester, in front of Murdac and Guy.

Sir Ralph Murdac had fled Nottingham. After the battle of Linden Lea, he had been chased to its very gates by Sir Richard's men, whereupon he had barricaded himself in the keep and defied the Templars for more than a month. But, at the news that King Richard had landed in England and was coming north to Nottingham, with all his men-at-arms, to take possession of his royal castle, Murdac had gathered his chests of silver and a few loyal men and fled to the protection of relatives in Scotland. He had been informed, by the Templars naturally, that the King wished to interrogate him about the whereabouts of much of the tax silver that had been raised in Nottinghamshire and Derbyshire the previous year to pay for the forthcoming great expedition to the Holy Land. Murdac, we subsequently discovered, had spent a good deal of the King's cash on the Flemish mercenaries, who, after Murdac's departure, had made their own deal with King Richard and had entered his service without batting an eye. The King's ministers, the sheriff was told, felt that Sir Ralph had been skimming too much off the top of these tax revenues and the King was planning to make an example of him. Murdac was right to run, I discovered later; Richard was indeed planning to remove him, but not because he was especially angry about the sheriff's shenanigans with his revenues. In fact, the King was planning to remove more than half the senior officials in England, purely as a money-raising exercise. Richard badly needed more money for his holy war, and a new sheriff, constable or bishop would gladly pay the King a fat fee for the appointment. A rich knight called Roger de Lacy had begun negotiating for the shrieval appointment in Nottinghamshire almost before Murdac's bags were packed.

Tuck's announcement that Robin and Marie-Anne were man and wife was greeted with a massed roar of shouted congratulations, and a few bawdy suggestions for the wedding night. Hugh, the saintly Bishop of Lincoln, seated near the royal party, frowned at this unseemly levity and Robin had to quieten his men with a hand gesture before order was restored. Then the venerable Bishop rose from his seat. Hugh was a tall, thin man, passionate and fearless, and after a curt blessing on the union of Robin and Marie-Anne, he launched into a harangue about the Holy Land, exhorting the audience to take the Cross and join King Richard on the great expedition to recover Jerusalem from the infidel.

Most people yawned through this religious rant – priests had been preaching it regularly for two years now – but one man seemed to be paying an inordinate amount of attention. Robert, Earl of Locksley, was apparently agog. When the old Bishop came to the end of his speech with the ringing words, 'Who then will take this symbol of faith from me and vow that, with God's blessing, they will not rest until Jerusalem is recovered?' Robin leapt to his feet. 'By God, I will,' he said in a loud sincere voice. And kneeling before Bishop Hugh he received a blessing and a scrap of red cloth which had been cut into the shape of a cross.

'Wear this symbol of Christ's love on your cloak, my son,' said the Bishop, 'and remember that you are guaranteed a remission of your many sins and a place in Heaven if you die on this perilous journey in God's name.' I caught Robin's eye as the prelate made him this promise, and I could have sworn that, the solemnity of the occasion notwithstanding, my master winked at me.

Other knights shuffled forward to receive the Cross, but the solemnity was spoilt somewhat by King Richard, who leapt out of his chair, strode across the hall and enfolded Robin in a great embrace, grinning like a regal mountebank. Somehow, in the few days they had both been at the castle, King Richard and Robin had become fast friends. Prince John, still seated, watched the pair of them as they slapped each other on the back, his face a study in contempt. Queen Eleanor was hugging Marie-Anne, who looked happier than I had ever seen her. I had expected her to be surprised, even shocked by Robin's sudden decision to go off to fight a war on the other side of the world, perhaps never to return, but she showed not a trace of anxiety. And I realised, of course, that the whole thing had been a piece of theatre.

Robin had struck a bargain with Sir Richard that terrible night after the first day of battle, as we bound up our wounds in Linden Lea and waited for death at the hands of Murdac's soldiers the following dawn. And Bernard, of course, had been Sir Richard's emissary. I too had played my part, albeit unwittingly. The single dove that I released at dawn, trailing its slim red banner, had been the signal to Sir Richard that Robin accepted his proposal. Bernard had explained it all to me in the days after the battle, when we who were fit enough laboured to clear the reeking field of the hundreds of dead and give them a decent burial.

'It's all about leverage, really,' Bernard had told me, as I hoisted the dead body of a skinny old man over my shoulder. 'The application of the right amount of pressure at the right time. Of course, the Templars are past masters at this sort of thing. And they nearly always get what they want, one way or another.' Bernard was being insufferably smug that day, the result I suspected of another conquest among Queen Eleanor's ladies. He played no part in the gruesome task of carrying the bodies to a common pit, but hovered around me and my team of bowmen, talking happily and getting in the way as we lugged the corpses to their final resting place. As we paused for a slug of wine, he continued: 'In this case, Sir Richard had long wanted Robin to join him on his great holy adventure. He wanted his bowmen, you see. He wanted the men who could do this,' he gestured at a body, a mailed knight in Murdac's colours, whose corpse was stuck with more than a dozen arrows. 'That cunning fox had probably been plotting to get Robin to take the Cross ever since he was captured.' Bernard chuckled, and then casually poured about a pint of Bordeaux wine down his throat.

After leaving us at Linden Lea before the battle, Bernard informed me, Sir Richard had ridden to join his brother Templars, and Queen Eleanor and her train, at Belvoir Castle, twenty or so miles south-east of Nottingham. There he had learnt that Murdac's forces had been reinforced with four hundred Flemish mercenaries, cavalry and cross-bowmen. He had realised that, with Murdac now so unexpectedly powerful, Robin was almost certain to be destroyed in the coming fight and, quite apart from his friendship with Robin, that would not have suited Sir Richard's plans at all. So he sent Bernard on a fast horse with a message to Robin. Sir Richard would bring a powerful force of Templar knights to Robin's aid, if Robin would promise to lead a mercenary band of archers and cavalry on the holy pilgrimage to Outremer the next year. Robin had no choice but to accept Sir Richard's offer, and by the charade of taking the Cross from the Bishop of Lincoln today, the Earl of Locksley was signalling his intent to fulfil his part of the bargain.

The ceremony over, Robin convened all his senior men in a small buttery off the great hall where we would soon be dining in some splendour with our royal hosts. Hugh, Tuck, Little John, Will Scarlet and I crowded into the small space and made ourselves free of one of the opened butts of ale in there. Hugh raised a wooden mug brimming with liquid and said jovially: 'I think we would all like to congratulate my brother on his wedding and wish him and his lovely wife Marie-Anne many years of happiness. Robin and Marie-Anne!' We all drank, except Robin, who put down his mug untasted.

'We have some business to conclude before we celebrate my nuptials,' said Robin in a voice as cold as hoar frost. He looked straight at Hugh. I noticed that John and Tuck were standing right next to Robin's older brother, as close as gaolers. 'What business is that?' asked Hugh lightly.

'I know it was you, Hugh,' said Robin, his voice grating. 'At first it was just a suspicion, and I dismissed it. I said to myself: my own brother would not betray me, never. My own flesh and blood? A man whom I have helped, saved, loved . . . The traitor cannot be him.' He paused, fixing his gaze on his brother, waiting for him to speak. Hugh said nothing, but the blood was slowly leaving his face. 'But then, at Linden Lea, I was deceived, by you, about the strength of their numbers. The Flemings, you told me, could not possibly be there for at least a week.'

'I made a mistake,' Hugh said. 'Intelligence is never exact. My sources said—'

Robin cut him off: 'The size of Murdac's force was nearly double what we had supposed. The mangonel . . .' Robin appeared perfectly calm, but he had to stop and take a breath. 'We were not luring Murdac into a deadly trap, he was luring us. Sir Ralph knew what we had planned from the very beginning . . . because you had told him.'

Hugh was frantically shaking his head. 'It wasn't me, Robin, I swear. It must have been another—'

'I know it was you. Don't insult me further by pretending it was not. Just admit the truth. For once, Hugh, just admit the truth.'

'I swear . . . I swear in the name of Our Saviour Jesus Christ—'

'Enough!' Robin's voice cracked across the small room. He pulled a bench out from the wall and, putting his arm around Hugh, he led him to the seat and sat him down, taking the place next to him. 'Hugh,' he said, his voice weary and kindly, like a parent talking to a recalcitrant child. 'You are my brother, I love you, but I know it was you. Just tell me why you did it and I swear I will not harm you. I swear it on all that I hold dear.'

'But Robin—' Hugh began, and his voice had a whining edge. Robin shushed him with a finger to his lips.

'Just tell me why you did it, that's all, and I will not harm you. Just tell me why. Please. Please, Hugh. Was I not kind to you, did I not help you when you were down, raise you up—'

Suddenly Hugh sat up straight; he threw off Robin's embracing arm. 'I am the elder brother,' he cried. '*I am*. First William, then me, then you. That's how the order goes. That is how God had ordained it. And look at you now, my little brother, an Earl, with the friendship of the King.' His voice had a sneering tone. 'I remember you when you were still shitting in your napkin and suckling at the wet nurse's teat. And now . . . and now . . .' Words seemed to fail Hugh. 'You have everything and I have nothing. No home, no money, no woman, no children. I am a lackey, a servant . . . to you!'

'When did Murdac first approach you?' asked Robin in a quiet voice. The whole room was spellbound by Hugh's words. The man dropped his balding head into his hands. Robin said nothing. The silence stretched longer and longer, became thin, unbearable . . .

'You don't understand,' said Hugh forcefully, lifting his head with a jerk. 'I did it for you, to save your soul. Your immortal soul is in terrible danger with this foul witch-craft that you practise, this pagan devil worship. You think it is mere pageantry – but you are wrong, you are so wrong. It is an abomination. You are damning your soul to Hell for eternity with these filthy practices. And you are encouraging others, simple country folk, to throw away their chance of Salvation. They said, Murdac said, that the Church would receive you with joy, that Christ would receive you. They would cleanse you of all sin before your death and guarantee you immortal life. In Heaven, in the company of saints. I wanted that for you! I wanted you to be saved.'

'How did Murdac approach you? When?' asked Robin quietly.

'You don't understand.' Hugh was nearly shouting by now. 'You don't understand: I approached him. Somebody had to stop you. After you humiliated His Grace the Bishop of Hereford, a great man of God, and slaughtered his holy men, I knew you were in danger of damnation. I had to act. I had to. And they promised me that you would be saved; that after your capture you would receive the blessing of Holy Mother Church and your soul would be for ever in Christ's keeping.' Hugh was suddenly sobbing. 'In Christ's keeping,' he repeated.

'And Thangbrand? And Freya? And all those men and women cut down in the snow? You wanted to save their souls, too?' said Robin, icily calm.

'They were already damned; they were Godless outlaws, pagans, priest-murders—'

'They were your friends,' snapped Robin. He rose from the bench. His kindly demeanour was gone. 'I've heard enough,' he said in a voice empty as a tomb. He pulled Hugh to his feet. 'Get out of my sight,' he said, pushing him to the pantry door. 'If I ever see you again, I swear I will kill you on sight. Now, get gone.'

Hugh stared at him through tear-blotched, empty eyes. Robin turned away, and I caught, just for a moment, a look of immense sadness on his face, before it hardened again into a cold mask. Then with his back to his brother, he snapped: 'Get out!' and Hugh turned, his body limp, defeated, as he made his way slowly towards the door.

We all pulled back to give him room; as if nobody wished to touch him. But then, to my left, there was a blur of motion, and John was past me in a whirlwind of muscle and anger. He took two steps, reached out with his great hands and wrapped them around Hugh's long neck, just as Robin's brother reached the door. Then he squeezed. Every ounce of strength in his huge body was concentrated on the double grip that entirely filled the space between Hugh's chin and his shoulders. Nobody moved; we were all frozen in surprise. Hugh's face began to swell and colour, cherry red and then purple, then grey blue. His own hands scrabbled at John's great fists, scratching and trying to pull them away as they squeezed the breath of life out of him. Suddenly there was a hideous popping click, and Hugh's head flopped to one side and, at the same time, we heard a great farting rush of fluid, and the buttery was filled with a rich meaty stench as his bowels emptied. Urine drizzled around his ankles, forming a yellow pool at his feet. John shook the body once, jiggling the unstrung head, and then dropped the carcass to the piss-soaked floor.

'John . . . what have you done?' asked Robin. His voice was weak, uncertain, quavering. He sounded like an old man. Still nobody moved. Then John bent over the body for a moment. He had a knife in his hand and I saw him prise open the dead man's mouth, pull forth the limp tongue and make one swift cut. He released the lolling head and it fell back on to the stone floor with a dull clunk.

'I gave him my word I would not harm him,' said Robin. His voice had a disbelieving quality; he seemed appalled by John's actions.

'By God's great swinging testicles, I did not,' said John, tucking the scrap of red flesh into the pouch at his belt. 'He needed to die, if any man ever did. And you would have given him forgiveness? You? He needed to die, if not for you, then for all those good men, your men, who died at Linden Lea. That is justice.'

Robin still seemed dazed by his brother's death. He stared down at the body. For the first time since I had met him he seemed almost weak. 'I'm an Earl now,' he said slowly, 'a companion of the King, a knight sworn to the Cross. I am no longer a common outlaw, a murderer. I have fought so long, so hard to get to this point . . . Does an Earl break his oath, murder his brother, mutilate men?'

'In my experience, that's exactly what Earls do,' said John.

Historical Note

On Sunday September 13, 1189, Richard, Duke of Aquitaine, was crowned king of England at Westminster Abbey to enormous popular acclaim. He immediately started preparing to embark for what later generations would call the Third Crusade. Henry II had left a decent sized treasury in England when he died, but Richard, his war-loving son, needed a lot more money for the glorious adventure he was planning to undertake.

Although he was now King of England, Richard's heart always remained further south in his mother's homeland of Aquitaine and, during his ten-year reign, he was to spend no more than ten months in his northern realm. Indeed, he seems to have considered England as a sort of enormous piggy bank, valuable only because of the money he could extract from it. To fund his crusade, however, Richard was not able to increase taxation upon the people of England: the Saladin Tithe, instituted by his father in 1187 to pay for a future expedition to recapture Jerusalem, had squeezed the country almost dry.

So Richard decided to auction off all the titles, rights and positions that were within his gift – a perfectly normal kingly practice in the 12th century. Roger of Howden, a contemporary chronicler, wrote of Richard: 'He put up for sale everything he had – offices, lordships, earldoms, sheriffdoms, castles, towns, lands . . .' Indeed Richard himself said, half-jokingly: 'I would sell London, if I could find a buyer.'

The result was a massive influx of cash and a major political reshuffle right across the country – Henry's men were out and Richard's were in. Of the twenty-seven men who had been sheriffs at the end of Henry's reign, only five retained their office, and the new men paid handsomely for their appointments. One such casualty of Richard's need for quick cash was Sir Ralph Murdac, the sheriff of Nottinghamshire, Derbyshire and the Royal Forests (there was no such position of sheriff of Nottingham until the middle of the 15th century). He was removed from his position and replaced by Roger de Lacy in 1190. Ralph Murdac was a real man but, personal facts about 12th-century individuals being rather thin on the ground, I have invented almost everything else about him apart from his name. The same is true of other historical characters in my story, such as Ralph FitzStephen, the constable of Winchester; Robert of Thurnham, the loyal king's man who held a castle in Kent; his brother Stephen, and Fulcold, Eleanor's chamberlain.

Piers, the unfortunate sacrificial victim is, of course, an invention, but the way he died is based on archaeological evidence of Celtic human sacrifices, specifically that of the Lindow Man, a mummified corpse from the 1st century AD found in Cheshire in 1984. The Lindow

Man, a high-status individual, quite possibly a druid, had been hit on the head, strangled and then had his throat cut as part of a pre-Christian ritual, before being thrown in a peat bog where the body was perfectly preserved for hundreds of years.

There is little evidence that paganism was widespread in 12th century England; indeed, most scholars now agree that the country was almost universally Christian. But I like to believe, perhaps fancifully, that there would have been pockets of people, in the wild inaccessible places, who still clung to the older gods, who still practised witchcraft and magic and who were fiercely resistant to the spiritual authority of the ubiquitous Church. To my mind, Robin Hood himself is an incarnation of a wild forest spirit; a manifestation of all that is non-urban, uncivilised and unchristian. And I think that part of his enduring appeal lies in that exciting 'otherness'.

So was Robin Hood a real man? This is a tough question. Was there once an outlaw named Robert who hid in Sherwood Forest, or perhaps Barnsdale, during the high middle ages and made a name for himself by robbing travellers? Almost certainly. In fact, Robert being a common name, robbery being the last resort of many a starving peasant – and the choice of many an impecunious knight – there were probably several men who could fit that description. Perhaps dozens. Would we recognise any of these pretenders to the title as the Robin Hood of our modern legends, stealing from the rich, giving to the poor, trading quips with his merry men while slapping a green-clad thigh? Almost certainly not.

In literature, Robin Hood first makes an appearance in a 1370s poem by William Langland, known as the

'Vision of Piers Plowman'. In it, there is a lazy cleric who knows the popular stories of Robin Hood better than he knows his prayers. So we know that the soap-opera-style tales of Robin were a byword in the second half of the 14th century when Langland was writing his poem. But some scholars even claim to have traced the man himself. The first references to a possible Robin Hood figure occur in legal documents in the first half of the 13th century. In 1230, the sheriff of Yorkshire accounted for the goods he had seized from a fugitive called Robert Hood. Another Robert Hod of Burntoft, County Durham, is mentioned as owning property in a legal document of 1244. He subsequently lost his property, so could this man have become an outlaw? The issue is further confused because by the second half of the 13th century the names 'Robinhood' and 'Robehod' occur frequently in the court records of several northern counties. Were they real names, or a generic word for any highwayman, or aliases given by criminals hoping to borrow some glamour from the association with a famous outlaw? I don't think we will ever know. But what we can assume is that Robin Hood, if he existed, operated during the beginning of 13th century or earlier. And I have chosen to set my stories at the end of the 12th century and start of the 13th century purely because the films and TV programmes that I watched when I was growing up set Robin's exploits in this era.

Whether Robin was a real person, or the personification of a pagan woodland sprite, or a 'brand name' co-opted by boastful criminals, or an amalgamation of several outlaws, I still find the stories about him strangely gripping. I hope you do, too; and I hope you will enjoy the next book in the series, *Crusader*, published in 2010, which deals with Robin and Alan's adventures on the long, dusty road to the Holy Land.

Angus Donald
Kent, January 2009

Acknowledgements

This book has taken nearly seven years to turn from idle pub chat to actual printed volume, and during that time I have been helped enormously by a great number of people: literary professionals, librarians, journalists and historians, friends and family. I'd first like to thank my agent Ian Drury, of Sheil Land Associates, who spotted some potential in the few rough chapters I sent him; I'd also like to thank David Shelley at Sphere for agreeing to publish this book and his colleague Thalia Proctor for doing such a good editing job. The staff of the British Library have been brilliantly helpful over the years, as have the kind folk at Tonbridge Library. I'd also like to thank Kieron Toole for being so patient while he was teaching me to stalk deer.

My long suffering friends and former work-mates at *The Times*, I thank, for putting up with endless conversations in The Caxton about me and my literary ambitions, when we could have been talking about much more interesting things (such as them and their literary ambitions). My brothers, Jamie, John and Alex deserve a special mention, too, as we have worked out many a knotty plot point together while tromping through the fields of Kent on a Sunday morning, or while getting outside a pint or three to refresh us afterwards. My parents Alan and Janet have been very helpful, too, bringing me old books and relevant newspaper articles, offering suggestions and, of course, for giving me more than forty years of love and support.

Some of the people who have been most helpful, I have not had the plesure of meeting, namely those professional historians whose books I have enjoyed: I particularly want to thank John Gillingham for his masterful work *Richard I*, Alison Weir for *Eleanor of Aquitaine*, A.J. Pollard for *Imagining Robin Hood*, Mike Dixon Kennedy for *The Robin Hood Handbook*, which always sits beside my desk, Robert Hardy and Matthew Strickland for *The Great Warbow*, and David Boyle for *Blondel's Song*.

I apologise in advance for any historical errors made; despite the huge amounts of help I have had in writing this book, these mistakes remain entirely my own.